"THE GREAT MARVEL OF KING'S SERIES IS THAT SHE'S MAN-
AGED TO PRESERVE THE INTEGRITY OF HOLMES'S CHARAC-
TER AND YET SOMEHOW CONJURE UP A WOMAN ASTUTE,
EDGY AND COMPELLING ENOUGH TO BE THE PARTNER OF
HIS MIND AS WELL AS HIS HEART." —*The Washington Post Book World*

MORE PRAISE FOR
LAURIE R. KING'S BESTSELLING MYSTERY

The God *of the* Hive

"*The God of the Hive* is mesmerizing—another wonderful novel etched
by the hand of a master storyteller. No reader who opens this one will
be disappointed." —Michael Connelly

"The Mary Russell series is the most sustained feat of imagination in
mystery fiction today, and this is the best installment yet." —Lee Child

"Gloriously complex...utterly absorbing reading...puzzling and up-
lifting." —*Booklist* (starred review)

"Her storytelling is robust, confident, and lightly sprinkled with grace
notes reflecting the author's background in theology."
—*The Seattle Times*

"The excitement and suspense build.... Throw in the Baker Street
Irregulars, several well-concealed London bolt-holes, some Holmesian
cunning, and a rousing finale, and you have all the ingredients of another
winning entry in the Laurie King canon." —*Mystery Scene*

"A spy thriller at its best." —*The Historical Novels Review*

"All it takes is the very first page of the newest installment in Laurie R.
King's brilliant series and you're gone...disappearing into an artfully
creative and crafted world." —M. J. Rose

"Laurie R. King's *God of the Hive* is not for those looking for just one more Sherlock Holmes story. This is a rich, complex portrait of the Holmes-Russell extended family, nuanced well beyond the simplicities of Sir Arthur's tales. As usual, King delivers far more than a 'mystery': Indelible characters and telling observations of England after the Great War make this real Literature but without pretension." —Leslie S. Klinger

"*The God of the Hive* will astonish and delight even the most seasoned of Holmes' devotees." —Katherine Neville

"From thrilling plot to lyrical prose, Laurie R. King's *The God of the Hive* is a spectacular finale to the unforgettable *The Language of Bees*. With nearly a continent separating them in this tale, Mary Russell and Sherlock Holmes take on a foe so powerful he has nearly eliminated not only their family but them. Without a doubt, King is the master of Sherlockian authors." —Gayle Lynds

The God
of the Hive

The God
of the Hive

A novel of suspense featuring
Mary Russell and Sherlock Holmes

Laurie R. King

Bantam Books Trade Paperbacks
New York

2011 Bantam Books Trade Paperback Edition

Copyright © 2010 by Laurie R. King
Excerpt from *Pirate King* © 2011 by Laurie R. King
Map copyright © 2010 by Jeffrey L. Ward

Published in the United States by Bantam Books,
an imprint of The Random House Publishing Group,
a division of Random House, Inc., New York.

BANTAM BOOKS and the rooster colophon are
registered trademarks of Random House, Inc.

Originally published in hardcover in the United States by Bantam Books,
an imprint of The Random House Publishing Group,
a division of Random House, Inc., in 2010.

This book contains an excerpt from the forthcoming book *Pirate King*
by Laurie King. This excerpt has been set for this edition only and
may not reflect the final content of the forthcoming edition.

LIBRARY OF CONGRESS CATALOGING-IN-PUBLICATION DATA

King, Laurie R.
The god of the hive : a novel of suspense featuring Mary Russell
and Sherlock Holmes / Laurie R. King.
p. cm.
ISBN 978-0-553-59041-8
eBook ISBN 978-0-553-90768-1
1. Russell, Mary (Fictitious character)—Fiction. 2. Women private
investigators—England—Fiction. 3. Holmes, Sherlock (Fictitious
character)—Fiction. 4. Holmes, Mycroft (Fictitious character)—Fiction.
5. Married people—Fiction. 6. Fathers and sons—Fiction.
7. Granddaughters—Fiction. 8. Conspiracies—Fiction. I. Title.
PS3561.I4813G64 2010
813'.54—dc22   2009052807

Printed in the United States of America

www.bantamdell.com

2 4 6 8 9 7 5 3 1

Book design by Virginia Norey

In memory of Noel,
who would have loved Robert Goodman

Prologue

Two clever London gentlemen. Both wore City suits, both sat in quiet rooms, both thought about luncheon.

The younger was admiring his polished shoes; the older contemplated his stockings, thick with dust.

The one was considering where best to eat; the other was wondering if he was to be fed that day.

One clever man stood, straightening his neck-tie with manicured fingers. He reached out to give the silver pen a minuscule adjustment, returning it to symmetry with the edge of the desk, then walked across the silken carpet to the door. There he surveyed the mirror that hung on the wall, leaning forward to touch the white streak—really quite handsome—over the right temple before settling his freshly brushed hat over it. He firmed the tie again, and reached for the handle.

The other man, too, tugged at his tie, grateful for it. The men who had locked him here had taken his shoes and belt, but left him his neck-tie. He could not decide if they—or, rather, the mind in back of *them*—had judged the fabric inadequate for the suicide of a man his size, or if they had wished subtly to undermine his mental state: The length of aged striped silk was all that kept his suit trousers from tumbling around his ankles when he stood. There was sufficient discomfort in being hungry, cold, unshaven, and having a lidded bucket for toilet facilities without adding the comic indignity of drooping trousers.

Twenty minutes later, the younger man was reviewing his casual exchange with two high-ranking officials and a newspaper baron—the true reason for his choice of restaurant—while his blue eyes dutifully surveyed the print on a leather-bound menu; the other man's pale grey gaze was fixed on a simple mathematical equation he'd begun to scratch into the brick wall with a tiny nail he'd uncovered in a corner:

$$a \div (b+c+d)$$

Both men, truth to tell, were pleased with their progress.

BOOK ONE

Saturday, 30 August–
Tuesday, 2 September
1924

Chapter 1

A child is a burden, after a mile.

After two miles in the cold sea air, stumbling through the night up the side of a hill and down again, becoming all too aware of previously unnoticed burns and bruises, and having already put on eight miles that night—half of it carrying a man on a stretcher—even a small, drowsy three-and-a-half-year-old becomes a strain.

At three miles, aching all over, wincing at the crunch of gravel underfoot, spine tingling with the certain knowledge of a madman's stealthy pursuit, a loud snort broke the silence, so close I could feel it. My nerves screamed as I struggled to draw the revolver without dropping the child.

Then the meaning of the snort penetrated the adrenaline blasting my nerves: A mad killer was not about to make that wet noise before attacking.

I went still. Over my pounding heart came a lesser version of the sound; the rush of relief made me stumble forward to drop my armful atop the low stone wall, just visible in the creeping dawn. The cow jerked back, then ambled towards us in curiosity until the child was patting its sloppy nose. I bent my head over her, letting reaction ebb.

Estelle Adler was the lovely, bright, half-Chinese child of my husband's long-lost son: Sherlock Holmes' granddaughter. I had made her acquaintance little more than two hours before, and known of her existence for less than three weeks, but if the maniac who had tried to sacrifice her father—and who had apparently intended to take the child for his own—had appeared from the night, I would not hesitate to give my life for hers.

She had been drugged by said maniac the night before, which no doubt contributed to her drowsiness, but now she studied the cow with an almost academic curiosity, leaning against my arms to examine its white-splashed nose. Which meant that the light was growing too strong to linger. I settled the straps of my rucksack, lumpy with her possessions, and reached to collect this precious and troublesome burden.

"Are you—" she began, in full voice.

"Shh!" I interrupted. "We need to whisper, Estelle."

"Are you tired?" she tried again, in a voice that, although far from a whisper, at least was not as carrying.

"My arms are," I breathed in her ear, "but I'm fine."

"I could ride pickaback," she said.

"Are you sure?"

"I do with Papa."

Well, if she could cling to the back of that tall young man, she could probably hang on to me. I shifted the rucksack around and let her climb onto my back, her little hands gripping my collar. I bent, tucking my arms under her legs, and set off again.

Much better.

It was a good thing Estelle knew what to do, because I was probably the most incompetent nurse-maid ever to be put in charge of a child. I knew precisely nothing about children; the only one I had been around for any length of time was an Indian street urchin three times this one's age and with more maturity than many English adults. I had much to learn about small children. Such as the ability to ride pickaback, and the inability to whisper.

The child's suggestion allowed me to move faster down the rutted track. We were in the Orkneys, a scatter of islands past the north of Scotland, coming down from the hill that divided the main island's two parts. Every step took us farther away from my husband; from Estelle's father, Damian; and from the bloody, fire-stained prehistoric altar-stone where Thomas Brothers had nearly killed both of them.

Why not bring in the police, one might ask. They can be useful, and after all, Brothers had killed at least three others. However, things were complicated—not that *complicated* wasn't a frequent state of affairs in the vicinity of Sherlock Holmes, but in this case the complication took the form of warrants posted for my husband, his son, and me. Estelle was the only family member not being actively hunted by Scotland Yard.

Including, apparently and incredibly, Holmes' brother. For forty-odd years, Mycroft Holmes had strolled each morning to a grey office in Whitehall and settled in to a grey job of accounting—even his longtime personal secretary was a grey man, an ageless, sexless individual with the leaking-balloon name of Sosa. Prime Ministers came and went, Victoria gave way to Edward and Edward to George, budgets were slashed and expanded, wars were fought, decades of bureaucrats flourished and died, while Mycroft walked each morning to his office and settled to his account books.

Except that Mycroft's grey job was that of *éminence grise* of the British Empire. He inhabited the shadowy world of Intelligence, but he belonged neither to the domestic Secret Service nor to the international Secret Intelligence Service. Instead, he had shaped his own department within the walls of Treasury, one that ran parallel to both the domestic branch and the SIS. After forty years, his power was formidable.

If I stopped to think about it, such unchecked authority in one individual's hands would scare me witless, even though I had made use of it more than once. But if Mycroft Holmes was occasionally cold and always enigmatic, he was also sea-green incorruptible, the fixed point in my universe, the ultimate source of assistance, shelter, information, and knowledge.

He was also untouchable, or so I had thought.

The day before, a telegram had managed to find me, with a report of Mycroft being questioned by Scotland Yard, and his home raided. It was hard to credit—picturing Mycroft's wrath raining down on Chief Inspector Lestrade came near to making me smile—but until I could disprove it, I could not call on Mycroft's assistance. I was on my own.

Were it not for the child on my back, I might have simply presented myself to the police station in Kirkwall and used the time behind bars to catch up on sleep. I was certain that the warrants had only been issued because of Chief Inspector John Lestrade's pique—even at the best of times, Lestrade disapproved of civilians like us interfering in an official investigation. Once his point was made and his temper faded, we would be freed.

Then again, were it not for the child, I would not be on this side of the island at all. I would have stayed at the Stones, where even now my training and instincts were shouting that I belonged, hunting down Brothers before he could sail off and start his dangerous religion anew in some other place.

This concept of women and children fleeing danger was a thing I did not at all care for.

But as I said, children are a burden, whether three years old or thirty. My only hope of sorting this out peacefully, without inflicting further trauma on the child or locking her disastrously claustrophobic and seriously wounded father behind bars, was to avoid the police, both here and in the British mainland. And my only hope of avoiding the Orcadian police was a flimsy, sputtering, freezing cold aeroplane. The same machine in which I had arrived on Orkney the previous afternoon, and sworn never to enter again.

The aeroplane's pilot was an American ex–RAF flyer named Javitz, who had brought me on a literally whirlwind trip from London and left me in a field south of Orkney's main town. Or rather, I had left him. I thought he would stay there until I reappeared.

I *hoped* he would.

Chapter 2

The wind was not as powerful as it had been the day before, crossing from Thurso, but it rose with the sun, and the seas rose with it. By full light, all the fittings in the Fifie's cabin were rattling wildly, and although Damian's arm was bound to his side, half an hour out of Orkney the toss and fret of the fifty-foot-long boat was making him hiss with pain. When the heap of blankets and spare clothing keeping him warm was pulled away, the dressings showed scarlet.

Sherlock Holmes rearranged the insulation around his son and tossed another scoop of coal onto the stove before climbing the open companionway to the deck. The young captain looked as if he was clinging to the wheel as much as he was controlling it. Holmes raised his voice against the wind.

"Mr Gordon, is there nothing we can do to calm the boat?"

The young man took his eyes from the sails long enough to confirm the unexpected note of concern in the older man's voice, then studied the waves and the rigging overhead. "Only thing we could do is change course. To sail with the wind, y'see?"

Holmes saw. Coming out of Scapa Flow, they had aimed for Strathy, farther west along the coast of northern Scotland—in truth, any village but Thurso would do, so long as it had some kind of medical facility.

But going west meant battling wind and sea: Even unladen, the boat had waves breaking across her bow, and the dip and rise of her fifty-foot length was troubling even to the unwounded on board.

Thurso was close and it would have a doctor; however, he and Russell had both passed through that town the day before, and although the unkempt Englishman who hired a fishing boat to sail into a storm might have escaped official notice, rumour of a young woman in an aeroplane would have spread. He hoped Russell would instruct her American pilot to avoid Thurso, but if not—well, the worst she could expect was an inconvenient arrest. He, on the other hand, dared not risk sailing into constabulary arms.

"Very well," he said. "Change course."

"Thurso, good." Gordon sounded relieved.

"No. Wick." A fishing town, big enough to have a doctor—perhaps even a rudimentary hospital. Police, too, of course, but warrants or not, what village constable would take note of one fishing boat in a harbour full of them?

"Wick? Oh, but I don't know anyone there. My cousin in Strathy—"

"The lad will be dead by Strathy."

"Wick's farther."

"But calmer."

Gordon thought for a moment, then nodded. "Take that line. Be ready when I say."

The change of tack quieted the boat's wallow considerably. When Holmes descended again to the cabin, the stillness made him take two quick steps to the bunk—but it was merely sleep.

The madman's bullet had circled along Damian's ribs, cracking at least one, before burying itself in the musculature around the shoulder blade—too deep for amateur excavation. Had it been the left arm, Holmes might have risked it, but Damian was an artist, a right-handed artist, an artist whose technique required precise motions with the most delicate control. Digging through muscle and nerve for a piece of lead could turn the lad into a former artist.

Were Watson here, Holmes would permit his old friend to take out his scalpel, even considering the faint hand tremor he'd seen the last time they had met. But Watson was on his way home from Australia—Holmes suspected a new lady friend—and was at the moment somewhere in the Indian Ocean.

He could only hope that Wick's medical man had steady hands and didn't drink. If they were not so fortunate, he should have to face the distressing option of coming to the surface to summon a real surgeon.

Which would Damian hate more: the loss of his skill, or the loss of his freedom?

It was not really a question. Even now, Holmes knew that if he were to remove the wedge holding the cabin's hatch open, in minutes Damian would be sweating with horror and struggling to rise, to breathe, to flee.

No: A painter robbed of his technique could form another life for himself; a man driven insane by confinement could not. If they found no help in Wick, he might have to turn surgeon.

The thought made his gut run cold. Not the surgery itself—he'd done worse—but the idea of Damian's expression when he tried to control a brush, and could not.

Imagine: Sherlock Holmes dodging responsibility.

Standing over his son's form, he became aware of the most peculiar sensation, disturbingly primitive and almost entirely foreign.

Reverend Thomas Brothers (or James Harmony Hayden or Henry Smythe or whatever names he had claimed) lay dead among the standing stone circle. But had the corpse been to hand, Sherlock Holmes would have ripped out the mad bastard's heart and savagely kicked his remains across the deck and into the sea.

Chapter 3

The man with several names edged into awareness. It was dark. The air smelt of sea and smoke. Fresh smoke. Memory was...elusive. *Transformation?* Yes, that was it—long plotted, sacrifices made, years of effort, but...

He'd expected physical reaction, but not this pain, not that smoke-filled darkness. Could what he felt be the birth pangs of the Transformed? *Blood and pain are companions of birth*; he himself had written it. If the right blood had been loosed—but no. The wrong blood had been spilt on the altar stone.

His own.

Certainly the pain was his. He groaned, and became aware of a woman's hands, then a man speaking, and the sudden bright of an opening door followed by more voices. After a time came the suffocation of a rag soaked in ether, and with a sharp vision of the sun black as sackcloth and the moon stained with blood, everything went away.

It was broad daylight outside the hovel when he woke. The woman lifted his head to trickle in a jolt of some powerful drink. The nausea of the ether receded. His chest was aflame, and his head was flooded with the memory of fire and gunshot, but the whisky helped settle his thoughts as well as his stomach.

"What time is it?" he croaked.

"What's that?" the woman said.

"Time. What time is it?"

"Oh, dearie, let me see. It's near noon. Saturday, that is."

Mid-day Saturday. To the north, over the pure, cold sea, the sun would be edging back from its darkness, the eclipse fading—and with it, opportunity. All his work, long months of meditation and planning, gathering the reins of Authority, feeling the power rise up within him (oh, exquisite power, exquisite sensations—peeling away a goose quill with the Tool, the sweet dip of nib into spilt crimson, concentrating to get the words on the page before the ink clotted: perfection), power that welled up like a giant wave from that vast sea, carrying him across the world to this exact place at this exact time, to midnight at an altar surrounded by standing stones with the perfect sacrifice, the one who mattered, lying helpless and expectant with his throat bared . . .

Snatched from him, at the very peak of the Preparation. The sacrifice had turned and summoned fire—the lamp, that was it. Damian had managed to fling out his arm and smashed the lamp. But what followed was unclear: noise and confusion and hot billows of flame, and . . . others? The impression of others—two of them?—and then a boom and a giant's fist smashing his chest, and nothing until he had wakened to the smell of sea and smoke.

Who could they have been? Enemies? Demons? Figments of his imagination? Not that it mattered: They had robbed him of Transformation. The Great Work lay shattered. A waste of years. His hand twitched with the urge to strangle someone.

And the child? She who was to have been his acolyte, his student, the daughter of his soul? Had the two demons stolen her? Or was she still in that burnt-out place where he had taken refuge?

Mid-day: She would be awake. Sooner or later, she would find her way out, and be seen. He had to get away before they came looking for him.

"Gunderson?" he whispered.

"He'll be here tomorrow morning." This was a man's gravelly voice.

"MacAuliffe."

"That's right, Reverend Brothers. You know what happened to you?"

With an effort, Brothers got his eyes open, squinting into the smokey light. "Shot?"

"Aye." The man grinned and reached down to whittle a slice from the sausage on the table, popping it between his yellow teeth and chewing, open-mouthed. "Only thing that kept you from the pearly gates was that book in your chest pocket. Weren't for that, the lead would've gone straight into your heart. As it is, we dug the thing out of your shoulder. Can you move your fingers?"

The wounded man looked down and saw a hand arranged atop a thick gauze pad covering his chest. The fingers slowly closed, then opened.

"There you go," MacAuliffe said, whittling off another slab of meat. "You'll be right as rain in no time."

"Is that my knife?"

The hired man held up the curved blade. "This yours? Wicked thing, nearly cut my thumb off with it."

"Give it!" The command came out weak, but MacAuliffe obeyed, wiping the grease on his trousers, then turning it so his sometime employer could take the ivory haft.

"I found it on the ground next to that altar thing, nearly stepped on it before I saw the handle. Didn't know for sure it was yours, but I didn't want to leave it behind."

Brothers' good hand slipped around the familiar object, his thumb smoothing its blade, the cool metal that had been given him on the very hour of his birth. He felt a pulse of temptation, to plunge the Tool into MacAuliffe's hateful belly, but he was not strong enough to do without assistance. Not yet. Not until he could summon The Friend.

Instead, he tucked the knife under his weak hand, as if the Tool's strength might transfer to flesh. "I need you to send a telegram to London."

Chapter 4

When we reached the coastal track and turned towards Kirkwall, the light strengthened with every step. Earlier, I had been forced to choose between the dangers of blind speed and the threat of being seen. Now I hitched the child up on my hips and leant forward into a near-jog. Her light body rocked against mine, and her own arms had to be getting tired, but she did not complain.

Half a mile down the road, I spotted a farmer coming out of a shed, to climb onto a high-sided cart. A tangle of shrubs marked where the farmyard lane entered the road; I let Estelle slip to the ground behind them, stifling a groan as my shoulders returned to their proper angle. I hunkered beside her (my knees, too, having aged a couple of decades in the past hours) and said in a low voice, "We have to wait until this man has gone by, and I don't want him to notice us. We need to be very quiet, all right?"

"Can we ask him for a ride?" she said in her loud, hoarse, child's whisper.

"No, we can't," I said. "Now, not a word, all right?"

I felt her nod, and put my arm around her tiny body.

The metallic sounds from the cart indicated milk canisters, and as I'd feared, it was headed towards town: We should have to wait until he was some distance down the road before we followed. This was clearly a daily ritual, since the reins were nearly slack and the cart was controlled less by the farmer than by his nag. Who was in no hurry—its pace was no faster than our own, and the high sides . . . I stared, then pushed aside the branches to see.

The cart was a purpose-built creation with a flat-bedded base on which had been fastened a large crate, some five feet on a side, tipped with the open top facing backwards. The dairyman sat in front, feet dangling, back leaning against what would originally have been the crate's bottom.

The only way he could see inside the cart would be if he were to walk around and look inside. Better yet, he had no dog.

I snatched up the child, warning her again to silence, and trotted forward, grateful now for the blustering gusts that concealed my footsteps. Aiming at the rattling cans and hoping for the best, I tossed the child into the shadows and hopped in beside her. As the noise had suggested, the cans came nowhere near to filling the space, and there was room for us to creep around behind them. The road was rough enough that the driver took no note of the shift our boarding caused, and if the horse noticed our weight, he did not complain.

Estelle snuggled against me. The milk cans rattled; the waking island scrolled past the rear of our transport. We dozed.

The cart slowed, and stopped. I wrapped my arms more securely around the child, placing my finger across her lips. The farmer's boots crunched to the road, the cart jerking as his weight left it. I followed the sound of his footsteps, braced for sudden flight, but the steps continued away from us a few feet, paused, then returned, moving more slowly and with a hitch in their gait. A figure suddenly loomed at the back of the cart, and another canister of milk swung inside. He added a second, then climbed back onto his seat and chirruped the horse into motion.

He repeated the milk pickup half a mile down the road. Once we were moving, I worked my way towards the back, to ease the heavy canisters to one side. The road was smoother here, which meant that our sudden exit would be difficult to conceal. I waited for a rough patch, but before one came, I caught a faint odour of distillery, and knew we had run out of time.

I gathered the child in my arms and more or less rolled off the back to the road. The horse reacted, but by the time the startled driver had controlled the animal and reined it to a halt, Estelle and I were squatting behind a wall.

The man would have seen us, had he got down and walked back, but to him the jerk of the cart must have felt like a result of the horse's shy, not the cause of it. After a moment, I heard him repeat the noise between his teeth, and the music of milk cans retreated down the road.

I rose to get my bearings, and found that we were a scarce half-mile from where Captain Javitz had set us down.

"Can you walk for a bit, Estelle? We're nearly there."

In answer, she slipped her hand into mine and we set off up the road. It took two tries to find the correct lane, but to my relief, the 'plane was there, in a long field surrounded by walls and a hedgerow. Lights shone from the adjoining house, and I led my charge in that direction.

I stopped outside the gate to tell the child, "My friend Captain Javitz, who drives the aeroplane, may be here. There's also a nice lady and her son. But, we don't want to talk to them too much. We'll only be here for a few minutes."

"And then we'll go in the aeroplane? Into the air?"

"That's right," I said, adding under my breath, "God help us."

I knocked on the door.

It opened, to a man pointing a gun at my heart.

Chapter 5

At noon, the air began to stink of herring. Soon they came to Wick, dropping anchor inside the crowded harbour. Damian was pale, but the dressings remained brown.

Holmes picked a woollen Guernsey, much-mended and reeking of fish, from the pile atop Damian, pulling it on in place of his overcoat. He added a cap in similar condition, then took the glass from the oil lamp and ran a finger over the inside, washing his hands and face with a thin layer of lamp-black.

When he glanced down at Damian, the lad's eyes were watching him, and the bearded face twitched in a weak smile. "You look the part."

"Aye," Holmes said. "I'm rowing into the town to find a medical person who can pull that bullet out of you. Best if we do it here, rather than toss you in and out of a dinghy." His voice had taken on the flavour of the north, not a full Scots but on the edge.

"Still think you should've done it yourself."

"I might yet have to. Gordon will stay here with you."

"I'd kill for a swallow of tea."

"I'll let him know. Lie still, now." He turned to go.

"Er, Father?"

"Yes, son?" They had known each other less than three weeks: Both men still tasted the unfamiliar words on their tongues.

"Do you think—"

"Your daughter is safe. Without question. Russell will guard the child like a mother wildcat."

"And my..." He was unable to say the word.

"Your wife? Yolanda died, yes. I saw her body. No question."

"You are certain it was Hayden? Back at the Stones?"

"Yes." This was not the first time he'd answered the question.

Damian swallowed, as if to force down the information. "If I'm here, then...Her funeral?"

"Mycroft will take care of it." Which Holmes hoped was true—surely his brother's inexplicable tangle with Scotland Yard would be a temporary state of affairs?

"Would you," Damian said, his left arm working under the cloth mound. "—my pocket?"

Holmes pulled away the covers and felt Damian's pockets, coming out with a leather note-case.

"There's a picture," Damian explained.

Not a photograph, but an ink drawing he had done of his wife and small daughter, intricate as the shadings of a lithograph. There were headless nails in the rough wall near Damian's head; Holmes impaled the small page on one that lay in Damian's line of sight. A woman with Oriental features and a cap of black hair sat with a not-so-Oriental child with equally black hair: Damian had captured a look of wicked mischief on both faces.

Holmes stood.

"I'm sorry," Damian said. "About...everything."

The apology covered a far wider span than the preceeding three weeks, but Holmes kept his response light. "Hardly your doing. It's a nuisance, having the police after us, but it's not the first time. Once we patch you up, I'll deal with it."

"Hope so."

"Rest easy," Holmes said, and went up the ladder.

Twelve minutes later, a final hard pull on the oars ran the dinghy up on a sandy patch at the edge of the harbour. Holmes tied the painter to a time-softened tree trunk above the reach of the tide, then tugged at his cap and set off for the town, walking with the gait of the sailors around him. When he saw a police constable strolling in his direction, he raised his pipe and a cloud of concealing smoke, giving the PC a brief nod as he passed.

At the first chemist's shop, a bell tinkled when Holmes stepped inside, but the customers took little notice: Stray fishermen were a commonplace. On reaching the counter, Holmes asked for sticking plasters, a box of throat lozenges, and a tube of ointment for Persistent Rashes and Skin Conditions. Picking the coins from his palm, he then said, "M'lad on the boat picked up a baddish slice, mebbe should have a coupla' stitches. There a doctor in the town?"

"There was, he took ill. Got a locum, though. His cousin."

"He'll do," Holmes grunted, and asked for directions. The chemist grinned as he gave them, but it wasn't until the door to the surgery opened that Holmes realised why. The doctor's *locum tenans* was a she: a short woman in her late twenties with hair the red of new copper and the colouration that went with it: pale and freckled, with eyes halfway between green and blue set into features that might have been pretty had they not been pinched with the anticipation of his response.

"Yes," she said tiredly, "I'm a girl, but yes, I'm a qualified doctor, and no, my cousin won't return for two weeks or more, so unless you want to take your problem to Golspie or Inverness, I'm your man." Her accent was Scots, but not local. St Andrews, he decided, or Kirkcaldy—although she'd spent time in London and much of her youth in . . . Nottingham?

The analysis ran through his mind in the time it took him to draw breath. "Can you stitch a cut?"

She cocked her head at him, considering his matter-of-fact tone. "I said I was a doctor, didn't I? Of course I can stitch a cut. And deliver a bairn or set a leg or remove an appendix, for that matter."

"Well, I dinna require obstetrical care or major surgery, but I've a lad needing attention, if you'd like to bring your bag."

Her surprise made him wonder how many times she'd watched would-be patients turn away. "Amazing," she said. "And he hasn't been bleeding quietly for a week before you decided I'd have to do?"

"Just since midnight."

She shook her head, donned her hat, picked up her bag, and followed him out onto the street.

"Where is the cut?" she asked, half-trotting to compensate for his longer stride.

"Over the ribs."

"How did he come by it?"

"Oh, I think you'll see when you get there."

"And where is 'there'?"

"Fishing boat. Moving him starts up the bleeding, I thought it best to have you look at it where he lies."

"If there's much motion, we'll have to bring him to shore."

"We'll face that if we have to. Come, the dinghy's along there."

"Can't you bring the boat up to the docks?"

"Not worth hauling anchor, it's nobbut two minutes out."

He led the doctor down an alleyway, around the back of a herring shed, and through mountains of precisely stacked whisky barrels, which was hardly a direct route but he'd spotted the PC down the lane, and didn't want to risk a second encounter. By the time they hit the small beach, the doctor was scurrying to keep up, and Holmes had become aware of a helmeted presence behind them.

He strode ahead of the diminutive doctor and had the boat untied and floating free before she caught him up. "Are we—" she started to say, but he seized her shoulders to lift her bodily in over the last bit of mucky sand, letting go before she was fully balanced. She plopped onto the seat with a squeak of protest; he stepped one foot inside and shoved off with the other, nearly toppling her backwards as the small craft shot away from the land and rotated 160 degrees. Two quick pulls of the oars completed the turn-about, and they were soon beyond shouting distance, leaving a puzzled PC on the shore, scratching the head beneath his helmet.

The doctor, with her back to the town, noticed nothing apart from her escort's haste. She straightened her hat, tucked her black bag underneath the seat, and scowled at the man working the oars. "As I was about to ask, are we in a hurry?"

"Tide's about to turn. I didn't want to risk losing the dinghy, but we're all right now. I hope you'll be having a scalpel in that bag of yours?"

"Of course. But why should I require a scalpel to stitch a cut?"

"Ah, about that. There is a hole in the lad's epidermis, all right. Unfortunately, there's a small lump of lead as well."

"A lump of—do you mean a *bullet*?"

"That's right."

"What have you dragged me into?" At last, she sounded uneasy. High time, thought Holmes sourly, and allowed the Scots to leave his diction.

"In fact, you're walking on the side of the angels, although I'd recommend in the future that a person who barely clears five feet might do well to ask a few more questions before she goes off with a strange man. Our situation here is . . . complicated, but all I need is for you to cut out the bullet and patch up the entrance hole, and we'll set you back safe and sound on firm land." *Although I fear,* he added to himself, *some distance from where you began.*

She gaped at him, then turned about as if to see how far she might have to swim to reach safety. The constable was still visible, but his back was turned, and she'd have needed a megaphone against the sharp breeze. When she faced Holmes again, she was angry beyond measure, and the flush in her fair skin made her eyes blaze blue.

"I don't know what you're about, but kidnapping is a felony."

"You're merely making a house call. Or, boat call," he amended. "I intend to pay you, generously. I swear to you, neither I nor the wounded man have done anything remotely illegal." Yet.

She studied his face, and the anger in her own subsided with her fear. "If you've done nothing illegal and yet he's been shot, why not go to the police?"

"As I said, the situation is delicate at present. A misunderstanding. And being far from home, difficult to clear up."

"Where is home?"

"Manchester," he said promptly, and then they were at the boat, and Gordon was reaching down to help the doctor aboard.

"Captain," Holmes said before the fisherman could speak, "this is

Doctor Henning. However, I think it may be best for everyone if we leave our names out of this. If she does not know our names, she need not worry about the consequences of speaking freely."

Gordon stared at the petite figure at the other end of his arm. "This is a *doctor?*"

Chapter 6

The Reverend Thomas Brothers, seated before the peat fire in the Orkney cottage, smiled freely at the wording of the telegram MacAuliffe had brought him:

> IF HEALTH PERMITS MEET ME TUESDAY ST ALBANS
> GUNDERSON·HAS DETAILS.

Health did not permit, not really. But with Gunderson at his side, he might be able to make it—and the chance to actually meet The Friend after all this time made it worth the effort. Besides which, as any leader knew, it was never a good idea to reveal weakness to one's lessers, not if one might need them for whatever the future held.

Three days, to make his way down the length of the country; three days to reconsider what failure meant.

If failure it was. One thing Brothers knew was that the Fates took a mysterious hand in all human acts. If his long and laboriously constructed Great Work had fallen apart, if the blood on the Stenness altar stone had failed to unite with the timing of the solar eclipse, if an accumulation of blood and Energies had spilt out for naught, then either the Fates were cruel, or he had not understood the demands of the Work.

He wished he had someone to talk this over with. MacAuliffe had as much sense as one of the sheep bleating outside the door, and Gunderson was little more than a useful tool. Yolanda would be the ideal ear, willing, if uncomprehending, but his one-time wife was dead now, in what he had thought would be a key element of his Work.

Which brought him in a circle again: What had happened?

Brothers shifted in the chair in front of the smoke-blackened stones, wincing as the sharp pain grabbed at his breast. The powerful home-brew in the glass helped take the edge off it, but the prospect of travel was not a happy one.

Gunderson would help. With all kinds of problems.

Chapter 7

The clever young man stood at the wide window with a glass in his hand, looking through his reflection at midnight London. Standing as he was, his head's shadow engulfed most of the houses of Parliament, the white streak over his temple overlaid the face of its famous clock, his chest engulfed Westminster Bridge and the hungry, flat, greasy River Thames, while his raised right elbow rested on the palace of the archbishop.

God of all he surveyed.

His presence in this place was a quirk, an anomaly that would have surprised all who knew him, were they ever to be invited here. Grey and invisible minions of government did not live among the warehouses of London's South Bank, no more than did men whose ambitions encompassed government as his reflection encompassed Whitehall. Not that any of his colleagues knew of his ambitions, any more than they knew of his home.

The building had belonged to his grandfather, who had lost it—or, from whom it had been stolen—along with the rest of the family inheritance. The grandson was on medical leave in 1917, following the bullet that left him with a streak of white in his hair, when his restless wanderings brought him here, to an empty and derelict warehouse, part of its roof taken off by a zeppelin attack. He had made a surreptitious and scandalously low offer for it—a steal, one might say—and in his first deliberate act of self-concealment, become its owner. After the Paris talks he had returned to London and a new position, and now he stood at the big north-facing window in the modern flat raised up from the top floor, his outline a frame over the powers of the empire.

So appropriate, that dim outline. Nothing overt, no splashes of the politician's mark or estate magnate's hammer. Merely a shadow, colouring all it overlay.

He'd found it every bit as easy to construct a hidden life as it was to construct a charismatic façade or the reputation for front-line fortitude. Men liked him, women, too, and beguiled by the wit and easy charm, none of them noticed that they knew nothing about the man underneath.

Even Whitehall scarcely knew he was here. Few so much as suspected a presence among the anonymous halls.

Mycroft Holmes was one. He thought that, in recent months, Holmes had caught a faint trace of someone at his heels: Why slim down and take up with a lady, unless in a pointless drive to reclaim youth? However, he'd been looking over Holmes' shoulder since 1921 without giving himself away—how else would he have known about the letter from Shanghai?

The few in this vast hive below who could put his face and a name to an act were all career criminals, who mattered less than nothing. Criminals could be bought or disposed of; as for Mr Holmes, well, it was all in the works now.

His current situation reminded him of a Vaudeville act he'd once gone to see at the urging of, oddly enough, Churchill. On the stage, a dapper gent juggled an increasing number of ever more disparate objects— a cricket ball, a roast leg of goose, a lit candle, a yelping puppy. The key element of the act had been the insouciance, even boredom, with which the fellow had caught each additional oddity thrown his way, incorporating it casually into his motions. The whole was intended to be madly humorous, as indeed the low-brow audience found it, but he thought it more effective as a paradigm: One's raw material matters less than one's confidence.

Take the telegram from the primitive reaches of the British Isles.

Brothers had been—predictably—shocked at his failure to achieve the immortality of Divine Transformation up in Orkney, yet he overlooked the real question: How could a man, armed with knife, gun, and heavy narcotics, not only fail at murder, but manage to get himself wounded as well?

Another ill-matched object to keep up in the air.

Ah, well. That was what one got from depending on elaborate plots with many moving parts. It had all been far too beautiful, too gorgeously complex and inexorable—until an artist had inexplicably failed to die, and dropped a spanner into the clockworks.

Still, it wasn't a total loss. Parts of the machine were still turning nicely, and since they were dependent only on his own actions, they would continue to run. From here on out, he would abandon the complex, and keep things simple, and brutal.

The clock across the way told him it was time for sleep: He had a seven o'clock appointment, a full day of meetings, and a trip to St Albans to arrange. He drained his glass and went to bed, where he slept without dreams.

Chapter 8

The grey-haired man in the dusty stockings stood in his London prison and studied the equation on the wall. The odd dreaminess of his imprisonment made it an effort to direct his mind to the formula and what it represented; still, it was what Buddhists called a *koan*, a focal point for the mind, a conundrum with a puzzle at its core.

$$a \div (b+c+d)$$

Ironic, to use schoolboy maths—beaten into him when Victoria still wore colour—to develop a theorem for the most complex and dangerous political manoeuvring of his career.

As ironic as the entire situation being based on a simple truth of governmental bookkeeping: A department immune to budget cuts is the most powerful department in the government.

$$a \div (b+c+d)$$

The a in the formula was his position in His Majesty's Government, a job his brother Sherlock had once whimsically described as "auditing the books in some of the Government departments." It was an apt description, in both the meanings of auditor: one who examines the accounts, and one who listens.

He had listened to a lot of secrets, in his career.

In his first draughts of this formula, a had represented himself, but he had revised that and replaced the person with the position; b was the age of the present incumbent. Not that he felt old, but he had to admit, the looking-glass in his bath-room startled him at times. *c* stood for the Labour Government, new, fragile, and perceived by many as a vile Bolshevik threat. And *d*, of course, was his own heart attack last December, the subsequent convalescence, and the lingering sense of vulnerability and impermanence.

He pinched the nail between his fingers, and paused.

His *e* was to be he, himself, the sum of nearly half a century of auditing the books of the empire. But on which side did that fifth element go: debit, or credit?

Once, that old man in the glass had been strong and flexible in mind and body. Now, he lived in an age where youth was all, where flightiness was virtue, where a man of a mere seventy years was made to feel outdated. Where Intelligence had become a Feudal stronghold, with peasants clamouring at the gates.

Once, he'd lived in a world where one could tell a man's profession and history by a glance at his hands and the turn of his collar, but now every other man spent his days in an anonymous office, and even shop-keepers wore bespoke suits.

Perhaps his time was past...

But, no; *e* was himself and the rest was mere doubt: He added an up-right to the horizontal line he'd scratched, and the equation read:

$$a \div (b+c+d) + e$$

e, after all, was Mycroft Holmes. Lock him in a dank attic, withhold his meals, force him to use his neck-tie as a belt and a slip of metal for a pencil, starve him of information and agents and human tools, ultimately there was no doubt: He would walk away. Sooner or later, his mind would cut through solid wall, build a ladder out of information, weave wings out of words and clues and perceived motions.

He found that he was sitting on the floor; the angle of light through the translucent overhead window had shifted. Odd. When had that happened? For a moment, a brief moment, he entertained the possibility that lack of adequate sustenance was making him light-headed.

But surely the past eight months of denying the body's surprisingly strong urges, shedding 4 stone 10 in the process, would have hardened him to thin rations?

No, he thought. It was merely the disorientation that comes with a pro-longed lack of stimulation. Still, he could not help wishing that he had been gifted with his younger brother's knack of using hunger to stoke the mental processes. Under present circumstances, Sherlock's mental processes would be fired to a white-hot pitch that would melt the walls.

Personally, Mycroft found a growling stomach a distraction.

Chapter 9

The business end of a gun is remarkably distracting. It dominates the world. So it wasn't until the weapon fell away that I looked past it to see the familiar scarred features of my pilot, who swore and reached for my arm. "There you are! I've known some troublesome girls in my time, but sweetheart, you take the—oh, hey there, honey, come on in," he added in a very different voice, and the hand at his side shifted to hide the gun completely. He peeled back the door to encourage us to enter, standing almost behind it so as not to frighten the child at my side.

"I didn't see you there, little Miss," he said. His voice was soft with easy friendship, and it occurred to me that he might have had a family, back in America before the War and the 'plane crash that left his face and hand shiny with scar tissue. "Do come in, it's chilly out there and Mrs Ross would be happy to set some breakfast in front of you. That's right, in you come, and pay no attention to the big ugly man who met you with a growl."

Estelle glued herself to my side. When the door was shut, she peered around me at Javitz. I looked down and said, "Estelle, this is the man with the aeroplane. He didn't mean to frighten you."

"What's on your face?" she asked him.

He gave no indication of the distress it must have caused, this first re-action from any new acquaintance. "I got burnt, a long time ago. Looks funny but it doesn't hurt."

"Did it hurt then?"

"Er, yes. It did."

"I'm sorry."

After a minute, he tore his gaze away from her to look at me. "Where have you been?"

"Probably best you don't know, just yet. Why the, er, armament?"

"Someone tried to jigger with the machine last night. I happened to be outside and heard them, so I stood guard to make sure they didn't get another chance. The lad took over at daybreak. I was about to set out and look for you."

"Well, I'm here. Is the 'plane ready? Can we go before the wind gets too strong?"

"What, both of you?"

"Estelle can sit on my lap."

"Where are her—" He caught himself, and looked from me to her.

"Her parents asked me to look after her for a couple of days. We'll meet them up later."

"My Papa's hurt," she piped up, contributing information I had given her some hours earlier. "His Papa is taking him to a doctor."

Javitz raised an eyebrow at me. I shook my head, warning him off any more questions, and asked, "Estelle, I'd bet you would like a quick bite of breakfast, wouldn't you?"

"Yes, please," she said emphatically. Javitz laughed—a good laugh, full and content, which I had not heard before—and led us towards the odours of bacon and toast.

The kitchen was warm and smelt like heaven. Javitz strolled in as if the room were his, and asked his hostess if she'd mind stirring up a few more eggs. I had met Mrs Ross briefly in another lifetime—the previous afternoon—as well as the lad currently out guarding the aeroplane, but there was still no sign of a husband. I decided not to ask.

The mistress of the house was a bit surprised at my reappearance with a child in tow—particularly a child with such exotic looks—but she greeted us cheerily enough, and stretched out a hand for the bowl of eggs. I stayed until she had set two laden plates on the table, then tipped my head at Javitz. He followed me into the hallway.

"Who do you think was trying to get at the machine?" I asked.

"All I saw was a big fellow who ran away when he heard me coming."

Which indicated it wasn't the police, I thought: That would have made things sticky. "Well, as soon as Estelle has eaten, let's be away. How much petrol have we?"

"She's full. I didn't know if you'd want to go beyond Thurso, but there was nothing for me to do here except fetch tins of petrol."

"Yes, sorry. Is the lad big enough to turn the prop for us?"

"Should be, yes."

"Good. I'd like you to take us back to Thurso—perhaps this time we can find a field closer to the town? Estelle and I will catch a train from there, if you don't mind making your own way back to London." It was all very well to risk my own neck bouncing about in mid-air and alternately roasting and freezing in the glass-covered compartment, but I felt that the sooner I could return my young charge to terra firma, the better. Thurso might carry a risk of arrest, but at least I would get her away from Brothers. And with luck, Javitz could land and quickly take off again, all eyes on him while Estelle and I slipped into town and away: There might be a warrant out for Mary Russell, but I thought it unlikely that any rural constable, seeing a woman with a child getting onto a train, would call that warrant to mind.

Javitz looked as if he would object to the plan, but considering the trouble we'd had on the way up here, he could hardly insist that the air was the safest option.

I wiped Estelle's face (Mrs Ross tactfully suggested a visit to the cloakroom for the child, a nicety I'd have overlooked) and led her out through the garden to the walled field. There it sat, this idol of the modern age, gleaming deceptively in the morning light. It had tried its hardest to kill me on the way up from London; I was now giving it another chance—with the child thrown into the bargain. I muttered a Hebrew prayer for travellers under my breath and climbed inside. Javitz passed Estelle up to me, and as he climbed into his cockpit before us, I let down the glass cover.

In the end, Mrs Ross herself pulled the prop for us, yanking it into life while her son oversaw operations from the top of the stone wall. Estelle's nose was pressed to the glass that covered our passenger compartment, watching the ground travel past, first slowly, then more rapidly. She shot me a grin as the prop's speed pushed us back into our seats; I grinned right back at her, and pushed away thoughts of Icarus and his wings.

Then we tipped up, took a hop, and were airborne. Estelle squealed with excitement when the wind caught us. She exclaimed at the houses that turned into sheds and then doll-houses, the horses receding to the size of dogs and then figurines, a motorcar becoming a toy, and a man on a bicycle who became little more than a crawling beetle. We rode the wind up and up over the town, then Javitz pulled us into a wide circle and aimed back the way we had come, roaring lower and lower. The houses, animals, and figures grew again as he prepared to buzz over the Ross rooftop—and then I glimpsed the man on the bicycle, only he was not simply a man, he was a man with a constabulary helmet, and he was standing on the Ross walkway craning up at us.

Five minutes later and he'd have caught us on the ground.

Estelle kept her face glued to the glass, her bony knees balanced on my thighs. I tucked most of the fur coat around her, and tried to ignore the frigid air brushing my neck and taking possession of my toes. It was less than forty miles to Thurso as the crow flew—although slightly longer for a Bristol Tourer that kept over land for much of the time. In any event, under less than an hour we would be trading our hubristic mode of transportation for the safety of a train, to begin our earth-bound way southward, towards civilisation and the assistance of my brother-in-law. Who would surely have reasserted his authority by then.

We approached Thurso as we had left it, over the coast-line between the town and Scotland's end at John o' Groats. The wind was powerful, but nowhere near as rough as it had been when we fought our way north. From time to time, Javitz half-rose in his cockpit to peer at the ground past the high nose of the 'plane, making minor corrections each time.

Unbidden, a thought crept into my mind: Would it be irresponsible of me to turn over the duties of nurse-maid to Javitz—just for the day— while I returned to the islands to see what could be done about Brothers? Clearly, the pilot had friends in the area. And he seemed to know better than I how to communicate with children. Yes, I had promised Estelle's father that I would watch over her; but surely removing the threat of Brothers would offer a more complete protection? Or was this merely what I wanted to do, and not what I should do?

We had shed altitude as we followed the coast-line south. Before the town began, Javitz throttled back, correcting his course a fraction each time he stood to examine the terrain. We were perhaps a hundred feet from the ground, and even I in my seat could glimpse the approaching harbour, when a sinister chain of noises cut through the ceaseless racket: a slap, a gasp, and an immediate, high-pitched whistle.

Javitz had been half-standing, but he dropped hard into his seat and wrenched at the controls, slamming the aeroplane to the side and making its mighty Siddeley Puma engines build to a bone-shaking thunder.

Estelle shrieked as her head cracked against the window. I grabbed for her, pulling her to my chest as her cries of fear mingled with the engine noise and the untoward whistle of air. Then in seconds, the sideways fall changed and everything went very heavy and terribly confusing. I was dimly aware of something raining down on my arm and shoulder as— I finally realised what the motion meant—we corkscrewed our way upwards. *Glass*, I thought dimly, falling from a shattered window. I pulled the protective fur coat up around the cowering child and shouted words of reassurance, inaudible even to my own ears.

In the blink of an eye, the world disappeared, and we were bundled into a grey and featureless nothing. Following one last tight circuit of the corkscrew, our wings tilted the other way and we grew level. I could feel Estelle sobbing, although I could scarcely hear her against the wind that battered through the broken pane. I rocked the armful of fur as my eyes darted around the little compartment, trying to see where all that glass had gone.

But what drew my gaze was not the jagged glass: It was the neat hole punched through the front wall of the passenger compartment.

Javitz spent a moment settling the controls, then gingerly swivelled in his seat to see if we were still intact. As his eyes came around, they found the hole: From his position there would be two—one in the partition between us, and one through the bottom of his seat. Had he been seated, the round would have passed straight through him. We looked through the glass at each other, and I watched his eyes travel to the smashed window, then to the child in my arms. I saw his mouth move, and although I couldn't have heard if he'd shouted, I could read their meaning.

I lifted the coat until my lips were inches from the child's head. "Estelle, are you all right? Estelle, child, I know you're scared, but I need to know if you're hurt at all."

The head stayed tucked against me, but it shook back and forth in answer. I smoothed the coat back around her and mouthed to Javitz, "We're fine. What happened?"

In answer, he raised his right hand and made a gun out of it. Yes, I thought—although it had to have been a rifle, not a revolver. Before I could say anything, he turned around again and set about getting us below the clouds.

I studied his back, seeing the motion of his head and shoulders as he consulted the instruments and worked the control stick between his knees. The grey pressing around us thinned, retreated, and eventually became a ceiling.

Javitz craned over the side at the ground, made a correction on the stick, then hunched forward for a minute before turning to press a note-pad to the glass between us. On it was written:

NOT THURSO, THEN. WHERE?

All I could do was shrug and tell him, "South."

He looked from the window to the lump in my arms, then wrote again.

SHALL I LAND SO WE CAN FIX THAT WINDOW?

I shook my head vigorously. If he could survive in the unprotected front of the 'plane, we two with our fur wrapping could hold out until we had reached safety.

Wherever that might be.

Chapter 10

We flew on through the grey, light rain occasionally streaking back against the glass. I had hoped the warm furs and steady course might reassure the child, but she remained where she was, a taut quivering ball.

Could I remember being three and a half years old? Not really, but my childhood had been a comfortable place until I was fourteen and my family died. This soft creature in my arms was too young to have a sense of history, too new to understand that terror passes, that love returns. In the past month—for her, an eternity—her mother had disappeared (died, although I was not going to be the one to tell her) and left her with a strange man (who had, in fact, been the one who killed Mother) until Papa came and joined the man for a furtive series of trains and boats to a cold, empty, smelly house, where she had wakened to find herself in the possession of a strange woman. A woman who had then hauled her through the night and pushed her into a noisy machine that was fun for ten minutes before it turned very scary.

My hand stroked the child's back, counting the faint vertebrae and the shape of her shoulder-blades. What must it be like, to be so without control that one would submit to a stranger's comforting?

But my hand kept moving, and after a minute, I bent to speak to the scrap of black hair and pink ear that emerged from the fur. "Shall I tell you a story, Estelle?"

There was no response, but I kept stroking, and started talking.

"Once upon a time there was a lady from America. She was a singer, a beautiful singer, who—sorry, did you say something?"

She turned her head slightly, and the faint murmur became words: "My Grandmama was a singer."

"I know, and this is a story about her."

I constructed a tale about the woman, a sort of *midrash* based on the little I knew about her, depending more on the drawings Damian had done of his childhood home than actual fact. The story was about opera, and her grandmother's cleverness, and the French countryside, and it was a distraction as much to me as it was to her. Slowly, the child in my arms grew more solid as a sleepless night and the ebb of terror did their work. Eventually, she shuddered and went limp.

I finished the story, and wrapped my arms around the warm little body. For the first time in hours, I had nothing to do but sit quietly and fret. Instantly, a wave of thoughts rose up and crashed over me.

A *sniper*, in Thurso? Brothers might have got away from the Stones alive, but he'd been in no condition to place a rifle to his shoulder—although he'd had assistance on Orkney before, and after the War, firing a rifle was hardly an unusual skill. How difficult was it, to hit a low-flying aeroplane? As difficult as hitting a deer, or a soldier on the other side of no-man's-land?

I did not even consider the possibility of an accidental discharge—if we'd been peppered with stray birdshot, perhaps, but this had been a single round. Someone had wanted to bring us down.

Not the police. Even if they had been unaware of the child on board, my crimes hardly justified a deadly assault.

It had to be Brothers or one of his men—and yet he'd wanted the child: Back in the hotel, I'd found a forged British passport for him and Estelle. Had he decided that if he couldn't have her, no one should? Had he given the order, not knowing I had her? If not Brothers and his local assistance, then who?

My thoughts went around and around, considering the possibilities of what had happened, what it meant, what came next. I blame that pre-occupation, along with the distraction of fear and the weight of responsibility, for missing the obvious. Of course, there was little I could have done even if I had known—ours was not an aeroplane with dual controls in the passenger compartment. Still, it took a shamefully long time for me to make note of the placement of the holes, to calculate the trajectory between the back of Javitz's seat and the overhead window-pane, then compare it to the actual position of my pilot when the round passed through.

When I had done so, I felt a cold that had nothing to do with the blast of air. I loosed an arm from the coat and stretched out to rap against the glass. Javitz slowly turned: The hesitation of his movements told me all I needed to know.

"How bad?" I mouthed.

He pretended not to understand. I grimaced, and began to trace the letters of my question, backwards against the glass.

HOW BAD IS YOUR LEG?

I could see him waver on the edge of denial, but my glare changed his mind. He wrote on his pad, and held it up:

BLEEDING, BUT USABLE. I PUT A TOURNIQUET ON IT.

In reply, I traced:

PUT DOWN AS SOON AS YOU CAN FIND A PLACE.

He shook his head, so decisively I could tell there was little arguing with him, so I changed it to:

GIVE IT AN HOUR? TO PUT US WELL CLEAR OF
BEING FOLLOWED.

He started to turn back when he saw my gesture and waited for me to add:

LOOSEN THE TOURNIQUET EVERY TEN MINUTES
OR YOU'LL LOSE THE LEG.

He nodded, and showed me the back of his head. We flew on through the morning, a trapped woman, a sleeping child, and a pilot slowly bleeding to death at the controls.

Chapter 11

H e's bleeding to death," Sherlock Holmes said with forced patience. It was good he'd had so much practice with stubborn females. Why couldn't this one be more like Watson, who at least placed medical needs before debate? Although Watson had never been shanghaied by having an anchor raised while he was below decks. Come to think of it, perhaps he should be grateful Dr Henning hadn't turned her scalpel on him.

"He'll lose it all the faster if my scalpel jerks. I'll not cut until this boat is still."

Holmes ran his hand over his hair, staring down at his half-conscious son. Without a word, he climbed up to have a word with Gordon.

"We need to keep the boat on a steady keel again for a while."

"How long?"

"Half an hour, perhaps longer."

"I did say we should stay in t'harbour."

"I couldn't risk it."

"Well, if you're thinking to anchor in a nice quiet bay, you picked the wrong coast of Scotland."

"Short of a bay, can you give us calm?"

"If I keep heading before the wind."

"Do that, then."

"You do know the farther out I go, the harder it will be to beat our way back?"

"Can't be helped."

"You'll buy me half a boat by the time you're finished," Gordon grumbled.

"I'll buy you the whole boat if you get us out of this in one piece."

"I'll hold you to that."

Holmes helped Gordon adjust the sails, then lingered on deck as the boat settled into its new course. He rested his eyes on the Scottish coastline, directly astern now and fast retreating. If Russell—

No. He turned his back on the land and on problems beyond his control. Brothers was dead, Russell was in no danger, and the rest was travail and vexation of spirit.

With the change in direction, the boat's troubled passage was replaced by an easy roll. Down below, he raised an eyebrow at his captive. "Will that be sufficient?"

"What if I say no?"

"Then you'll have to stand by and watch me do my best with your scalpel."

She bent her head for a moment, judging the motions of the hull, then asked abruptly, "How did you know my name?"

"Your diploma is behind the desk in your surgery."

"You have good eyes, if you saw the print from across the room."

"I don't miss much," he agreed.

"And this is your son, and you don't wish to come into contact with the police, yet you swear you have done nothing wrong."

"Correct. On all three counts."

The whole time, her concentration had been on the boat's rhythm, and now her head dipped once in grudging approval. "I can manage, if it doesn't get worse. Boil a kettle. And I'll need clean towels, a better light, and a bowl. A well-scrubbed bowl."

"Yes, ma'am," he said, and moved the kettle onto the stove, tossing more coal into its already glowing interior.

Her hands were small, but when Holmes watched them ease away the dried and clotted dressings, he found their strength and precision reassuring. Her fingertips marched a slow exploration of the patient's side, lifting as Damian's breath caught, then going on. When she sat back, Holmes spoke.

"Those two ribs are the reason I didn't want to move him before the bullet was out."

"A punctured lung is not a pretty thing," she agreed. "However, I think they're only cracked, not fully broken. Help me turn him so I can get at his back—I want to take care not to twist the ribs further."

The bullet had ricocheted off stone before hitting flesh. Had it hit a few inches higher, it would have reached the heart or lungs, and Damian would be the one lying dead on the standing stones' altar, not Brothers. Had it retained more of its initial energy, it would have smashed through the ribs into the heart or lungs, and they would have a three-and-a-half-year-old orphan on their hands. Instead, the bullet had burrowed a track between bone and skin until it was stopped by the powerful muscles attached to the shoulder-blade.

Dr Henning's fingers delicately probed the clammy skin. "My hands are like ice," she complained. "Could you slide the hatch shut, please?"

"Your patient is pathologically claustrophobic," Holmes told her.

She looked down at the face that lay inches from her knees, then up to the hatch atop the companionway ladder, held open on the deck as it had been since leaving Orkney. "I don't carry chloroform in my bag."

"Not needed," Damian replied, his voice gritty but firm.

"Very well, we'll make do with morphia."

"No!" both men said in the same instant. Her eyes went wide as she looked from Damian to Holmes.

"Drugs are not a good idea," Holmes explained, in bland understatement.

"I see. So, no sedation, and I work with cold hands. Any other problems you'd like to tell me about? Haemophilia? Hydrophobia? St Vitus' Dance?"

"Just the bullet," he assured her. She shook her head, and went back to her examination.

At long last, the doctor was satisfied that she had all the evidence her fingers could give her. She arranged pillows and bed-clothes around her patient, shifting his limbs as impersonally as she would the settings on a tea-tray. Holmes went to check on the kettle.

"Have you studied the sorts of wounds received in war?" he asked over his shoulder. He knew that she had spent time nursing wounds, but not where.

"This is from a revolver, not a rifle or bayonet."

Which response probably answered his question. "I was referring to the dangers of infection following a wound with a fragment of clothing in it."

"This will be my first *private* case of a bullet wound," she said, "but I worked as a VAD during the War. I have seen gas gangrene, yes."

"You must have been fifteen years old."

"Nineteen," she said.

When the water had boiled and the bowls and implements were clean, Holmes carried them over to the impromptu operating theatre. Dr Henning scrubbed her hands, leaving them in the bowl to warm while Holmes climbed onto the bunk, arranging his legs on either side of his son's torso. When he nodded his readiness, the deft hands dried themselves on a clean cloth and took up the scalpel, suspending it over the lump beneath Damian's skin. The boat tipped and swayed, riding out a swell, and at the instant of equilibrium, the fingers flicked down to make a precise cut in the flesh. Damian bit back a whine, but the cut was made, and in moments she was easing the bullet out as Holmes locked the young man's arching body into immobility. The fingers staunched the blood, then reached delicately down to retrieve a clot of threads that had ridden the bullet through the body. They looked at each other over the bloody scrap, and smiled.

Ten stitches, and four more to close the entrance wound in the front, then she was wrapping a length of gauze tight around Damian's ribs. When they eased him flat again, he cautiously drew breath, and his mouth twitched with relief. He met her eyes. "Thank you."

"My pleasure," she said.

Chapter 12

I may have wrapped my arms more tightly around the child, following the realisation of our pilot's condition. I know I prayed.

We had been flying for a quarter hour or so when I became conscious that my lips were moving, and that the words they shaped were Hebrew: *Yehi ratzon mil'fanecha*, the prayer of the traveller begins. *If it be Thy will, to lead us towards peace, to guide our footsteps in the way of peace, to have us reach our destination of peace.* The repetition of *shalom*, meaning both peace and health, is said to calm the nerves. Mine could certainly use some calming.

But *how* had Brothers followed us? The man was a religious charlatan, not some master criminal with a platoon of armed men at his beck and call. Yes, he had Marcus Gunderson, but I'd questioned Gunderson myself, at the point of a knife, and there had been no indication that he was one of a platoon of Thugees.

Brothers' mumbo-jumbo was the spiritual equivalent of eating an enemy's heart. He believed that by spilling blood at carefully chosen places and times—lunar eclipse, summer solstice, meteor shower, today's eclipse of the sun—he would absorb the loosed psychic energies of his victims. However, he appeared to have kept this aspect of his teaching to himself: I had seen no evidence that he used any of his Inner Circle in his quest to become a god; only Gunderson.

With Brothers in my thoughts and the Hebrew on my lips, my mind turned to the nature of gods. The Hebrew Bible does not say that the gods do not exist, merely that we are not to worship them. For a Christian, doubt is a shameful secret, a failure of faith, but the rabbis have long embraced doubt as an opportunity for vigorous argument. For the rabbis, the existence of God is no more of a question than the existence of air: Doubt is how we converse with Him.

Small-*g* gods might be considered a sort of concentrated essence: Loki the impulsive, Shiva the destroyer, Wayland the craftsman. The local gods were why Brothers had come to Britain, a country littered with Norse and Roman deities. The Holmes brothers were a bit god-like: generous and well meaning towards lesser mankind, but capricious and sometimes frightening in their omniscience. What, I wondered sleepily, would Brothers have embodied, had he succeeded in becoming a god? For that matter, what god would carry the attributes of flying machines? Which deity would be represented by the rifle?

As I sat in the deafening, cramped and frigid compartment, behind a dying pilot, holding a child for whom I could do nothing, incredibly, imperceptibly, I drifted into sleep.

The grey scraps of cloud outside, tossed like leaves in a fitful breeze, shifted, becoming wind-tossed foliage. I was sitting not in a fragile device of metal and wood, but on a hillside, warm and secure in an ancient land. The foliage remained, a hedgerow bordering a field of summer wheat. The grain rippled with the breeze, the green wall danced, until in the midst of the leaves—or the scraps of cloud—I became aware of a Presence among the moving scraps of green or grey: a pair of eyes that were there and then gone, that met mine and were hidden again. Green, grey; there, gone; comfort, threat.

I must have made a noise, because the child in my arms stirred, pushing away the heavy coat to rub her eyes and look around her.

"What did you say?" she asked me.

"I didn't say anything, honey."

"Yes, you did," she insisted.

"I fell asleep, and was dreaming. It must have been something about that."

"I'm cold," she complained.

"It won't be much longer," I said. She gave me a look that declared her lack of reassurance at the statement. "Here, snuggle back under the coat," I suggested.

This must be what it felt like to be an Elizabethan noblewoman before a roaring fire, I thought: toasty warm in front, frigid in back.

"What was your dream about?" Estelle asked.

"Only a silly dream. A face peeping out from leaves."

"My Papa made a painting like that."

"Did he? Oh yes, I remember." I'd seen it in a London gallery—heavens, only two weeks before? *The Green Man*, Damian had called it, a Surrealist rendering of the ancient pagan spirit of the British Isles, the surge of life in this green land. The figure was carved into church ceilings and pews, painted on the signs of public houses, leading processions. He was often shown as a face with branches bursting from his mouth and nostrils and twining about his head in the exuberance of life: a divine creature, speaking in leaves.

Jack-in-the-Green, Will of the Wisp, Wild Woodsman: The figure represents not just life, but the cycle of birth and death and birth anew. His authority and mystery stand behind such diverse characters as Robin Hood and Puck. Damian's painting began as a study in green, a canvas entirely covered with leaves so precise, they might have been the colour photograph of a hedge. Only after examining the wall of greenery for some time, searching for meaning in the shades and shadows, did the viewer become aware that two off-centre points of light were not drops of water on leaves, but reflections from a pair of green eyes. Unlike the foliate heads carved into the stones of churches, nothing could be seen of the features—or rather, the skin seemed made of leaves instead of flesh—but the sense of watching was powerful. Not threatening, necessarily, just...eerie. Disturbing.

At the time, my thought had been, *Next time I walk in the woods, the back of my neck will crawl.*

Now I pulled my arms more snugly around the artist's child, and raised my eyes to what I could see of Javitz. He had stayed reassuringly upright; there was no indication that he was about to faint away and send us spinning to earth. Still, I wanted to get down as soon as we could.

The hour I had given him was less than half over, but the man urgently required medical attention.

I stretched out an arm to knock on the dividing glass. I could tell he heard me from the tilt of his head, but it took a minute for him to turn.

When he had done so, I held out my hand and slowly lowered it, palm down, to indicate that I wanted us to descend. He put up a finger, telling me to wait, then bent over his pad for a minute. He held up the message:

> I'M FINE. BLEEDING STOPPED. NO REASON
> NOT TO MAKE INVERNESS OR FORT WILLIAM.

Inverness was some eighty-five miles from Thurso, or less than an hour with the wind at our back as it was. Fort William was nearly twice that. I shook my head firmly, mouthing, "Inverness, not Fort William."

He shrugged, which I would have taken for capitulation except that I had a feeling that those scars were hiding an expression of stubbornness. He started to turn back, but I rapped hard on the glass, and spelt out in front of his eyes:

> KEEP LOOSENING THE TOURNIQUET.

Not bleeding: *Right,* I thought. *So why are you surreptitiously reaching down now to work the tie loose on your upper leg?*

The first thing I'd learned about this aeroplane was that its 230 horsepower engine would take it 500 miles on a tank of petrol. On the trip up here, we had failed to come anywhere near that, but—so far—it appeared that our curse of mechanical problems was in abeyance. Theoretically, 500 miles would take us near enough to London to smell the smoke—although if Javitz's hands were no longer on the controls, it could as easily land us in Ireland, France, or the middle of the North Sea.

How to force a man to your will when you could not reach him—could not even communicate if he chose not to turn his head? It was maddening, and his masculine pride was putting this child in danger.

I might have to break the pane of glass that separated us, even if it meant Estelle and I were in the full blast of air. The butt of the revolver would do as a hammer—but as I was reaching for it, I saw that Javitz had turned again, and was holding to the glass a longer message:

> I KNOW YOU'RE WORRIED ABOUT THE LITTLE GIRL, BUT HONEST, IF I FEEL MYSELF GOING THE LEAST BIT WOOZY, I'LL TAKE THE CRATE DOWN, NO HESITATION. I'VE BEEN WOUNDED BEFORE, I KNOW HOW IT FEELS TO BE SLIPPING AWAY, AND I WON'T TAKE ANY RISK WITH THE TWO OF YOU.
>
> BUT I CAN'T HELP THINKING ABOUT A MAN WITH A RIFLE IN THURSO, AND WONDERING HOW MANY MORE OF THEM MIGHT BE SCATTERED AROUND SCOTLAND. THE FARTHER SOUTH WE GET, THE GREATER THE CHANCE WE LOSE THEM. WHOEVER THEY ARE.
>
> IF YOU REALLY INSIST, AND YOU DON'T THINK THEY'LL BE WAITING FOR YOU THERE, I'LL TAKE US DOWN IN INVERNESS.
>
> UNLESS THERE'S A WHOLE ARMY OF THEM, THEY WON'T HAVE A MAN WAITING IN FORT WILLIAM. OR GLASGOW.
> YOUR CALL.

The farther you go, the harder it will be to catch Brothers, said a voice in my mind. I looked down at the burden in my arms, and pushed the thought away.

Javitz and I studied each other through the cloudy glass, me searching for a sign that his injury was worse than he was admitting, he waiting for my decision. Estelle stirred, and his eyes went to her, then came back to mine. His expression had not changed, and I could see neither doubt nor truculence there.

I mouthed, "Fort William."

He turned back to his controls; the noise from the engine picked up a notch.

Chapter 13

Chief Inspector Lestrade picked up the latest report from Scotland, then threw it down in disgust. It said the same thing all the other reports had said: no sign of them.

Lestrade was not a man much prone to self-doubt, not when it came to his job, but in the eight days since he'd posted the arrest warrants for Sherlock Holmes and his wife, he'd begun to wonder if he might not have been rash. Granted, their outright refusal to appear and be interviewed had left him with little choice in the matter, but even then, a part of him had refused to believe that the man had anything to do with the death of that artist's wife down in Sussex.

Yet, he was involved somehow. The name Adler could be no coincidence—the artist had to be related to Irene Adler, even if French records had been too thin to show precisely how.

Still, even if Damian Adler was a blood relation to the woman, what right did Holmes have to take matters into his own hands? An amateur investigator was a danger to society, and the man's attitude towards the police was outmoded, self-important, and frankly offensive. It happened every time Holmes appeared on the borders of a police investigation. It hadn't taken much urging for Lestrade to agree that it was high time to let Holmes know that a Twentieth-Century Scotland Yard would no longer tolerate his meddling and deceptions.

No matter how often the man had solved a crime the police could not.

No matter the respect Lestrade's father had held for the man.

No matter the reverence with which politicians and royals alike spoke of him.

Time to bring the old man down a peg, him and that upstart wife of his.

(If he could only lay hands on them.)

Except that now the man's brother had vanished as well.

He'd had Mycroft Holmes in two days before, and—surprise—the man had answered not one of his questions to his satisfaction. He'd been even more irritated when, half an hour after the man left, an envelope with his name on it was brought up—left by Mycroft Holmes at the front as he went out. Having spent two hours in Lestrade's office, he was now suggesting a meeting later that afternoon.

Lestrade had thrown the note into the waste-bin and got down to the day's work, but at five o'clock, he'd found himself going not home, but in the direction of the suggested meeting place.

But the man didn't show. Lestrade stood in the crowded halls amongst the children and the tourists, feeling more like an idiot every minute. He went home angry.

His anger had become slightly uneasy when the man's housekeeper telephoned bright and early the next morning to say that when she'd let herself into the Holmes flat that morning, her employer had been missing, and what was Scotland Yard going to do about it?

In fact, he'd been uneasy enough that he'd telephoned to the offices Mycroft Holmes kept in Whitehall. And when the secretary said that his employer hadn't come in that morning, and yes it was highly unusual, Lestrade had rung the caretaker at Mycroft Holmes' flat on Pall Mall: Mr Holmes had left Thursday morning, and not returned.

Not that there was much Lestrade could do about it yet. Mycroft Holmes was a grown man, and although he had not been seen since walking out the doors of Scotland Yard Thursday afternoon, there could be any number of reasons why he might have done so, and it was too early to assume foul play. The man had vanished on the same puff of smoke as his brother Sherlock, along with Mary Russell, Damian Adler, and Adler's small daughter. To say nothing of Reverend Brothers and his henchman Gunderson.

Nary a sign of any of them.

Chapter 14

An hour south of Thurso, I was relieved when the clouds at least grew light enough to suggest where the sun lay. However, its location also was a sign that we were not headed towards Fort William. Instead, Javitz was either aiming us at the other goal he had mentioned, Glasgow, or at Edinburgh to its east. Both cities were approximately two hundred miles from the island where we had started the day: two and a half hours at cruising speed, a little less with the push he had on now.

Estelle fell asleep again. The weak morning sunlight took some of the bitterness from the cabin's chill. Or perhaps I was fading into hypothermia. If so, I couldn't rouse myself to object.

Two hours south of Thurso, the big engine showed no sign of slowing, and I could perceive no change in our altitude. Javitz remained upright, and his head continued to swivel as he studied the instruments before him, so I hunkered down in the furs and tried to emulate my granddaughter.

Our decision was made for us by the machine itself. I jerked awake at a change in the noise around me, registered briefly that we'd come a lot farther than Glasgow, then realised that what woke me was something drastic happening below. Javitz responded instantly by cutting our speed and nudging the flaps to take us lower.

A moment's thought, and I knew what the problem was: The hole in our hull had given way, and was threatening to peel the metal skin down to the bones.

Land now, or crash.

For the first time in hours, we dropped below the clouds, although it took a moment before my eyes could make sense of the evidence before them: Somehow as I slept we had passed over all of Scotland, and were now in the Lake District—that could be the only explanation of those distinctive fells, that stretch of water in the distance. But on one of the aeroplane's sideways lunges, I saw that below us lay not nice bare hillside, or even water, but trees.

Green, stretching out in all directions, unbroken and reaching up to pull us to pieces.

Oh, dear.

Javitz was no doubt thinking the same thing, only with profanity. I could see his jaws moving as he cursed the timing of our forced descent, then he pulled himself all the way upright and I caught my first glimpse of his injury: The clothing over the left side of his body, waist to knee, was stained with blood; the white silk scarf he had used as a tourniquet on his upper thigh ranged from dark brown to fresh red.

The flapping noise grew louder, while Javitz struggled to counteract the effects of an increasingly large metallic sail under our feet.

A giant hand laid hold of us and tugged, and the very framework around us began to twist: In moments, the aeroplane would be ripped to pieces.

Javitz turned and shouted, loud enough for me to hear, "Brace yourself!"

There was little bracing I could do, rattling around in my miniature glass house as I was. I threw my arms and body around Estelle, and told her in a voice that I hoped was firm and comforting that we were going to land but it would be a big bump so she was to stay curled up and not be frightened—but my words were cut short as the giant hand jerked us with a crack felt in the bones. Javitz cut the fuel. For a moment, it was silent enough to hear my voice reciting Hebrew. Then the world exploded in a racket of tearing metal and crackling trees, the screams of three human voices, and an unbelievable confusion of sound and pain and turmoil as we tumbled end over end and fell crying into the dark.

Chapter 15

A crying seagull woke Damian. His eyes flared open, then squeezed shut against the pain. When he had himself under control, he looked first at his father, who had sat all night on a stool between the bunks, then towards the lump of bed-clothes opposite that was the kidnapped doctor.

Damian licked his dry lips; instantly, Holmes was holding a mug of water for him to drink. When his father had lowered his head to the pillow, the young man murmured, "Where are we?"

"Halfway to Holland, more or less."

"Holland? Why on earth—?"

"It would appear that is where the wind and waves care to take us."

"But we can't go to Holland. What about this poor woman?"

"She, in fact, cast the deciding vote. Having treated you, she was loath to watch her work go for naught by permitting the toss of the boat to reopen your wounds." What the doctor had said was, *As the people in Wick seem disinclined to offer me employment, I may as well stay with the one patient who will have me.* A sentiment that Holmes not only appreciated as a benefit to the lad in the bunk, but agreed with. Dr Henning had proved a surprisingly robust personality; he wondered what Russell would make of her.

Damian closed his eyes again, this time in despair rather than pain.

"First a boat, then a doctor. I should have stayed in Orkney and let myself be arrested."

An infinitesimal twitch from the bed-clothes betrayed the doctor's reaction to that last word.

"If we are both in gaol," Holmes said in a firm voice, "there will be no-one to prove your innocence. As soon as I assemble the evidence, we shall present it, and ourselves, to the police. Until then, subjecting you to incarceration will serve no end. And I believe we now must bring Dr Henning into our confidence."

Without the slightest chagrin, the woman threw off the covers and sat up, blinking at the two men. "I'd like a cup of tea before we launch into explanations," she said to Holmes, and to Damian, "How are you feeling?"

Holmes moved over to the stove while the other two concerned themselves with the sensations beneath the gauze. The doctor decided, as Holmes had earlier, that healing was under way, and no infection had begun.

He distributed the mugs, then pulled on a pair of stinking oilskins and a coat, stirred several spoons of sugar into a third mug of tea, and managed to get up the companionway without pouring it over himself.

The young fisherman's face was gaunt with fatigue and his fingers were clumsy as they stripped off their gloves and wrapped around the mug. Holmes laid a hand on the wheel and, as the beverage scalded a path down the fisherman's throat, said, "Your sense of responsibility is admirable, but you have been on deck for twenty-four hours, and you would better serve us all if you had some sleep. I am perfectly competent to keep us on a straight course for two or three hours."

Gordon said nothing, just savoured the hot, sweet drink while studying Holmes' hands, the sails, the sea. When the cup was empty, he said, "If anything changes—anything at all—you'll wake me?"

"I imagine any slight change will rouse you before I can call, but yes. If so much as a bird lands on the deck, I'll shout you up."

Without another word, Gordon walked across to the hatch, looking half-asleep already as his feet hit the companionway. When his head had disappeared, Holmes felt as if he were drawing breath for the first time in thirty-six hours.

It was, in truth, precisely the sort of undemanding distraction he required at this point: his eyes occupied with the shapes and heading of other vessels on the North Sea water while his mind took the Brothers case from the shelf to examine it. He even managed to get a pipe going, to assist his meditations.

The need to spirit Damian away had taken priority—although the urgency of an investigation did tend to lag when its main actor died—but he hoped that Russell had lingered in the burnt-out hotel where Brothers had gone to ground long enough to unearth its secrets.

Not that she would have stayed until daylight: The police were sure to arrive there, and Russell would choose the child's safety and freedom over any gathering of evidence. She would have done the best search she could by candle-light, then slipped away—removing or destroying first anything that might lead back to Damian.

But competent as Russell was, it remained a frustration to walk away from a case before its conclusion. True, they'd had no sign that Brothers' acolytes had either participated in or were poised to resume their master's crimes, but there was an itch at the back of his mind, the feeling that some piece of pattern did not quite match the others. Although even now, with the first leisure he'd had in days, he could not decide where that ill-fitting piece lay.

Perhaps, Holmes suggested to the machine in his mind that chewed up information and spat out hypotheses, the sensation of an ill fit was due not to something missing, but to the very nature of the man at its centre? Everything about Brothers—ideas, appetites, impulses, reason—was unbalanced; why should that not taint the case itself? Plus, there was no doubt that the speed of events over recent days made it impossible for data to catch him up. That alone made the case seem incomplete.

It was vexing, being unable to reach Russell, not even knowing how long it would be before he could reach her. Or Mycroft, for that matter.

Which raised a further source of aggravation: Mycroft. If the gaps in the Brothers case made for a mental itch, what he knew of Mycroft's situation brought on the hives: Mycroft Holmes, taken in for questioning by Scotland Yard? Lestrade might as easily interrogate the king.

He had just knocked out his second pipe-load into the sea when a head of tousled copper hair appeared from the open hatch. The quizzical expression on the doctor's face indicated that she and Damian had been talking, and that his son had kept little back.

"Sherlock Holmes?" The rising tone was not quite incredulity, but made it clear that she was questioning her patient's clarity of mind, if not his outright sanity.

"Madam," Holmes replied with a tip of the head, and resumed his study of the eastern horizon.

"I'm supposed to believe that?"

"A lady physician might be inclined towards belief in many impossible things."

"That's scarcely on the same level."

He sighed. "You wish me to prove myself. I might show you identification, but papers can be forged. And I might recite the details of my professional life, but you would protest that I had merely read Dr Doyle's fanciful tales in the *Strand*. Shall I then put on a demonstration, trot out my own patented brand of common sense? Shall I tell you that I know from your voice that you were born in Kirkcaldy and educated in Nottingham? That your father was a doctor who has either died or become incapacitated for work, freeing you to adopt his bag when you qualified? That the books and equipment you added to the somewhat antiquated surgery in Wick assured me that your skills were both considerable and up-to-date? That I knew you also had nursing experience because of the distinctive scarring on your fingers, which one sees on a person who has been in continuous proximity to infected wounds? That your shoes and your haircut are approximately the same age, which tells me you have been in Wick less than four weeks? That you wore a ring on your left hand for some years, and took it off around the time you started medical school? That—"

"All right! Stop!" She studied her left hand for a minute, comparing it to her right, then thrust both into her pockets. "You are often doubted, as to your identity?"

"One tends to use pseudonyms."

"And . . . your son. Although his name is Adler."

"His mother thought it best."

She pulled her coat more tightly around her, and considered the

decking. "My father died in the 1919 epidemic. And it was an engagement ring—the one I took off. When my fiancé died, it was all I had of
him. I wore it until 1922."

Holmes said nothing.

"Mr Adler's wife was very pretty. To judge by his drawing of her, that is."

"So I understand," Holmes agreed, although she'd not been particularly lovely when he saw her in the mortuary, the plucky little idiot
whose infatuation with a lunatic had landed them all in their current
predicament—but that was neither charitable nor pertinent.

"He tells me she was murdered."

"Two weeks ago. Damian only learnt of it yesterday. Her name was
Yolanda, a Chinese woman from Shanghai. I never met her in life, but
her first husband, from whom she had parted before she met Damian,
turned out to be a madman convinced that human sacrifice performed
at key places and auspicious times would transfer the psychic energies of
his victims into him. He killed Yolanda and at least three other innocents. It was his bullet you retrieved."

" 'Psychic energies'?" He felt her gaze boring against the side of his
head. "You're joking."

"Would that I were."

"He planned to make himself into . . ."

"A sort of Gnostic *Übermensch*, I suppose."

Either she understood the reference to Nietzsche, or she was too distracted to hear it. "And the police find this difficult to believe?"

He glanced at her, surprised not by sarcasm, but by the lack of it. Most
people of his acquaintance would cavil at the reasoning of the mad:
Dr Henning spurned the distraction to grasp the essentials. Admirable
woman.

"They may reach the same conclusion eventually; however, I was
disinclined to hand Damian over to them until they did so. As I said,
his reaction to being enclosed is extreme."

"What do you intend to do?"

"Were the wind less assertive, I'd have put in along the coast of England,
found a safe haven for Damian, and made my way to London. Now, I shall
have to shelter him in Europe and make a more circuitous way home."

She spotted a sturdy basket that had come to rest beside the capstan, and upended it, sitting with her face turned towards the long-vanished Scotland. "He says he's only known you a short while."

"We met briefly in the summer of 1919. After that, he went to Shanghai. I lost sight of him until he appeared on my terrace in Sussex, nineteen days ago."

"And in that time his wife died at the hands of a crackpot, and you solved the case, then uncovered several other deaths, and eventually tracked the murderer to far distant Orkney, where Mr Adler was wounded. And this mad religious leader was killed."

"An adequate précis, yes."

"You killed the man?"

"A gun went off; he died."

"And yet you say that you have committed no crime."

"Homicide in defence of self or family is not a crime. My son saved my life."

She blinked, not having expected that her patient was the man with the gun. After a minute, she asked, "The man was about to kill you?"

"Damian was his intended sacrifice, to coincide with yesterday's solar eclipse over the sixty-fifth latitude. I intervened; there was a struggle."

"Well," she said. "You've certainly had a busy three weeks."

"My wife did much of the work."

"Your wife." The flat syllables indicated that Damian had neglected this part of the tale.

"She read theology at Oxford."

"Of course she did."

"What do you mean by that?"

"Nothing. How do you intend to get the police to listen to you? Or will Mr Adler be forever in hiding?"

"That would not do at all. I have resources, and they will listen. However, I need to reach them first, without attracting police attention."

"Hmm. And may I ask, where is Mr Adler's daughter? He'd got as far as the confrontation on Friday night before exhaustion took him."

"The child is with my wife."

"Where?"

"Orkney, when last I saw them."

"Mrs Holmes was on Orkney as well?"

"She goes by the name Russell, but yes, she was there. Damian's memories of the incident at the Stones may be uncertain, but she and I were both present. However, with Damian injured, we could not risk having the child to slow us down. So we split up, and Russell and Estelle remained behind."

"You left your wife and a child to explain to the police about a dead madman?"

"I should be astonished if Russell was still there when the police arrived."

"She, too, is evading the police?"

"Dr Henning, you heard me say that all three of us have warrants out for our arrest, from before this. And all three of those warrants are unjustified. I say again, you will come to no harm, apart from the inconvenience of this voyage. For which I sincerely apologise."

He met her gaze then, grey eyes locking on green, and in a moment, she surprised him. Her eyes began to dance, and her mouth twitched, and then she was laughing, with full acceptance and good humour and not a trace of the hysteria one might expect of a woman in her situation. She laughed so hard, the basket jumped out from underneath her and left the doctor sitting on the grubby deck.

"Oh, my," she said, fishing out a handkerchief. "My, my, my. And to think that mere minutes before you arrived in my surgery, I was making an inventory of supplies that I'd counted ten times already and wondering if it was too late to take a position of public-school nurse that I'd been offered in Edinburgh."

"Yes, well," Holmes said, "my wife does not tend to complain of boredom."

"I can see that." She stretched her legs out straight and clasped her hands on her skirts, a gesture of decision. "Very well. I should tell you that I happen to have a relative on the Dutch coast. Would you consider that 'safe haven' for your son?"

Chapter 16

I coasted through the darkness on silent wings for a time, and then snapped back into a confusion of pain and terror and the stench of petrol. Some furious creature was struggling against me, a knife was buried into my kidneys, and my head felt like a football: kicked about and swollen with air.

Directed less by thought than by animal instinct aimed at making the noise and pain go away, I patted at the furious struggling creature. After a while its noises and struggles diminished somewhat. Nothing I could do about the vacant pounding inside my skull, but, continuing the patting motion, I eased the creature off my belly, which reduced the stabbing of the knife.

I had no idea where I was, but I emphatically did not want to be there: topsy-turvy with walls pressing in on me, the crackle of broken glass accompanying my every motion, noises of distress beating at me. And not only noises—the enclosure was jumping in time to a pounding from outside.

My unoccupied hand came up of its own will and looped my dangling spectacles back onto my ears. With clarity came awareness: The panel in front of my nose had a hole in it. A bullet hole?

Suddenly the heavy reek of petrol was intolerable, and my entire body was seized by the need to be away—*away!* Whatever this enclosure was, it moved alarmingly with every blow from that person on the other side.

My mouth formed some words—*Stay there*, perhaps?—and my body convulsed with the effort of turning the right way around.

On my knees was better than on my back. And my hands could grasp the lower (upper?) edge of the enclosure and tug: heavy, but it moved. The pounding and noise cut off abruptly, and I tugged again, but it was impossible to brace myself, crowded into this tiny space with another.

I would have more room to move if the small creature were not pressing against me—but what to do with it? I returned my grip to the lower edge of my cage, and said, "Get out when I lift this."

And I lifted, straining with all my might and biting down on a scream of pain. The gap between hands and ground grew: two inches, then five, and now on a level with my hips. Quivering with effort, my skull near to explosion, I gasped, "Out!" and felt the creature squirm past me, beneath the dangerous weight of this structure, wailing in protest but obeying. A tiny pair of shoes gave a final kick against my knees, and then I was alone in the trap. I let the impossible weight settle down around me and collapsed against the side, panting and near to blacking out again.

The pounding started up again, with renewed urgency. A few of the accompanying words began to register: *Petrol* was chief among them, then *fire*.

A child's voice from without joined the chorus, twining around the *fire*-person's masculine bellows. My head—oh, my head! If they would only be quiet for a moment.

Estelle, that was the small creature's name. And with her gone I could—just—manoeuvre myself into a half-standing, hunched-over position, my back against what was, in fact, the upturned floor of the enclosure. Which did me no good, since I couldn't very well lift the weight and crawl out at the same time, but perhaps—

"Estelle? Estelle!" Shouting sent a bolt of agony through my head; it took me a moment to notice that she was no longer wailing and the man no longer shouting.

"'Stella, I need you to find something to prop under the back of the 'plane"—yes, there was an aeroplane in the equation—"when I lift it up. Can you find a big, heavy stick, about as tall as you are?" Could she? She was a mere child; I had no idea what she could do.

I heard her voice, although I couldn't make out her words. She seemed to be moving towards my right, which indicated some kind of response to my command. The voice stopped, then started up again. It did this two or three times. A conversation? Did small children hallucinate? Or was it normal to converse with imaginary friends at times of stress?

"Estelle, can you find a stick, please? It's really important, honey."

"No, I—"

But her protest was cut off by a shudder in the enclosure, and without stopping to reflect on the unlikeliness of a child of forty months (even if she was Holmes' granddaughter) understanding the fulcrum principle, I responded by pushing upwards with all my strength against the floorboards.

The machine rose, tail-end first, leaving the heavy engine off to my left. Tentatively, I let my knees sag a fraction; when the load remained up, I dropped to the ground and dove out from under the remains of the 'plane.

"Good work, Estelle," I started to say, but then I saw her, thumb in mouth, staring towards the tail end of the machine. I took three steps forward, and saw the person responsible for lifting the burden.

I say *person*, but my concussed brain knew full well that it was indulging in a few hallucinations of its own, and that I had conjured up the creature of my recent thoughts and mythic dream. The being on whose shoulders our tail assembly was resting might have been spawned by the trees all around us: a wiry figure, all beard and hair, clothed in dark brown corduroy trousers, a lighter brown tweed jacket with an orange patch on one sleeve, a once-red shirt, a lavender tweed waistcoat, and a cap the green of the branches behind him. The cap had a feather in it. I glanced down, half-expecting hooves or fur where his trousers stopped, but he wore boots, their leather the colour of the soil.

I met a fool in the forest, a motley fool, my mind recited idiotically.

I became aware that he had said something. This creature of the woods had made speech. I blinked at him, and he repeated it, more loudly, but I was distracted by a presence at my side. A small child—Estelle. Estelle had both arms wrapped around my leg, as if clinging to a rooted tree in a hurricane. My hand smoothed the back of her head; I was dimly aware that she was sobbing, and only the woodman's urgency forced a key word from his thrice-repeated warning into my awareness.

"Petrol!"

Petrol. Fire. Javitz—and the poor devil already bore the scars of flame.

Some dim awareness of a long-ago situation that had involved a child in need of distraction penetrated my mind, causing my hand to reach for an object that I didn't know was there until I drew it out: a delicate porcelain dollies' tea-cup, slipped into my pocket days before. I pressed it—miraculously unbroken—into the child's hand. She looked at the familiar toy and unwrapped her arms from my leg, making sounds of exclamation while allowing me to usher her away (*away! from the fire!*) and settle her on the ground. I then moved with alacrity back to the remains of the machine.

The wreck was little more than a cigar-shaped tube—both wings had shredded, the propeller was gone, and the whole thing had flipped over. I squatted to look underneath, and blinked at the sight of Javitz's head and shoulders, upside-down on the earth while his legs disappeared upwards. He worked to turn his head around.

"My foot's caught," he gasped. "Get out of here. The petrol will go up any moment."

It was already dripping down the control-stick and across the pilot's clothing.

"What can I do?" I asked him.

"Let me have your revolver, and then run."

My thinking processes, far from clear, failed to connect the weapon with a means of freeing a caught foot. However, I could think of another weapon that might do it.

I dropped my jacket and the gun on the ground, then called to our hirsute rescuer, "Can you keep the machine absolutely still? If it shifts and makes a spark, we'll both be trapped."

"I can," came the reply.

Javitz protested furiously all the while I was inching my way in beside him.

His right boot was caught on something invisible in the broken belly of the aeroplane. Ignoring his furious commands, I slid the knife out of my boot and walked both hands up a trouser leg sodden with petrol: knee; calf; ankle. When I reached his boot, my fingertips found the bit of metal snagging the laces. He had fallen silent, rigid with dread; I needed only whisper my warning: "Brace yourself."

The knife point slid under the laces and the tough cord parted. He grunted as his full weight settled onto his bent neck. I held his foot away from the metal snag, waiting for him to pull away.

The only direction he could move was out, under the hanging body of the aeroplane, both of us praying that the buttons and ties of his clothing did not create any friction. Head, shoulders, torso, legs, and finally his feet—one booted, one bare—were pulled past my own feet and disappeared from view. My face was mere inches from his toes as I followed, fast as my legs could scrabble.

Out of the corner of my eye I spotted the fur coat and rucksack, spilt from the compartment. As I rose to my feet, I stretched out a hand to snatch them up: The pack came without hindrance; the fur caught briefly on something before coming free.

As it did so, a faint clang came from the depths of the machine. I took three panicked leaps, halfway to Estelle, and then the *Whomp!* of igniting petrol shoved at me and I caught her up in a somersault that ended in a tangle of legs, leaves, and fur among the trees.

If the petrol tank had not been down to its last quarter, the explosion would have incinerated us all. Still, there was plenty of fuel to set the machine instantly ablaze.

I stuck up my head, taking a census. Estelle sat, wide-eyed, covered in leaves, shocked speechless. I threw aside the fur and went to pick her up, although on closer examination, she seemed less terrified than amazed. Javitz, on the other hand, had come to a halt with his back against a tree and was staring white-faced and shuddering at the flames. Our rescuer— our rescuer was nowhere to be seen.

I set the child down next to Javitz, thinking that comforting her might at least distract him for a moment, then scrambled in a wide circle around the pulse of flames. I expected to find our Good Samaritan either aflame or impaled—but the dirt-coloured boots came into view, waving from the shrubbery beneath a slab of propeller quivering from a tree-trunk. The boots sank, and a head took their place. He stared open-mouthed at the propeller, the fire, and at me. His eyes, I noticed with the peculiar clarity of the concussed, were the very shade of Damian's *Green Man*.

Then he laughed. "Ha!" he shouted, a bark of pure joy at the ridiculousness of life. "Ha ha!"

His head disappeared into the shrubbery, which convulsed madly until he emerged from their back side, brushing half a bushel of dried leaves from his clothing. He retrieved his cap from a branch, slapping it against his leg before pulling it onto his hair, then climbed onto the dirt track to stand, hands on hips, grinning at the dying flames. He looked like a village lad at a Guy Fawkes bonfire; I half-expected him to gather some branches to toss on.

"Ha!" he barked again.

Then his head turned to find the three of us and the beard parted in a wide grin, which seemed remarkably full of very white teeth. "Who knew this day would hold such drama?" he said cheerfully.

My brains were so thoroughly scrambled, I could only grin back at him. We watched the flames for a while—they were, in fact, remarkably interesting—until I reluctantly woke to my responsibilities and looked around me.

Estelle was patting our blood-soaked, terror-stricken pilot on the head, comforting him instead of the other way around as I had intended. His eyes were tightly shut as he struggled for control, and I kept my distance while this strong man pasted on a deathly smile, dismissing her services when what he wanted was to curl over and howl with terror. I gave him time, and when he was restored, I approached.

Estelle had sat down on the bedraggled fur. She was holding the teacup in one hand and an acorn-cap about the same size in the other, scowling between the two. I shook my head in wonder: I'd been in charge of this small life less than twelve hours, and I could already feel an ulcer coming on. How did parents survive?

I dropped to my knees beside Javitz. His face was contained, his left hand clamped around his upper thigh. Fresh blood oozed around the fingers. The once-white scarf had all but torn free, but I did not think this patch of roadway was the best place in which to examine his injuries.

A pair of dirt-coloured boots came into the corner of my vision, and I said, "He needs a doctor. Is there a town nearby?"

"No!" Javitz protested. "If there's a town, there'll be police."

I glanced upwards to see what impression this statement had on the bearded man—expecting, perhaps, that a man who reacted to flames with childish glee would be childish in all things—but his raised eyebrows spoke of a mind quick enough to put together the situation. Although he did not seem alarmed.

"Three master criminals fleeing the law in an aeroplane," he reflected. "I have fallen into a *Boy's Own* adventure."

His voice. I peered more closely at him, trying to see beneath the herbage. He might look like a resident of the wilderness—a charcoal-burner, perhaps, or a rat-catcher—but he sounded like an Oxford don.

I opened my mouth to pursue this oddity, but a small groan brought me back. *Focus,* I told myself: *Your brains have been knocked about and all the world looks odd.* "His injuries want attention," I repeated.

The hairy man dropped into an easy squat, and a pair of surprisingly clean hands gently pushed aside the larger man's blood-stained fingers. He looked into the pilot's eyes and asked, "The bone's not broken?"

"No," Javitz answered through clenched jaws.

"This didn't happen here."

"I was shot."

The green eyes travelled from Javitz to me and over my shoulder to Estelle, who had turned her back, literally, on the adults and was laying out a tea-party, supplementing the porcelain cup with acorn-caps and leaf-plates. He frowned, then jumped up and walked around to face her. She raised her head, and the green eyes went wide.

I found I had got to my feet and taken a step towards him, but he did not notice. Slowly, he lowered himself to his haunches. I watched, un-certain, as the two of them studied each other for the longest time. I could see his face clearly, but I could not begin to guess what he was thinking. He studied her face as if its features contained a message coded just for him.

Eventually, his gaze shifted, and he turned to scrabble at the leaf-mould, a small noise that startled my ears into noticing that the incessant engine noise was gone, that the noise of the flames was dying, that the ringing in my ears had given way to silence, blessed and profound.

He found what he was looking for, and held it out for Estelle's approval: an acorn cup. After she had accepted it and added it to the others, he broke the stillness with a question. "Would you like to come to my house?"

"Yes, please," she answered, without hesitation.

"Put those in your pocket, then. We'll make some tea to go in them."

"Thank you, Mr..."

"Goodman," he supplied, and held out a hand to her. "But you can call me Robert."

"My name is Estelle Adler," she announced, and gave his hand two solemn shakes.

"Pleased to meet you, Miss Adler," he said, and helped her to her feet.

Then he came back to us, with Estelle trailing after. He told Javitz, "If it's not broken, there's no point in a splint. Grit your teeth, friend." And without so much as a grunt of effort, the small man slid his hands under the big American and lifted him like a child.

Goodman took half a dozen steps and vanished among the trees. I retrieved the fur coat, helped Estelle stash the last of the acorn cups in her pockets, and led her to the place where the men had disappeared. The narrow path between the trees would have gone unnoticed unless one had seen them go in. I glanced back at the now-smouldering wreck and took Estelle's hand.

Three steps inside the green, she dug in her heels. With an ill-stifled groan, I bent to pick her up. She was not, in fact, heavy, and my tired arms forgot their bruises to welcome her.

Perhaps that was the answer to my earlier question, of how parents survived.

"It will be all right, Estelle," I said. "I'm here."

"But," she piped in a worried voice, "shouldn't we leave crumbs, so we can find our way out again?"

So it hadn't been just my concussion: It would seem that we were actually setting forth into a fairy-tale.

Chapter 17

The fairy-tale impression only grew stronger as we followed our rescuer, whom my abused brain insisted on calling Mr Green. I had not known that England still possessed areas of ancient woodland such as this. The light, here in what could only be called a forest, was so dim that I followed him more by sound than by the occasional glimpses I caught of his back. Once, when the child in my arms grew heavy with sleep, I stopped to wrap the fur more securely around her; when I stood again, the noise ahead of me resumed.

It began to rain lightly, more a background susurration than actual drips through the leaves. We travelled through the green nowhere, never seeing more than a few feet to either side, following the rhythm of firm footsteps. The journey was timeless, the landscape featureless, my companions noisy ghosts.

Then the noise ceased. In moments, I stepped into a clearing, and glanced involuntarily upwards to check the sky: yes, still cloudy, which meant it was the real England. And despite the heavy grey, I thought no more than an hour had passed since the crash.

Goodman's home confirmed the sensation that Hansel and Gretel could not be far away—or perhaps Titania and Oberon. The structure—hard to think of it as a house—stood off-centre in a lush meadow encircled by forest and punctuated by one magnificent oak tree. Once upon a time, the dwelling may have been a woodman's hut, but was now a gallimaufry of elements: A yellow-brick shed leant against a lichen-blotched stone hut butting up against a red-brick shack that was in turn held upright by a wooden lean-to that might have been built yesterday, the whole variously roofed with old moss-covered tile and slick new black slate and two sheets of rusted corrugated iron. The water tank perched on top looked like a joke, or a nesting-place for herons. The huge oak rose up thirty feet from the door, and might have been the home of fairies. At a slight remove stood another shed, this one wooden and apparently windowless, with a wired chicken-coop leaning to its side.

The faint aroma of wood-smoke in the air was the most real thing about it.

He had left the front door open, and I looked through into an unexpectedly light room of colour and wood. As I stepped in, I caught sight of Javitz's legs, stretched out on a neatly made bed through an inner doorway. The Green Man—no, he had a name: Goodman—was in the act of spreading a thick duvet on the floor beside it. I followed him, going down on one knee to ease my sleeping burden onto the down pad; she made a faint protest in the back of her throat, then curled onto her side and was still. I left the fur around her and stood, kneading my upper arms and wondering why mothers didn't resemble stevedores.

From the outside, the building had suggested an uncomfortable series of cramped spaces, but on the inside there were only two rooms. The bedroom was scarcely twice the size of the narrow bed it held, but the main room was spacious—or would be for a single inhabitant. It had a fireplace faced by two highly civilised soft chairs, a window with a long, padded window-seat at its base, a simple but sturdy wooden table, and a small kitchen consisting of a sink with a tap, a tiled work-surface, and a small wood-burning cook-stove.

As a whole, it resembled a windowed cave furnished by a jackdaw—or a child. One wall, floor to ceiling, was a collage of bright paper and small shiny objects, many of which looked as if they had been dug up in the woods: blue medicine bottles, bright labels from food tins, cut-out colour illustrations from ladies' magazines, coins so old the features were worn away, bits of broken mirror glass, two mismatched hair-combs. In the centre was a spray of half a dozen feathers; around the wall, a wide arc of horseshoes from pony to draught-horse traced a path through the jumble. The rest of the room was similar: a Japanese tea-pot without a spout held a handful of wildflowers; none of the curtains matched; the original upholstery of the chairs was hidden beneath a length of brilliant orange-flowered curtain and a blue and green Paisley, respectively. Still, it was surprisingly clean and smelt sweet, as if the floor had been strewn with rushes until an instant before we walked in.

Our host had tossed sticks onto the fire and set a kettle over the heat, and was now divesting himself of his outer garments. When hat and coat were on their hooks—a randomly arranged nest of sawed-off antlers—he finally turned to me, a short, slim man showing no effects of having carried over thirteen stone of man through the woods for three quarters of an hour.

It was difficult to know how old he was. Even without all that disguising hair, he had the kind of skin that conceals a man's age until he turns eighty overnight. He moved like a man of thirty but spoke like someone twice that; when his face was still, he had the ancient gaze of a trench soldier; when he grinned, his teeth were uneven and slightly oversized, like an adolescent who had yet to grow into his mouth.

"Thank you for coming to our rescue," I told him. "I'm Mary Russell. That man you've been carrying is my pilot, Cash Javitz. He's an American. The child is my husband's granddaughter, Estelle."

"Robert Goodman," he said.

It was on the point of my tongue to say, *Not Robin Goodfellow?* but that was the concussion speaking.

Oddly, a twinkle in his emerald eyes suggested that he guessed the fanciful direction of my thoughts. I shook off the idea: stick to facts. "We started this morning in Orkney. I think Mr Javitz had hoped to make it to Manchester, but the machine rather came to pieces around us."

"So I saw. Something to eat, then?"

"I think—"

But he had already snatched two large onions and a handful of carrots from a basket under the work-table, and set them beside a small knife and a heavy iron pan. "Chop these while I see to your pilot."

I eyed the proceedings dubiously—I am no cook—and instead followed

Goodfellow to the bedroom. There he gently removed the half-conscious man's remaining boot before pulling a long, well-honed knife from somewhere about his person and, with one deft motion, slit the blood-soaked remnants of the trousers from cuff to belt.

He looked over the leg without touching it, then picked up a flowered bowl and bar of soap and pushed past me to spill water into it from the heating kettle. I was encouraged to see him scrub his hands. He even poured that water into the sink and refilled the bowl before bathing Javitz's wound.

It was messy, a ten-inch furrow up the outside of his thigh. Because of the circumstances, it had bled a lot, but bar infection, I thought it would heal without permanent effect.

"Would stitches help?" I asked my host.

He shook his head. "They'd pull."

I watched him work, cleaning the wound and examining the portions that were still bleeding, but those stubby hands knew what they were doing. "You've done this sort of thing before," I remarked.

"He...A friend..." He stopped to concentrate on the wound. "*I* was an ambulance driver in the War. Lent a hand in the dressing stations when I was needed. One picks things up."

It was a peculiar idea, Ariel strolling through the fourth act of *Henry V*—then I pushed the thought away, hard: Clearly, it would take a while for my brain to settle.

I left our unlikely medic to his repairs, and went to address the problem of the onions and carrots, about which I will say only that I succeeded in not giving my host another major wound to dress.

Chapter 18

The remainder of Saturday passed in snippets of memory, cut from whole cloth and rearranged by the blow my head had taken:

After we ate, I lay dozing on a surprisingly comfortable if much-repaired deck chair beneath the big oak tree. The late-afternoon sun had broken through; someone had put a warm wrap over me.

Estelle and Goodman were sitting on a pair of upended firewood rounds, a third round between them as a table. On it the child had arranged an impromptu tea-service. The participants were Estelle, Goodman, and a bedraggled once-purple stuffed rabbit lifted from his sitting room wall, with a fourth setting for the fawn he had told her might come by. The plates were mismatched saucers from Goodman's kitchen, the cups were two acorns, a small tea-cup, and her treasured porcelain dollies' cup. The tea-pot was a creamer lacking a handle, decorated with the Brighton Pier and a generous stripe of gilt. A silver salt bowl and spoon made for a scaled-down sugar bowl. A clean khaki-coloured handkerchief was the tablecloth.

Goodman solemnly stirred a spoonful of nonexistent sugar into the dollies' cup, which was scarcely larger than the salt spoon. He raised it to his lips and sipped noisily, then held it out to admire.

"This is very pretty," he remarked.

"I have the others, at home," she informed him. "That's in London."

"You only brought the one?"

"Mary brought it. She found it where I'd left it, at a friend of my Mama's."

"That was thoughtful of Mary."

"Papa bought it for me in Shanghai, before we left. He gave it to me so I would have a reason to remember how beautiful the city was. But I don't, really."

"Still, it was a nice thought."

"Mr Robert, do you think the baby deer will come out? Or should we give his serving to the bunny?"

Later that afternoon: I was now on a settee before the fireplace, while Estelle helped prepare supper, scrubbing potatoes while our host kneaded bread on a board.

"There's a lot of potatoes," she said in mild complaint.

"You can stop if you're tired."

"No, that's all right."

"Sometimes when I'm doing a tedious job, I keep myself busy by singing."

"I like to sing."

"I thought you might. Do you want to sing something for me?"

She happily launched into a merry song with Chinese words. Despite the foreign tonality of the melody, her voice was pure and precise, skipping up the half tones without missing a one. At the end, Goodman clapped in an explosion of flour. I joined him, although the impact reverberated through my skull.

"Ha!" he laughed. "That was very fine. You must teach it to me one day."

"You sing now," she ordered.

Perhaps the task at hand or the demands of the kneading rhythm brought the song to mind: Goodman threw back his head and, in a rich and unexpected baritone, began to sing.

There were three men came from the west their fortunes for to try,
And these three made a solemn vow, John Barleycorn must die.

I stirred and tried to catch his eye, but he was well launched into the song and beat his bread dough with gusto. I subsided; surely the child was too young to understand the words?

It is a rousing tune, to be sure, and he did skip over the more adult verses—it is a very old song, and whether it is a paean to fertility sacrifice, an evocation of Christian Transubstantiation, or simply a drinking song, John Barleycorn is put through the wringer—hacked, beaten, ploughed, sowed, and buried—before he is reborn as beer, and finally sprouts up anew. Goodman sang and thumped his bread, raising a fine mist of flour in the room.

To my relief, when the song ended, Estelle did not enquire into the significance of the words. She merely demanded another. Goodman started "Frère Jacques." Instantly, she joined him. In French to his English, the high child's voice and the man's baritone wound around each other, creating sweet harmony from an unlikely cottage in a Lake District clearing.

During the afternoon, he juggled for her, four round oak galls, then threw himself into a game of hide-and-seek that had us both grinning with Estelle's infectious giggles. Later, they went out to fetch the day's eggs from the hen-house, stopping on the way to examine a flower of some kind.

"Let Nature be your teacher," Goodman said—or rather, pronounced.

"I don't go to school yet," Estelle told him.

"It is never too early to have a teacher. Or too late," he said, with a note of surprise.

"How is Nature a teacher? Does she stand in front of a classroom with a stick?"

"I believe Mr Wordsworth merely meant that we can learn much from the world around us."

"Is Mr Wordsworth a friend of yours?"

"We have many friends in common, Mr Wordsworth and I. Such as the hedgehog you shall see this evening."

Their voices trailed off then, in the direction of the hen-house.

* * *

Dusk. The mouth-watering odour of baking wheat permeated the universe, and although I had been up and around, I was again on the settee in front of the fire. Estelle and Goodman were seated side by side in the open doorway, waiting for a hedgehog to emerge after a saucer of milk. Every so often he reared back his head to look at her; he seemed fascinated by the shape of her eyes.

"There it is!" Estelle squeaked.

"Shh, don't frighten him. Not to worry, he'll come back in a minute. See, there's his nose, sniffing to make certain the world is safe."

"We won't hurt it."

"Hedgehogs are shy."

"What does *shy* mean?"

"Shy is when a person is frightened of many things."

"I'm shy."

"Ha! I don't think that's so."

"I'm frightened of aeroplanes."

"That only makes you sensible."

"I'm afraid of our neighbour's dog. It's big."

"That's probably sensible, too."

"Are you scared of anything, Mr Robert?"

"Look, he's finished the milk and is looking around for more. Greedy thing."

"Shall we give him more?"

"No, we don't want him to forget how to find his own food. Milk is a treat, not dinner."

"What do hedgehogs eat?"

"Roots. Grubs."

"Ew."

"Carrots are roots. You ate those."

"Because Mama says I have to be polite and eat what I'm given."

"You don't like carrots? Then I won't serve them again."

"But I don't eat grubs."

"True. But a hedgehog likes them. He would probably say *ew* if you offered him a chocolate biscuit."

"Let's try!"

"Ah, the scientific approach. No, I don't wish to introduce him to the taste of chocolate. What if I'm wrong and he likes it, and that one morsel condemns the poor creature to spend the rest of his life in unrequited longing for the taste of chocolate?"

"You talk funny, Mr Robert."

"People before you have told me that."

"So, are you frightened of anything?"

"Logic *and* persistence—I fear you will go far in this world, Estelle Adler."

"Are you?"

"Yes."

"What?"

He sighed. "Fear," he said, and turned to look down at the child by his side. "I am afraid of fear."

Then he jumped to his feet. "If you can say the word *pipistrelle*, I will take you to watch the bats come out."

Evening, and I might have curled up to sleep fully clothed except it had occurred to me that children required putting to bed. Estelle and Goodman were in front of the fire, he on the floor with Damian's sketch-book on his knee, she stretched with her belly across the tree-round he used for a foot-stool, narrating the drawings for him. I had found the book in my rucksack, astonished that it had survived this far, and leafed through its pages before I gave it to her, making sure it contained none of his detailed nudes or violent battle scenes. Some of the drawings I had found mildly troubling, but doubted a small child would notice.

"That's Papa," she said. "His face doesn't look like that, much."

"I'm glad to hear that," Goodman replied, and I had to smile: Damian's self-portrait might have been an interspecies breeding experiment, his face oddly canine down to the suggestion of fur.

"And that's Mama," she said.

"She's very pretty." *I must tell him about Estelle's mother,* I thought. *Tomorrow.*

"Papa says I have her hair."

"Doesn't she miss it?" he asked.

It took her a second to understand the joke. Then she giggled and called him silly, explaining that her Mama had her own hair, of course!

A vivid picture of that heavy black hair spilling over a cold slab flashed before my eyes; I shuddered.

The sound of a page turning, and then silence. I knew what sketch they were looking at, since I had lingered over it myself.

Estelle, yet not Estelle. In this portrait, Damian was looking forward through time to put an adult shape on his small daughter's face. One might have thought it was Yolanda, from the clear Chinese cast to the features, but no one who knew Holmes could possibly mistake the imperious gaze from those grey eyes.

"I think that's Mama," the child said, sounding none too certain.

"No, it's you," Goodman said.

"I don't look like that."

"You will. Your Papa thinks you will."

She leant forward, her nose near to touching the page.

"He loves you very much," Goodman said.

"I love him, too. Mr Robert, is Papa all right?"

"Yes." Goodman's voice was absolutely certain, and my fingers twitched with the impulse to make a gesture against the evil eye.

Estelle did not respond, not immediately. Instead, a minute later I heard her feet cross the room, and opened my eyes to find her standing beside me, the sketch-book in her hand. "Can you take this out for me?" she asked.

I pushed myself upright, taking the book. She pointed to the drawing of her older self and ordered, "Take it out."

I only hesitated for a moment before deciding, with the complete lack of logic that had permeated the last two days, that if Damian had wanted the drawing, he shouldn't have let himself be duped by the charlatan who had murdered his wife. I reached down to my boot top for the knife I kept there, ran its razor-sharp point along the edge of the page, and handed it to her.

I thought Goodman was not going to accept it. He swallowed, shaken by the gift, before reaching out and taking it by the edges. After a moment, he stood and took it to the decorated wall. "Where should I put it?" he asked her.

She pointed at 'a handsbreadth of bare wood. Instead, he removed the bundle of feathers that marked the wall's focal point, and mounted the drawing in its place.

She watched solemnly, then asked, "Is that the kind of feather that's in your hat?"

"The very same," he said, and began to work one of them free.

"Why do you wear a feather in your hat?"

"*Ich habe einen Vogel,*" he replied.

I choked, and he cast me a twinkle of his green eye.

"What does that mean?" she asked.

"It means *I have a bird.* Or at least, one feather of a bird. And now so do you. This is for you," he said to her. "It's from the owl who lives in the big tree. She sometimes gives me one of her feathers, to thank me for sharing my mice with her."

She fetched her hat and brought it to me, demanding that I work the feather into the hat's crown.

I did so, trying not to laugh all the while: The colloquial English for the German *Ich habe einen Vogel* is *I have bats in my belfry.*

When the feather was installed, I suggested it was time for bed. Rather to my surprise, she accepted the command, although when she was tucked into the makeshift bed, the hat and its feather stood on the floor beside her head.

She wished us both good-night, and curled up with her face towards the wall, banishing my own thready memories of prolonged stories and prayers and glasses of water.

At long last, I was free to take to my own bed. I removed my shoes and sat on the window-seat I had been assigned, then realised that Goodman was still in the bedroom doorway, his eyes on the sleeping child. He felt my gaze, and turned to look at me. His eyes were liquid with tears. " 'A simple child,' " he said, " 'that lightly draws its breath/And feels its life in every limb...' "

Then turned and walked out of the house into the night.

Slowly, I arranged the wraps over my legs.

My paternal grandmother had been much taken by the poems of Wordsworth, the bard of the Lake District, and had read and recited them, over and over, when I was at her house in Boston. Thus, my mind could now supply the line about the child that Goodman had left off:

What should it know of death?

Chapter 19

On Tuesday at half past five, Reverend Thomas Brothers' taxi stopped in front of a house in St Albans. His left arm was in a sling, his overcoat rested on his shoulders, but he was in better condition than he'd anticipated, after the long journey south. The town itself pleased him, built as it was on the blood-sacrifice of a Roman: The site was propitious. "This town was known as Verulamium," he told Gunderson, who had closed the taxi door and was now paying the driver. "It was the most important Roman town in the south of England. Named after an executed soldier, martyred as a Christian in the year 304."

"Yes, sir," the man replied.

Gunderson had never been the most responsive of employees. Still, he'd been surprisingly efficient, during these past months. Perhaps it was time to give him a small rise in salary.

Gunderson picked up their valises and followed Brothers up the steps, waiting as the door-bell clanged inside. The door came open, and Brothers stepped up, his right hand already out.

"We meet at last," he said, for the man could not possibly be a servant, not in that suit. "Thank you, sir, for your longtime assistance to the cause."

The man with the white streak in his hair replied, "Reverend Brothers, how do you do?" He took Brothers' hand, although he still had his gloves on against the chill of the house. "Gunderson, you can leave those bags here. Come to the back, Mr Brothers, I have the fire going."

Gunderson took the coat from his employer's shoulders, and accepted Brothers' hat and scarf.

When Gunderson came into the garden room, where the curtains were drawn and the air was cool despite the glowing gas fire, Brothers was well launched in his explanation of what had taken place over the past two weeks. He had claimed the chair nearest the heat, and allowed the other man to hand him coffee, accepting it as he might have from a servant. It was clear that Brothers considered himself the important person in this room, the other two mere worshippers at the altar of Thomas Brothers.

He poured out his heart to his two acolytes, blissfully unaware that heresy was in the offing.

Then he paused, and gave an embarrassed little laugh. "I have a confession to make, sir. I have to admit that I do not recall your name. I'm sure you told me, but I meet so many people, and our communications have been of the sort that names were not used."

The man with the white streak in his hair had not, in fact, ever given Brothers his name. Nor had he shown himself to Brothers, although he'd gone to the man's church once, early on, just to be sure that Brothers did not rave too outrageously in public. "Peter James West," he said, putting out his still-gloved hand for another, ceremonial clasp.

"I am so glad to get this chance to talk with you, Mr West. You and Gunderson have been my faithful friends, my helpmeets, as it were, ever since I arrived in November. So I hope that you can help me find my way to understanding the events of this past week. I know we expected considerable results from the events of Friday, and I was at first deeply puzzled, even dispirited, at what appeared to be the failure of my sacrifice. However, as *Testimony* says, *'The greater the sacrifice, the greater the energies loosed.'* I have had some days to meditate on it, and I should like to put before you my thoughts, to see if you are in agreement with my understanding. And also to get your thoughts about where I might go, since England looks to be a bit hot for me at the moment. I was thinking perhaps America, where they—"

"Brothers, I'm sure Gunderson is as tired of this nonsense as I am."

Brothers gaped at him. "*What* was that you said?"

"You heard me. I put up with your claptrap because it made you such a useful tool. I brought you from Shanghai because of it."

"*You* brought—for heaven's sake, West, don't be absurd!"

"Your name came to my attention last August, when I was searching for potential weak spots in a colleague. Your former wife provided a link—she'd married an artist in Shanghai, who I discovered was my colleague's nephew. That made you useful."

"Do you mean Damian Adler? The man has no family, he told me so himself."

"Then he lied. However, we all know that you are in the habit of hearing only what you wish to hear, which makes your companionship, at times, most trying. So instead of your filling the air with verbiage, let me tell you a story.

"Certain government agencies keep themselves in the shadows. Some men regard this as an opportunity, others a responsibility. I work in such an agency, but I have an associate possessed by an overly grand and unfortunately archaic sense of his own importance. His presence is obstructive, for those of us concerned with this country's ability to move into the Twentieth Century, but he is as thoroughly entrenched as Buckingham Palace itself.

"Three years ago, I discovered his flaw. Ironically enough, its very existence kept me from doing a thing about it. Then thirteen months ago, I found a wedge beneath his massive façade: I happened to see a letter he had received from Shanghai, addressing him as 'uncle' and referring to a service rendered years before. The nephew was writing to ask for my colleague's assistance in establishing British citizenship, for himself and his new family.

"I immediately set into action a full investigation of this man and his wife. Which led me to you, with your small congregation of gullible spinsters and other neurasthenics. You received a letter in August from Sicily, suggesting that England was a rich but untapped bed of theological synthesis? You thought it came from Aleister Crowley, but it was, in fact, from me. I was prepared to offer further incentives, including a sit-uation that would drive you from Shanghai under threat of arrest, but in the end, you readily seized on the idea of transplanting your hare-brained theories to the land of your fathers, and were here before the Adlers arrived.

"I paved the way for you. I suggested where you could find an assis-tant such as Mr Gunderson here. I helped him arrange for your change of identity, your house, and hiring a church hall. And I stood by as your delusions took you over, and you began to slaughter various useless peo-ple in search of—whatever it was you imagined you would find."

"I don't—" Brothers said. "What do you . . . I mean to say, *Why?*"

"My . . . colleague has always appeared absolutely righteous, untouch-ably ethical, unquestionably moral. A god among lesser mortals. I'd thought at first I might use the bohemian morality of his nephew—a drugs party, perhaps, or an orgy—to lift the edges of that mask. All I needed was an event linked to my colleague that might plant a seed of doubt among his even more self-righteous superiors. One small doubt was all I needed, but you—good Lord, you gave me a harvest of them! I have to hand it to you, Brothers, I'd never expected to have it so easy—a few minor adjustments to the evidence, and the nephew became the chief suspect for Yolanda's death. I owe you and your mad theories con-siderable thanks."

"*Mad!* But, the Transformative—"

"Oh, for pity's sake. Let me see your knife."

"My—you mean the Tool?"

"That's right."

"Why?"

"Mr Brothers, let me see it for a moment, please?"

The voice was so reasonable that Brothers automatically reached for his collar, to loosen his clothing and retrieve the holy object he wore always near his skin. He withdrew it from its soft, thick leather scab-bard, dark with decades of his body's sweat, and contemplated the wicked object. "I don't know that you should touch it," he told West. "It is an object of considerable power, and your hands are not—oh!"

West took a quick step back.

The three men gazed at the ivory hilt protruding from Thomas Brothers' shirt-front.

In no time at all, the energies of Thomas Brothers were freed to explore the Truths of the life beyond.

BOOK TWO

*Sunday, 31 August–
Thursday, 4 September
1924*

Chapter 20

Sunday morning, the last day of August, I woke from my cushions beneath the window to the sensation of being watched. Closely watched. By a child bent so low over my face, I could feel her breath on my right cheek. Which was about the only part of me that didn't ache.

"Good morning, Estelle," I said without opening my eyes. "Did you want something?"

"I'm hungry," she said. "And Mr Javitz is snoring."

The American did have a prodigious snore, which I had been given cause to admire all the night long. I gingerly pushed away the much-abused fur coat that had been my bed-clothes on the window-seat; with motion, all the previous day's contusions made themselves felt, from wrenched ankle to bruised scalp. The previous evening, mine host had examined the glass cuts along my back, putting three quick stitches in one of them. I did not want to rise up; I did not want to cater to this child. If I moved, yesterday's headache might return.

"Where is the Green—Mr Goodman?" I asked her.

"Mr Robert went out. And he left me these," she said, holding her two fists half an inch from my nose. I pushed them back until a pair of carved deer came into focus, a doe and a buck with small antlers.

"Very nice," I said. "But you shouldn't call a grown man by his given name. Call him Mr Goodman."

"But he told me to call him—"

"I know. But let's be polite and call him Mr Goodman."

"Should I be polite and call you Missus Russell?" she said, sounding sulky.

"I—oh, never mind, Mr Robert is fine."

I had to agree, the usual formality did not fall naturally from the tongue when it came to Robert Goodman. She repeated her demand to be fed.

It occurred to me that perhaps I should be concerned by Goodman's absence, but really, if the man wished to turn us over to the police, he could have done so the day before and spent the night in his own bed. I did not know where he had slept, but a glance at the table showed that he'd been in, leaving a basket of eggs. Odd, that I had not heard him stir about.

Estelle withdrew her hovering self far enough for me to struggle more or less upright. My skull gave a warning throb, but eventually I was standing. I tottered to the bedroom, propping a shoulder against the frame as I studied my pilot. He appeared to be sleeping as comfortably as could be expected, so I closed the door and went to search out the means by which to feed a small child.

I managed toast, although her efforts with the toasting fork were more successful than mine. I then had to scale a foot-stool to reach the pot of honey I could see but not stretch my arm for, then ascended the stool a second time when Estelle informed me that she and her two deer preferred the strawberry preserves. I was interested to see that much of the contents of the hermit's cupboards were not willow baskets heaped with gathered nuts, dried berries and wild honeycomb, but ordinary store-bought jars and packets.

There was even a tin of aspirin tablets from the chemist, for which I was grateful.

By the time Goodman returned, three hours later, my headache had retreated and I was able to stand with something of my usual ease, walking over to help him unload his rucksack.

He had brought a large bundle of sausages wrapped not in butcher's paper, but in the week-old news. I looked at it askance, but he mistook my doubt.

"A child needs meat, and your pilot, if he is to heal," he said. "A neighbour killed a pig two days back. I knew he'd have extras."

He was right: We had to eat, and last night's bean soup would only go so far in building the injured American's strength. Still: "You and I need to have a talk," I told him.

"Very well," he replied, taking a large black skillet from beneath the work-table.

I glanced at Estelle, underfoot as usual. "Later."

"She wants to talk to you without me hearing," the child explained to him.

Goodman let a rope of sausages spill into the pan, and asked her, "Is that rude, do you think?"

She thought for a moment. "Not very."

He gave me a green twinkle. "You and I shall go for a walk after we eat," he said.

We propped Javitz before the fire with Estelle, and I followed Goodman outside. He went to the shed that stood at a little distance, coming out with a hatchet stuck through his belt. He set off briskly across the meadow, to slip into one of the larger pathways that led to the outer world—this one distinct enough that a deer might be able to follow it. I followed. Twenty minutes later, his hand came out to stop me.

"Do you see?" he asked.

I looked at the trail ahead, circling past a rocky outcrop. "See—oh. The branch?"

One branch of a low-growing tree was tied back against the next tree with a piece of strong twine. Careful not to touch, I stepped around Goodman, searching the ground until I saw the fine, dirt-coloured twine: a trip-wire.

It was a booby-trap, not deadly but powerful enough to swat a person backwards down the path, breaking a nose or arm in the process. I looked up from where I was squatting to ask, "Do you have many of these?"

"It is a private estate. This helps keep away visitors."

"So I should imagine."

Satisfied that his warning had got through to me, he walked on.

After a time, Goodman slowed, and began to peer at the under-growth. I decided this was as good a time as any to have our conversation, so I started by expressing my immense gratitude that he had not only saved our lives, but given us shelter as well. He grunted, then pulled out the little axe and laid it to the base of a young sapling, twelve feet tall with an odd bifurcation halfway up, as if something had bitten off its growing tip and driven it to generate twin alternatives.

I raised my voice. "I ought to take my companions away as soon as I can."

"His leg should rest."

"Well, at least let me move the others into the main room with me, so you can sleep at night."

"The shed is comfortable," he said.

I studied what I could see of his face, wondering at the thoughts underneath all that hair. The precipitate arrival of three demanding strangers into his quiet retreat seemed to trouble him not in the least—apart from a few mild comments, he had been remarkably incurious about our situation, our history, or our plans. One might almost imagine that the dreamy, fairy-tale quality of his surroundings had permeated his mental processes, as well, leaving him incapable of questioning even the most unlikely events.

That approach did not much help me, however. Even if we were welcome to stay here until Javitz could walk, my own mind was by no means dreamy, and worries pressed in on me: What was Brothers up to? Where were Holmes and Damian? What about Mycroft in London? Where could I find safe hiding for Javitz and Estelle near here?

Wherever *here* was.

"Where are we, exactly?" I asked.

The sapling fell. Goodman chopped off the twin tops, then exchanged the hand-axe for the thick knife he wore, stripping away the branches as he answered.

Exactly, it would seem, was not a term that applied to this location, although it was well short of the Forest of Arden setting I had begun to suspect. We were, as I'd thought, in the Lake District, approximately midway between two villages I'd never heard of. But if one drew a line between Grasmere (the bustling centre of the Wordsworth industry) and Ravenglass (on the Irish Sea), we should be halfway along that. Or perhaps a bit closer to the east. And south, he thought.

"Where do you shop?" I asked him. "When you're not buying sausages from a neighbour?"

He named a village, adding, "I give the shopkeeper a list of requirements, then pick them up when next I go. I gave him one this morning."

"What, on a Sunday?"

"He was at home, of course, preparing for church. I told him I'd be back tomorrow."

I looked at him uneasily. "I wish you'd consulted with me first. It's not a good idea to have it be known that you are sheltering three strangers. Someone's sure to have found the wreck by now, even out here."

He finished reducing the branches to stubs, slid the knife into its scabbard, and sighed. "Very well. Tell me your story."

"It started when Estelle's father came to our door in Sussex," I began. We walked, he listened, with little response apart from a noise of pain when I told him that Estelle's mother was dead.

"She doesn't know," I said.

He gave me a look over his shoulder.

"I haven't had a great deal of free time in the past thirty-six hours," I protested. "In any event, I can't decide if I should tell her, or wait for her father to do so. I rather think it should be him."

"Yes," he said. I waited for any further response, but there was none, so I went on. I told him our problem, or enough of it to make him understand the danger: serious enemies with unknown but potentially considerable resources; scattered companions whose situation was unknown; a mad religious fanatic and his acolytes; the remaining threat against us. "We thought Brothers was dead, but by the time I got back to the hotel, it was pretty clear that he had escaped," I told Goodman. "And, he somehow managed to alert a subordinate in Thurso that we were coming."

"And that subordinate took a shot at your aeroplane."

"I do not know who else it might have been."

"It could not have been an accident?"

"I'd like to think so, but it beggars the imagination to picture a stray bullet cleanly puncturing the centre of an aeroplane two hundred feet overhead. Nor can I accept that the northern reaches of Scotland is so rife with madmen that we could find a religious fanatic and a man who takes pot-shots at passing targets within twenty miles of each other."

He nodded, conceding my point.

"I have to assume that Brothers is somehow related to the sharp-shooter. And if he has two assistants—one on Orkney, one in Thurso—he could have more."

"Which requires that you keep your heads down for a time."

"Until I meet up with my companions and we pool information, I cannot know who, or why. Or, I will admit, even if."

Goodman walked, head-down with the stick across his shoulders, leading me in a wide circle through the untouched woodland as I told my tale—although since I was forced to leave out many of the details so as not to enmesh him in danger, I found it was a story I would mistrust myself, were I to hear it.

At the end, I described the rapid disintegration of the aeroplane mid-flight, and said, "Captain Javitz brought it down in the clearest patch he could see, although it proved not quite clear enough. And you know the rest."

Back now where we had started, Goodman sat down on a fallen tree, studying the rambling structure on the far side of the clearing: tree in front, shed behind, a glimpse of orchard at the back. After a minute, I sat beside him. Even with a clear head, the meadow resembled the dwelling-place of some mythic creature. Could there possibly be a deed some-where with Robert Goodman's name on it? I thought it more likely that the aeroplane had delivered us to another world, one in which official land deeds and telegraph lines did not exist.

"The whole story sounds terribly alarmist and melodramatic, I know. But short of giving you all the details, and the names"—*which would absolutely guarantee that you did not believe me*, I mentally added—"it's the bald truth."

"Good. So you won't be leaving momentarily?"

"Not if you don't mind having us, for two or three more days." If nothing else, I owed it to Javitz to let his leg heal before moving him.

"Good," he repeated, adding, " 'Dull would he be of a soul who could pass by/A sight so touching in its majesty.' " I stared, then followed the line of his gaze: A hundred feet away stood a magnificent stag, its antlers each showing six or seven points. The creature's liquid eyes studied us with as much interest as we studied him. *Majesty* was the word.

Which was, again, that of Wordsworth. " 'Westminster Bridge'?" I asked.

He looked at me as if I were mad. "No, red deer."

And so saying, the little blond man set out across his meadow, causing the stag to leap away and me to grin at my companion's retreating back. The stripped sapling rested across his shoulder like a rifle barrel. Or the first support for a child's swing.

I thought it safe to leave the two men with the child for a bit longer—indeed, Estelle seemed happier with either of them than she did with me—and the walk had begun to loosen my sore muscles, so I skirted the edge of the meadow and followed what looked like an overgrown horse-track to the west. In twenty minutes, I came to the house that explained the estate.

A square, unfussy Georgian box of a house in the middle of an abandoned garden, weeds growing through the gravel of its drive. The boards across all the ground-floor windows and some of the upper storeys suggested that it was vacant. I circled it, seeing no sign of life.

A broken gutter-pipe had been recently repaired, although not painted—and I thought this might explain Goodman's presence. A country estate whose family did not wish it to deteriorate entirely would want it cared for; permitting this odd sort of man with a love for simple things to make a home nearby was a sensible precaution.

Although he was an unusual sort of caretaker, I reflected as I turned back towards the meadow. His accent and education spoke of the officer class, but his skills confirmed his claims of ambulance service. One might assume that some physical shortcoming had disqualified him from active service, but he showed no signs of infirmity now.

One of the small objects on Goodman's wall of decoration was a bronze Croix de Guerre. It could have belonged to anyone, of course—he had not personally worn any of the twenty-three horse-shoes on the wall either—but I suspected it was his, even though governments did not often give medals to lowly ambulance drivers.

In any case, a man living in the deep woods six years after Armistice had probably not had an easy War. But then, I had known that since the moment I saw those old eyes in the young face.

Back on the dead tree, I sat massaging my neck, stiff from yesterday's violence and the source of my persistent headache. It was just as well he hadn't agreed that we should leave, I thought: I'd have collapsed before we reached the crash site.

Goodman came down the front steps and went over to the enormous tree, retrieving a garden fork that he had left leaning against its trunk. He absently patted the trunk, a gesture remarkably similar to my mother's touch on the *mezuzah* at our door, then headed towards his little walled vegetable garden beside the shed.

My eyes went back to the tree. I had seen no sign of fairies. Perhaps it was instead Yggdrasil, the World Tree where the gods hold court. Although that was an ash, and this an oak. And the dark preoccupation with Norse mythology belonged to Reverend Thomas Brothers, not Robert Goodman.

The name opened a door in my mind and out flowed all the anxiety and speculation that I had kept dammed up when talking to our rescuer. If Brothers was not dead, where had he gone, and who was helping him? Should I have directed a telegram to Chief Inspector Lestrade, to inform him that Holmes' suspect was at large in the wilds of Scotland? Or would that simply further endanger the child?

Thoughts chased around my head, making my skull ache again, and I was glad when Goodman reappeared around the side of his motley construction with a full bushel basket. I climbed from my perch and went to the house, where I found Estelle setting out another dollies' tea-party, this time with Javitz, the two deer Goodman had given her, and a two-inch-tall rabbit, crude but rich in personality. She had given the American the porcelain cup of honour, making do herself with an acorn, and was chattering happily about a doll she had at home. I could only wonder at the indomitability of the very young.

I settled to the tangle of dried beans in want of shelling, and she instantly trotted over with two acorn cups, giving me one. I thanked her, and she presented the other to Goodman, watching in anticipation for his reaction. Javitz shot me a father's amused grin, while I wondered how one was to play the game, but Goodman did not hesitate. He raised his cup to his lips, took a noisy sip, and swallowed, the very picture of satisfaction. The verisimilitude of his act made me glance involuntarily at my own tiny woodland cup and to wonder, for an instant, if his might not contain actual tea.

Chapter 21

$$a \div (b+c+d) + e - (\tfrac{1}{2}\,c)$$

Mycroft decided on Monday that the election of the Labour government might have a larger role in his current predicament than he had originally allowed; however, because it was not entirely to blame, he only deducted half of it.

He thought it was Monday, although it was difficult to be certain. Distressingly difficult. He had the impression that some of his food and drink contained sedatives—not a lot, just enough to make him drowsy. He hoped so. Humiliating to think that mere solitude might affect the control of his mind.

The room provided only two sources of external stimulation: the window overhead, and the gaolers.

In the roof a dozen feet over his standing head was a sky-light, four feet square, of translucent glass—or rather, regular glass that had been whitewashed at some time in its history, now darkened by decades of grime and generations of passing birds. He rather wished that the man wielding the brush had been less diligent, and thus provide a prisoner with a tiny glimpse of the sky. Instead, he had a featureless square that became visible at dawn then faded at dusk, propelling a diffuse patch across floor and walls in the hours between. (Logically, this prison might be constructed with an outer roof and fitted with an artificial light that rose and fell, confusing his time sense and rending the regularity of his meals false—but that would be elaborate and to what purpose? The very idea was diabolical and intolerable, and in that direction lay a path to madness.)

Yesterday (was it yesterday?) a faint scratching from above had caused his heart to race, but it had only been pigeons. And every so often, if he lay staring up for long enough, a quick shadow would pass across the whitened glass; once it had been an entire flock of birds, which played across his internal vision for a long time.

As for the gaolers, there were two. The younger one with the City shoes came in the mornings. His athletic stride sent brisk echoes down the corridor outside, hard heels making impact on the worn surface. The older, heavier, slower man who wore scuffed boots and had a slight hitch in his stride was in charge of the afternoons and most late-night visits.

In either case, food and drink were placed in a tiny pass-through that was walled about on the corridor side. Mycroft pictured a sturdy metal-lined box fastened against a hole cut in the wall, its top unlatching to deposit the food and refill the cup. One morning he'd kept the cup to see what would happen, and his gaoler—the younger man—had simply poured the water onto the floor of the pass-through and left.

The younger man, twice at the beginning, had trailed a faint aroma of bay rum after-shave. The older man smelt of gaspers and had the phlegmy cough that went with them. Neither responded to his questions, although the younger man would pause to listen.

The younger man interested Mycroft considerably.

The food and drink (drugged or no) were delivered at regular intervals: seven in the morning, three in the afternoon, and eleven at night—he could hear Ben tolling from the Houses of Parliament. The morning delivery in the sharp shoes was timed as precisely as the quick footsteps: within two minutes either way of seven. The older man was more lax, especially last thing at night, when the eleven o'clock "meal" often preceded the three-quarter ring of the bells. But no matter the time or the footsteps, what his gaolers brought was the same: a bread roll, a boiled egg, a cup of water, and an apple. That morning, the apple had been an orange. He had spent nearly an hour fretting over the significance before deciding just to eat the dratted thing.

Breaking open the peel had at least improved the smell, for a while.

His prison was in the top floor of an unused warehouse near the river, whose traffic he could occasionally hear. The shade of the bricks combined with the direction of the clock meant that if he was turned loose, he could point directly to his prison. The débris in the corners and the floor-boards indicated that over the years the space had held a variety of goods: tea leaves and turmeric, a palimpsest of dye-stuffs, the gouges of metal parts. He'd found a fragment of Chinese porcelain, which came in handy, and a William IV farthing coin, which was less so.

The district outside was moribund—he could barely discern the vibrations of daytime activity rising from below—and that alone had made him hesitate to attempt breaking the window: If he did manage to break it, no one would hear his calls, and the cold nights pouring in might finish him off. In any event, the only thing heavy enough to do the job was his toilet bucket, and he preferred not to empty its contents onto the floor.

His mind was wandering, yet again. He pulled his thoughts from useless speculation and re-addressed himself to the schoolboy algebra on the wall.

$$a \div (b+c+d) + e - (\tfrac{1}{2}\,c)$$

The first letter drew his eyes, yet again. *a* for *Accountant*, as a child's book might have it. Had Damian ever drawn a book of ABCs for the child? Estelle was her name, *e* for Estelle—no, *e* stands for Mycroft Holmes, who calls himself an accountant, the man who oversees the books of the British Empire.

In recent years, his bookkeeping—the financial and political balance sheets of nations—had begun to take on elements of the ethical as well. What in earlier years had been a fairly straightforward enterprise, as black and white as numerals on a page, slowly took on shades of grey, and even colour. He had come to recognise that a government bound up in its own purposes required an outside mediator. Even if the government did not acknowledge its need. Even if Mycroft Holmes was an ironic choice for the arbiter of ethics.

He went back to the formula on the wall, staggering a bit as he got to his feet, and scratched another element:

$$a \div (b+c+d) + e - (\tfrac{1}{2}\, c) - (f)$$

Absently sucking the bloody patch on his finger—the scrap of porcelain was adequate against mortar, but viciously sharp—he thought about the *f. f* was the sum of those times when Mycroft Holmes had acted at deliberate cross-purposes to his government. He had always thought of it as acting directly for the king, by-passing the evanescent Prime Ministers, but in fact, the choices had been his alone. Three times in his career, he had stepped beyond the mere gathering of Intelligence, taking into his hands a decision that others were incapable of making; twice he had used his authority to further his own interests.

The third time he would have done so was cut short, four days ago (he thought) by an armed abductor at the very gate of New Scotland Yard.

Not that Mycroft Holmes had any ethical dilemma with playing God. He could look his conscience in the face; if there were elements in his past of which he was not proud, he was content that he walked the line of justice.

No: What had begun to concern him this past year was the face in the looking-glass—the thinning hair, the sagging jowls, the old man looking back, even though he was barely seventy.

It was all very well and good for Mycroft Holmes to play God, but who was to say that the next man, the man who took his place in the accounting house, would have as untarnished a conscience?

Chapter 22

On Monday, my headache had retreated to the back of my head, although sudden motion made me queasy. I told myself that another day of rest would not be the end of the world, and put aside any plans for leaping into action.

After breakfast, Goodman presented Estelle with a second lively wooden rabbit and a fully articulated three-inch-tall bear with leather thongs for joints.

In the middle of the morning, he finished making a crutch for Javitz out of the sapling. He had trimmed the split top to make a rest, added rags, then neatly bound the padding with buckskin. It rode so easily under the big man's arm, the sapling might have been grown for that express purpose.

After lunch, Goodman returned to the nearby village for the shopping he had requested. He took with him my letter to *The Times*, enclosing a pound note and the request that they run a message for me until the money was used up. The message was designed to attract the eye of an amateur beekeeper like Holmes:

> **BEEKEEPING is enjoyed by thousands, a reliable and safe hobby, practiced on week-ends alone from Oxford Street to Regent's Park.**

A telegram was a more complicated proposition. I had not yet decided if the risk of a telegram to Lestrade was worth the slim chance that he would actually issue a warrant for Brothers. Or if one to Mycroft would be the same as one directed to Scotland Yard.

Goodman returned bearing an enormous parcel, which he set with a resounding thump onto the kitchen table. Estelle hopped up and down as our resident St Nicholas unpacked the load: A change of stockings and shirts all around were, I supposed, required, as were the trousers and boots for Javitz, since he'd lost everything in the wreck, but my own pullover was far from unwearable (although the back of it was rather the worse for wear—the blood had washed out, but the darning was clumsy). Certainly I did not require a skirt, particularly one three inches too wide and two inches too short. And for a hermit to purchase not one, but two frocks for a small child was not only unnecessary, but foolish.

He saw my disapproval, and knew the reason. "The village is fifty miles from nowhere."

"You don't think the 'plane has been found by now?"

"You needed clothing," he said firmly. "And here's your *Times*."

He no doubt thought to distract me from the purchases at the bottom of the pack: a set of jackstones, collected in a red cotton bag, and a small soft doll that he slipped into Estelle's hand. I'd have had to be considerably farther away than the clearing to miss her squeals of pleasure.

I gave up and carried the newspaper outside.

Monday, 1 September. I ran my eyes methodically down what Holmes called the agony columns of small adverts and messages. Two or three posts attracted my attention—one for the health benefits of honey, the other a notice for a ladies' motoring school, since my skills at the wheel were a longtime source of criticism from my partner—but in the end I decided that neither held hidden meaning.

For lack of better entertainment, I read the paper all the way to the shipping news, paying particular attention to reports of a terrible earthquake in Japan—I hoped the friends we had made there in the spring were safe. I folded it neatly to give to Javitz, thinking that he, too, might appreciate a reminder that the outer world had not faded away.

But when I had finished, there was nothing for it but to go back inside and join my granddaughter's dollies' tea-party.

Complete with iced biscuits, bought for the purpose by an unrepentant wild man of the woods.

Tuesday morning, my head was clear and my bruises healing. Goodman was gone when we woke, but returned while the morning was young. Later, he and I set out together in the opposite direction from his previous day's trek, leaving Estelle in the care of Javitz—or perhaps vice-versa. I had spent the evening making adjustments to the skirt, thinking it might render me less noticeable than a pair of trousers with a ripped knee and ground-in soil, but it was not a garment readily suited for a rough walk through the woods, and I was forced to stop every few minutes to disentangle the tweed from a snagging bramble or branch.

I also noticed two more of the bent-branch booby-traps. Robin Goodfellow he might be, but this hermit had no intention of permitting others to come upon him unawares.

After five miles, we came to a high wall with a narrow metal gate. The gate was speckled with rust; the sturdy padlock was not.

"I need to go into the village alone," I told him, brushing my skirt and checking that my boots were not too caked with mud.

"A woman by herself would stand out almost as much as a woman with me," he said, pocketing the key and pushing open the gate.

I glanced at him, surprised at this perceptive remark from a man who showed less sign of interest in the mores and customs of the outer world than the hedgehog might have done. "By myself I can invent a reason for being there. With you, there's no chance."

"As you wish. How long will you be?"

"An hour at most. You're certain there's a telegraph office?"

"There's a post office," he replied. "It has a telegraph."

"If the telegraphist isn't off fishing or caring for his aged mother, you mean?"

"Buy some milk, for the child. And I think she needs another warm garment—"

"Oh for heaven's sake," I said. "Look, you will be here when I return, right?"

"Or in the village."

"Well, just wait half an hour before you come in. And if you see me, don't give on that we know each other."

I stepped out onto the road and marched into the village.

I was, I realised, in luck: The village was on a lake, and the lake was on the Picturesque Sites of Olde England tours. A steamer had recently deposited a load of earnest sight-seers, all of them wearing sensible shoes and clutching guide-books and pamphlets. I did not fit in, precisely, lacking hat, book, and earnest expression, but being one stranger in the vicinity of a dozen others made invisibility easier.

In the village shop, I gathered up three post-cards, a copy of the day's *Times*, and a tin of travelling sweets, then stood in the queue to buy stamps. Once there, I enquired about sending a telegram. The rather befuddled but undeniably picturesque woman in charge of the village's postal service admitted that there was a telegraphic device fitted to the shop's post office, but suggested that I should be much better off to return across the lake to the town and use their service, because her husband, the man in charge of this daunting machine, had taken to his bed with a touch of the ague and was not to be disturbed.

This message was profusely illustrated with woe and took six long minutes to deliver. The queue behind me was now to the door. I was sorely tempted to clamber over the counter and tap out the message myself, but knew that this would not help my aim of invisibility. Besides which, the sharp sniff coming from her young assistant at the mention of *ague* suggested that the cause might be something other than germs.

So I waited until the postmistress had dithered to an end of her story, then batted my eyes at her and told her that I truly needed to send a telegram, now please, and it would be such a pity if I found I could not, because I should then have to speak to my uncle in the telegraphs office down in London and let him know that the village wanted attention.

She put up her window and fetched her husband.

I gave them both a sweet smile and let myself into the crowded back of the shop.

The man moved in a cloud of gin, freshly swigged in an (unsuccessful) attempt to steady his hands. I permitted him to run the first part of the message, but in a short time he found himself eased to one side while this chipper female, twittering all the while about how her uncle had been amused to teach her Morse when she was a tiny thing, finished the dots and dashes.

This is the telegram I had decided to send, addressed to Mycroft:

ALL WELL COMING HOME SOON BUT ORKNEY BROTHERS REQUIRE URGENT ATTENTION STOP MESSAGES IN THE USUAL WAY WILL REACH ME STOP RUSSELL

It was a risk, but almost as much as the message about Brothers, I wanted to reassure him (and possibly, through him, Holmes) that we were safe. Besides, it gave nothing away other than its place of origin, and with any luck, we would be far away by the time Scotland Yard came looking.

I thanked the gentleman (who was now looking quite ill indeed) and went to pay his good wife. As I opened my purse, motion out of the corner of my eye had me looking out of the window, at Robert Goodman.

The shopkeeper noticed the direction of my gaze and hastened to reassure her dangerous customer with the powerful London relations. "Don't worry about him, dearie, that's just the local loonie. Perfectly harmless."

One green eye winked at me through the glass. "You're certain?" I asked.

"Absolutely. Mad as a rabbit, that one, but he pays his bills."

I did the same, and left, but all I saw of Goodman was the brush of his coat as he went into the next shop.

Well, with Robert Goodman in the village, the residents would take no notice of me.

We met again where we had parted. Over his shoulder was slung another load of foodstuffs and fancies with which to ply his guests. I had *The Times*—which again had failed to yield a message from Holmes, or even Mycroft—and the post-cards and tin of sweets, bought for disguise.

Also, two small Beatrix Potter picture-books.

Chapter 23

By Tuesday, Sherlock Holmes was beginning to feel that a nice cosy gaol might be preferable to his current situation.

On Sunday afternoon, he'd been glad just to reach Holland, having spent the day on deck as Gordon's crew, a sustained physical effort that made him all too aware of his age. He'd had little conversation with Dr Henning, once the decision was made to take refuge with the man she described as a second cousin, twice-removed. He'd had even less with Damian, who slept.

Their goal was a small fishing village roughly a third of the way from Amsterdam to the Hook of Holland. The place appeared, he had to admit, eminently suited as a hideaway—no one in his right mind would look for Sherlock Holmes there. Rumour of their presence might take months to reach England.

As they neared the coast-line, the doctor had come on deck to direct Gordon. She also informed Holmes that Damian was running a fever.

"Not much of one, yet, but it is essential that we get him to a place of quiet and stillness."

"I have been trying to do that for two days."

"I am not criticising, merely saying, he needs quiet."

"And this cousin of yours can offer that?"

"Well, stillness certainly. Although now that I think of it, the quiet will depend on how many guests are in residence."

He turned on her a raised eyebrow. "Guests?"

"Never mind. If the main house is full, he'll put us in one of the cabins."

"Dr Henning, it is not too late to—"

"No no, it'll be fine, don't worry. Eric regards himself as a patron of the arts. He's very wealthy and quite a character. He's also an expert on the American Civil War, and he occasionally stages re-enactments of the major battles. However, they never last more than a day or two. Of course, there's also the artists. When Eric retired ten years ago, he decided the best way he might serve the arts was to provide a congenial place in which they might concentrate. So he bought up half this village, and invites painters and sculptors to live here while they are working."

"This is most unfortunate."

It was her turn to raise an eyebrow. "You object to artists?"

"By no means. But have you not discovered in the course of conversation with your patient that Damian is an artist?"

"Half the people in London regard themselves as artists," she said dismissively. "Those that aren't poets or playwrights."

"Damian Adler is the real thing. He is, in fact, rather a well-known painter, among certain circles. A collective of artists is not an ideal place in which to keep him under wraps."

"I see," she said.

Holmes rubbed his face in self-disgust. When he was young, lack of sleep had only sharpened his faculties. Now, it only took two or three sleepless nights to turn his brains to cold porridge. He was soft, old and soft, and easily distracted by thoughts of bed and bath and how much he disliked this beard under his finger-nails.

Holland. What other choices were there? He had a colleague in Amsterdam—or not precisely a colleague: The man was a criminal who ran a series of illegal gambling establishments, but he had proved useful once or twice.

But trust the fellow? The temptation to sell Damian to the police might prove too great.

"We'll have to keep Damian closeted, and avoid using his name," he told the doctor. "As soon as he can be moved, we'll be on our way."

"I am sorry, I didn't think to mention it."

"The fault is mine," he said in a tired voice, and went down to explain the situation to the patient.

Two hours later, they were nearing the mouth of a small bay. Holmes stood at the rail beside the doctor, watching the approach of a noble white house with several acres of lawn spreading down to the water and six small white cottages back among the trees. The whole resembled a plantation mansion, complete with slaves' quarters, more at home in colonial Virginia than on the coast of Holland.

"That's it. We can put in at the boat-house," she said, and turned to call instructions to Gordon. That was something, at any rate: A boat-house would reduce their chances of being spotted, and of being asked inconvenient questions as to passports and permissions to dock.

When they had tied up, Henning stepped lightly to the boards and trotted off to the big house. When she was halfway across the lawn, a round man in a brilliant white suit came down the steps to greet her. She disappeared inside his embrace, then freed herself, straightening her hat as she gazed up at him. Explanations took but a moment before the man turned to the figures on the terrace behind him to wave orders. Three of the figures turned instantly away to the house, two of them returning with an object that, as they drew nearer, became a rolled-up Army stretcher.

Getting Damian up the boat's tight companionway was tricky, but the servants managed. They marched away in the direction of the farthest white cottage, the doctor scurrying after.

Holmes, Gordon, and the second-cousin-twice-removed studied each other in bemusement. Holmes put out his hand. "Terribly sorry about this, we had a bit of an accident on this boat we'd hired, and your... Dr Henning said the best thing for it would be to inflict ourselves on you for a day or two, while the lad mends. Our good captain," he continued, warming to the tale he was constructing—

However, the would-be plantation owner was not interested in the details of their presence. The rotund gentleman, who had been introduced as Eric VanderLowe, cut in, "Would you two mind posing for us?"

"Posing? As in, for drawing?"

"Precisely. I have a group coming in the morning. We'd arranged for two lads from the village, but they've been called away. It would help my artist friends a great deal."

"Er, perhaps we might talk about it tomorrow," Holmes suggested. "We're all a bit tired."

"Of course, tomorrow will do nicely." And so saying, VanderLowe summoned a manservant to take their few possessions to the guest cottages.

That night, despite the prescribed quiet, Damian's fever mounted. Holmes and the doctor stayed at the young man's bed-side, applying wet cloths in an attempt to cool him. Damian thrashed and sweated, cursing in three languages and carrying on broken conversations, in Chinese with Yolanda and in French with his mother.

Finally, towards morning he grew quieter. Gentle snores arose from where the doctor sat, well bundled against the breeze pouring through the open windows. Holmes stood at the foot of the bed, studying his son's resting face.

An hour later, Dr Henning stirred, then jerked upright at the silence. "He's sleeping," Holmes said in a low voice before she could react further.

She stood, to feel the pulse on Damian's free wrist and tug his bed-clothes back up to his shoulders, then rolled her neck and shoulders with a grimace.

"You go and sleep," Holmes told her. "I'll fetch you if anything happens."

She nodded, although she seemed in no hurry to move away from her patient. "Twenty days, you've known him?"

"Today being Monday, it is three weeks."

"Who was his mother?"

"A woman who out-smarted me. More than once."

"Does he resemble her? The way you look at him . . ."

"He does now."

Monday was endless; Holmes had discovered early that there was not a copy of *The Times* within twenty miles.

Damian slept. Holmes turned the sick-room over to Dr Henning and took to his own bed at last, but in the afternoon he gave in to the pleas of his host and sat for ninety minutes while half a dozen oddly assorted artists—four men, one woman, and a person of indeterminate gender—bent over their drawing tablets. Gordon took his place for an hour, and when he escaped (outraged at their request to shed his clothing) he stalked away to scrub down the boat.

At five o'clock, Holmes leant against the cottage's open doorway, listening to Damian's steady breathing and feeling the inner seethe of frustration. Shadows inched across the lawn. He found himself wishing for soldiers of grey and blue, blasting at each other with antique firearms: Pickett's Charge or the Battle of Antietam would provide a nice distraction. Instead, there was music coming from the house that made his fingers twitch for a violin; the tobacco in his pouch was running low; and the doctor's bag sat on the table beside Damian's bed, its open top an invitation, tugging at his attention every time he went through the room.

He had no intention of using the narcotic distraction it offered; he had long outgrown that habit. But the mere fact that he noticed the bag was irritating.

"You don't need to stay in shouting distance," the doctor's voice came from behind him. "He's sleeping nicely, and I have a book."

He did not answer, but eyed the half-mile of lawn between the cottage and where Gordon was working, shirt off and head down over the boat's decking.

"Go," she urged. "Physical labour will help you to sleep tonight."

He opened his mouth to ask why she imagined he might have trouble sleeping, then changed it to, "My friend Watson could tell you that I have never been good at following doctor's orders."

"Then think of it as a friendly suggestion."

He glanced down at her, and had the disconcerting impression that the wee thing had overheard his inner dialogue with the black bag. Quite impossible. She must have picked up on his general agitation—although that was a bad enough sign in itself, that he was giving himself away to a near-stranger.

Still, she was right. There was nothing like hard labour to take one's mind off of frustration.

He gave a glance back at the sleeping Damian, then set off across the lawn, rolling up his shirt-sleeves as he drew near the dock.

Work helped. But still, Monday was endless.

So it was that on Tuesday, shaking off the sensation of prison, Holmes trimmed his beard, changed some pounds to guilders at the house, put on his only suit (miraculous, that he had managed to retain his valise during the past week's eccentric travels), and asked Dr Henning if, seeing as how he was taking the train to Amsterdam, there was any person to whom she might like a telegram sent.

Surely Wick would have noticed by now that their doctor was missing?

Chapter 24

The train to Amsterdam was small and antique. In a country more tolerant of dilapidation, this rural transport would have devolved into a threadbare state, but here it was so scrubbed it could only be considered worn.

Two other passengers boarded at the tiny station, a long-married couple (two wedding rings, worn thin) that Holmes would have dubbed "elderly" had he not suspected they were younger than he. They waited for him to enter, he gestured for them to go first, and all three might have stood on the platform being polite until the train pulled away had the conductor's whistle not broken the old woman's nerve. They took seats at one end of the car, and Holmes walked to the other, settling behind his newspaper.

It was a Dutch paper, bought as much for camouflage as to provide him with distraction during the journey, but the reaction of the old couple was telling: They had known him for a foreigner without him opening his mouth.

Three stops up, Holmes folded the paper and joined the disembarking throng of two office workers (one had the chronic stains of an accountant's ink on his cuffs, the other's fingers betrayed long hours on a typing machine). He followed the two as far as the station's news stand, saw at a glance that the offerings here were no more sophisticated than the station at which he had begun, and returned to the train. At the last minute, he changed direction to fall in behind a louche young poet (the scrap of paper sticking from his pocket betrayed a sonnet) ambling towards the next car up, and boarded that one instead: not that he expected anyone to trace his movements, but Holmes had not lived to grow grey by neglecting to lay false trails.

He shook open the paper, making an effort to damp down his simmering impatience. There was no point in leaping from his seat at every stop to search for a copy of *The Times*. No point whatsoever. He would soon be in Amsterdam, and given a wide choice of international newspapers.

They would, he knew, contain nothing of interest. It was, after all, only Tuesday. Taking into account the presence of a child, and the sparse provisions of transportation out of Orkney, Russell might well still be working her way down from the northern reaches of Scotland.

The probability of finding a message from her in *The Times* agony column was decidedly thin.

On the other hand, there was Mycroft to account for. Holmes still found Russell's report of a Scotland Yard raid on his brother's flat hard to credit. Could it have been a false rumour? Chief Inspector Lestrade was obdurate, but the man had never before displayed signs of outright insanity.

This, thought Holmes, half ripping a page as he turned it, *this* was why he'd avoided family ties for so much of his career: It made matters so much more difficult. He felt a bit like the boat whose hull he'd attacked the previous afternoon, thick with barnacles and sea-washed débris. If he didn't have Damian on his hands; if Russell didn't have the child—

He grimaced, and violently folded away the newspaper. One might as well say that Russell was a drag on his progress. Or Mycroft. Which was not the case. Or, rarely the case.

He spent the rest of the journey listening to accents, accustoming his ears to the peculiarities of the language and rehearsing the shape of a few key phrases.

When the train pulled into central Amsterdam, Holmes made his way, with deliberate Dutch politeness, down from the train and towards the news stand. As he suspected, the only *Times* the man possessed was

Monday's. Still, he bought that and a copy of a Paris newspaper, enquired when the Tuesday editions of both would arrive, and walked down the street until he found a clothier with a French name.

One does not need to be invisible, merely explicable.

He left with his English clothing in a parcel under his arm, looking for the barber the salesman had recommended. When he had finished there, he carried his purchases down the street to a small café, requesting *een kopje koffie en een broodje, alstublieft* in a thick French accent. He lit a French cigarette, passed a manicured hand over his newly trimmed hair (both hair and beard trimmed into the latest Parisian *mode*), and sat in his new Parisian collar and Lyonnaise neck-tie, the very picture of a *monsieur* in Amsterdam. Only when the tiny cup and roll were placed before him did he open the English paper.

He'd been deciphering the grumbles and whispers of the agony column for more than a half century; his eyes knew its texture the way a sculptor's hands knew a lump of stone. One glance told him that there was nothing of interest among the close-packed print. Still, he read his methodical way down each column before he permitted himself to be certain: Neither Russell nor Mycroft had left their mark there.

He dropped some coins and both newspapers on the linen cloth and set about the day's tasks.

His first stop was a post office. There he mailed the letter to *The Times* that he had prepared early that morning: a notice for the agony column that began, "Bees may thrive in foreign lands."

However, the untoward actions of Scotland Yard made him question the wisdom of depending on the Royal post. Letters were too easy to open. What he required was a private and less easily breached means of communication: a telephone. And there was, on the surface of it, no particular reason why he could not go into a public telephone office to make his trunk call.

But why should that phrase, *on the surface of it*, make him think of an incident that had taken place this past spring, late one evening in the midst of the Pacific Ocean? He'd been at the rails in conversation with Russell, idly tracking a bit of flotsam off the bow, paying no conscious attention to the object except that the back of his mind kept nudging his eyes towards it. Only when the insistent pressure reached forward, making him aware of the unlikelihood of a floating object keeping pace with a ship, did his eyes suddenly give the thing a shape and an identity: the dorsal fin of a disturbingly large shark.

He needed to concentrate on the Brothers case, but Lestrade's uncharacteristic audacity kept protruding from his thoughts like that bit of flotsam from a moonlit sea.

It might be that a trap was being laid. Granted, it was equally plausible that Lestrade had lost first his mind and then his job, and that Mycroft was even now settled at his desk in that anonymous governmental office, savouring a morning coffee and considering the state of the world.

He shook his head: one matter at a time. Once Damian was free from danger, there would be time enough to focus on Mycroft. Still, there was no harm in being cautious. Without data, he might be jumping in for a swim beside a shark the size of a motorcar.

He found what he wanted twenty minutes from the station, a grand hotel that showed signs of renovations aimed at a modern traveller. He asked for, and received, a suite of rooms that was not the most expensive the hotel offered, but close to that, and informed the manager that his bags would follow by evening. To be certain, he enquired after their facilities for international telephone calls, and was assured that they had installed the most up-to-date equipment, and that if the exchange could handle the call, the hotel could support it.

Satisfied, he allowed himself to be escorted to the room, high up in the east wing, giving the bellman a tip that compensated for the lack of bags. He took off his hat, sat at the desk before an elaborate arrangement of fresh flowers, and lifted the earpiece.

A trunk call from this address did, as he'd expected, receive priority treatment. Within a quarter hour he was speaking with a familiar Cockney voice, the line crackling and occasionally dropping words, but tolerably clear as these things went.

The two men had known each other more than thirty years, since the eight-year-old Billy had introduced himself by attempting to pick Holmes' pocket. On being caught, the young thief's cheeky intelligence led Holmes to hire him on the spot, eventually to appoint him the most unlikely page-boy ever to grace Mrs Hudson's kitchen. More importantly, Billy had become Holmes' liaison with the street-boys he had dubbed his "Irregulars." Now, the two men exchanged the sorts of greetings designed to communicate that they were both alone, and as secure as might be expected. Then Holmes got down to business, avoiding as always the unambiguous meaning and the personal name—one could never tell when a bored exchange operator might be listening in.

"I need you to get into touch with my brother," Holmes began.

"You know he's been arrested?"

"*Arrested?* My—" He bit back the name before he could finish it; the Bakelite earpiece creaked in his grip.

"You didn't know?"

"I'd heard there was a raid, but an *arrest?* For what?"

"Truth to tell, the arrest's speculation, like. Only, I heard he was picked up Thursday and taken in for questioning, and he hasn't been seen since. You want me to go by his place and check?"

"No." He tried to imagine what on earth could be going on, to result in the arrest—*arrest!*—of Mycroft Holmes. That was taking the game of cat-and-mouse to an extreme. It had to be some Scotland Yard brainstorm: A play for power amongst the Intelligence divisions would be more subtle. Whatever the reason, it was most inconvenient. He'd been counting on the use of Mycroft's connexions.

"No, I think you should steer clear of his apartment, and do not make any approach to Scotland Yard. If you hear that my brother is at home again, you might give him a ring from a public box, but don't go beyond that. I'll be back in a few days, I'm sure it's a misunderstanding."

"I hope so." The Cockney voice sounded apprehensive: Billy thought Holmes had meant that the arrest was due to a misunderstanding, not that Billy had misunderstood Mycroft's absence to be an arrest. Still, there was no point in correcting him. In any event, if the Dutch operators were anything like the English, he risked being cut off soon. However, he had to venture another question before getting down to business.

"What about . . . the rest of my family?"

"Your wife?"

"Yes." No one but Mycroft and Russell—and now Dr Henning—knew who Damian was.

"Haven't heard from her. You want me to ask around?"

"Don't worry, she's been out of town. I expect she'll get into touch before long."

"Anything you want me to tell her when she does?"

"To keep her eyes open. The same goes for you."

"I understand."

"I need you to do something."

"Anything."

"A man who calls himself Reverend Thomas Brothers, who runs a somewhat shady church called the Children of Lights on—"

"The Brompton Road, yes."

No moss grew on Billy when it came to the goings-on in London, that was for certain. "See what you can find out about Brothers, and about his assistant, a felon named Marcus Gunderson, who did time in the Scrubs."

"Marcus Gunderson," Billy repeated. "Thomas Brothers. Anything in particular?"

Holmes had had time to think about the ill-fitting elements in the Brothers case, and here was the place where the design was most baffling—and although it would have been far better to investigate it himself, Billy would make an adequate stand-in. "I want to know how Brothers managed to create a new identity for himself in such a short time. He stepped foot off the boat from Shanghai last November, and in no time at all had a new identity, a house, an assistant like Gunderson, and a building to start his new church."

"You think he had friends before he came here?"

"I think he was in touch with the criminal underworld, yes. I want to know how." He did not say to Billy that such information might provide Lestrade with a more attractive suspect than an artist who wakes up one morning and decides to murder his wife in cold blood. Brothers' death would be a complication. However, with both Gordon and Dr Henning at hand to bear witness to Damian's injuries, the police might quietly decide that to have lost a man like Brothers was not entirely a bad thing.

"And, Billy? Brothers is dead, although it is possible no-one knows that yet. Watch how you walk: I don't know what ties he might have had to the crime world, so I don't know if it was merely a business matter or if they would be out for revenge."

"I had this teacher, once, schooled me always to keep my eyes open."

"Good man. You remember the place where my family and I leave messages for each other? Don't say it."

The lengthy dim crackle down the line was Billy reflecting on the likelihood of this conversation being overheard. However, whatever Holmes suggested . . .

"I remember," the younger man said.

"I want you to visit that place for a few days. If we need you, we'll leave a message there."

There came a longer pause, while Billy worked it out.

"In the morning, right?" Billy asked.

Holmes smiled in relief: *The Times* was a morning paper. "Correct. And if you have any message for me, you can do the same. Although I'm sure you're a busy bee these days."

"A busy—ah, right you are, Gov. And if there's anything else, anything at all, don't hesitate to ask."

"We won't."

Holmes returned the earpiece to its hooks. After a minute, he took it down, then hung it up again, and sat thinking. No, he decided: He might get into touch with the Dutch gambler tomorrow, but not today. Instead, he plucked a white rose-bud from the floral arrangement on the desk to thread into his button-hole, put his (new, French) hat back on his head, and left the hotel.

Half an hour's walk later and a mile to the north, he stepped into a telegraph office to send reassurances to Wick and to Thurso, for his inadvertent companions.

The rest of the day was given over to the tedium common to so many investigations, with time crawling as the apprehension gnawed at the back of his mind. He told himself firmly that Russell and little Estelle were sure to be fine, that Damian was as safe in the artists' community as anyplace on earth, that he would soon be back in London where Mycroft would tell him what the deuce was going on. That an enforced holiday did no one any harm. He walked the canals, visited a museum, ate a leisurely luncheon he did not want, and addressed everyone in the purest of French. He shopped, including a change of clothing for the doctor—who had been forced to borrow an ill-fitting frock the previous day—and for Damian—whose choice of apparel was distinctly bohemian and thus far from invisible. In the window of a stationers, he spotted a handsome sketch-book, and added that and a set of pastels to his parcels: They might keep the lad occupied, once his arm began to heal. And down the street, a shop sold him French cigarettes and English pipe-tobacco.

The newsagent had said the foreign papers would arrive by three o'clock. At twenty minutes past the hour, Holmes returned to the small shop near the station, and asked for both papers. The French one was in, the English one was expected any time. He gave the man a very French shrug, bought the one, and went back to the café.

It was after four when he spotted a small delivery van pulling up to the news stand. He finished his long-cold second cup of coffee, leaving a tip to acknowledge his long occupation of the table, and strolled back to the shop. Wordlessly, the man held out the day's *Times*. Holmes tucked it under his arm and walked to the station, passing the time until his train arrived by examining its front pages.

He had not actually expected to find a message, had he? So why should he feel so let down?

The train came, and he began the voyage back to the village by the sea. With every mile, he pushed away a growing conviction that he needed to be heading out of Holland, not settling more deeply into it.

Chapter 25

Peter James West looked down at the figure in the chair. Curious, he thought, how small the dead become.

"He put that knife right in your hand," Gunderson said in astonishment. "Never occurred to him you might use it."

"Remarkable, considering how ruled Brothers was by his imagination."

"Deluded to the end, he was."

The two men glanced at each other, a quick and unspoken dialogue passing between them.

You'd better believe it's occurred to me, Gunderson's eyes said.

So you've told me, replied West.

Which is why I also let drop about that little insurance policy I set up. Just in case you ever think I'm no longer useful.

But West turned away before Gunderson could see his reply: *Yes, and I'm glad you mentioned that letter, my friend, since it allowed me to take care of it. It wouldn't do, to leave that sort of thing lying about.*

The criminal classes were such refreshing employees: Money and fear were what men like Gunderson understood. Of money, it took surprisingly little to purchase muscle and a modicum of brain-power. One had only to remember that money might buy service, but not loyalty: For that, one required fear.

After tonight, Gunderson would think twice about betrayal.

West took off his suit coat and gloves, then rolled up one sleeve of his shirt, methodical as a surgeon, before retrieving the knife. Blood welled, but, without the heartbeat to propel it, there was neither gush nor splatter. It was a lesson to remember: A quick death leaves little mess. He wiped the blade on the victim's trouser leg, then pulled a clean handkerchief from Brothers' breast pocket to finish the job, tucking the scrap of linen back into place when he was finished. He held the vicious blade to the light.

"I understand he thought this to be meteor iron."

"That's what he said."

"One might almost believe him. It's a handsome thing." West bent again to free the scabbard, then slid the knife into the leather and the whole into his coat pocket. "You failed at the aeroplane, then."

"Looks like. I thought I'd hit it, but I haven't heard anything about it coming down. Have you?"

"No. Never mind, it was a slim chance and not our last. Do we know if the woman was in it?"

"MacAuliffe heard that she and the child were both in the 'plane."

"Leaving the men to their fishing boat, I suppose. Any idea how much nosing around she got up to before she left Orkney?"

"Far as I know, none at all. There wasn't a word of her between the time she and the American landed and when they took off."

"Good."

"However, Brothers left his passports behind. In that hotel he had MacAuliffe set fire to the week before."

"What, he and Adler were staying there?"

"That's right."

"Idiot. Well, the passports are clean, never mind. What about the others in Orkney?"

"What about them?"

"Don't act the imbecile, Gunderson, it doesn't suit you."

"They're still breathing, if that's what you mean."

"Was that wise?"

"Tiny place like that, three bodies would've been noticed—getting rid of MacAuliffe and his woman might've been explainable, but adding to it the doctor who patched Brothers together seemed risky. I didn't think you'd want a trail of bodies pointing at you."

"What about the telegram I sent?"

"Burned."

"Perhaps we ought to consider the telegraphist as a fourth candidate for attention. A clever investigator might ask all kinds of questions, and find it odd that a man like MacAuliffe would send a wire to London."

And the brother, Sherlock, was nothing if not clever. And tenacious.

"So you want me to go back up there and take care of them all?"

"Not yet," West said. Gunderson tried to hide his uneasiness, but it was there: For some reason, the man disliked killing women. He could send Buckner—but no, Buckner had the wits of a turnip. Cleaning Orkney required a deft touch. However, there was no rush: Even after Brothers was found, and identified, it would take days for news to trickle north to alarm MacAuliffe. After tomorrow night, Gunderson would be free; then he could go north and finish things up.

Gunderson started around the room with a handkerchief, wiping down surfaces. West joined him, taking care to cover the same places Gunderson had treated, on the off chance the man might think to set him up. At the end, they went through Brothers' valises, transferring several items into a worn rucksack.

When it was fully dark, Gunderson left, taking the rucksack with him. West watched him closely, then shut the door, satisfied: Gunderson had avoided meeting his eyes whenever possible. The lesson of fear had got through.

He climbed the stairs to open a window on the back of the house, returning to sit in the chair opposite the dead man. The room was quite cosy now.

"Once the flies get inside, I'm afraid there won't be much left of you," he told the would-be god. "It's a shabby way to treat a friend, Brothers, but I've no doubt you would have done the same to me, had it proved necessary."

The two men sat together for another hour, one man cooling while the other grew uncomfortably warm. The warm man spoke from time to time. He found the dead restful: They never argued, rarely raised any objection to one's actions, and encouraged the sort of calm reflection that was difficult around the living. At the end of their conversation, both agreed how appropriate it was that the archaic madness that had driven Brothers would help unseat the dinosaur of Intelligence, and free it to become a piece of modern machinery.

Eventually, Peter James West buttoned his overcoat and took his leave of the man who had, all unknowing, been so useful to him. He turned the gas down a fraction, switched off the lights, and locked the door.

On the way to the train station, West paused to slip the house's key into a storm drain.

Just in case.

Chapter 26

The train reached King's Cross shortly after ten-thirty Tuesday night. West was one of the last to disembark, and he walked past the left luggage office where Gunderson would have stored the rucksack. He would send another to retrieve it.

Just in case.

He had the taxi take him to the office, deserted but for the night staff. There he checked his mail, made a few notes for his secretary, and read the reports that had come in since the afternoon. Among them was one concerning the disappearance of Mycroft Holmes.

When his desk was clear, he walked on to his more private office in the shadow of Westminster Cathedral, where he read with greater interest the unofficial reports from the British and European ports. He then sent three coded telegrams and placed a long telephone call to Buckner, giving him the change in the next day's orders.

Back on the street, a light drizzle had begun to fall. He lit a cigarette in the portico of the building, then set off on foot in the direction of the river.

He was damp through by the time he unlocked the door of the quiet modern apartment in its deceptive warehouse. He hung his coat and hat to dry, and stuffed newspaper in the toes of his shoes before adding them to the airing cupboard.

He bathed, and ate. It was one o'clock Wednesday morning before he took up his god-like post at the window, drink in one hand and cigar in the other.

It was not that West enjoyed killing. During the War, of course, it had been part of the job—although it was hard to compare that hellish cacophony with the calm execution he had performed hours earlier in St Albans. Still, he had to confess (to himself, in that quiet room, alone) that on the few occasions when he had been required to end a life, the exercise of ultimate power had brought him a certain frisson of satisfaction. And without a doubt, death was a process that held considerable fascination for a thoughtful individual such as himself, transforming a complex, breathing machine, the image of God and little short of the angels, into so much cold meat.

No, Peter James West only killed when necessary. For the most part, he merely ordered a killing. But it was good to know that when the personal touch was required, his hand did not hesitate.

He put down his drink and laid the half-burnt cigar into its cut-glass bowl, to take up the leather scabbard that Brothers had worn against his skin. The oily texture of the leather was repugnant, but the knife itself was a thing of beauty. The blade, whether or not of meteor iron, was the work of a true artist, shaped to perfection and beaten until the surface shimmered with depth. The hilt might have been carved to fit his own hand, the warm ivory coaxing his fingers to wrap around it and hold the blade to the light.

It was the kind of knife that whispered, *Use me.*

A year ago, he would not have considered using a knife on Mycroft Holmes. Now, however, the old man had dropped a tremendous amount of weight: A six-inch-long blade would easily pierce his vitals.

Would it, West wondered, feel like regicide?

He regretted talking so much, in St Albans before Gunderson left. That was the problem with an audience of nonentities: One tended to overlook their capacity for action. Yes, the criminal classes could be bought and be kept in line by fear, but the moment they imagined they had the stronger weapon, they could turn vicious. Which would be inconvenient.

Not that he had given away any secrets—if he'd been stupid enough to do so, he'd have been forced to leave Gunderson lying on the floor next to Brothers. Which might have been a bit tricky. However, once this was over, Gunderson would have to be removed.

Let it be a lesson to you, Peter James: Never talk before the staff.

But he was grateful for the knife, a unique object in so many ways. An unexpected gift. But then, wasn't this entire affair an unexpected gift? He'd never have thought it possible, three years ago, when the Secret Intelligence Service budget was being pared to the bone, Smith-Cumming was so ill it was a surprise to see him each morning, every man was snarling to defend his small corner, and the distasteful "arrangement" was being imposed on them, weakening every aspect of the Service. The one person without a look of panic on his face had been Mycroft Holmes, who wandered the halls as fat and as enigmatic as ever. And only he, West, had thought to question why.

Mycroft Holmes, the ethical, the incorruptible. Who had laid a façade of virtue over a foundation of corruption, constructing a massive edifice almost entirely hidden by the grit and grief of lesser enterprises. Who answered to no higher authority than the face in the mirror.

It had been a hard two years, knowing the flaw but being unable to use it. Two years, before he'd heard of a letter from Shanghai.

Holmes called himself an accountant. Well, every accountant should know that there comes a day of reckoning.

West felt he'd played with the man long enough: drugs in his drink, disguised footsteps every morning, carrying a cloth dabbed with bay rum cologne. A private game, childish, perhaps, and at the end of its run. Time for Mycroft Holmes' final service to his country.

West finished his drink, crushed out the cigar, and took himself to bed.

As he slept, the curved knife lay on the bedside table.

The next morning, he put it into his pocket before he left the flat.

And carried it with him as he made his way to the attic prison of Mycroft Holmes.

Chapter 27

$$a \div (b+c+d) + e - (\tfrac{1}{2}\, c) - (f) = g$$

g, Mycroft decided on Wednesday, was The Opponent. *g* was the one who kept him here, who had granted him a neck-tie for a belt, who (this last was hypothesis, but he felt it a strong one) came down the prison's corridor on City heels and smelt occasionally of bay rum.

Mycroft's December illness had damaged his heart, but cleared his vision. He'd grown so accustomed to power, it took a spell of weakness to make him see just how immense his authority was. His job did not exist; his position was largely outside the government and therefore essentially without oversight. His was a power based entirely on ineffable agreement and hidden secrets: Mycroft Holmes is unshakably ethical; he is the nation's moral authority; all sides that matter accept him as the ultimate authority and mediator; he may have whatever he requests, to get his job done.

Three decades ago, he had made a decision that was not his to make. A decision that made everything possible. A decision that only he and one living man knew had been made. Before December, he'd managed to all but forget it, himself.

It was a beautiful thing, and a fragile thing, to place an empire's moral welfare in the hands of one man. Six months ago, he had come face to face with the knowledge that it was also a terrifying thing, and foolish beyond belief.

$$a \div (b+c+d) + e - (\tfrac{1}{2} c) - (f) = g$$

A *koan*, a conundrum, now beginning to disappear with the setting sun. If *g* was the man who had put *e* here, then it followed that *g* wanted to replace *e*. That *g* had looked at the rôle of the accountant and lusted after its authority—rather, its perceived authority, since the power behind *e* remained well hidden. And as soon as the *g* had been scratched onto the wall, Mycroft could only wonder that he was not yet dead.

Not that *e* objected to the delay of his death. Mycroft was actually growing accustomed to the hunger, and the cold, and even the stupefying boredom.

However, one possible explanation of his continued immobility was that in the outside world, *g* was busy assembling his weapons. That he was pulling together—call them *m* and *s* and *n* and *i*: Mary and Sherlock and Nephew and Infant. Adding to *g*'s side of the equation. Making *e* into a tool of his own.

Which raised the further question: Was this person *e*—this most ethical and moral of men—required to act on his suspicion? Was he obligated, as a servant of His Majesty, to remove a potential tool from enemy hands by using this bent nail to open a vein in his own wrist?

His grim thoughts broke off: a sound, where customarily there was none. It was too early for his evening visitation, too heavy for one of the pigeons, too near for street noise. He grabbed the solitary brick that his chip of porcelain and farthing coin had between them freed from the wall, then scrambled to his feet. Tightening his silken belt, he faced the approaching sound.

He wished that he might have been permitted to shave, before they came for him.

Chapter 28

On Wednesday, Goodman tried to teach Estelle jackstones. However, mature as her mind might be, her small hands lacked sufficient coordination to toss, snatch, and grab. She grew increasingly frustrated, and was not far from tears when he bundled the game back into its cloth bag and brought out his knife and a chunk of pine instead, asking her what kind of animal she wished him to carve next.

We were all relieved when she permitted herself to be distracted, to decide on a hedgehog.

So he carved Estelle a family of hedgehogs.

When I looked for him after lunch, he had disappeared again. Estelle and I gathered fallen apples from his orchard and managed to cook them without burning the place down. We helped Javitz hobble out to the garden, and had a fierce contest on who could spit a plum-pit the greatest percentage of their height (Javitz won). Fortunately, our host reappeared before I was driven to assemble an evening meal, bringing with him a *Times*, half a dozen fresh-baked scones, a bag of fresh-ground coffee, a jar of bilberry preserves, a piece of beef (which he would cook for us but not eat, as he had not eaten the sausages), a tiny silver hair-brush, and a diminutive pink pinafore.

My BEEKEEPING message was in the agony column, but no other.

* * *

On Thursday afternoon, our host walked to the lakeside village and returned with a box of soft chocolates, three varieties of cheese, two packets of biscuits, and that day's paper.

My message was there—and, halfway down the far right side, another:

> **BEES may thrive in foreign lands yet, lacking protection, meet peril close to home on Saturday.**

I nearly danced in relief: They were safe, Holmes and Damian both, somewhere far from London or Sussex, and he would post our meeting-place in Saturday's column.

Things were moving, at last! Tomorrow I would make my way to a train, and be in London when the Saturday papers hit the streets. The only question was whether I should remove Javitz and Estelle from this rustic establishment, or return for them once Holmes and I had joined up. And that decision, I knew, would have to wait until I could speak to Goodman without being overheard.

At the moment, he was instructing the child on the art of the plum crumble, she standing atop a stool at the sink measuring sugar into a bowl, her tiny form enveloped in one of his shirts as a stand-in apron, he beside her, buttering an oven bowl. I helped myself to a second cup of the stewed tea he'd made when he came in, and took it into the afternoon sunlight for a leisurely perusal of the rest of the day's news, which had rather begun to resemble distant drum-beats heard from a jungle fastness.

I read about the status of the German economy and the doings of the Royal Family, followed by an article concerning a film actor and a scientific report on a new radio device. I casually turned over a page, read a follow-up on the earthquake in Japan, and turned the next. With one swallow of bitter tea yet in the cup and the light fading from the sky, the page with the obituaries came into sight.

A name leapt off the page at me, electrifying my brain and driving the breath straight out of my chest:

Mycroft Holmes, OBE

Chapter 29

Tuesday night, the wind that had shoved against the European coast-line for the past week finally died away. Before Wednesday's sun cleared the eastern horizon, Gordon cast off from the private dock and slipped into the North Sea, a generous bank draught tucked into his pocket.

To Holmes' surprise, Dr Henning had declined to accompany Gordon. She claimed that she'd scarcely got the smell of fish out of her hair, and said that she would wait for a nice large steamer for the return trip. She seemed in no hurry to be home, or to abandon her patient.

Following a luncheon brought over from the house, Holmes resumed the French clothing that he had bought the day before and arranged to have the VanderLowe driver take him to a different, more southerly train station. There he bought a packet of Gitanes and a day-old Paris news-paper, was greeted by the ticket-seller in French, and inhabited the stance and accents of his French persona as he rode the train to Amsterdam, arriving shortly before three in the afternoon. Holmes made his way to the same news stand; this time, the day's *Times* had arrived. He sought a café in the opposite direction from the one he had patronised the day before, spread out the pages with a snap of impatience, and felt a great burden lift:

> BEEKEEPING is enjoyed by thousands, a reliable and safe hobby,
> practiced on week-ends alone from Oxford Street to Regent's Park.

"Safe": Russell and the child were well, and she proposed a rendezvous on the week-end in the bolt-hole that lay between Oxford Street and Regent's Park—more precisely, in the back of a building that opened onto Baker Street. She would no doubt see his own message in the agony column, possibly tomorrow, or for certain on Friday; when no contradictory message followed, she would read that as an agreement.

He folded the paper, saw by his pocket-watch that he had half an hour before the return train set off, and used that time to buy the good doctor another change of clothing. This time he had a closer idea of her taste, and the frock he paid for was considerably less dowdy than the brown skirt and white shirt he'd taken her the day before.

The following day, Thursday, Holmes made his third trip to Amsterdam, and found them waiting for him.

Had he gone earlier in the day when the two men were fresh, they might have had him. Had he relented from his obsessive and life-long habits of vigilance, had he been less rested or more preoccupied with the telephone call he wished to place, he might have walked straight into their arms.

Had he not looked at flotsam and seen a shark, he might even have approached them openly.

As it was, his train was one of dozens the two men had watched pull in that day, and he was both alert and unremarkable, one of a thousand men in dark suits and city hats.

He spotted the first watcher while the train was slowing to a halt, a big man tucked into a niche near the exit, giving close scrutiny to every passing male, and to those females of a greater than average height. Holmes went still, his grey eyes boring into the nondescript figure on the far side of the crowded platform, instantaneously considering and discarding a hundred minute details of dress, stance, hair, attitude. There came a brief gap in the stream of passengers, and two things happened: The man shifted, as if his feet were sore, then he glanced across the station. The watcher had a partner.

Police? Not that the nearer man had trained as a constable, or even as a soldier—no man who'd pounded the pavements would fail to wear comfortable shoes for day-long surveillance. Plain-clothes detectives? But they were not local: No Continental tailor had cut those suits, and Holmes could place the source of both men's hats to a specific London district.

Mycroft's men? He was conscious of a sudden taste of optimism in the air; nonetheless, he kept his seat in the emptying car. Certainly the two had the look of the men his brother employed, quiet, capable, and potentially deadly. And the cut of the first man's coat suggested a gun, which Mycroft's agents had been known to carry.

However, these two were actively looking for him, searching for his face among the crowd. If Mycroft had wished to throw his brother a link, wouldn't he have instructed his men simply to take a stand in some prominent location and wait for Holmes to approach them?

This pair was not offering themselves to Holmes: They were hunting him.

Ten seconds had gone by since he'd seen the first man, and although he wanted nothing better than to sit and explore the meaning of it, he had to move. He discarded the day's paper and made a number of small adjustments to hat, collar, and tie that changed their personality, then moved smoothly to the door, where an ancient hunched dowager hesitated to commit her ivory-handled cane to the descent. *"Kan ik u helpen?"* he asked politely. The old woman peered up at him with suspicion, adjusting her fur collar with a diamond-studded hand. In the end, she either decided that she knew him, or that he was better than nothing, and tucked one gnarled hand through his arm. He helped her down from the car, bending his ear (and thus his spine) to her querulous and incomprehensible monologue, punctuating his nods with the occasional *Ja!* or *Het is niet waar?* as they went. They tottered down the platform, adding a finishing touch to the picture of an elderly couple, shrunk by age and forced by reduced circumstances to make their own way into an inhospitable city. Not at all what the two English agents had been told to watch for.

At the taxi rank, Holmes handed the woman into a cab and let it pull away.

He was sorely tempted to double back and turn the tables on the man with the gun. All it needed was a moment's distraction for him to slip a hand inside the coat and make the weapon his. A short walk to a quiet place, and he could ask who had sent the two men.

But there *were* two. And Holmes did not know the city intimately, nor did he speak the language with anything approaching fluency. If it weren't for Damian... but no, getting himself arrested would leave the lad dangerously exposed. Discretion never felt less a part of valour; on the other hand, walking away permitted the formulation of a plan.

What he required was a place to ruminate. Were he at home, he would settle into a nest of cushions with some shag tobacco and stare into nothingness, letting his mind chew its way through the facts and inferences. Here he had neither cushions nor shag, nor even a violin. He could, however, achieve the nothingness.

The cinema house was only half full, its patrons caught up in a romantic farce that would have been every bit as impenetrable in English. He threaded his way to a seat in the back, slid down against the upholstery, and lit his first cigarette.

The lights rose and faded twice while he sat, motionless but for the act of smoking.

The sight of the Englishman in the train station had hit his mind like the reagent in a chemical experiment: When the fizz of reaction subsided, what remained was not the same substance.

Two days ago, he had been investigating the Brothers case (albeit at a remove of some 200 miles across the North Sea) only to be confronted with a new puzzle: Why should Scotland Yard move against Mycroft Holmes? But, intriguing as his brother's problems might be, his son's welfare came first. Once he had evidence sufficient to convince Lestrade that Damian was innocent—or, at any rate, guilty of nothing more than extreme naïveté in his choice of wife—then he could risk approaching Lestrade.

But the Brothers case had abruptly become something much larger.

It was a rare investigation that achieved one hundred percent solution. Human beings are untidy, and the evidence they leave behind is equally complex: One of the main tasks of an investigator is to know which small facts are incidental and which are revealing.

The Brothers case, like many others, had minor points that had thus far escaped explanation. Holmes had no doubt that, once he was given the leisure to pursue the investigation unhindered by arrest warrants and emergency surgery, he would come to a solution that would prove satisfactory even to the official police.

It was one of those apparently peripheral gaps that he had asked Billy to look into for him: how it was that Brothers so readily slipped into a world of fairly sophisticated criminal activity. False identities and thuggish assistants are not everyday needs for the majority of individuals, and yet, before coming to England, the only obvious criminal tendency Brothers had evinced was the methodical fleecing of his flock of believers. Before coming to England, the man's beliefs seemed to have been entirely theoretical; as far as anyone knew (and by *anyone* he meant Mycroft's gifted agent in Shanghai, Captain Nicholas Lofte) only when he came to England did Brothers flower into homicidal mania.

Which came first, the criminality or the belief?

In fairness, Holmes would leave his mind open to the possibility of coincidence. It was unlikely, but within the realm of possibility, that there were two separate cases here, one involving Brothers, the other the shark moving through the waters, all but unseen until a swirl of motion— Mycroft's arrest—gave him away.

Mycroft: arrested. Nearly as unthinkable, the warrants issued for himself and Russell. The ease with which James Harmony Hayden had slipped into the skin of Thomas Brothers, and the ease with which Thomas Brothers had found a man to be his bulldog. Finally, two armed and hard-eyed Englishmen in the Amsterdam station. All points that a lesser mind might dismiss as coincidence, but made Holmes reflect that a man capable of issuing a command to Scotland Yard might also send agents to Holland.

And what of Mary Russell?

If it hadn't been for her message in the paper, he'd have begun to feel uneasy.

Was Thomas Brothers the shark whose fin stuck above the moon-dark sea? Had his true self been concealed beneath the façade of a religious nut-case? Was the speed with which he slipped into England related to the speed with which the two men had located Holmes?

Had Holmes, all unknowing, been trailing blood in the waters for the shark to follow, from Scotland to Amsterdam? A shark who was both incredibly fast—deploying men to Amsterdam at the drop of a hat—and powerful—having the men to deploy in the first place.

How long before they thought to search the private docks along the Dutch coast?

He dropped his cigarette on the floor, pressed past the knees of the cinema-goers, and turned towards the town centre, away from the train station. Let those two watch the mouse-hole until their feet wore off; it was more urgent to get Damian away than to question one of them. As for 'phone calls, well, any further information he might obtain from Billy would have to wait.

He found a copy of Thursday's *Times* at a news stand near the tram stop, and tucked it under his arm as he trotted towards the approaching tram.

Forty minutes later, much jostled and aware that he was on edge, he forced himself to pause on the steps of the latest in a series of tram-cars and survey the street. There appeared to be no-one watching—no-one even standing still, at this time of day. Pedestrians and bicyclists wove along the streets and pavements, intent on their evening meal; the only stationary person in sight was a small boy hawking paper twists of warm peanuts.

Since the two men at the central station possessed three times the peanut-seller's bulk and had shown no inclination for disguise, Holmes thought he was safe enough.

He made his way up the street to the train station, several stops from the town centre. A cautious survey of the platform was similarly reassuring: Either they (whoever *they* might be) were sanguine that he would appear in central Amsterdam, or their numbers were too limited to cover the outer reaches of the town.

Which might have been reassuring had it not been for the inner voice that whispered, *They're searching the coastland instead.*

He bought a ticket for the next southerly train's final stop; unfortunately, the train would not be here for an hour. An inn directly across the street had a promising-looking restaurant, but he would not sit in a well-lit room a stone's throw from a station; instead, he walked back the way he had come, to a tiny hotel as neat as anything else he'd seen in this country. This place, unlike the larger hotels, required that he pay before he was given the key, although they, too, accepted without question his statement that his luggage would catch him up later that evening.

He was given a quiet room overlooking a row of gardens and clothes-lines. He laid his hat and coat on the bed and dropped into a soft chair, stretching out his tired legs. After a time, he opened the paper.

During his tram-journeys, he'd scanned the agony columns and seen that his own message was there—"BEES *may thrive in foreign lands...*" He'd also noted the repetition of Russell's, but that was as far as he'd got. Now, he went over the columns more closely, on the unlikely chance that he had missed a message placed by Mycroft at his most diabolically subtle. But there was nothing.

He let the paper collapse onto his knees, glowering down at the ser-ried gardens. Mycroft was the cleverest man he knew, but it was stretch-ing the bounds of credibility to think that his brother could have found him by deduction alone. He'd have had to know not only that they'd been in Wick, but why; then extrapolate that they would choose the path of least resistance because of Damian's wounds; and after that, make a close enough analysis of winds and tides to plot a likely course over the waters to Holland. His brother was a genius, but he was not god-like. And for someone other than Mycroft to have done the calcula-tions? Even Russell couldn't have done it.

Ergo, whoever was responsible for those men had known where he was.

And none of his companions could have given his location away. Had it been Gordon or the doctor, the big Englishmen would have knocked on the VanderLowe front door, not stood for hours in a draughty train station.

No, the betrayal had been his own. And his only points of contact with the world had been the trunk call to Billy—whom he'd as soon mis-trust as he would Russell—and the telegrams to Thurso and Wick.

It was true that the men had the look of Mycroft's agents. Was it possible that he had mistaken their aggressive attitude? That their scrutiny was not due to hostile intent, but, in fact, desperation? Were they trying to keep him from some unseen threat?

Holmes stared at the darkening window, trying to construct an hypothesis to explain Mycroft's having sent the pair, but it was only wishful thinking: His data were insufficient to fill in the too-large gaps in his model. Until he could reach London, he had to assume that an unknown enemy lay out there. Someone who swam in the murky depths beneath Thomas Brothers. Someone with authority over both Scotland Yard and the SIS. Someone who had decided the time was ripe to sink his teeth into Mycroft Holmes.

Whatever had driven Lestrade to issue the warrants and make the arrest, it had not been bribery: Of that Holmes was sure. But any man with family was vulnerable—as he was learning—and it would not take much to nudge Lestrade's self-righteousness into outright action.

A criminal gang who could not only intercept telegrams or telephone calls (perhaps both) but also move a man like Lestrade to their whims was a dangerous thing indeed.

He could only pray he was a step ahead of them.

First he would make Damian safe. Then he would set his face to London, where all desires are known, from whom no secrets are hid.

He took out his pocket-watch: twenty-three minutes to waste before leaving for the station. He got up to twitch the curtains shut, then turned on the light and picked up the paper.

He read with care every mention of criminal activity, but he could discern no pattern, and found none of the expected indications of a powerful gang pushing for dominance.

Again he took out his pocket-watch to check the time: four minutes. He put it away, turned the next page, and felt his heart stop:

Mycroft Holmes, OBE

Chapter 30

Inspector Lestrade turned the page, hiding the obituaries. He felt sick, as if the king himself had died. Worse, died on Lestrade's watch.

It was not his fault—of course it was not. He'd been more than fair to both Holmes brothers all his career, but just because he'd respected the two men did not mean that he should change the law of the land for their convenience.

When Mycroft Holmes had vanished last week, he'd given the man until Monday, because any man had the right to a week-end away. But when Lestrade had telephoned to Whitehall again early Monday morning and been told Holmes was still missing, he'd put out a bulletin about the disappearance.

Now the man was dead, and Lestrade did not know why. Or even how. Nor would he—or apparently any other member of the Metropolitan Police—be permitted to find out: When the body was discovered, His Majesty had ordered it seized before it could undergo the usual examinations. Word was, the petty meddling of one of the Yard's detectives was the reason.

Thursday had been the most hellish day in his career. It had begun with a ridiculous incident involving a missing person in Mayfair, some middle-aged Mama's boy who hadn't come home, and Mama knew the sorts of high-ranking officials who could demand that a chief inspector of New Scotland Yard turn out to do a constable's job. Then the minute he'd walked into his office—ten minutes late because he'd had to stop in Mayfair—Lestrade had been called upstairs. There, he'd been unofficially reprimanded for searching Mycroft's flat the week before and taking the man—albeit briefly—into custody. His protests that it had not been an arrest, and that he had been more or less ordered to carry through with it, had fallen on deaf ears. Mycroft Holmes had held a high position in the shadowy world of Intelligence, far above the reach of a lowly Scotland Yard inspector, and Lestrade was lucky the victim's employers might be willing to forgo an official enquiry into the matter.

The underlying message being: Your job would be at risk if Whitehall didn't want to avoid drawing further attention to the matter.

Then to top it off, he'd crept back to his desk like a caned schoolboy, and the first telephone call he'd had was from the biddy in Mayfair, blithely saying that her boy had come home and not to worry.

A note of farce to end the morning, leaving him to sit and stare impotently at the obituary.

He did not know where Mycroft Holmes had been for six days, or what he wanted to tell Lestrade that he could not have said in the office.

He did not know where Sherlock Holmes or his wife was.

He did not have any idea where Damian Adler or the other principals in the Brothers case were.

He had not even been able to prove that Damian Adler the painter was in any way related to Irene Adler the singer.

What he did know was, Mycroft Holmes was dead, and the last person known to have talked to him, a week ago, was Chief Inspector John Lestrade.

Chapter 31

Peter James West re-read the obituary with a smile:

Mycroft Holmes, OBE

Mycroft Holmes, long-time employee of His Majesty's Accounting Office, was found dead late on Wednesday evening outside of a club that had been the subject of numerous recent police raids. Scotland Yard report that he died of knife wounds, and ask for help from anyone who may have been in the vicinity of The Pink Pagoda late on Wednesday evening. His Majesty's Government have issued no comment regarding the site of Mr Holmes' death, but private statements indicate that Holmes had been unwell in recent months, and evinced a number of changes in his interests and way of life. Mr Holmes was presented the OBE in 1903 for his long service in uncovering incidents of fraud and corruption. Private services will be held Sunday afternoon at St Columba's cemetery, London.

A neat piece of fiction, West thought with satisfaction. Poor Mycroft, getting on in years and suddenly discovering the wilder things in life (and the things for which The Pink Pagoda was known could be extremely wild). Reading between the lines (his lines, in fact), Mycroft was something of an embarrassment to his government, a busybody ("incidents of cor-ruption") on the surface and something more distasteful below.

Yes, Gunderson had done a neat job of it, disposing of the meddler while Peter James West was in clear public view, all that day and into the night. It had made for a fraught fifteen hours, every moment of it spent tensed for news that his plan had gone awry, but the new day had come and all was well. Holmes was dead, Gunderson had placed him for dis-play and then spirited him off, and was now on the train north to deal with the stray ends in Orkney. And when the brother and his American wife appeared at the funeral, if Gunderson hadn't returned, he and Buckner would manage.

Then, Peter West could get on with his work.

He closed the morning paper and gazed at the adverts and notices, a bleating chorus of the city's personal concerns.

Bees and beekeeping, indeed.

BOOK THREE

Thursday, 4 September–
Sunday, 7 September
1924

Chapter 32

Y ou don't understand," I said to the two men. It was dark outside, had been dark for a while, although I had no idea what time it was. The hours between reading Mycroft's obituary and walking back into Goodman's cabin were already lost, a time spent on the fallen tree at the far side of the clearing, watching the sky go from robin's egg to indigo to black.

It was impossible. Unimaginable. Mycroft was a force of nature, not a man to be killed at whim. Why couldn't these two grasp that? And why could they not see that I had to be on the first train south in the morning? Alone.

I struggled to gather my thoughts. "Mycroft Holmes is—was—enormously important in the government. In some ways, he has—had—more power than a Prime Minister, who comes and goes at the whim of the voters."

"But this obituary says he was an accountant," Javitz protested.

"That's somewhere between a joke and a figure of speech. He was an accountant in the sense that it was his responsibility to account for—" I broke off: I had no right to divulge what I knew of the nation's Intelligence machinery, nor could I reveal that one of its key members answered to no authority beneath His Majesty. What Mycroft accounted for went far beyond guineas and pence. And anyway, telling them who I was married to and getting them past their disbelief had already eaten up far too much time.

"It doesn't matter. Mycroft was powerful and he was family, and I must return to London immediately. I cannot take you and Estelle with me; I am forced to ask you to watch over her; so we have to decide where would be a safe place for you both."

"I thought you said we wouldn't be safe until we had that maniac behind bars?"

I felt as if someone fleeing Vesuvius with me had stopped to fret about the carpets. The obituary had buried any lesser consideration: To my mind, the Brothers case was in a box and temporarily closed away. Who would worry about a mere killer when the world was being engulfed?

Still, Javitz was right..In my concern over having freedom of movement once in London, I could not overlook the lesser dangers, such as the one that had brought us from the sky. Even if that had not been Brothers, there was no doubt that, if he could find us, he would attempt to seize the child. I could not overlook the one responsibility in the interest of the other. God, I wanted Holmes by my side!

"Exactly," I agreed, to simplify things. "Brothers wants the child. One of his passports had her on it."

"You don't think it was Brothers who killed your brother-in-law?"

The question stopped me dead. "I don't—no, I shouldn't think so. How would he have made any connexion between Damian and Mycroft? No-one knows." I was thinking aloud. "Except now you two. Plus that, he was wounded just five days ago—could he have made it to London, found Mycroft, and got close enough to kill him with a knife after being shot? No, it wasn't Brothers."

"This happened last night?" Javitz said, and reached for the newspaper to re-read the obituary. "Very quick reporting."

"He was an important man," I said. Why didn't they understand that? I wanted to shout at them, except that would have awakened the sleeping child.

"Estelle and Javitz will be safe here," Goodman said, for the third time.

"No offence," the pilot said, "but if I stay cooped up here much longer, I'll go stir-crazy."

"So where—" I took hold of my irritation, and lowered my voice. "So where can you go?"

"Someplace that no-one would think to look for me, you said? That pretty much rules out old friends and the couple of cousins I have."

He, too, was thinking out loud, and since we had already been over this ground twice, I did not hold much hope for an answer from him. I was considering two or three places, but that decision would have to wait until I could lay hands on a telephone.

I pushed back my chair and started to stand, but a sharp, urgent hiss cut my motion. Goodman had turned towards the window, half-open to the night; one hand was raised and outstretched. I froze, straining to hear whatever had attracted him. I heard nothing at all.

Our host did, however. He snapped into motion, twisting the controls of the lamp into darkness and bolting across the room to the door.

"What—" I started, but the door closed and there was only stillness.

Javitz whispered, "Have you any idea what is going on?"

"He heard something. You stay here. I'm going to see if I can tell what it was."

I felt my way towards the faint rectangle that was the doorway, wishing that the moon were more than five days old, and eased my boots down the two stone steps. When I was away from the house a few feet I stopped, head cocked: nothing.

I stood for five minutes, then six, but all I heard were a series of thumps from Javitz's crutch moving across the floor and the cry of a fox. I was about to turn back when a faraway crackle of brush was joined by a sharp yell.

"What was that?" came Javitz's voice behind me.

I grinned. "That was Mr Goodman 'misleading night-wanderers and laughing at their harm.' One of our host's booby-traps." I had to assume there was more than one man, and that they did not mean us well.

"Someone's coming?" he asked.

"It may be nothing, but I think we should move back among the trees. Can you see without a light?"

"A little," he said. "You?"

"My night vision is not great," I admitted, "but I'll manage. You go around the back of the house. I'll bring Estelle."

He started to protest, but immediately realised that a man with a crutch was not the best candidate for carrying a child. Without another word, he felt around for his coat on the rack, and went with caution down the steps.

I, too, retrieved my coat, checking to make sure the revolver was in its pocket, then patted my way inside the bedroom. The child gave a sleepy protest when I lifted her, but I murmured assurances and she nestled into my arms, bringing yet again that peculiar blend of animal pleasure coupled with the dread of responsibility.

I held her in close embrace, through the cabin, down the steps, across the uneven ground. Halfway to the trees, my whispered name drew me towards Javitz. Nearly blind once the depth of the forest sucked up all light, I felt out with each toe before setting down weight; I was first startled, then grateful, when his hand touched the back of my arm.

"Sit down," I breathed at him.

"Don't you think we should move back some more?"

Oh, for a man who did not have to discuss everything! "I need to fetch our things and I don't want to lay Estelle on the ground."

"I'll go—"

"Javitz! If she wakes, she'll cry, and you can't hold her for long if you're standing. I know it's uncomfortable, but—sit!"

Gingerly, radiating humiliation, he sat. I transferred the child into his arms, then took the revolver from my pocket and pressed it into his hand.

I left before he could protest.

Back inside, I stood for a moment, pulling together a memory of where our few things lay. Money; clothing; Estelle's shoes; and the books I had bought her. In the kitchen, I remembered the wooden creatures Goodman had made for her and gathered them into the rucksack, adding bread, apples, and cheese, slinging it and the now-disgusting fur coat across my shoulder.

Javitz and I sat shoulder to shoulder in the darkness and waited. Only minutes passed before my eyes reported some vague motion, followed by a deliberate scuff of a boot against soil.

I clicked my tongue against my teeth and the woodman was there, panting lightly and smelling of fresh sweat. He'd been running, I thought in astonishment—how could anyone run through a pitch-black forest?

"Who are they?" I murmured.

"Strangers, five or six of them," he snarled, "with a local boy who knows the woods. They'll be here in ten minutes. Longer, depending on how many more trees they walk into." His voice put a twist of vicious pleasure on the last prospect, and it occurred to me that his panting might be due not to exertion, but to fury.

That many strangers at this time of night could only be here for one reason: us. And with Javitz on crutches, and a child as well, this was no place to make a stand.

"We're ready, let's get farther back into the woods."

Goodman did not respond. I put out a hand to his arm, and found it taut and trembling. "Goodman, believe me, I understand how you're feeling. I really, *really* want to know who they are. But do we want Estelle in the middle of a potential battleground?"

"T-take her," he ordered, stammering with fury.

"I wouldn't make it a mile in these woods."

He stood, torn between the choices I had given him. It might be nothing. A charabanc of travellers benighted and looking for help. A band of Wordsworth fanatics looking for a host of golden daffodils by moonlight. Even some of Mycroft's men coming to our assistance—that last made for a lovely thought. But until I knew for certain, we had to treat this as an invasion, and I hated the idea that this damaged man's generosity of spirit had brought an abrupt loss of his hard-won peace. I felt him wrestle with the decision, then his muscles went slack.

"Very well. I'll take you out."

"Thank you," I said, and let go of him.

But when I bent to take Estelle from Javitz, she woke, and cried aloud at the dark strangeness. I shushed her, pulled her to my chest to muffle her wails, and tried to quiet her with what had worked with this odd child up to now: a rational explanation.

This time, however, she was having none of it. She heard my words but only shook her head at the need to leave, at the arrival of yet another threat, at yet another demand for silence. "No!" she repeated in sleepy fury, until I was forced to contemplate a physical stifling of her noise.

Then she shifted to, "Want my *dolly.*"

"Your dolly? It's right—oh." Books, shoes, the carved menagerie, even the tatty coat she'd become so attached to, but the doll that Goodman had bought for her was left behind in the tangle of bed-clothes.

"I'm so sorry, honey, but—wait, stop—please, just hush!"

"Want Dolly!"

I couldn't throttle her, couldn't even threaten her as I might an adult, so what—ah: bribery. "Estelle," I said in quiet tones, "if I get Dolly for you, do you promise to be quiet? Absolutely quiet?"

Her thumb crept up to her mouth, and she nodded.

I sighed. I doubted Sherlock Holmes had ever faced such a maddening comedy of errors in one of his adventures. "I promise, Estelle, I will get you your dolly."

"I'll get it," Goodman told me.

"Wait," I said as an idea blossomed. "What if—would you mind awfully taking Estelle and Javitz away now, then coming back for me? It would be enormously helpful to know who these people are."

"Give me an hour and I'll hand you their heads."

It was temporary outrage speaking, not serious proposition—a man who had driven ambulances during the War and who lived in the woods without so much as a shotgun was not about to commit mass homicide.

"Please, Goodman—Robert: Take these two to safety. I will be perfectly safe here until you return."

Javitz, hearing the decision being made, tried to give me back the revolver. "No," I said. "You may need it to protect her."

Putting him in charge of protection may have restored a modicum of his masculine dignity. He put the gun back into his belt, and struggled to his feet.

In thirty seconds, I was alone.

Chapter 33

I tripped once on an unseen obstacle in the clearing, and once inside, gave my hip an agonizing gouge on the unexpected corner of a table. Long minutes later my fingers located the texture of firm stuffing amidst the soft bed-clothes; I stuck the doll in my waistband and turned to go.

A brief flash of light shot across the clearing from the east, the direction we'd come from the first night. I leapt into the bedroom, pulled up the window, and dropped to the ground outside.

The smell of fermentation led me to the apple tree, halfway between the house and the out-building and wide enough to conceal me from a casual inspection. From there I could see something of the meadow, where brief flickers of light drove away all thought of friends or poetry fanatics. The approaching men were experienced, using their lights sparingly as they spread out in near-complete silence around the dark buildings. The circle grew tight, and tighter, until a voice called, "The door's standing open."

I could not see that side of the house, but I imagined that two of the men entered in a swift rush, because the sounds of banging were followed by a minute of silence. A torch went on inside. Thirty seconds later, a head stuck out of the bedroom window and a beam played through the orchard, not quite reaching my tree. The head pulled back. A voice reported, "They're gone."

Three torches immediately went on, one of them barely ten feet from me, and bounced over the ground as the men went to the front. The lamp went on inside. Wary of others lingering in the dark, I crept forward until I was directly underneath the open window. I could hear their words: five men.

"—paper, it's open at the obituaries," said a deep London voice.

"The lamp was still warm," said another.

"Any sign of the girl?"

Did he mean Estelle, or me? Could Brothers have summoned the means to direct five violent men here, to retrieve the child he was determined to keep?

"There's two chairs pulled out from the table."

"Could mean nothing."

"Is this the kind of food a man on his own would have?" a new voice wondered.

I was startled when the next voice came inches from me: "Someone's been sleeping on the floor in here."

"This is the place, all right. Where do you suppose they've got to?"

"Ten feet away, they'd disappear," said the first voice.

"Want to sit and wait?"

"No point, I shouldn't think. Let's have a look at that out-house. Then we can leave a little thank-you for the hermit."

I did not at all care for the sound of that. I backed away from the house to consider my options.

Taken one at a time, I might be able to overcome them, and I would very much like to take at least one of them captive for questioning, but five men together? With at least some of them—I had no doubt— armed?

I am, I should say, very good at throwing things—darts, knives, cricket balls, chunks of stone. People tend to over-look the advantages of an accurate throwing arm, when it comes to weaponry.

No doubt if the men before me had witnessed me grubbing around my feet for large rocks, they would have thought it funny.

They made it easier by bunching together and shining all of their torches: I could hardly miss. The phrase *shooting fish in a barrel* came to mind, as my arm calculated the trajectory required, and let go, launching a couple of the missiles high into the air so as not to betray my position.

Seven fist-sized stones rained down on them; all seven hit flesh. Before they had the sense to shut off their lights and scatter, I saw two of them fall to the ground and one hunch down with his arms around his head. I also saw three handguns, and made haste to step back behind the old apple tree.

In the darkness, I heard groans and curses along with furiously whispered queries and commands. What I did not hear was gunshots. Which told me without a doubt that the men were experienced enough not to blaze into the darkness at an unseen assailant, wasting bullets and giving away their positions.

I'd have been far happier had they been amateurs. Reluctantly, I let go the possibility that I might get one alone.

They fell back to the house with their wounded. There they drew the curtains, closed the front door, and lit the lamp. To my satisfaction, in the muddle of this house-of-many-structures, although they closed the bedroom curtains, the connecting door remained half-open.

I walked silently up to the window and eased the curtain join apart, which allowed me a glimpse of the men gathered around the table.

They were assessing their injuries. One man went past with a white flash of dishtowel in his hand, and I heard a sound of ripping. All of a sudden the bedroom door flew fully open and a man came straight at me. I bolted sideways down the house, but no torch beam shot out of the window, and the tiny thread of light from the crack in the curtains remained as it was. Gingerly, I eased back to the window-sill, then held my eye to the crack again: This time, the bedroom door had been left open far enough to reveal several men, one of whom was ripping a large sheet of fabric—he'd been after the bed-sheet.

They bound wounds, washed bashes, cursed fluently. One man groaned. The others argued. Their faces were not distinct, because of the uncertain light and the number of shadows cast, but the accents told me that they were far from home, and they spoke more like criminals, or hardened soldiers, than police.

One man, the deep-voiced Londoner whom I had first heard speak, was adamant that they needed to stay until morning. The others objected loudly. Back and forth they went, until the voice that had been swearing pointed out that they'd be no safer during the day, once among those trees.

Even the Londoner fell silent at that reminder.

"Fine," he said after a moment. "We'll go as soon as Mack here can walk, but we'll set fire to the place before we go. Pour out the bastard's lamp on the floor and—"

I did not stop to think, I simply moved. Burning down the household of this poor man whose only sin had been to help a trio of strangers? Absolutely not. My right hand reached forward to yank one of the curtains from its rod, while the other snatched the knife from my boot, snapping it through the air. The sliver of steel left my fingers, passing through two rooms to plant itself in the man's upper arm. He bellowed and disappeared, and I made haste to vanish, as well—it was not a serious injury, the angle and the limited target had guaranteed that, but it would serve to frighten them. With luck it might also deliver the warning that the woods held a corporeal sylvan who disliked this talk of burning.

Five minutes later, motion in the darkness materialised into the Green Man of the woods. "Come," he said.

"One moment," I responded.

He hunkered down beside me. The night was quiet again, and I was braced for the beginning crackle of flames. Instead, the torches appeared at the front of the house, and five shadows limped away, across the clearing to the path down which they had come.

I stood. "I need to see if they left my knife behind," I told him.

"Why do they have your knife?"

"One of them was talking about torching your house. I wished to discourage him."

He held my arm back with his hand. In a moment, I heard the same crackle of loosed branches I'd heard before, followed by shouts of pain and outrage.

Robert Goodman, hermit and Robin Goodfellow look-alike, chortled in pleasure. "Wait here," he said. I heard him trot away. The window gave a dim light for perhaps two seconds, then went dark. Seconds later, I heard a faint squeak—the hen-house door. But why . . . ?

Before he pressed the handle of my knife against my palm, I had worked out the meaning of that squeak: Goodman anticipated being gone long enough that his chickens would starve.

He grasped my hand, and pulled me away into the black expanse of his woods.

Chapter 34

D o you wish a motorcar?" Goodman's enquiry was polite, as if offering me one lump or two in my tea.

"Do you have one?" I asked in astonishment. Puck with a motorcar?

"Theirs is on the road. We could reach it before they do."

"Mr Goodman," I said in admiration, "you have a definite aptitude for low trickery."

He chuckled, then shifted course and sped up.

I was blind. Only the wordless eloquence of his hand in mine kept me from injury, if not coma: His fingers told me when to go left and when right; a slight lift of the hand warned me of uneven footing; a pull down presaged the brush of a bough against my head. In twenty minutes, I sensed the trees retreating and knew that we were on the cleared soil of a forest track.

Now he broke into a fast trot, pulling me along in childish companionship. It was terrifying at first, then strangely exhilarating, to run at darkness, trustingly hand in hand with a wood sprite. I could only pray that his attentive guidance would not waver. In eight or nine minutes, he slowed, and I became aware of the smell of burnt petrol: the crash site.

He stopped to listen to the night, then said, "We have three or four minutes. If I push the motor, there is a slope in half a mile that should be sufficient to start it."

"Wait—can we risk a light?" I asked.

"Briefly."

"I may be able to circumvent the ignition lock." His footsteps went around to the passenger side while I felt my way in behind the wheel— groping first for the keys, but finding them gone—then contorted myself sideways until my head rested against Goodman's knee, half under the instrument panel. He lit a match, shielding it as best he could with his body, and I saw that the motorcar was my old friend the Austin 7, which must have been a tight fit for five men and their local guide, but made my task easier. If only my mind hadn't been taken up by the rapid approach of five angry men with guns...I pulled at the wires, followed their leads, and let him light another match when the first one burnt to his fingers. At the third one, I had it: A yank and three quick twists, and the car would be mine.

I touched the wires together: The starter spun into life. I jerked upright, slammed my door, turned on the head-lamps, and slapped it into gear. We jolted forward, and the woods exploded in a fury of gunfire.

Had it not been for the trees, the bullets might have hit us, but we were safely away long before the shooters reached the track. I eased my foot back on the pedal, and let out a nervous laugh. "A bit closer than I'd have wished."

"Driving like that, we could have used you on the Front," he said.

"I do hope Javitz and Estelle are in this direction? It might not be a good idea to turn around."

"Two miles north," he agreed, "then ten minutes' walk."

"Is that all? If those men come after us, they'll catch us up."

"Why should they? We could be making for Carlisle, or Newcastle. They'll turn back to the village."

"I hope you're right," I said uneasily.

"Do you know what they want?"

In truth, I did not. "One of them said something about 'the girl,' but I don't know if that meant Estelle, or me."

Two miles up the track he had me stop. The head-lamps dimmed, then went dark as I separated the wires; the silence was loud over the tick of cooling metal. Had we come far enough that the men would not notice the sudden cease of motor noise, and renew their pursuit?

Goodman got out, and I quickly whispered, "Don't slam the door."

"No," he said. I was again blind. His feet rounded the motorcar's bonnet towards me; the door creaked open. "You can't see?"

"I'm sorry," I said. "If we wait a—"

His hand found mine, to lead me again into rough ground; leaves brushed my legs and arms. It required an intense commitment of trust that this man was not leading me off a cliff or into a tree. The earlier run through the dark had been terrifying, but my brief return to control and capability—to say nothing of vision—brought a strong impulse to freeze. Every step was a decision: to trust, or rebel? In the end, the only way I could continue to follow him was by imagining that the hand in mine belonged to Holmes, whom I had followed blindly into circumstances worse than this.

Once I had half-convinced myself of that, the going became easier.

It was probably not much more than the ten minutes he had suggested before we found Javitz and Estelle, although it seemed like an hour. Judging by the relief in his voice, Javitz had felt the press of time, as well, sitting alone in the darkness—thankfully, Estelle was fast asleep. I relieved him of the bundle of child and fur, and heard him struggle to his feet.

"I'll support you when I can," Goodman told Javitz in a low voice, "but the path is narrow. Use the crutch and put your free hand on my shoulder. Miss Russell, you follow. Yes?"

"Let's go," Javitz said. I shifted Estelle into my left arm and inched forward until my fingers encountered his shoulder, and we moved off.

We walked like a platoon of gas-blinded soldiers. It might have been easier had we been on flat ground and able to march in step, but between the unevenness of the terrain and our various impediments, we stumbled at a turtle's pace, and made so much noise I could feel Goodman's disapproval, even with Javitz between us. An entire night passed, longer, a nightmare of stumbling, cursing, tangling, and growing fear.

Finally, our guide could stand it no longer. He stopped, causing us to pile up into him, and spoke. "I will come back for you."

Before either of us could speak, he was gone. Gratefully, I sank to the ground and let the weight go off my arms. Javitz stayed upright, propped on his stick. Neither of us spoke.

Five minutes went by; eight. Javitz stirred, and said, "He will come back."

"Yes." In truth, I did not much care: I was quite prepared to sit here, warm under the fur and the small body, until light dawned.

But Goodman did return, without so much as a rustle before his voice whispered, "All clear. Just a hundred yards more."

I struggled upright, hushed Estelle's sleepy protest, and laid my hand on the pilot's shoulder.

Never have I been more grateful to feel a rustic track underfoot.

With some effort, we folded Javitz into the back of the motorcar, and I deposited Estelle in his lap. I whispered, "You are all right, holding her?"

"I can't do the driving," came his voice in my ear, "so I might as well hang on to her. She's a good kid," he added.

"Isn't she just?" I replied gratefully, and resumed my place behind the wheel.

I went less than a mile, then stopped, leaving the engine running.

"Mr Goodman, I appreciate all you've done for us, but there's no reason to take you any farther. I'd suggest you be very cautious about your house for a time, since there's no knowing if they mightn't come back, but I think you could manage that."

"I will c-come with you."

"There's no need for—"

"Go!" he roared.

We went.

With our five pursuers to the south, we were forced to motor north, eventually to circle around. The forest track thinned and nearly died altogether, but eventually grew more confident, giving way to a wider track, which led to a more-or-less metalled stretch, until eventually our tyres hit a surface recognisable as roadway. I was grateful that our villains had thought to fill the petrol tank before they had ventured into the wooded places. Their thoughtfulness meant that we had fuel sufficient to reach civilisation.

Or if not civilisation, at least a crossroads with two buildings. One was a neat stone house, darkened at this hour. The other appeared to have been a smithy from time immemorial, converted now to the Twentieth-Century equivalent: a garage. A shiny petrol pump stood in the fore-court, illuminated from above by a hanging lamp, an altar light over a shrine to modernity.

It was still well before dawn and none of the shrine's attendants were stirring. However, I for one needed to stretch my legs, step into the bushes, and consider our next move.

I pulled into the station's forecourt and put on the hand-brake, then fumbled to separate the ignition wires. They spat and the motor died. In-stantly, a small sleepy voice piped, "Where are we?"

Good question.

We climbed from the motor and took turns paying visits to the shrub-bery. I gave Estelle some biscuits and a cup of water from a tap behind the petrol station, which woke the dog tied behind the dark house, which in turn roused the owner. The man stuck his head out of the upstairs win-dow, shouted the dog to silence, then demanded what we thought we were doing.

I launched into speech before any of my companions could respond, a tumble of apology in a cut-glass accent with words designed to soften the heart of the hardest working man: *took a wrong turning* came in early, and *ill mother* and *emergency summons* and *child*, followed by *des-perate* and *terribly sorry* and *frightened* and *hungry*, but it wasn't until I hit *plenty of money* that the window slammed down and a light went on inside.

"Look hopeless, you two," I suggested, at which Javitz leant heavily on his stick while Goodman did him one better by stepping away into the night. Clutching Estelle, who by this time was fully awake and curious about it all, I waited beneath the light for the man above to tug on his trousers and come down.

By the breadth of his shoulders, he had been the smith before the petrol engine took over his occupation—his hands were permanently stained with the grease of engines, but they showed signs of regular use of an anvil and hammer as well. The rôle of the smith in the mythic landscape of England required that the man be addressed with considerable respect, and more than a little care: A smith answered only to himself.

However, silver placates the most irascible of gods. A display of our tribute soon had him working the pump, but it was my air of respect and Javitz's of interest that led to the grudging admission, once the tank was filled, that he generally woke near to now anyway. I glanced at the sky, and noticed the faint fading of stars to the east. I gave him a wide smile and asked brightly, "If you're about to make yourself some tea, I don't suppose you'd like to sell us a cup?"

He grimaced, but then went into the house, which I took for agreement.

While he was away, I took advantage of the light over the pumps to go through the motor's various pockets.

It was, as I'd expected, a hire car, from a garage in Lancaster—the size alone promised they hadn't come from far away in it. This suggested that the men had come up from the south on a train, having got news of an aeroplane crash followed by the odd purchases made by one of the more colourful local residents. They'd either been remarkably efficient or damnably lucky, to find us so quickly.

The other items in the pockets were uninformative, although the maps would be useful. The most suggestive thing about the motor was its size: With five men already crammed inside, they hadn't intended to take us prisoner.

I carried two of the maps around the front, spreading them across the bonnet with the three-shilling Lake District sheet on top. Javitz joined me, Goodman reappeared, even Estelle tried to peer between my elbows until I lifted her onto the warm bonnet, where she sat supervising, Dolly in lap and chin in hand. I was eerily visited by the shade of her grandfather, finger on lips as he awaited information.

I tore my gaze from the child to compare the map with the few road-signs I had glimpsed, tracing our location forward. Oddly, the place where we had begun our journey was relatively devoid of the usual signs and markings: It was a vast private estate, which explained the unharvested woods and lack of public footpaths. That part of the map might as well have borne the old cartographic label *Here be monsters.*

"This is where we are," I said, laying my finger on a join of thin lines, then exchanged the large-scale sheet for one of the entire country. "I must be in London by Saturday morning, but we need a safe place for you as well. I was thinking that—"

Goodman abruptly thrust his hands in his pockets and half turned away. I raised an eyebrow, but he simply stared at the trees pressing in on the road, caught up in some obvious but unguessable turmoil.

"Did you have a suggestion?" I asked.

He took a step back, running one hand over his bush of hair. Another half-step, as if about to make a break for the woods, then he stopped. "I...he..."

His face seemed to convulse, as if a current had been passed through the muscles. It was an alarming expression, one I had seen before in the shell-shock wards of the hospital during the War: minds broken by the trenches, struggling so hard to produce words, it made the tendons on the men's throats go rigid.

One's impulse is to provide words, any words. "We could—"

He held up a hand to stop me, then turned his face towards Estelle, the youthful gargoyle on our bonnet. We waited. He swallowed, and when he spoke again, it was in an oddly thick and methodical voice, as if he were removing each word from his throat and laying it onto a platter. "He...*I*...have f-family."

The idea of this man with relatives struck me as even more unlikely than his having a motorcar, and it was on the tip of my tongue to ask if their names included Loki or Artemis. Fortunately, the awareness of his distress stayed my flip remark. I said merely, "Where?"

He turned from Estelle to the map; from his reluctance, the paper might have been made of burning coals. One fingertip tapped lightly at the western edges of London's sprawl. "D-d." He stopped, swallowed hard, and began again, with that same palpable deliberation. "Distant family. But they would m-make you...they would make *us* welcome."

"Would the men behind us be able to find them?"

"No-one here knows my name." Monosyllables seemed to present less trouble.

"What about in the house? Is there anything that would lead them to your relatives?" I asked. "Letters, official papers, anything?"

"Some. From a s-s-solicitor. He lives in Italy. It would t-take time."

I lifted an eyebrow at Javitz, who said, "I was going to suggest an old friend from the RAF, but I haven't seen him in a couple of years, and his house is not much larger than that cabin."

My intent had been the country house of friends currently in Ireland, but since our pursuers were not looking for the man of the woods, it would, as Goodman said, take them some time to uncover any link. "Fine," I decided. "Richmond it is."

The petrol station owner came with the tea, although he did not offer to return to the house for an additional cup for our party's fourth member, summoned out of the night. The beverage was hot and strong, and we shared it out gratefully. When the cups, the pot, and the jug of milk were all drained, I placed the tray back in the man's hand.

When Estelle and Javitz were settled once again in the back of the motorcar, I reached down for the wires. I waved my hand at the smith-turned-garage-owner and put it into gear, roaring up the north road over protests from two of my three passengers.

I continued blithely on my way for three minutes, then slowed and manoeuvred into a many-sided turn before heading back south. Half a mile from the garage, I shut off the head-lamps, leant forward over the wheel, and said to my still-grumbling critics, "Now, everyone keep still, please."

With the engine turning over at little more than an idle, we rolled, dark and silent past the station. The owner had gone back into his kitchen, and did not look out of his window as we passed. The dog did not bark. I continued down the southward leg of the crossroads for a hundred yards, then pulled on the head-lamps and pushed my foot down on the accelerator.

Chapter 35

Two hundred fifty miles takes a lot longer to motor than it does to fly over. On the other hand, when a tyre went flat outside of Wigan, the mechanical difficulty did not result in us falling out of the sky. I found this infinitely reassuring.

Goodman, however, seemed less reassured the farther south we went. While our tyre was being repaired, we made our way to a nearby inn for a lunch. We were so far from our starting place as to be safe, nonetheless, looking at the motley crew unfolding itself from the motorcar, I could not help thinking that we were not the most invisible of travellers.

At the door to the inn, Goodman spoke into my ear: "Order me something." Before I could protest, he walked away. Estelle was tugging at one hand, the other was holding the door for the pilot. If the hermit did not want to join us, that was his loss.

The inn was a relief to the spirit, dim and quiet but with promising odours in the air. We crept to a table near the fire. Javitz ordered a triple whisky and a pint, and when I looked askance, snarled, "My leg hurts like the devil."

I gave our hostess a wan smile. "I'll have a half of the bitter, thanks, and a glass of lemonade for the child. And do you have anything left by way of luncheon?"

Under other circumstances, I might have regarded her offerings as predictable and unenticing, but after the past nine days—much of which

had been spent either in the air or in a cabin catered by a vegetarian—
the dishes sounded exotic, complex, and mouth-watering. We ordered,
and I included an order for our missing companion. When she brought
the drinks, Javitz tossed his whisky down his throat and closed his eyes.
Gradually, the tension in his face began to relax. He opened his eyes,
winked at Estelle, and reached for his beer.

We were nearly finished with our meal when the inn door opened and
a clean-shaven, spit-polished young man came through it. He paused,
noticed us sitting before the fire, and came in our direction. My fork
went still as he approached, until I noticed the green eyes. I dropped the
implement in shock.

"Good Lord," I said.

"Yes, well," the oddly congested voice replied, "I couldn't very well
greet f-family disguised as a bear."

"Mr Robert!" Estelle exclaimed. "You cut your beard!"

"And my hair, too, didn't I?" he said. "You save me some food?"

Javitz and I resumed our meal, but neither of us paid it much attention. The man before us was smooth in more ways than his skin: In removing his hair, he had put on another, less obvious disguise, one that
was jarring to a person accustomed to the hermit's quiet ease. This
Robert Goodman would have seemed at home in a London night-club,
brash and bold, with quick movements and nervous fingers.

I couldn't help thinking, he must be little short of frightened of this
family we were about to meet.

However, in the end, Goodman's relatives were not there to greet us,
merely the serving staff left behind. We pulled up to a grand three-storey
stone building with Sixteenth-Century bones and Eighteenth-Century
additions, its windows glittering in the sun that neared the horizon. A
boy of about twelve stood in the doorway, his mouth open. After a
minute, an elderly man appeared, hastily adjusting the neck-tie he had
clearly just that moment put on: a butler, caught off-duty. He was followed by a round, grey-haired woman in her early sixties, emitting the
sorts of exclamations usually reserved for a long-lost son of the household.

Goodman reached out a finger and laid it gently across her lips; she fell silent, but the pleasure in her eyes was eloquent.

I thought that the trio's relative dishevelment and the sequence of their appearance suggested that the family was away and the servants were bored silly. And indeed, once the housekeeper was freed to speak by the removal of Goodman's stifling finger, her rush of words included a lament that the family had left for a wedding in Ireland, and would not return for a fortnight.

Goodman swayed, then walked off a few steps. After a minute, he cleared his throat, then vaguely suggested the provision of rooms and the concealment of our motorcar.

But his voice—that strangled deliberation had gone, leaving his speech as light and humorous as it had been before his home was invaded, before he had been forced out into the world, before he had made the decision to lead us to a family that clearly overwhelmed him with an unbearable apprehension. I wished I had figured it out before this: I might have saved him a day of great distress.

The servants scurried to obey, even the boot-boy. Their boredom, it would seem, was acute.

Although it was well into the dinner hour, tea was hastily summoned to a room glowing with the day's last sunshine, its furniture hastily cleared of sheets and its French doors flung open to the terrace. Loath to spend more time in the sitting position, we carried our cups out of doors, watching Estelle solemnly explore the sculpture garden in the company of the boy while we stood and sipped and waited for our ears to stop ringing.

"I'll go into Town first thing in the morning," I told my two companions.

"I'll come with you," they chorused.

I scowled at my cup. Why were men so woefully infected with the urge to chivalry? If I weren't very firm about this, I would find the entire cohort stuck to me like sap to the shoe, forcing me to march to war in the company of a crippled daredevil, a fey three-year-old, and Puck himself.

And towards war I was going, I could feel it in my bones. Before our woodland idyll had been invaded, even before reading of Mycroft's death, events had been pressing in on me, a creeping sensation that all was not right in the country I loved.

In the three and a half weeks I had been back—the last two of which, admittedly, spent on the run—English life had struck me as oddly loud and fast. At first, I had thought it was the sharp contrast between London and our peaceful South Downs retreat. Then I told myself that travelling out of the country for eight months had made me forget what England was truly like. And, of course, the Brothers case had been guaranteed to fill me with unease—not only for itself, but for the awareness that throughout history, religious mania had gone hand in hand with dangerous political and social turmoil.

Were five armed men another symptom of unrest?

Or was this simply what modern life would be, a place where a homicidal charlatan is embraced as wise, where children can be shot out of the sky, where a Good Samaritan can be driven from his home by armed intruders?

I wished I had Holmes to talk with about this.

I did not know the face of the enemy. I could not see how a sniper or a group of armed men in the Lake District could be connected with Thomas Brothers. I did not know why Mycroft had died, or at whose hand. I had no way of knowing if Damian and Holmes were still safe. I did not want to abandon Damian's daughter to her own devices, and I emphatically did not wish to place her in the path of danger; however, she seemed as happy with Javitz, the housekeeper, and the boy as she was with me, and three times now—with a sniper's bullet, a 'plane crash, and armed men in a motorcar too small for hostages—keeping her at my side had nearly been the death of her.

I prayed this time I might walk away from her without fear. If a child could not be kept safe in a private house, then no place in the British Isles was secure.

Nonetheless, a compromise was in order. I looked over my cup at Javitz. "I shall have to ask you to stay here, and guard the child."

Chapter 36

Holmes huddled on the aft deck, inadequately sheltered against the vaporised ice pouring down the North Sea, and wondered if he'd made the right decision.

It was a damnable choice. Leaving Damian behind had felt remarkably like turning his back on a man holding a knife—why hadn't he anticipated the problem, and cajoled Gordon into staying on? But trying to take a tall, injured young man and a diminutive red-haired Scots female on what were sure to be closely watched ferries would have required intense tutoring on the arts of disguise, and he simply did not have the time. Nor had he the leisure to find a Dutch replacement for Gordon willing to smuggle three British citizens (only two of whom had passports) during daylight hours.

He'd done the best he could. On disembarking from the train the previous night, he had hired a taxi at the village station and burst into the VanderLowe cottage, going light-headed when he found his son and the doctor sitting peaceably before the fire, reading to each other from *The Pickwick Papers*.

He'd distributed just enough information to put the fear of God into them, and when the lights were out in the main house, he had borrowed one of the motorcars—well, not to put a fine point on it, he'd stolen the thing—and spirited his mismatched pair away from the artists' community.

Then he spent the next twelve hours playing a sort of shell game with the two of them, aimed at baffling any pursuit: into Leiden, stashing them in an hotel, leaving the stolen motor near the central train station, and walking through the deserted town to a large hotel where at first light he hired a motorcar, ditching the driver (fortunately with trickery, not violence) and retrieving the young people to transport them in what amounted to a wide circle, ending at a small seaside watering-hole a scant forty miles south of where they had begun the day.

He established their identities as a young French aristocrat and his paid English nurse who were keeping out of his family's way after a falling-out with an older brother. Drilling them both on the absolute necessity to speak as much French as possible and to keep to their rooms as much as they could bear, he emptied his purse into the doctor's hands, and left to make his way to the Hook of Holland. There he deposited his second stolen motorcar, in a street where it would not be found until Monday at the earliest, and walked the last two miles to the Harwich steamer.

Even then, his day was not finished, for one who lacks both funds and time must resort to creativity. Reminding himself that there was no virtue like necessity, Holmes performed his third virtuous act in twenty-four hours, stooping to theft of the lowest kind. With twenty minutes to spare before the boat left the dock, he brushed against a banker who was admiring a fat infant in a perambulator, and picked his pocket.

The Fates had the last laugh, however, for the Moroccan leather note-case was worth more than what it contained, and there had been enough to cover the cheapest single ticket to England, but no more. Rather than chance another theft in the tight boundaries of the ship, Holmes spent the journey on the open deck, where the cold wind helped to numb the pangs of hunger.

Nothing, however, would alleviate the gnaw of anxiety, for family both behind and ahead. Oh, things had been so much simpler when the only person whose safety he'd agonised over was John Watson, M.D.

When the ferry at long last bumped against its pier, he joined the off-loading passengers, wan with hunger, red-eyed from a lack of sleep and a surfeit of wind, fighting at every step the impulse to howl and launch himself like a footballer down the gangway and towards London.

A man stood among those waiting, a large man in a warm overcoat. He might have been brother to the watcher in Amsterdam.

Chapter 37

Peter James West pushed away the impulse to shout with triumph at the report in his hand. His instincts had been right: The fishing boat Sherlock Holmes had hired in Thurso landed not in England, but in Europe. With the agency's men still in Scandinavia—sent there, in delicious irony, by Mycroft Holmes—they had been readily re-deployed when the trunk call was placed from Amsterdam. Did Holmes' brother imagine they would overlook his longtime associate, simply because the two were no longer partners?

It was almost disappointing, how easy this was proving.

And although the men had lost sight of Sherlock Holmes, and their pursuit of the son and that rural lady doctor they'd picked up in Scotland had yet to bear fruit, it did not matter.

Sunday would be the funeral. Neither Holmes nor his wife would miss that.

Chapter 38

Late on Friday night, Chief Inspector Lestrade stood up from his desk, his eye drawn yet again to the folded newspaper notice of the funeral for Mycroft Holmes. Hard to comprehend, that larger-than-life, demigod of a man, snuffed out by a blade. Impossible to avoid, that Lestrade's own actions had somehow led to that death.

He did not believe Mycroft Holmes had been murdered because he had ventured into a wild night-club.

He could not shake the sensation that the death was tied to the unofficial near-orders—an urging, but difficult to overlook—that he bring into line Sherlock Holmes and his wife.

He was quite certain that there was some link between Holmes and the artist Damian Adler: That canny detective would not have stuck his nose into Yolanda Adler's death merely because her body was found a few miles from his home.

He felt like a man in a whirlwind, with nothing firm to grasp, all his familiar landmarks obscured. Nonetheless, he was more at peace than he had been for some days, because late that afternoon he had withdrawn the arrest warrants for Sherlock Holmes and Mary Russell.

If nothing else, it would permit him to keep his head high at Sunday's funeral.

Chapter 39

Goodman was in the breakfast room when I appeared early Saturday morning. I was dressed in clothing the housekeeper had chosen (and hastily altered during the night) from a wardrobe of items left behind by guests. None of them fit me well; none of them, I dared say, had been abandoned by accident.

My stand-in host was freshly shaved and wearing a suit of light grey wool with a public-school tie. His upper lip bore a pencil-trace of moustache; his nails were clean and clipped. The only vestiges of the woodsman were the emerald eyes and the unruly hair which, despite an application of oil, had a barely suppressed energy, as if any moment it would spring wildly upright.

"That's a handsome suit," I said.

"My cousin's sister's husband's," he replied, proudly looking down at the costume. He straightened the handkerchief in his breast pocket, brushed away an invisible crumb, and dropped his table napkin beside his plate. When he rose, it became clear that the gentleman in question was an inch taller in the leg and an inch narrower in the shoulder.

Clothes, however, make the man. Certainly, Goodman moved differently in this garb, his spine straighter, the boundaries of his body tighter, as if braced against the press of crowds and the pounding of pavements. The butler motored us to the train station, and when I stepped away from the ticket window and looked around for my companion, I nearly looked past him. On a weekday he would be almost invisible in a crowd of young businessmen, until one noticed the eyes beneath the light summer hat, and the faint idiosyncrasy of an owl feather in its ribbon. The Green Man had become the Grey Man, the colour of the city around him.

The newsagent was laying out the morning papers, and I paid for a copy of *The Times*. We took our seats and when I spread the fold open, Holmes' message reached out like a touch of the hand. I wondered how far from me he was now. If he might be stretched out with his feet to the fire of one or another of his bolt-holes, waiting for me to find him.

"Do you have a plan?" my companion asked.

"Yes. There's a message here for me, telling me to meet him at the funeral. However, there are one or two places to go first."

I was feeling rather like Holmes who, when frustrated by lack of progress in a case, was apt to shout, "Data! I require *data!*" Before I could go much further, I needed information and I needed assistance: For both, I knew where to go.

At Waterloo, Goodman and I disembarked and made our way out of the steamy cacophony towards the exit. Long ago, in his days as an active consulting detective on Baker Street, Holmes had employed an ever-changing tribe of urchins he called his Irregulars. The core member of these troops was a quick, clever, nimble-fingered, unhandsome child with a gin-soaked mother and too many fathers, whose work for Holmes re-shaped his life away from outright crime towards an eventual adult profession of enquiry agent.

Billy had proved quite successful in his work. He would have been even more so—financially speaking—had he not chosen to remain in the district where he had grown up. He now kept an office in a part of the South Bank that did not actually frighten away monied clients, but he still lived two streets from the house where he had been born, and had built his own army of operatives out of cousins, neighbours, and childhood friends, a good number of whom had felony records.

If anyone, Billy could provide both manpower and information.

South of the Thames, the business of empire is less politics and finances than goods and services; consequently, the London sprawl that lies below the busy riverfront is less comprehensively served by modern transport. Half a mile to the north, we might have transferred to the Underground; here, we set off into the familiar by-ways.

Except they felt not entirely familiar. Surely I had not been away for that long? Each step I took, the sensation of wrongness grew, until in the end I murmured to Goodman, "Come," and stepped into a rather run-down café. He followed me to a table that was sticky with spilt break-fasts, and I ordered coffee from the harried waitress.

The coffee that arrived thirty seconds later had already been doused with cream and sugar. Goodman raised an eyebrow at his cup, but I just leant forward, trying to avoid a puddle of egg yolk, and told him, "There's something wrong here."

"Indeed," he agreed. Then he raised his eyes from the liquid, which was developing an interesting scum of coffee dust and flecks of half-spoilt milk solids, and saw that I was not referring to the drink. He changed his agreement to a query: "Indeed? What?"

Good question. I did not know London as thoroughly as Holmes did, but I had spent many days in the city, and had been in this area any number of times, including eight o'clock on a Saturday morning. "I don't know what it is, precisely. But the district feels *wrong.*"

Another man might have looked askance, but this was a man who knew his forest so intimately, he could run among its trees in the dark. "Something you've seen? Smelt?"

"Sounds," I replied slowly. "And things not seen. Two streets back, generally on a Saturday one hears the racket of a piano teacher at one end of the houses and a young man drowning her out with a gramophone at the other; both of them were silent. And not only is the district generally quiet, but people are missing." I craned to look out of the steamy window, and then indicated the corner opposite. "Every time I've been on this street I've seen an elderly Italian man perched on a high stool. He's the lookout for an all-hours gambling racket upstairs."

"Constabulary tidying?" he suggested.

I pursed my lips. "A police operation would not affect children. Where are they? It's a Saturday morning, they should be all over."

I paid for the untouched coffee and we went back out onto the street.

As we walked, my senses were heightened: a shop door closed here that I had never before seen shut; the gang of adolescent toughs that normally inhabited an alleyway there, missing; a shopkeeper who hired his upstairs rooms to a couple of the local ladies, watching through his window with a wary expression; the street itself, normally boisterous and carrying an edge of threat, gone still and indoors.

I liked this less and less, until I decided that to go farther into Southwark risked walking into a trap.

Three streets from Billy's home was a greengrocer's with a public callbox. I stepped into it, fed in my coin, and listened to the buzz of the ring.

A voice answered, a male on the uncomfortable brink of manhood, whose control slid an octave in the first two syllables of his reply.

"Is that young Randall?" I asked. "This is Mary Russell. Is your father—"

The voice cut in, so tense it warbled. "Pop said to tell you: Run."

"But I need to see him," I protested.

"He's where you first met. Now, run!"

I dropped the telephone, grabbed Goodman's hand, and ran.

Chapter 40

Down the street we flitted, diving into a courtyard slick with moss from a communal well and ducking through the narrow covered walk at the far end. I did not think we had been seen, but as I scuttled through the damp passage, I pulled off my cardigan and yanked the blouse from the skirt's waistband, letting it fall to my hips. The first ash-can I came to, I snatched up the lid and stuffed inside the cardigan and both our hats. Then I seized the back collar of Goodman's jacket, stripping it from his back in one sharp yank, and would have added it to the other things had Goodman not grabbed it back and bundled it under his arm, then retrieved as well the feather from his hat. I dropped the lid on the bin, palmed my spectacles, and made for the street, slowing to a brisk but unexceptionable walk as we emerged from the alley. With a convenient piece of choreography, a red omnibus stood at the kerb twenty feet away. I pulled Goodman inside, paid the conductor, and scurried up the curve of stairs.

With a hiss and a judder, the 'bus pulled out. To my great relief, there was no shout raised from the pavement below, no pounding of feet. We took our seats, and when I put my spectacles on, I found that Goodman no longer resembled the successful young office worker he had when we started out: Hatless and in his shirt-sleeves, he looked even younger than he had, and decidedly rakish. He looked...not entirely trustworthy. More a part of our surroundings than I did.

His eyebrows were raised.

I explained. "The person on the telephone was the son of the man I wanted to see. The father runs an enquiry agency, and he'd left a message for me: to run."

"How far?"

"At the moment, I am to meet Billy—the father—at a park on the other side of the river, although we have a stop to make first. After that, we'll see. Are you sure you don't want to—"

"I will stay."

I nodded, by way of thanks, and kept my head down as we crossed over the bustling river traffic and entered the city proper.

The place where Billy and I had first met was a small green square not far from the theatre district. That was in 1919, when an evening at the opera with Holmes had ended with Billy bashed unconscious and the old-fashioned carriage he was driving left in shreds. After that auspicious beginning, I had met him perhaps a score of times, and although I did not know him well, we had, after all, been trained by the same man. However he and his son were communicating, he would not be surprised if I took an hour to make a two-mile journey, especially not following that urgent warning.

So instead of going directly there, we rode the 'bus through the crowded shopping districts, disembarking two streets away from one of the handful of bolt-holes Holmes still maintained across London. Each of them was well hidden, nearly impregnable, fitted with an alternate escape route, and well equipped with food, clothing, basic weaponry, sophisticated medical supplies, and the means for disguise. Revealing them to strangers was unheard-of, grounds for shutting the place down. This would be the only time I had done so.

This bolt-hole was on the Marylebone Road around the corner from Baker Street, and had originally been wormed into the space between a discreet seller of exotic undergarments and a firm of solicitors. It had been threatened a few years earlier when the merchant of stays and laces had died one day amongst his frothy wares, but to my amusement, the business that opened in its place was a medical firm with a speciality of cosmetic surgery that, as the need for patching together soldiers faded, had turned to tightening sagging skin and removing unsightly bumps on noses. As I'd commented to Holmes, if ever our disguises failed us, we could now pop next door and have our faces altered.

Inside the building vestibule, I let the frosted-glass door shut behind us and told Goodman, "I am not going to make you cover your eyes, since you'd probably find this place blind, but I'd like a promise that you'll forget where it is, or even that it exists."

"What place is that?"

"Thank you," I said, and stretched up to press the triggering brick. On the other side of the vestibule, the wall clicked, and I pulled open the glass-fronted display case to climb through. With his bark of amusement, Goodman followed: up a ladder, sidling down a tight corridor, across a gap, and through the back of a disused broom-cupboard.

I could, I suppose, have left Goodman nearby and returned, supplied with the means of concealment—we would not find much clothing here for a man his size, anyway, although his thick hair might keep the hats in the cupboards from settling over his ears. I was glad he'd kept the jacket. But I brought him . . . I was not altogether sure why I was bringing him, other than I found his presence strangely reassuring, like a warm stone in a cold pocket.

Reason enough to open this secret place to him.

It was a relief getting into clothing that was not only clean, but fit me: a lightweight skirt and white blouse; a jacket that could be reversed to another colour; shoes so ordinary as to be invisible in a crowd; and two scarfs, orange and eau de Nile, so as to instantly change the appearance of hat, blouse, or jacket. I sat before the big, brightly lit looking-glass to change the shape of my face and the colour of my hair, replaced my spectacles with those of another shape and material, slipped a modern and nearly unreadable wrist-watch onto my left wrist and a row of colourful Bakelite bracelets onto my right, and screwed on a pair of screamingly bright earrings to match.

Then I turned to the man who had watched the entire process (less the actual changing of garments) with the bewitched curiosity of a child. "Shall we go?"

Any other man might have demanded, "Who the devil *are* you?" This one picked up his straw hat, adjusted the owl feather in the ribbon that matched his new breast handkerchief, and opened the door to the broom-cupboard.

We approached the little park a bit after mid-day, strolling up and down the surrounding district, lingering on a street-corner while I made ostentatious glances at my watch, and finally meandering towards the park, swinging hands like a pair of young lovers.

Being hand in hand with Robert Goodman, even as part of a disguise, ought to have been an uncomfortable sensation—I was, after all, a married woman. Yet I found that the press of his palm and the grip of his fingers possessed not the least scrap of adult, or perhaps masculine, awareness. It was like holding the hand of a taller, more muscular Estelle: companionable, child-like, and providing an ongoing and subtle form of nonverbal communication. His hand told me when he was alert, when he decided a passer-by was harmless, when he was amused by the antics of two children shrieking their way around and around a tree. His palm against mine spoke of trust and ease. And his fingers threaded through mine told me when he spotted Billy, slumped on a bench with a newspaper draped across his face.

I tightened my own fingers briefly, letting him know that I had seen the sleeping figure, and cleared my throat loudly as we passed the bench. The newspaper twitched. Five minutes later, Billy came around the back of the washroom building.

He looked tired, and I thought his unshaven face was more necessity than disguise. He had been living rough for some days; a darkness about one eye testified to recent physical conflict.

"You can't stay in Town, and you mustn't go to Mr Mycroft's funeral," he blurted out. His voice was pure raw Cockney, which happened only when he was upset.

"It's nice to see you, too, Billy," I said calmly.

"I mean it," he insisted, stepping forward in what I decided was an effort to intimidate me into obeying him—which would have been difficult even if he was not three inches shorter than I. Goodman put his hands into his pockets, looking more interested than alarmed.

"Billy, what is going on? Why did you tell me to run? And why have all the criminals in Southwark gone to ground?"

"You noticed."

"It was hard to miss. Are they all under arrest?"

"No, just as you say, gone to ground. I told 'em to hike it."

"But why?"

"There's something big up. I don't know what it is, but there's coppers in the rafters, sniffing under the dustbins, listening in at the windows."

"You're sure they're police?"

"Nah, that lot're not police, but they're not honest criminals either. They're hard men, that's what they are, and they're looking for you and Mr 'Olmes."

"Is that why you had Randall tell me to run? Because someone was listening at your windows?"

"I didn't want to be the one to lead you to 'em. I've been sleeping away from home for three days now because I was afraid they'd follow me to you. I wouldn't risk that."

"You're a good friend, Billy," I said, which was both the unvarnished truth and an attempt to calm him down. "But tell me about these men. If they're not police, who are they?"

"They're working with the police, but they're sure as sin not local boys, or even the Yard."

"So, it's some kind of a criminal gang moving into new territory?"

"No," he said in an agony of impatience. "They're not a gang—or they are, but not criminals."

"I don't understand."

"A criminal gang wouldn't pick me up for questioning and then let me go. But Scotland Yard wouldn't threaten my family if I didn't cooperate. Randy's the only one left at home, and that's because he's decided it's time to play the man."

I had to agree, this sounded very wrong. "I see what you mean. When did this start?"

"Thursday."

"The day after Mycroft was..." It was hard to say the word. Billy's face went even darker.

"I heard about that first thing in the morning, and they were at my door an hour later. They let me go at tea-time and I bundled my family off to—" He glanced at Goodman for the first time, suddenly aware of a new hazard.

"Sorry," I said, and made the introductions. The two men shook hands, Billy eyeing the owl feather with curiosity. "Well, Billy, I suggest you collect your son and join your family until we get this sorted. Holmes should—"

He cut me off. "I've sent the family away, but that doesn't mean I'm hiding. This is my town, they can't pull me in and beat me up and expect to get away with it. When I'm finished for Mr Holmes I'll go home and sit tight."

Goodman stirred, putting together the bruises on Billy's face with the situation as a whole.

I smiled at the irate Cockney. "Somehow it doesn't surprise me to hear that."

"And I don't think Mr Holmes knows about it—any rate, he didn't on Tuesday. I told him that Mr Mycroft hadn't been seen of late, but that was all I knew." The *H* had returned to *Holmes*.

"You've talked to Holmes?"

"Down the telephone," he said. "And there's another thing. He was phoning from Amsterdam—"

"*Amsterdam?*"

"That's what he said. And I know I'm probably not up on this modern machinery," Billy admitted, "but the timing's dead fishy. Mean to say, he rings me Tuesday, there's hard men in the neighbourhood Wednesday, Mr Mycroft dies late Wednesday, and I'm picked up and questioned Thursday."

"So you talked with him before Mycroft..."

"Right. And afterwards he could've told anyone that he'd talked to me. Or, Southwark could have nothing to do with Mr Mycroft. But like I say, it's just . . . fishy."

"Well, I expect to see Holmes soon. Certainly by tomorrow. But, why did he ring you?"

"To ask me to look into this Brothers bloke. To see if he had any ties to a criminal gang, maybe a new one making a push into London from the East."

"Does he know Brothers is still alive?"

"He is? Are you sure?"

"Almost certainly."

"No, he told me Brothers was dead, but that people might not know yet. Mr Holmes wanted me to look for what the man's ties might've been to a gang, and if they'd want to do anything more than cross him off their books."

"Revenge, yes. And have you found anything?"

"I put out the word, but people were only starting to get back to me when my usual lines of communication got . . . disrupted. I did find that the bloke what works for Brothers, Marcus Gunderson—he came into steady employment 'bout a year ago. Got himself a nice flat, stopped associatin' with his usual friends."

"When was this?"

"Hard to pin down."

"Might it have been November? He started working for Brothers then."

"That lot, it could've been last week and they'd be hard-pressed to be sure. Do you think this Brothers might have anything to do with Mr Mycroft?"

"Other than the timing being, as you say, fishy, most of the links are pretty feeble. I know you and I were trained by the same man, but you have to allow that events can be simultaneous but unrelated."

He looked unhappy, but then, so did I.

"I'm thinking of getting my hands on one of them, asking a few questions of my own," he said abruptly.

I opened my mouth to object, but then closed it. Memories of brutalising information from Brothers' man Gunderson two weeks earlier were still strong enough to make me queasy, but the fastest way to find out what the devil was going on in London was to ask one of the villains. However, I definitely wanted Holmes there to supervise. "They're certain to show up at the funeral. We'll see what we can do about separating one of them from the pack after—"

But he stepped forward with a look of panic, grabbing my arm. "You're not going! Promise me you're not going to stick your head up there!"

"Ow, Billy, stop!" He relaxed his grip, but not his urgency. "Look, I can't not go to Mycroft's funeral." Besides which, if Holmes failed to show up at the bolt-hole—always a possibility—I should have to look for him at the funeral.

"They'll take you. You'll be dead as he is, and then what will Mr Holmes do?"

I was touched by the worry contorting his face, and amused at Holmes' concerns being his priority. And although I was very aware that he could be right about the threat, I could think of one way to mitigate the risk.

"You may be right," I said, and began to smile. "Do you suppose some of your kith and kin would like to attend as well?"

Chapter 41

Funeral services, according to the newspaper, would be conducted at graveside, at four on Sunday afternoon, some twenty-seven hours from now. I had no idea if Mycroft's will had specified the arrangements—frankly, I'd have thought my brother-in-law would prefer the simple disposal of a cremation—but if he had not made them, who had? His grey secretary, Sosa? His housekeeper, Mrs Cowper? Whoever was responsible, they knew Mycroft well enough to leave the Church out of the picture.

The need to see Holmes was an ache in the back of my mind, although I had grown accustomed to Goodman's presence, and even grateful for it. From a practical standpoint, any police officer looking for a tall young woman in the company of an even taller American with burn scars—and possibly a child, depending on how up-to-date their information was—would not look twice at a tall young woman accompanied by a short, blond, green-eyed Englishman. But more than that, I found Goodman combined the amiability of a retriever with the bounce of a Jack Russell terrier. He was quite mad, of course, but his was a very different kind of lunacy to what had taken Mycroft, this dark madness I could feel growing around me like electricity. If the unseen threat was an approaching thunderstorm that raised one's hair into prickles, Goodman was a bucket of water atop a half-open door: an unsubtle but refreshing distraction.

Still, I longed for Holmes.

I looked at some boys dashing across the lawn after a football, and made up my mind.

"I need to leave you for a time," I told him. "Perhaps two hours. Do you want me to return here, or shall I meet you elsewhere?"

He, too, eyed the football. "I shall be here."

It was both a relief and unexpectedly nerve-wracking to set off across the city on my own. When I reached the first of my destinations, I had to sit for a while and let my jangles dissipate.

Holmes was not here, in the second of his bolt-holes, tucked within the walls of one of London's grand department stores. The Storage Room, as he called it, had been the first bolt-hole I had seen, in the early years of our acquaintance. Holmes had not been there then, and he was not here now.

Nor was he at any of the other four I checked, although two of them showed signs that he had been there with Damian the previous month.

If Holmes was in London, he was lying very low.

I rode back to the theatre district in a taxi, looking at streets that had gone unfamiliar to my eyes, infected with strange new currents, new and unpredictable and dangerous. Men with rifles sent at an instant's notice to the farthest reaches of the land. The ability to trace the source of telephone calls. Men who were neither criminals nor police, but both. The brutal murder of one of the king's most loyal and powerful servants.

These bustling pavements could be hiding any manner of threat; the wires overhead might even as I passed be singing my fate to the ears of a sniper; the helmeted constable on the corner may as well be a "hard man" with a very different view of London from my own.

Brave new world, that has such creatures in it.

In this strange London, I found that I looked forward to seeing Robert Goodman again, a small and cheerful man in whose blood moved the ancient forests of Britain, who rescued three fallen mortals from the hubris of a flaming sky-machine, who took joy in simple, silly things and looked on modernity as a jest, who overcame vicious armed men with the prank of a taut tree branch.

I spotted him sitting cross-legged on the lawn, grass-stains on his cousin-in-law's knees, coat shed, shirt-sleeves rolled up, playing mumblety-peg with four young girls while their mothers looked on with a peculiar mixture of fondness and dubiety. They were as disappointed as their daughters when I made him fold away his lethally sharp pocket-knife and come away with me.

I was not certain that Goodman's woods-awareness translated into city streets, but leaving the park, I was wary enough for the both of us, glancing in the reflections of polished windows, stepping into various shops to study autumn fashion or newly published titles while looking out of the windows at passers-by—and even more carefully, at those who did not pass by. I saw three uniformed constables and two private guards in mufti, but try as I might, I could see in the area surrounding Mycroft's flat no police presence, and no "hard men."

When we had been in the vicinity for twenty minutes, I stepped into a passage called Angel Court. Three steps to a doorway, and we were gone.

"Stand still," I whispered into the damp and echoing darkness, feeling along the wall for the box of matches. My fingers found them; light flared, then settled onto the candle in its glass-shielded holder. I lifted it high to light our path through the narrow labyrinth to Mycroft's flat.

At the far end, I set the candle on its ledge and took up the key from its invisible resting place, sliding the cover from the peep-hole that showed Mycroft's windowless study. The low light he kept constantly burning showed enough to be certain the room contained no intruders.

I slid the key into its concealed hole and breathed to Goodman, "There's no one in the room directly inside, but I can't speak for the rest of the flat."

"I will go first."

"No," I said.

"If they take me, what does it matter? If they take you, others will suffer."

He meant that Estelle would suffer. I said, "Very well, but don't turn on any lights." I turned the key and put my shoulder to the wall. The bookshelf moved, and I stood back to permit him entry. Once inside, he pushed the hidden door nearly shut. Through the crack I watched him walk on silent feet across the carpet and out of the room.

My mind began to count the seconds as I waited, one hand on the door to pull and the other set to turn the key.

And waited.

He made a thorough job of it, and had time to look under beds and inside wardrobes before he reappeared, chewing an apple. I breathed again—disappointed that Holmes was not there, but relieved no one else was. I pushed the door fully open and stepped into the familiar book-lined room.

"What are we looking for?" He was curiously examining the shelves, which were as idiosyncratic as those of Holmes—although where the younger brother's shelves were devoted to crime and art, Mycroft's concentrated on crime and politics.

"Mycroft tends to keep his business to himself," I said. "I know where his office is, more or less, and I've met his secretary, but I don't even know the name of his colleagues. A desk diary or address book would be nice. What I'm hoping for is a hidden safe. Which, being Mycroft, may well be concealed behind a less-hidden safe."

Goodman flashed me his young-boy's grin and clasped his hands behind his back, turning to a contemplation of the walls.

Most men conceal personal valuables in a bedroom, professional treasures in a study. Mycroft would only choose those sites if he had decided on a double blind, but trying to outguess Mycroft would set one on the road to madness: One might as well flip a coin.

I knew this study, the guest room, and the sitting room reasonably well, and thought that over the years, I might well have caught some indication of a hidden safe in one of those rooms. Instead, I would begin with Mycroft's bedroom.

But not before ensuring our security. I walked through the flat to the dining room, intending to jam one of the chairs under the front doorknob, and there saw an envelope with my name on it, propped against the fruit-bowl in the centre of the table. Battling an urge to look around me for a trap, I picked up the envelope and tore it open:

Miss Russell,

I have withdrawn the warrants for you and your husband. Please accept my condolences over the death of Mycroft Holmes. And please, come in to talk with me at your earliest possible convenience.

Yours respectfully,
John Lestrade (Chief Insp.)

My first reaction was less reassurance than a feeling that I had just seen a predator's spoor: I made haste to take a chair to the front door and work it into place. But with pursuers thus slowed, I read the words again, more slowly. Lestrade had proven himself generally competent and thoroughly tenacious, but he had never evinced the cold cunning needed to lay a trap under these circumstances.

It was the underlining of the words that pushed me towards accepting it at face value: Three words, using a considerable pressure on the pen, suggested a degree of urgency, even desperation.

Earliest possible convenience.

I read it a third time, then folded it away and returned to my search.

In his bedroom, I was unprepared for the powerful sense of Mycroft's presence that washed over me. For a moment, my large, complicated, terrifyingly intelligent brother-in-law moved at the edge of my vision.

Then memory crashed in, and I found myself on the chair in the corner, blinking furiously, swallowing hard against the lump in my throat.

Mycroft Holmes was not a loveable man, but to know him—to truly know him, every unbending, impatient, haughty, and self-centred inch of the man—was to respect him, and eventually, reluctantly, to love him. I loved him. The thought of him dead in an alley filled me with rage. I wanted to find the man who had done that and rip into him, for making the world a less secure, less blessedly interesting place. But first I wanted to sit and weep.

This was an age of the death of gods.

I stood and brusquely wiped my face. I had no time for the distraction of tears. I forced myself to open drawers and search the backs of shelves, to pull up carpets and quietly shift furniture. I examined the underpinnings of his remarkably stout bed, pawed through the unwashed laundry in his basket, and lifted the lid of his toilet's cistern. I emptied his bathroom wall-cupboard of medicines and felt the boards, knelt by the bathtub and felt the tiles, stood on a chair and felt the light fixtures.

Then I did the same in the guest room.

In the study, I found Goodman sitting in a chair in the centre of the room, looking at one of the walls. He might have been in a gallery studying an Old Master: *Still Life of Odd Books.*

"I had a thought," I said, and took the work-lamp from the desk, transferring it to the plug nearest the bookshelf entrance and carrying it into the dim passageway. I held it up so its beam fell onto the bricks, new on one side, ancient on the other, searching for any anomaly. A moment later, Goodman's hand came into view and he took the lamp from me, holding it so I could continue my search unencumbered.

Twenty minutes later I had reached the edge of the light's beam, having found nothing but walls.

I returned the lamp to its place. "Well, it was just a thought."

"There's something odd about this shelf," Goodman said.

I looked at him in surprise. "Very good. Not many people would notice."

Mycroft had contrived a hidden recess the size of one of the shelf spaces. Now I unloaded the books and felt around for the slightly protruding nail head towards the back, which freed the back to drop forward into my hands.

It held ordinary valuables—money in several currencies; passports in false names that fit the descriptions of Mycroft, his brother, and me; and a piece of paper with a row of numbers on it, which when translated into mathematical base eight gave one the European bank account where he kept his foreign savings. Nothing to suggest his real secrets. Nothing to connect him with the world of Intelligence, either large or small *i*.

I decided to leave the study to last, on the theory that if an ordinary man keeps his secrets close, an extraordinary man keeps his far from him. Having made this decision, I turned for the sitting room, only to have the stillness of the flat shattered by a jangling telephone. "Don't answer it," I said. We both watched the machine, waiting for many rings before it fell silent.

I worked my way down the hallway towards the sitting room, rolling up the carpet runner, groping along the floorboards and skirting, unscrewing the switch plates, peering behind the pictures.

When I got to the end, my clean clothes were no longer and I had broken a fingernail prising at one of the boards.

Sucking at the finger, I kicked my way down the rolled carpet until it was flat, only then realising that I ought not to have started in the bedroom. Mycroft had commanded that Mrs Cowper's kitchen be renovated, shortly after an enormous dinner for important guests—a goose, all the fixings, two pies, and several dusty basement-stored bottles—had first stuck, then come crashing down four stories in the dumbwaiter. It was the same time at which he had installed his secret entrance, using the dust of one building project to conceal the other.

And, I now saw, it would have been the ideal time to install a well-concealed safe in an unlikely place—why hadn't I thought to look in the kitchen first and saved myself the knowledge of his laundry and nostrums?

Chapter 42

Mycroft occasionally cooked in this kitchen, on Mrs Cowper's holidays or days off, but for the most part, it had become the housekeeper's room. Her ruffled apron hung from a hook on the back of one of the swinging doors; a photograph of her grandchildren stood beside the warming oven; an enormous portrait of the king beamed down upon her labours from the wall where the late and unlamented dumbwaiter had once opened—loyal as he was, I doubted the portrait would be Mycroft's choice of decoration.

The room was tidy, as Mrs Cowper always left it; there was no knowing when she had last been here.

And this, naturally enough, was where I found Mycroft's stash, in a place both difficult to reach and seemingly inappropriate for treasures: the frame of a notably modern oven. The temperatures alone should have guaranteed that any nearby paperwork would disintegrate in a matter of days; however, appearances were deceiving: What looked solid was not; what looked heated was cooled.

I drew from the narrow panel with the invisible hinges an inch-thick metal box the dimensions of foolscap paper. I settled on the floor with my back to the wall, lest Goodman come upon me without my noticing, and opened the box.

Inside were sixteen sheets of paper, typed or hand-written, none from the same machine or hand. All sixteen were condensed confidential reports, all concerned the behaviour of leaders in colonies or allied countries. I could not avoid a quick perusal, although I did not wish to compromise the Empire's security by knowing what I should not; even that light survey made it clear that any one of these pages could instigate a revolt, if not outright war.

But that was not the extent of Mycroft's secrets.

The box's cover had two layers to it, with some insulating substance such as asbestos between them to protect the contents. However, as I returned the pages in their original order and applied a dish-towel to the metal so my finger-prints would not be on it, the top of the box felt a fraction thicker than the sides and bottom. I put down the cloth and turned the top towards the light, and saw: The top itself had a hidden compartment.

In it was a single sheet of paper, in Mycroft's hand.

Dear Sherlock,

If you are reading my words, the chances are good that I am dead. I congratulate you on finding this, for I did not wish to make it easy.

Please, I beg you, destroy the outer contents of this box. The international repercussions of their revelation would be terrifying, and without me to oversee what might otherwise be described as blackmail operations, the papers themselves will be of no further use to anyone.

If as I imagine you will be loath to set match to them, please, I beg you, ensure without a fraction of a doubt that they will be destroyed upon your own death. The enormity of reaction should they be revealed would taint our name forever.

Finally, I commend to you two individuals, in hopes that you will care for their future needs. One is my housekeeper, Mrs Cowper, a woman of many hidden talents. The other is my

*secretary, whom you met long ago, a person who has helped me
Interpret all manner of data over the years.*

Wishing you joy on the great hunt of life,

*Your own,
M.*

It was signed with the initial alone, but my eyes seemed to see his usual signature, in which the cross of his *t* swirled into an ornate underscore. I set the letter down long enough to examine the box, making certain it contained no further secrets, and return it to its place. The letter I kept.

I was still sitting against the wall, pondering Mycroft's message, when the swinging doors parted to admit Goodman's head. I scrambled to my feet, folding away the letter into a pocket.

"Did you discover your safe within a safe?" His gaze wandered along the shelves and pans that I had left every which way.

"More or less," I answered vaguely. "You didn't find anything else in the study, then?"

"Only this." He stepped inside, holding out a key.

I took it with interest. I had not seen it before, an ordinary enough shape but with an engraved Greek *sigma* on its flat head. "Where did you find it?"

He walked away; I turned off the lights and followed.

Unlike the rest of the house, which I had left speaking eloquently of either a hasty search or a minor tornado, the disruption in the study was confined to two precise spots: the shelf niche with the money and passports, and below and to one side, a place where the wood of the shelf itself had been hollowed out. The thin veneer fit in behind the facing of the shelf, and would have been invisible unless one were lying on the floor, staring upwards, with a powerful light to hand. Even then, a person would have needed to know the hiding place was there.

I for one had not, although I'd spent countless hours in that very chair.

"How on earth did you find that?"

He frowned, then said, "The shelf did not match."

"What, the wood?"

"No. The contents." He could see I did not understand, so he tried to explain. "In the forest, a place where there was once a road or a house is betrayed by the varieties of trees that grow there, the shape of the paths cut by animals aware of the difference. Here, a man set out the contents of this shelf with a degree of . . . distraction, perhaps? As if this shelf had a different history from the others."

I could recall no particular difference between the books on this segment of shelf and the books on any other, although it did contain a small framed photograph of a thin young man in an Army uniform, all but unrecognisable as Damian Adler. "I hope you have a chance to talk with my husband," I told him. "You two would have much to say to each other."

The key was the only object inside this highly concealed compartment. I looked at it under the light, but it was unexceptional, apart from the Greek letter. In the end, I added it to the contents of my pocket, along with the money, the bank account code, and the passports.

Mycroft had no further use for any of them, and with any luck, I could soon hand the collection over to Holmes.

I went to the guest room and changed into some of the clothes I kept there, then went through the other rooms so they bore the same disruption as the rest of the flat. I removed the chair from under the door-knob, noticing with a pang that Mycroft's walking stick stood in its umbrella stand. He used it mostly for the regimen of afternoon strolls he had begun, following his heart attack; if he'd been carrying his stick that night, would he have had a chance for self-defence?

When we let ourselves out of the secret doorway, the only things left behind were Mycroft's sixteen political thunderbolts and one considerable mess.

The bobbing light accompanied us along the passageway to Mycroft's other hidden exit, on St James's Square. Again, I stowed the candle and peered through a peep-hole to make sure our emergence from a blank wall would not be noticed, then worked the mechanism.

In the outer world, the low sunlight made the autumnal leaves glow;

in sympathy, perhaps, a small corner of my mind began to light up, and I fingered the letter in my pocket.

Mycroft Holmes had a Russian doll of a mind. He was a man whose secrets had secrets. Any layer of hidden meaning was apt to have another layer, and one below that.

At opposite ends of the flat, he had left a letter to his brother and an unidentified key. With any other man, one would assume the two were unrelated. With Mycroft, there was the very real possibility that he had left two clues that by themselves were without meaning, that only together—if one persisted in *the great hunt of life* and found both—created a third message: *The key is in the Interpreter.* Or a fourth meaning. Or fifth.

There was also the likelihood that I was ascribing to my departed brother-in-law an omniscience he lacked: Even Mycroft Holmes would hesitate to lay out clues that his brother would not think to follow.

I badly wanted to talk to Holmes about this; however, I did have another set of remarkably sharp eyes with me.

"Let's take supper," I said, the first words either of us had spoken for at least ten minutes.

Down a side street lay a tiny Italian restaurant where I had once had an adequate meal. They were not yet serving, but were happy to ply us with wine and *antipasti*. When the waiter was out of earshot, I pulled Mycroft's letter from my pocket and laid it on the table-cloth before Goodman.

"I found this in a place where not one man in a million would think to look. I'd like you to read it, keeping in mind that its author was the man who designed and arranged those bookshelves. Tell me if anything strikes you."

He read it, twice, then folded it and handed it back to me. "There is hidden meaning there."

"Yes," I said in satisfaction. "I thought so."

"Something to do with the secretary, I should have said. Who, unlike the housekeeper, goes nameless."

I unfolded the page, and my eyes were drawn, as they had been each time before, to that unlikely capital *I* on the verb *Interpret*.

"Wait here," I told him, and slipped out of my seat and onto the street outside.

Ten minutes later, I sat down again, finding a laden platter of glistening morsels and a full glass of red wine. I laid my purchase on the table.

A glance at its table of contents gave me the page number, and a review of the story took a few minutes. I gazed into space for a bit, and when the waiter drifted past, I woke and asked, "Have you a London telephone directory?"

"I am sure we do. Which letter were you looking for?"

"*K*. I think."

He went away, confused but cheerful about it, and Goodman said, "Not *S* for *sigma*?"

By way of answer, I placed the book before him, open at the twenty-year-old short story "The Greek Interpreter."

Unless the capital *I* had been a slip of the hand, which I found hard to credit, it was a teasing directional arrow left by Mycroft for his brother. Mycroft's first appearance in Dr Watson's tales had been in the adventure of the Greek Interpreter, when Mycroft's upstairs neighbour, a pathologically naïve freelance interpreter named Melas, was sucked into a case of theft and deception, nearly losing his life in the process.

The Christian name of Mr Melas is not given, but the victim of the would-be theft, who died in the event, was a young man named Kratides. Key to his troubles was a sister named "Sophy." A name that in Greek begins with the letter *sigma*.

There was nothing under *S*, or the name "Sophy" or "Kratides." But when I hunted through the *M* listings, there was one Melas. The given name began with an *S*.

Perhaps Mycroft's message was to be read: *The key* is *the Interpreter*.

Chapter 43

The address attributed to S. Melas was a quiet, tidy yellow-brick house in Belgravia, less than a mile from Mycroft's door. In the swept front area a pot of bronze chrysanthemums flamed. The bricks were scrubbed, the paint was fresh, the brass knocker gleamed.

A maid answered the door. I handed her a card with a name that was not quite my own, apologised for the late hour, and asked if I might speak with Mrs Melas.

Instead of asking us in, she took the card and left us on the front step, looking at a closed door. Caution clearly ruled over societal niceties in this household.

We did not wait long before the maid returned. She led us to an airy, slightly old-fashioned drawing room that smelt of lavender and lemons. In a minute, the lady of the house herself came in.

Sophy Melas was a tall, dignified woman in her late fifties, whose Mediterranean heritage had kept all but a few strands of white from the thick black hair gathered atop her head.

I apologised for our unannounced visit, but beyond that, could see no point in anything but bluntness. "Madam, were you related to a Mr Paul Kratides?"

Her near-black eyes went wary. "Paul was my brother, yes."

"You married a Greek interpreter named Melas, who some years earlier had attempted to rescue you and your brother from villains?"

"I think you should leave."

"My brother-in-law was Mycroft Holmes," I told her.

She swayed a fraction, as if a sharp breeze had passed through the room, but said coolly, "How does this concern me?" Her accent was Greek overlaid with decades of life in England.

"I believe Mycroft may have left some information with you. I'd like to know what it was."

"Why would you imagine the gentleman left anything with me?"

I sighed, and held out the decorated house key, dropping it into her outstretched palm. "I could have fitted it to your front door, but I thought that ill-mannered. Do I need to do so?"

She rubbed the key's engraved letter with her thumb, then looked up at me. "It would not do you any good. I had that lock changed years ago. Still, you may as well sit. Would you like something to drink? Coffee?"

I allowed her to offer us hospitality, and when we had before us an elaborate silver coffee setting, she said, "I was sorry to hear of Mr Holmes' death. The world is a lesser place." It was a formal declaration, expressing no more emotion than the obituary in *The Times* had.

"What was your relationship with Mycroft, if I may ask?"

"I was . . . his friend. Occasionally I acted as his secretary."

"That must have been a recent appointment." I had last met the weedy and humourless Richard Sosa in December, when Mycroft was ill and asked us to take his secretary a letter one Sunday afternoon. However, all sorts of changes might have come about while I was out of the country.

"By no means recent. I have worked for him, on and off, for more than twenty years. Since I returned to this country and married Mr Melas," she added. Then she smiled, unexpectedly. "I did occasionally act as his type-writer, but my primary purpose was to provide eyes and ears. Sometimes this was in the manner of his other . . . associates, but generally my use was for Mr Holmes himself. Your brother-in-law liked occasionally to discuss his affairs with what he termed 'a pair of sympathetic and intelligent ears.'"

I looked at her with considerable interest. This woman not only knew of Mycroft's agents, she was claiming that she had been one of them. Moreover, it sounded as if he utilised her for a sounding board, as Holmes had done with Watson, and later me. Why had it never occurred to me that the brothers might be alike in this way?

If that was the case, it pointed to a degree of trust I would not have expected of Mycroft. This aloof and rather hard-looking woman could know secrets Mycroft shared with no one else.

"Do you know anything about his death?" I asked her. "All I have heard is that he was killed outside of a raucous night-club. The *Times* obituary made it sound as if he had been a client."

"Absurd," she said flatly.

"I agree. But why else would he have been there?"

"I can think of any number of reasons why Mr Holmes would have been in that area. He was apt to meet his associates in the oddest locations."

My rising hope was cut short by suspicion: Mycroft's intellect ranged far and wide, but physically, my brother-in-law kept to a rigorously limited circuit—as Holmes put it, his brother could not be bothered to go out of his way to verify a solution. "Interesting," I said mildly. "I thought Mycroft rarely went out to such meetings."

"That was certainly true in the past," she said. "However, when a man looks into the eyes of his own mortality, he confronts many demons. I believe that one of the demons Mr Holmes faced, after his heart attack, was that his disinclination to stir from his common rounds made him dangerously predictable. Either the world had changed, or his own unshakeable habits had created what he termed 'an eddy in the currents of crime' around him. In either event, he made an effort to change those habits."

And I had thought Mycroft's new régime of taking exercise was merely a weight-loss response to illness. I should have known there would be more than one meaning.

"So, who was he seeing at that club that night?"

"Ah, I'm sorry, you misunderstood my meaning. He occasionally spoke about his personal regrets—knowing that I of all his friends would understand—and even about his colleagues, but I was not privy to his secrets. Certainly not those to do with his work. And you have to realise, his remarks to me were often quite incomprehensible. In the

general run of such things, we would be in the middle of some quite ordinary conversation—music or art or a current scandal—when he would
drop an utterly unrelated and quite oblique remark. As if he wished to
see my unstudied reaction."

"Er, can you give me an example?"

"Let me think. Yes: Last month we went to the theatre to see a pair of
Shaw plays about deception, and as we strolled home, talking about the
strictures of drawing-room plays and the life of an actor, he asked me
what I thought about the wage demands of coal miners. A topic that was
much in the news at the time."

"I see. And he never happened to mention anything related to this
night-club?"

"Not that I remember. Although I believe something has been preying
on his mind, of late."

"What?"

"That I do not know. I only noticed that he seemed mildly distracted
the last two or three times I saw him."

Goodman spoke up from the sofa; I had all but forgotten he was
there. "Mr Holmes asked an odd question the last time you talked," he
said in a voice of certainty.

"Did he? Now that you mention it, yes he did. It concerned loyalty. At
first I was taken aback, because I thought he was making reference to *my*
loyalty, but it seemed that was not his concern."

"If not yours, then whose?" I asked her.

"I do not know."

"The exact words he used were . . ." Goodman coaxed.

"'Where does faith part from loyalty?'" she answered. "He had been
reading the Greek philosophers, a discussion of the Virtues. He said
something about one being legal and the other emotional. I'm sorry, I
have little education, and I often did not understand what Mr Holmes
was saying."

Faith, as the Latin *fidelis*, connotes an unswerving belief; loyalty is
linked with *lex*, a legal commitment. Faith is bone deep and unques-
tioning, whereas loyalty comes with a sense of threat and the possibility
of failure.

I asked, "Did you get the impression that he was talking about himself? Wondering if *he* should remain loyal, for example? Or someone else?"

She answered slowly. "It sounded—looking back, that is; I can't be certain what I felt at the time—but I should say it sounded as if he was trying to understand the underpinnings of someone's concept of loyalty. Not his own."

"But that's all he said?"

"It's all I remember. When I asked him what he meant, he laughed and changed the subject."

"To what?"

"Oh, just a question about a novel we'd both been reading."

Mycroft Holmes discussing a novel? For that matter, Mycroft discussing business with a woman he'd first met in the course of a crime? There must be unexplored depths to the woman—although Dr Watson's story intimated as much.

"When was this—your last conversation with him?"

"The twenty-seventh of August, a Wednesday. He had been very occupied for several days, to the extent of cancelling a musical engagement, but he rang me that morning to say he was free for a few hours."

That Wednesday, I had been flying to Orkney while Holmes was bobbing about the North Sea: It was, as she said, the first day in many that Mycroft had been free of us. This was also the day before he was taken in by Lestrade for questioning, and then disappeared.

"You said Mycroft occasionally talked about his colleagues. Any of them in particular?"

"Recently?"

"In the past few months."

"I'm sure he did, but nothing that stands out in my mind. Let me see. His secretary—his work secretary, that is, Mr Sosa—was out for some days with what I gathered was an embarrassing illness, although I couldn't tell you the details. One of his associates in Germany went missing for a period, in March, I believe it was, and My—Mr Holmes was quite preoccupied."

"Do you know if this associate reappeared?"

"I think Mr Holmes would have mentioned, had his worries been for nothing. To put my mind at rest."

A missing agent, I noted: Had Mycroft died in Germany, I should certainly know where to begin enquiries.

"Anyone else?"

"He talked about you and your husband a number of times during the winter," she replied. "He was relieved when you came away from India without mishap, and concerned later, when you had problems in California."

I blinked: That Mycroft would talk about business matters to a pair of "sympathetic ears" was surprising enough, but that he talked freely about his family was extraordinary.

"And very recently—that same Wednesday, it would have been—he told me a tale about a young associate who travelled from the Far East in record time. He loved it when one of his young people had a triumph like that. Let's see, what else? He mentioned Prime Minister MacDonald, once or twice. And there was a colleague, Mr West—Peter James West, he called him, with all three names—who had done something unexpected. Speaking up to his superior, I believe it was, although that was one of those cryptic remarks, nothing detailed like the other young man's trip from the East. Oh, but he did tell me about a conversation he'd had with the king a few weeks ago, when they both happened to be passing through St James's Park."

"Do you remember what that conversation was about?"

Her black eyes, unexpectedly, sparkled with inner amusement. "I believe it was to do with the *lèse-majesté* of ducks."

I laughed, joined by Goodman's shouted *Ha!* of humour.

I thanked Mrs Melas for her help, and made to rise. She seemed surprised, hesitating as if to ask something, but whatever it was, she changed her mind and got to her feet, holding out the key.

"Do you wish to keep this?"

"No," I told her. "I think its only purpose was to point towards you."

"Do you think so? I gave it to Mr Holmes many years ago, when he first helped me set up a household. It's nice to think he kept it as a memento. Even if I had changed the actual lock."

This was not at all what I had meant, but I could see no purpose in disabusing the woman of the notion that Mycroft's keeping the key had an emotional, rather than merely practical, use.

At the door, Mrs Melas asked, "Would—do you think anyone would object, if I came to the funeral?"

"Whyever would they?" I replied. Which rather begged the question of who was going to be there to object?

"Ours was, well, not a liaison he openly acknowledged," she said.

And only then, with her standing at my elbow, did my mind deliver up the question: Mycroft? Was the woman's cool exterior in fact a struggle to contain grief? Had she been about to call Mycroft by name, when telling me about his concern for his agent in Germany? Did this mean that my brother-in-law's diamond-hard mind and ungentle personality had a softer side? That Mycroft...that Mrs Melas...

I thanked her again, and made haste to get out the door.

Down the street, I became aware of Robert Goodman, a shadow at my side. I laughed, a shade uncomfortably. "From the woman's reaction, one might almost think..."

"One might," he agreed.

Ridiculous. Quite impossibly ridiculous.

Wasn't it?

Chapter 44

S he expected something, there at the end," Goodman observed some indeterminate time later.

"You mean when she looked as if she was about to ask a question?"

"More as if she was hoping you might ask."

I paused on the pavement, going over that portion of the conversation, her air of expectancy before she stood. "You may be right. I felt she was telling the truth, so far as it went. But holding something back as well. Was she waiting for me to give some kind of a password?"

"Somewhat melodramatic, that."

I laughed, both because Goodman was saying it, and because of the woman's history. "You didn't read the end of the 'Interpreter' story."

"You took it away before I finished."

"The two men who kidnapped Sophy Kratides, killed her brother, and assaulted Mr Melas, were later found dead in Buda-Pesht. It looked as if they had stabbed each other in a quarrel; however, a Greek girl travelling with them had vanished."

"More knives," Goodman murmured.

"Knives are personal," I commented. We walked on.

"Have you further plans?" he asked.

"I must speak with Mycroft's colleagues," I told him.

"Tonight?"

It was, I was startled to find, nearly ten o'clock. "Perhaps not. In any case, I'm not sure where to find the fellow she mentioned—Peter James West. He may attend the funeral; if not, it will have to wait until Monday. But Mycroft's secretary—his proper secretary, that is, not..." Whatever rôle Sophy Melas played. "Sosa lives not too far from here; we could at least go past and see if his lights are lit. However, we shall have to approach him with care—he will not talk about anything he regards as an official secret. He knows me—I wonder if we might be able to convince him that you're a part of the organisation? Can you stay silent and look mysterious?"

The expression Goodman arranged on his features was more dyspeptic than mysterious, but perhaps a bureaucrat would expect no less.

The grey-faced and humourless Richard Sosa was a life-long bureaucrat who for more than twenty years had kept Mycroft's appointments book and typed his letters. The man lived, with an unexpected note of upper-class levity, in Mayfair, in the basement apartment of his mother's house, around the corner from Berkeley Square. Sosa *mère et fils* had long settled into a mutually satisfactory state of bitter argument and disapproval, which occasionally blew up into more active conflict, such as the time his mother bashed him with a fry-pan for being late to a promised dinner.

Perhaps the "embarrassing illness" to which Mrs Melas referred had been another such episode.

At the top of the quiet street, I paused to study the noble doorways. Goodman murmured, "No-one awaits."

I was sceptical, as he'd spent perhaps thirty seconds in the survey. "How can you be certain?"

He did not answer; it occurred to me that I'd asked an unanswerable question, so I changed it to "*Are* you certain?"

"Yes."

Very well; I'd trusted his eyes in the night-time woods, perhaps I should do the same in this night-time city. "All right, let's see if he is home."

But he was not: The curtains were drawn, and a piece of advertising had been left against the door, which I had seen in none of the other houses. We went back onto the pavement, so as not to attract the attention of the man walking his dog or the tipsy couple, and kept our heads averted as we strolled down to the end of the street and turned towards the lights of New Bond Street.

"I'll wait here for a time," I said. "He may be in later."

"You plan on breaking in," my companion noted.

"Er. Perhaps."

"Do you need me?"

"I was going to suggest you find your way back to the hideaway."

"I will go and sing to the trees for a while, I think."

With no further ado, he turned in the direction of Hyde Park. I watched him go, wondering if he could possibly mean that literally. I only hoped he was not arrested for vagrancy. Or lunacy.

I circled corners until I was across from the Sosa door—or doors—and when the street was empty, I chose a low wall and settled down behind it. After ninety minutes that were as tedious and uncomfortable as one might imagine, the surrounding houses had all gone dark (for in Mayfair, no traces survive of the eponymous annual celebration of wild debauchery) and passers-by had ceased.

I waited until the local constable had made his semi-hourly pass. Then I climbed to my feet, brushed off my skirt, and went to break into the house of a spymaster's assistant.

The locks to the basement flat were impressive, the sorts of devices I could be cursing over for an hour, and the door was a bit too exposed for comfort. However, those who find security in large and impressive locks often neglect other means of entry—and indeed, the adjoining window, although well lifted up from the area tiles, was both wide and inadequately secured. Ten seconds' work with my knife-blade, and its latch gave.

Being Mayfair, the window-frame was even well maintained, emitting not a squeak as it rose. In moments, I was inside.

I stood, listening: The room was empty, and I thought the house as well. As I turned to pull down the window, something brushed against my toe; when the window was down (unlatched, in case of need for a brisk exit) I bent and switched on my pocket torch. It was a tiny Japanese carving called a *netsuke*, a frog with an oddly expressive face and perfect details. I left it where it lay, and walked through his flat, making sure the rooms were empty. Which they were, although the missing razor and tooth-brush, the empty hangars, and the valise-sized gap on a bedroom shelf suggested that he had not merely stepped out for the evening.

Richard Sosa's home was a handsome, self-contained flat made from those portions of the building once given to the servants, although more opulent than one might expect of servants—or of a man with a secretary's income. Some of its opulence was that of old money—much of the furniture had descended from the house above, receiving fresh upholstery in the process. But those things that reflected Sosa's personal taste—the delicate Oriental ivory carvings, two new carpets, the paintings on the walls—had not been bought with a governmental salary.

On the table just inside the front door lay a card: Chief Inspector J. Lestrade, New Scotland Yard, with a telephone number and in his writing:

Please telephone at your earliest convenience.

Back in the first room, I checked the remaining curtains to be certain that no light would escape. The first was overlapped, but the second showed a slight gap. As I tugged them together, something fell to the floor: another tiny *netsuke*, a rabbit, ears flat against its back.

Cautiously, I peered behind the fabric of the remaining window with my hand obscuring the head of the torch, and saw a third carved figure, this one a sparrow, perched on the window's upper rim. Its balance was precarious, nearly half its circumference protruding past the painted wood. And when I loosened my fist to allow a trace more light to escape, I could see the trigger: a thread, attached to the curtains, looped around the sparrow's ivory neck. With my other hand, I pushed the fabric away from the window, and the *netsuke* fell, its weight pulling it out of the loop of thread.

Well, well: The grey little secretary had picked up a few tricks.

I looked over at the window I had come in by. Thick carpet lay underneath the window, but would I have missed the sound of an ivory frog falling to the floor? Possibly.

I returned the rabbit and the sparrow to their perches, but I did not bother to loop the thread back—any man with the foresight to set up a sign of intruders would also know the angle at which he had left his traps.

The creatures were unexpected, in two ways: an indication of considerable care and sophistication, and an inescapable note of whimsy. Mycroft's secretary was not so grey as he appeared.

I searched the place with a nit-comb, taking my time so as to leave no evidence of my presence. The constable's footsteps went past four times, every thirty-four to thirty-seven minutes, as I uncovered the secretary's life. His office suits ran the gamut from pure black to dark charcoal, the neck-ties included those of a minor public school, and his leisure wear leant heavily towards flannel and mildly patterned jumpers. His stocking drawer was occupied by ranks of folded pairs, none of them with holes in them. His undergarments had been ironed.

His bathroom cupboard said that he suffered from angina, for which he had been prescribed nitro-glycerine, as well as dyspepsia, ingrown toenails, migraines, and insomnia. He wore an expensive French pomade, and possessed a curious electrical instrument that looked like a torture device but which I decided was to stimulate the growth of hair follicles.

I found two art books that might at a stretch be termed erotica (on an upper shelf in the library), the playbill for a slightly raunchy revue (three years old and buried in a desk drawer), and some modernist sketches that might, perhaps to the mother living upstairs, be considered risqué. I found no drugs, and no sign of female company (actually, of any company at all).

The desk in his small, tidy study had a telephone and a leather-bound 1924 diary. I went through it closely, copying various times and numbers, but Sosa either was cautious about writing down too much information, or trusted himself to remember the essentials: Appointments were often just an initial and a time, sometimes "Dr H" or "dentist" and the time. Three times he had written down telephone numbers, two of those with an abbreviated exchange. The last of the three was on the Thursday that Mycroft disappeared, with the same exchange Mycroft had, although it was not Mycroft's number. I could simply ring the numbers, but without knowing what alarms might be set off, it might be best to leave the task of identifying the numbers to Holmes.

I returned the book to its position by the telephone, and turned my attention to his desk drawers. One of them held files, a number of which contained carbon copies of letters from Mycroft, the ornate capital *M* he used as a signature indicating that these were official duplicates, not mere draughts. They were addressed to the current and the last Prime Ministers, to the owner of a large newspaper, to several Members of Parliament. Reading them, I was reassured that the contents were not particularly inflammatory: Whatever Sosa's qualities, sheer carelessness was not among them.

In the end, this is what his home revealed:

The notes from his diary

Six new and expensive paintings on the wall

The business card of a very high-class art dealer

Another card, from a house whose reputation I knew, a mile away

An ingeniously concealed wall-safe with a lock that took me nearly two full passes of the constable to circumvent.

Inside the safe I found a velvet pouch with a palmful of large-carat diamonds, three stacks of high-denomination currency (British, French, and American), a number of gold coins, a file with memos and letters signed with Mycroft's distinctive *M*, and a bank book dating back to 1920.

The file included a trio of carbon pages requesting information on Thomas Brothers and Marcus Gunderson. They were pinned to a copy of the Brothers photograph that Mycroft's Shanghai man had brought, and another of a glaring Marcus Gunderson.

The bank book was the most revealing. For years, the entries down the IN column varied little, and seemed to comprise his regular salary and periodic income from stocks and an inheritance fund. Until the past March, at which time round sums began to drop in at untidy intervals: twenty guineas here, thirty-five there. In the middle of June was one for a hundred guineas.

I had to smile sadly at the idiocy of criminals: caution and carelessness; locked doors beside vulnerable windows; scrupulously kept books recording illicit income.

Then I looked at the last page, and the smile died:

Friday 29 August: 500 guineas received.

The day after Mycroft disappeared.

Five hundred pieces of silver.

I left everything where I had found it: I had the name of the bank, the dates of the deposits—along with information on his art dealer, his newsagent, his housekeeper, his solicitor, and his mother. It would be of interest to examine the mother's account, although I did not imagine it would show those round sums in its OUT column.

It was nearly time for the constable to pass, so I stood at the curtains with my torch off, waiting for the deliberate footsteps.

Sosa was in his fifties, an age when some men looked up and saw not what they had, but what they lacked. This was particularly true when a man was under pressure—and between December and March, when Mycroft came back to work after his heart attack, the pressure on his assistant would have been considerable.

The major question in my mind was, when did Mycroft discover Sosa's hidden income, his secret life, his—call it what it had to be—treason?

It was hard to picture the grey man working day in, day out under Mycroft's very nose without giving himself away. But until this past month, I had not seen Mycroft since the early weeks after his attack, at which time he had been both ill and distracted. I could not deny the possibility, however remote, that he could have overlooked his secretary's treason until very recently.

Ten days ago Mycroft had talked to Sophy Melas about loyalty. *Where does faith part from loyalty?*

He knew then.

Did that knowledge get him killed?

Or had he known for some time, and done nothing, either because he was testing the limits of his secretary's betrayal, or—and this I could envision—because he was using Sosa to lay a trap for the man or men behind him? I could well imagine Mycroft keeping an enemy close for half a year in order to tease out the extent of a conspiracy. He might even have embraced the challenge of proving that his illness had not lessened his abilities: to work every day cheek-to-jowl with an enemy, blithely feeding him information, never letting slip once.

A Russian doll of a mind.

Had that hubris got him killed?

And was there any way in which Brothers entered this mix? There was no copy of the man's bible, *Testimony*, on Sosa's shelves, and I had not seen him in the Church of the Light services that I had attended. Was it possible that whoever was backing Thomas Brothers was also responsible for suborning Mycroft's secretary? As I'd told Billy, simultaneous timing did not prove consequence, but coincidence still bothered me.

The constable approached, then passed. I let myself out of the Sosa apartment, leaving the ivory frog where it lay, and managed to lock the window before I left.

Several late-plying taxis passed me on the walk to Baker Street, but sure knowledge of the conversation a taxi-ride would entail—either the driver would think a young woman out on her own at this time of night was no better than she should be, or he would wish to rescue her and watch over her every move until she disappeared through the doors of a house—forced me to walk, reminding myself at every step that I should dress as a man for every night-time expedition. However, the bolt-hole was not far out of the way from my next destination: I could effect a change there.

Under-slept, over-walked, and distracted is no way to approach a secret hide-out, and I was lucky the only person lying in wait was a blond imp, who dropped light-footed from a first-storey archway and scared me to death. I cursed him and came near to kicking him, and in an ill temper stalked towards the entranceway.

"Why are you out here?" I snapped. "Did you forget how to get in?"

"The city at night is a restful place," he said, which was no answer and was patently untrue—my own night in this city had hardly been restful. "I am happy to see that you were not arrested."

I looked up from the locking device, my eyes narrowed with suspicion. "How do you know what I've been doing tonight?"

"I don't. What have you been doing?"

"How—ah." I turned back to the lock: He was not talking about my house-breaking. "I neglected to tell you what was in that letter in Mycroft's flat. It would appear that the police have decided my husband

and I are no longer of official interest." I explained what the note had said, and who had sent it.

"So you can come out into the open? You and your husband?"

"Probably not. For one thing, it's possible that Lestrade might be thinking to lay a trap, either for us, or to lead him to Damian—my stepson, Yolanda's husband."

"Estelle's father," Goodman said, adding, "Who is too claustrophobic to go to gaol."

"Are you?" I asked. "Claustrophobic?"

"Not in the least."

"Good," I said, and opened the door to Holmes' bolt-hole, which was so snug and stuffy, a hibernating squirrel might become uncomfortable.

While Goodman set about exploring the nooks and crannies of the space carved into the interstices of the buildings, I did what I should have done on our earlier visit: Review the supplies and check the ventilation shaft, lest some bird had plugged it with a nest.

All was well: food, drink, electrical light, and air, along with entertainment in the form of books, a chess set, and playing cards. There was even a serviceable bathing facility, cramped but equipped with warm water diverted from the neighbouring building.

I showed Goodman where everything was, then told him, "If anything happens to block the entrance, the alternative exit is down here." He peered with lack of enthusiasm into the duct, but in an emergency, I felt certain, he would manage. "In the winter time it's a little tricky, because the building's furnace is at the bottom, but it should be fine for now."

"You are leaving again," he asked, although it was not a question.

"I have to speak with Lestrade. He may not be in charge of the investigation, but he'll have kept a close eye on its progress. I'm going to write a letter to Holmes before I go. If I'm wrong about Lestrade and he has me arrested, everything Holmes needs to know will be in the letter—if you see him, tell him it's here. But after that, I recommend you make your way as quickly as you can back to Cumberland. With, may I say, my considerable thanks."

I put him into the bedroom, warning him to turn on a light when he woke—even he might bash his skull by rising incautiously. When I was

alone, I changed my clothing, then sat down to record everything that
had happened since Estelle and I had parted from Holmes and Damian,
eight days before: the suggestive lack of police interest that night in
Orkney; the sniper in Thurso; the crash and rescue; five days in the Lake
District cut short by men with guns, and how they might have found us;
leaving Javitz and Estelle at the house in Richmond; what Billy had said
about the "hard men"; what I had found in Mycroft's flat (this I worded
with great care); the interview with Sophy Melas; and what Sosa's home
had told me.

I finished:

> I am going now to speak with Lestrade. I believe the sincerity of
> the note he left at Mycroft's.
>
> I may, of course, be wrong (yes, even I!) in which case you may
> need to stand me bail. However, I beg you, wait to do so until you
> have solved this case and ensured the safety of Damian and
> Estelle. I understand that one can get a great deal of mental work
> done in the confines of a cell.
>
> Finally, I commend to you Mr Robert Goodman, whose name
> might as well be Robin Goodfellow. A singular character whom
> I have no doubt will entertain you mightily.
>
> Your
> Russell

When I had finished, it came to six pages despite my attempt at suc-
cinctness. I then set about putting key sections of the thing into code: If
the letter was intercepted, Mycroft's sixteen inflammatory papers
would be safe enough, given my wording, but I did not care to give up
the location of Estelle Adler to unfriendly eyes. And there was no reason for Goodman to know that his innocent actions had betrayed us to
our enemies.

I folded the pages into an envelope, added Mycroft's letter, wrote Holmes'
name and our Sussex address on the front, and left it—stamped but un-
sealed—on the table.

Chapter 45

Chief Inspector John Lestrade lived in the house where he had been born, some forty-five years before. His father, also a Scotland Yard detective, had died during the War, bequeathing his son the house, a set of unfortunate facial features, a mind rather too quick for a policeman's desk, and a long-established relationship with that trouble-making amateur, Sherlock Holmes.

I had known for years where Lestrade lived, although I had not yet been inside the house. It was approaching three in the morning when I rounded a corner four streets down, stopping in the shadow of an overgrown lilac to survey the street.

Few watchers can keep still at three a.m. when nothing is happening. Even watchers too clever to light cigarettes still scuff their feet, move up and down, anything to alleviate the boredom of a fruitless watch.

I stood motionless for half an hour before I was certain that the stretch of front-doors and walled areas contained nothing more threatening than an amorous tabby cat atop a wall. Only then did I step into the open pavement, plodding and stooped with tiredness on the chance some insomniac was gazing from their window.

I continued up the rows of houses, then made a pair of right turns to survey the house's back: no service alley here, and a snuff and a tentative *whoof* returned my feet to motion—his neighbours had a dog.

Unfortunately, that left me with no choice but the direct approach.

I made another pair of right turns, and when I had reached the next house but two from Lestrade's, I hopped over the waist-high wall, hastily grabbing a bicycle toppled by the manoeuvre. The next low wall I took with more circumspection, creeping across the pavers to slip onto Lestrade's property.

The house was dark, as were all the houses save one three streets down. I moved noiselessly across the little forecourt to the door, grateful he did not leave a light burning there all night, and bent to work with my pick-locks.

Like most policemen, Lestrade was convinced of his invulnerability. The lock took me six minutes, working entirely by touch and hearing. When it gave way, I turned the knob and stepped inside, closing the door silently.

And stopped.

If it is difficult for a watcher to stand motionless, it is nearly impossible to remain utterly silent for more than a few seconds: the faint brush of clothing, the pull of breath through tense nostrils, the catch of air in the throat while the person tries to listen.

The hairs on my skin rose with the awareness of someone standing very close.

"Chief Inspector?" I said in a low voice.

A brief shift betrayed the other's position. I said, "I apologise for the intrusion, but it was important that I speak with you unseen. This is Mary Russell."

A sharp exhale of breath, the rustle of clothing, then the vestibule light blinded me.

I winced, and saw Lestrade: his thin sandy hair awry, his feet bare, in dressing gown and striped pyjamas, a cricket bat in his grip.

"I nearly took your head off," he said furiously. His low voice told me that either there were others sleeping in the house, or he too feared discovery. At this point, it did not matter.

"Good evening, Chief Inspector," I replied.

"Hardly evening. And what's good about waking to find someone breaking into the house?"

"You said at my earliest possible convenience. Which this is. I didn't want to wake your family."

"You triggered an alarm."

Perhaps I was hasty in judging Lestrade one of those too-confident policemen. "That note you left, at Mycroft's," I said. "Were you serious about withdrawing the warrants?"

He stared at me, shook his head in dismay, then leant the bat against the wall and stepped into a pair of beaten-down slippers left to one side. "Come in here, we can talk without disturbing my wife."

"Here" was the kitchen, two steps down towards the garden. I eyed the window, decided that to worry about his neighbours playing host to villains was to court paranoia, and continued down the steps. He indicated a chair. I sat.

"Have you eaten?" he asked, filling the kettle at the tap.

"Yes."

"Not been hiding out too badly, then?"

"Merely cautious. Were you serious—"

"Yes."

"What changed your mind?"

"I didn't like the idea of arresting you at a funeral. Besides, I wasn't entirely convinced in the first place that the threat served any purpose. Tea, or coffee?" The gas popped into life under the kettle.

"Uh, tea, thanks."

"Where's your husband?"

"I'm not sure. I haven't seen him in a week."

He dropped into a hard kitchen chair, looking tireder than a night's interrupted sleep could explain. "And Damian Adler?"

"Last I heard he was out of the country."

"What about the child?"

"She is safe."

His weariness snapped off. "You know where she is, then?"

"She's safe," I repeated, and before he asked again, I got in a question of my own, even though I was fairly certain of what the answer would be. "You're not in charge of the investigation around Mycroft?" Extraordinary, how difficult it was to use the words *death* and *murder* when it was personal.

"No. I'm sorry, by the way." He caught himself, and started again. "I mean to say, I was very sorry to hear of your loss. Mycroft Holmes was a fine man. He will be sorely missed. Which makes the whole thing all the harder."

"What is that? Who's in charge?"

"No one."

"I beg your pardon?"

"No one I know. It's being kept in-house, you might say. Seems that Mycroft Holmes is too important for the grubby likes of Scotland Yard."

I sat forward sharply. "Would you please explain?"

"I wasn't on duty, Wednesday night. The man who was got the call at a quarter to midnight: man found dead in an alley. Gets dressed, goes with the car, arrives, and finds a man in a suit there before him, flashing the kind of identity card you can go your entire career without once seeing. This fellow hands over the papers found on the corpse, tells my colleague that Intelligence takes care of its own, and leaves. Taking the body with him. My fellow scratches his head, can't think what to do about it, and goes back to his bed."

" 'Intelligence takes care of its own'—that's what he said?"

"The very words. I didn't hear about it until the next day. When I did..."

The kettle had begun to boil. He stood and went to the stove, pulling down tea and pot, keeping his back to me. "I had him in for questioning, ten days ago—Mycroft Holmes, that is. The very next morning, his housekeeper is raising a stink because he's not home. Nobody sees him for a week, until he's found in an alleyway, then snatched away by someone flashing SIS papers. So I get on the telephone and start hunting down the body. Twenty minutes later, my chief comes in and orders me to stop."

He finished making the tea in silence, fetched a bottle of milk in silence, brought two mugs to the table in silence.

I blew across the hot surface, thinking. Then: "Why were you at Richard Sosa's flat?"

"Who?" His face showed a moment of incomprehension, followed by puzzlement, as if he'd recognised the name but couldn't think why I had brought it up.

"Richard Sosa. In Mayfair? You left your card on the table?"

"I leave my card on a lot of tables. It's a steady drain on the finances, it is."

"But why were you there?"

"Oh, for—" He threw up his hands and reached for the sugar pot, flinging in two spoonsful, clearly irritated by a non sequitur. "He's a government employee with a busybody of a mother who is friends with the sorts of people you might imagine, living in Mayfair as she does. She got all in a tizzy when little Dickie didn't come home one night, and got onto the PM's office and he himself rang to me—at home, mind you—the next morning asking if I'd do him a favour and look into this missing-person case. Ridiculous—and to top it off, the son hadn't even been gone a day! But I went past on my way in, got the key from Mama, who lives upstairs, made sure her darling boy wasn't lying in a puddle of blood, left my card on his table, and told her she could report him as a missing-person the next day. Friday. Two hours later I'm in my office after one of the most unpleasant meetings I've ever had and the telephone rings and it's the butler—the butler!—ringing to say never mind, the boy's home. Not even Mama herself, and nothing resembling an apology. Biddies like her cause us a lot of trouble. Now are you going to tell me why you want to know about him, or are we going to go on to another completely unrelated crime?"

"Richard Sosa is Mycroft's secretary."

He stared at me. "Mycroft Holmes' *secretary*?"

"His right-hand man. Which may be a better explanation of why you were asked to look into his disappearance than a mother's connexions."

"Jesus," he said.

"You're certain he was home on Thursday?"

"Like I said, the butler rang. I did then ring back the house—Mrs Sosa's number—to make sure the call actually came from there. When the same voice answered, I let it go. Why, is he still gone?"

"I think someone broke into his house recently, causing him to panic and run." I described briefly the *netsuke* I had found, well aware that I was delivering myself up to yet more charges. How many books was one permitted in a gaol cell? I wondered.

"He's not staying there, and you say his mother has not seen him. Without going into too many of the sorts of details you might prefer not to hear, I can say that Sosa has information about Brothers in his safe, and his bank book records some hefty payments of nice round sums. Including one for five hundred guineas dated the day after Mycroft disappeared. One must ask oneself what the man knows."

He sat back in his chair, frowning. "That's a considerable sum."

"Mycroft was a considerable man."

"You think the secretary was paid to give him up?"

"I think you might like to talk to Sosa. And although the mother obviously frets when he doesn't come home, and one might ask if she made occasional gifts to her son, something Mycroft once said about Sosa indicated that he and his mother don't get on very well."

He looked thoughtful, rather than convinced. However, I had another question for him. "Chief Inspector, can you tell me if you've had news of a death in Orkney? Specifically, at the Stones of Stenness."

"A death? When?"

"A week ago Friday."

"No. Although there was an odd report from up there. What was it? A prank? That's right, some boys set a fire that sounded like gunfire, but when the local constable arrived he found only scorch-marks. Why? Who did you think had died?"

It was confirmation of what I had feared: The lack of police interest at the Stones that night was because there was no body. Which meant that, unless someone had retrieved his dead body almost instantaneously, Brothers remained an active threat. Perhaps more than active: Having his intentions for Transformation crushed would surely add a thirst for revenge to his murderous plans.

I did not answer directly. Instead I asked, "Do you still think Damian Adler murdered his wife?"

"What *is* the interest you two have in that young man?" he demanded.

I was glad to hear the question, since it meant he did not know who

Damian was. "As you are aware, Chief Inspector, Holmes attracts a wide variety of clients, including bohemian artists. Do you—"

"I need to question Adler. You need to tell him he's not helping himself any by avoiding us."

"I swear to you, Chief Inspector, that Damian Adler is not the man you are looking for in his wife's death."

"Well, he's certainly not the only one I'm looking for." He picked up the tea-pot to refill his cup. "I don't suppose you know where I might find this Brothers maniac either?"

"So you *are* looking for Brothers now?"

He slammed the tea-pot onto the table so hard liquid spurted from its spout, and snarled, "He's connected with two people dead of knife wounds and a third from gunshot, so yes, you might say I'm looking for him."

I protested, "Chief Inspector, we tried to tell you about Brothers and his church weeks ago. Don't—"

"Yes, and now everywhere I go, I'm tripping over you two. You're in Brothers' church; your finger-prints are all over his house, including a knife left stabbed through the desk blotter; you have the police in York ring me up to ask if I might shed some light on one of their deaths; and you bundle a villain like Marcus Gunderson into a carpet and have me come pick him up."

"A villain whom you then let go."

"What did I have to hold Gunderson on? He was the victim of assault in that house."

"Do you know anything about the man?"

"He's a thug. Spent some time in the Scrubs for robbery—bashed his upstairs neighbour and stole his cash retirement fund. Gunderson was lucky the old man had an iron skull, or it would've been a murder charge—but since then, he's been clean, as far as I can see."

"Do you know if he's familiar with guns? Not just revolvers, but rifles?"

"He wasn't in the Army. And hunting? Not likely for a city boy. Why?"

"Someone took a shot at me, a few days ago. Someone either very lucky or well trained with a rifle."

"And you think it was Gunderson? What, at the orders of Brothers?"

"Brothers looks to be behind everything else we've faced since we returned to the country." Precisely twenty-seven days ago—had I ever had a more hectic four weeks?

"Yes, and you keep saying that Adler has nothing to do with it, but then I find that he's done artwork for Brothers' book, and his wife was a devout follower of Brothers' crank religion—" (So he did not know that Yolanda had actually been married to the man.) "—and I've seen at least three paintings he did of Brothers—one that his wife had on her wall, another in Brothers' house, and a third in the gallery that's selling his paintings. So you can't tell me there isn't some kind of link between Adler and Brothers."

"Of course there's a link—Brothers is trying to kill him!"

"So help me stop it."

"Chief Inspector, I do not know where Damian Adler is, and the last I saw of Brothers was in Orkney last Friday, when he tried to murder Damian and was injured in the attempt."

As soon as the words were out of my mouth, I kicked myself for giving away more than I absolutely had to. Lestrade leant slowly back in his chair, eyes narrowing; his expression had me reviewing the exits, for when he made a grab for my wrist.

"You want to tell me how you know that?"

"You want to tell me why you took Mycroft in for questioning?"

His expression shifted, from a hunter with his prey in sight to a guilty schoolboy. "What does that have to do with anything?"

"It has everything to do with it, Chief Inspector. You're Scotland Yard. Mycroft was . . . Well, he was Mycroft. What on earth drove you to make a move against Mycroft Holmes, of all people?"

"He was standing in the way of a police investigation," Lestrade said stubbornly.

I wished my eyes when they glared went grey and cold like Holmes' instead of light blue, bloodshot, and concealed by spectacles. "Your going after him was not only unlikely, it was uncharacteristic. Add to that my growing suspicion that Brothers has been receiving help from high places, and . . ." I waved a hand. "That's why I picked your lock at three in the morning rather than walking into your office."

Lestrade's face changed. "Are you accusing me of being a corrupt officer?"

"I would not be sitting here if I thought that. But it is clear that Brothers had help, and from someone other than Gunderson. Some person helped him set up a new identity in this country, back in November. Someone helped him cover up his deeds. I began to suspect it even though I've been on the run for the past two weeks. What I am asking is, did that person reach out to you as well, and influence you to intercept Mycroft's wires and invade his home?"

He stood abruptly and went to rummage through a drawer, coming out with a mashed-looking packet of cigarettes. He got one lit, and stood looking out the dark window. The stove clicked as it cooled; somewhere in the house, a clock chimed four.

"It's possible," he said finally. He came back to the table, his face closed. "I don't take bribes.

"But you want to know if someone got at me, if I gave in to pressure against my better thoughts. The answer is yes.

"Look," he continued, "I follow orders. The nature of my job gives me a great deal of independence, but when orders are given, I follow them. And something very near to being a command came down to put some pressure on Mycroft Holmes."

"Down from where?"

"Doesn't matter. It didn't originate with the man who gave it, which means it was high enough that it might have come from outside the Yard entirely. And frankly, I didn't ask too closely about it. Society only works if the police are given a free hand to investigate where they will. No one should be above the rule of law. Even him. You and Mr Holmes have walked the edge any number of times, but always managed to keep close enough inside the bounds that I could tell the difference between personal affront and official wrongdoing."

"Is that why you issued warrants for Holmes and me as well?"

"Not directly, but it helped move me in that direction. Truth to tell," he said, "it wasn't the first time I'd wanted to put handcuffs on your husband."

"I know the feeling," I said. He blinked, and laughed.

"This time, it was Mycroft Holmes walking the edge, and over. It didn't take much to convince me that it was time to snap him back into line. Your brother-in-law is not God, you know."

"A week ago, I might have disagreed," I said sadly—and indeed, his use of the present tense testified that Lestrade himself was not altogether willing to quit his belief in Mycroft's omniscience.

"However, I've come to wonder if I may have been wrong," he said.

"About his divinity?"

"About treating him as the object of an investigation." He clawed his fingers through his thinning hair. "Mycroft Holmes asked me to meet him privately, that same day he came into my office. He left at one o'clock. Twenty minutes later, I was handed a note that he'd left for me, telling me to meet him at the Natural History Museum, the statue of Charles Darwin, just before closing. He told me to keep it entirely to myself, and to come alone."

"But you didn't go?"

"In fact I did, although I'd put it off to the last possible instant. He wasn't there. The next I heard of him, he was dead."

Chapter 46

The thud of that word, *dead*. Inconceivable, inescapable, dead: Mycroft.

I shook away the memory of his prodigious appetite and more prodigious memory, and—

Tell no one.

Come alone.

Where does faith part from loyalty?

I looked at Lestrade, thinking, *Russell, you need some sleep, before you forget how to think.* "Did you, in the end, keep the meeting to yourself?"

"I did."

"Surely being instructed to come to a meeting alone must raise a policeman's suspicions? You weren't concerned that it might be some kind of a trap?"

"Had it been another man, I'd have been a fool not to tell someone where I was going. But this was Mycroft Holmes—I did check, and it was he who left the message. And although in theory I know nothing about him, in truth I know enough to be sure that if the man wanted to dispose of me, he hardly needed me to come to him. No, I figured the reason for the meeting was the same reason he couldn't tell me in my office."

"That being...?"

"One possibility was, he wanted to test me, either to see if I'd do as he asked, or because he wished to propose something so illegal it could bring down his career or mine, and didn't want to risk being overheard. Or, he suspected a traitor in the ranks."

I mentally apologised to the man in front of me, for Holmes' disparaging remarks over the years.

"Your ranks, or his?"

"I thought at the time he meant mine. Why else did he want to get me away from the Yard? And although I have considerable faith in the trustworthiness of my officers, the bald truth is, there's always an apple in any barrel ripe for spoiling. Bribery or threat—a determined man can usually find a police officer to corrupt."

"Do you still think it's one of yours?"

He raised an eyebrow at me, a look that would have been pure Holmes had his features not resembled those of a sleep-ruffled ferret. "I'm not the one going into the ground tomorrow," he pointed out brutally.

I blew out a slow breath. "It does make one rather wonder."

"About what?"

"Who could have got close enough to Mycroft for him to let down his guard."

"You think his organisation—whatever that might be—could have a traitor? Is that why you asked about Sosa?"

"Mycroft was talking to a friend recently, and out of the blue, brought up the topic of loyalty. Who better to betray a man than his secretary? And what more painful treason?"

"What friend was that?"

I shook my head. "Mycroft passed on no information, merely indicated that the idea of loyalty had been on his mind."

"I need to know who he was talking to," he said sharply.

"I'm sorry, Chief Inspector, I am not going to tell you. You'll simply have to trust that if there had been anything more substantial to learn, I'd give it to you."

He mashed out the cigarette stub with unwonted violence, and snapped, "Tying my hands like this, we might as well turn the country over to the SIS and let us all go back to being rural bobbies."

"I think we'll find there're ways around it. You were asked to investigate Sosa's disappearance. Surely you would be expected to follow that up, until you can speak with the man himself?"

He looked at me. "I could lose my job." It was less objection than observation.

"I hope that's all you could lose."

He snorted in disbelief. "I'm Scotland Yard—they come after me with paperwork, not weapons."

"And Mycroft?"

After a moment, his eyes involuntarily flicked upwards, towards his sleeping family.

"Yes," I said.

"But Sosa is a secretary!"

"I was not thinking directly of Sosa. But it may be that someone has control over Sosa. Someone who has his hand on Scotland Yard as well."

"But who? And why Mycroft Holmes?"

I could think of any number of nations who would pay to end Mycroft's meddling. Sixteen of whom had written explosive letters currently resting beside Mycroft's oven. But without facts, I might as well throw darts at a spinning globe.

"That's what I need to find out. First off, can you find out more about Sosa?"

"I can try."

"And beyond that?"

"I'll be locked out of anything with international significance."

"Which is interesting, considering Reverend Brothers spent so many years in Shanghai."

Lestrade rolled his eyes. "Brothers again."

"If Mycroft's death and Sosa's disappearance are not *somehow* tied in with the machinations of Reverend Brothers, I may be forced to believe in coincidence. I'll never be able to look my husband in the face again."

Lestrade picked up his empty cup, and put it down again. "Do you want a drink? Hard drink, I mean?"

"No thanks. You have one, though."

"If I went to church with whisky on my breath, my wife would leave me. Look, maybe you're right. I'll see how far I can get before someone pushes back. That should tell us something."

"But about Mycroft. If I don't have to worry about being arrested, there's nothing to stop me from going to his superiors and asking what they know about Sosa, is there?" Nothing other than sharpshooters and hard men.

"God knows *I've* never been able to stop you from asking questions. I'm not sure how they would like it."

"What, a bereaved private citizen, broken-hearted over her brother-in-law's death, concerned that his assistant—to whom Mycroft was very close—might be even more troubled?"

He came very near to laughing, and said in admiration, "It's not a track I'd have thought of, but I wish you luck with it."

I glanced at the window, wondering if the darkness was less profound than it had been. Should I ask him to trace the telephone numbers? No: If he decided to search Sosa's flat, he would find the numbers himself. "One last thing. I know that, theoretically speaking, you have no knowledge of Mycroft's work. However, have you any idea how I might get into touch with a colleague of his by the name of Peter West? I think he may work for the SIS, and he may be more willing to talk than Admiral Sinclair would be."

"I've heard of him, haven't met him."

"I'd like to reach him before Monday."

"It might take some doing to hunt down an Intelligence fellow on a weekend."

"If you can locate West without having anyone take notice, it would be good if I could talk with him before the funeral. However, don't draw any more attention to yourself than you must." I drained my cup and stood, but he remained stubbornly in his chair.

"Miss Russell, I really need to speak with Damian Adler."

"I swear to you, Chief Inspector, I do not know where he is."

"And his daughter?"

"I am keeping her safe."

I looked at his tired face, feeling badly for having robbed him of what

little sleep he might have expected this night. However, giving him talk-
ative little Estelle would be giving him the information that Damian was
Holmes' son. And until Damian was safe, until he was no longer regarded as a suspect, I could not risk that.

I put out my hand. "Thank you, Chief Inspector."

He looked at it, then stood and took it. "Ring me later. I'll see if I can
come up with an address for Mr West."

"Thank you."

"And, Miss Russell? Watch yourself. Brothers and Gunderson are still
out there, to say nothing of Sosa's lot. All in all, a number of people you
don't want to be meeting in a dark place."

"I rarely want to meet anyone in a dark place, Chief Inspector," I
replied. At the door, I let him open it for me, then paused. "Will you be
at the funeral this afternoon?"

"I will."

"Thank you," I said. And astonished us both by leaning forward to kiss
his unshaved cheek.

Chapter 47

New experiences were salutary, Holmes reflected. In four decades of creeping through the back-streets and by-ways of London, he had never had quite such an unrelenting series of setbacks, and although his body might protest at being folded up into its narrow recess a dozen feet above the paving-stones, no doubt it was good for him to be challenged. He wished that, in exchange, he might learn a bit more about his pursuers than he had so far.

Take the man who had been waiting on the pier at Harwich.

The man had been standing among those waiting to greet the boat, but it would have taken a larger crowd than that to conceal his presence: large, alert, and armed.

Holmes saw him, and kicked himself for not having anticipated the problem. Short of an hour with make-up (neither of which he possessed) and a change of clothing (almost as difficult) there was no way of getting down the gangway without being seen. Which left him with two options: Stay on board and return to Holland, or use another exit.

The steamer's lavatories were conveniently near the exit, and its attendant had gone to assist with the disembarking process. When the last gentleman had finished, it was the work of moments to set a fire blazing in the waste bin (placing it by itself amidst the tiles, since he had no wish to burn the ship to the water-line) and slip away.

When the alarm was raised, every crew member within shouting distance responded at the run, leaving several tills unguarded. Holmes helped himself and made for the lower decks.

A sad story to a likely face (about a bill collector waiting on the docks, to a man whose nose bloomed with the veins of strong drink) and one of his stolen bills into a meaty palm, and Holmes became an honorary member of the crew off-loading Dutch goods and passenger rubbish.

He pulled on his newly acquired jacket and a cap he fervently hoped was not inhabited, then set a large bag of post onto his shoulder and joined the trail of laden men, trudging along the gangway, down the pier, and past the watcher. Few passengers trickled off the steamer now, and the feet beneath the tan coat—which were all Holmes could see of him around the burden—moved restlessly. Holmes moved down the boards to deliver his sack to His Majesty's waiting lorry, then kept walking, along the front to a warehouse. There he found a place where he could watch the watcher.

The man waited long after the last passenger came off, but he did not, Holmes was interested to see, then go on board and conduct a search. This could mean he had no authority to do so, or that he had been told not to draw attention to himself. On the other hand, it could indicate an excess of confidence in his own invisibility and his quarry's lack of skill.

Eventually, the man abandoned his position and strode down the pier. Holmes eyed the few remaining taxis, but the man did not turn towards them, nor towards the nearby parked motorcars. Instead, he went into the hotel directly across the way.

Checking out? Having a meal? Reluctantly, Holmes settled into his corner, but in the end, the man was back out on the street in four minutes, and walked directly to a car parked on the front. Holmes readied himself for a sprint to the taxis, but to his surprise, the man walked around to the passenger side, tossed in his hat and coat, and got in. There was a flash of white: a newspaper.

He was waiting for the next steamer.

Holmes stayed in the shadows.

Half an hour later, a boat drew in, but the man merely leant forward to see where it was docking, then went back to his paper.

He was not waiting for just any steamer, but specifically the next one

from Holland. Which would be the boat from Amsterdam, arriving in—
Holmes checked his pocket-watch—approximately two and a half hours.
Adding the forty minutes the man had waited before abandoning his
watch the last time, that gave a tired and hungry detective nearly three
hours in which to assemble the materials he required.

Holmes turned and went into the town.

He returned two and a quarter hours later, stomach filled, beard
trimmed, wearing a clean shirt, carrying the tools he needed to break
into the watcher's motorcar.

The motorcar was gone.

The old man in the tea stand informed him that the big man in the
tan great-coat had gone into the hotel, then come out and left in a hurry,
less than half an hour before. A telephone call, Holmes thought.

Another trail lost.

The delay in Harwich cost him five hours, and his residual wariness
drove him to take a most indirect path to London. An eleven-hour trip
from the Hook of Holland to Liverpool Street took nearer to twenty-
four, landing him in town well after dark on Saturday at London Bridge
station, which he judged to be nearly as unexpected for a traveller out of
Holland as it was inconvenient. And to prove it, there were no large men
lurking near the exits.

Nonetheless, things soon became very interesting, which was how he
found himself in a walled-up window, twelve feet above the ground.

Because of the question about the safety of telephones—any organisation capable of manipulating Scotland Yard would have no trouble
buying the services of telephone exchange operators—he had not tried
to reach Billy beforehand. He set off from the London Bridge station on
foot, keeping to the darker streets.

Even with all his senses at the alert, they nearly had him.

He was standing across the street from Billy's house, wondering if the
darkness of its windows and the lack of sound from within were possible
on a Saturday night, when the blast of a constable's whistle broke from
a window over his head. One glance at the men who emerged from both

ends of the street told him that, whistle or no, these were not the police—and then he was running.

Sherlock Holmes was unaccustomed to having difficulties making his way around London. He once knew intimately all the patterns and sensations of the city (although he had never much cared for the image of a spider web that the great romanticist Conan Doyle insisted on using) and in any neighbourhood within miles of the Palace, he knew the doors left ajar, the passageways that led nowhere, the stairways that gave onto rooftops, the opium dens full of men who would be blind for a trace of silver across their palms.

Then came the War, and the aerial bombing, and the inexorable changes in the city during the years since. He'd been retired for two decades now, and loath as he was to admit it, the speed with which life changed was growing ever faster. Added to eight months of absence from his home, it was making him feel like a man resuming a language once spoken fluently, whose nuances had grown rusty.

He did not care for the sensation, not in the least. And although the older parts of Southwark were little changed, even here his urban geography proved to be ever-so-slightly out of date, gracing a long-disused alleyway with builder's rubbish, filling an easily prised window with brick. He was grateful the builders had taken the short-cut of bricking the hole in from within, which left just enough of a sill outside for a precarious perch.

Perhaps it was time to acknowledge that his city had passed to other hands.

A figure appeared at the end of the passageway; a torch-beam snapped on. The man saw the scaffolding and came to give it closer consideration, not thinking to do the same to the walls on the opposite side. Holmes kept absolutely still, willing the man to come closer, to stand below him—but then a second torch approached, and this man went to join his partner.

When the passageway was empty again, Holmes cautiously shifted until he was sitting on the ledge, his long legs dangling free. When his circulation was restored, he eyed the ghostly lines of the scaffold. Instead, he wormed his way around and climbed sideways, following a route that he had practiced under the tutelage of a cat-burglar, twenty-three years before. In five minutes, he was on the roof; in forty, when the first faint light of Sunday's dawn was rising in the east, he was crossing Waterloo Bridge.

Not altogether shabby for a man of his years, working under outdated information.

Still, the day had proved sobering. He'd told Dr Henning that he had resources in London, were he only able to reach them, but with all else that had changed in this city, he was beginning to wonder if that was true. Lestrade bought off, Mycroft under arrest, even Billy driven from his house and his neighbourhood taken over. Would this new Prime Minister—a Socialist, after all—see Sherlock Holmes as a living fossil? If he could make it through the guards at the Palace...

No, he would not play that card unless he had no other.

He was free, fit, and on home ground. He paused at the end of the bridge, looking upstream. As the light strengthened, he could see the Embankment path, and in the farther distance, Ben's tower riding over the bulk of the Houses of Parliament and the brick monstrosity of New Scotland Yard. However, his eyes looked not at those centres of authority, but at the Underground entrance that stood, waiting.

Four stops up the Metropolitan Rail line to Baker Street. Half an hour to reassure himself that Russell had made it to Town, that she and the child were safe.

And if he did not appear? She would remain where she was as long as possible; when she did emerge, she would be even more cautious than usual.

He turned his back on the Metropolitan line. There was much to do before the funeral.

Chapter 48

Back at the bolt-hole, I found Goodman reading in front of a low-burning fire. He rose, stretching like a young whippet, and dropped the book onto the chaise longue.

"You look tired," he observed.

"Very."

"I, on the other hand, am rested and in need of air. I shall return."

I started to protest, then decided against it. Even two or three hours of sleep would make all the difference to the day. And after all, no one in the city was looking for Robert Goodman: He was the one person among us who could walk with impunity among police constables and hard men alike, invisible in his innocence. If he had wanted to give Estelle and Javitz to the police, he'd have done so long before this; as for leading the police back here—deliberately or inadvertently—I was safe, as he could have no idea where the back exit debouched.

I changed my protest to a nod, and reminded him to check his surroundings with care before he stepped into or out of the hidden entrance.

As I curled up on the sofa with the travelling rug, I wondered where in this almighty city Holmes might be hiding. I noticed my certainty, and smiled: I had not even questioned that he would be here.

Then the smile faded. If Mycroft lay cold in his coffin, who among us was safe?

* * *

When I woke, the coals were grey, the building was silent, and there was no sign of Goodman. I glanced at the clock, and saw to my surprise that it was nearly ten: I had slept almost five hours.

I took a cursory bath and dressed, and still no Goodman. As I took up the pen to write a note, telling him that I would be back shortly, I saw that the letter I had written to Holmes was not on the table. I had not been so heavily unconscious that I would not have heard him pass through, which meant that Goodman had taken it with him when he left.

Why?

I could think of no reason that did not make me uneasy. On the other hand, I could think of nothing Goodman had done or said to threaten betrayal. Perhaps he'd decided to deliver it himself—he knew where the funeral was. I shook off my apprehension, then walked the exit route nearly to its end before diverting into the adjoining building.

The surgeon's offices might well shut down their telephones with close of business on Friday, but on the other side was a firm of solicitors, some of whom had been known to come in on a weekend. Fortunately, none of the desks were filled with a hard-working junior partner; equally fortunately, the telephone earpiece emitted a lively buzz. So I helped myself to a desk in one of the more impressive offices, dragged a London telephone directory onto the blotter, and phoned Lestrade.

I'd caught him going out, he said, but before I could apologise, he told me to wait a minute. Footsteps crossed the floor, and I heard his voice and those of two females, one older and one young. I heard him say that they were to go ahead, he'd join them as soon as he'd finished this telephone conversation.

The voices retreated, a door closed. The footsteps came back.

"That's better," he said.

"I'm sorry to keep you from church," I said. "I was only wondering if you'd found a telephone number or an address for Mr West?"

"It took some time, the gentleman doesn't appear to want casual callers. The telephone number's more difficult, that has to wait until tomorrow."

"Whom did you have to ask?"

"Don't worry," he said, "my wife has an old friend who works with the voters' registration lists, she popped into the office for me and looked him up. She'll say nothing."

He gave me an address across the river from Westminster. I wrote it down, and remarked, "That doesn't seem very likely."

"I know, there's not many houses down there, but you'll always find one or two residences even in that sort of district."

"I'll try it," I said, and told him I hoped he enjoyed the sermon. A glance at the solicitor's clock told me I had plenty of time to stop at West's address before the funeral.

But first, another telephone call, this one to Richmond.

The butler answered. After a minute or two of silence, Javitz's loud American accents were assaulting my ear.

"Yeah? Is that Mary Russell?"

"Hello, Captain Javitz, I thought—"

"You gotta get us out of here," he said sharply. "Like, now."

Cold air seemed to blast through the stuffy office, and I found I was on my feet. "Why? What's happened?"

"You know who your crazy hermit Goodman is?"

"I know whose house that is, but—"

"But you don't know who *he* is?"

"No, who is he?"

"I'd have thought—oh, look, I really can't go into it here. Just, how soon can you come get us?"

"Hours. I don't know the train schedule."

"Then the kid and I are setting off now, we'll be at Waterloo when we can."

"Wait! You can't set off on crutches, you'll hurt yourself."

"I'm not staying here. Get a car and come."

"For heaven's sake, what *is* going on?"

"One hour, we leave." The instrument went dead.

I swore, and looked at my wrist-watch: It had to be twenty-five miles, even if I left this instant . . . But first, one last call.

"The Travellers' Club," the voice answered.

"I'm looking for Captain Lofte." Lofte was my last hope, this fleet-footed traveller from Shanghai, Mycroft's man who had given us key information about Brothers. No one working with Brothers would have given us what Lofte did.

"I'm sorry," the smooth voice said, "Captain Lofte is no longer with us."

For a horrible moment, I thought the man meant—but he went on. "I do not think he will be returning for some time."

"Has he gone back to Shanghai?"

"I am sorry, Madam, but The Travellers' does not divulge the destination of its members."

"This is terribly important," I begged.

Something in my voice must have taken him aback, because after a moment's silence, he said, "He left a week past. I believe the gentleman had a message on the Friday, directing him to return to the East."

Rats, I thought; Lofte would have made a resourceful colleague. Billy was beyond reach, Holmes was gone, none of Mycroft's other agents were beyond taint. I should have to make do with what I had. Namely, myself.

I thanked the person at the club, put up the earpiece, and scurried back into the bolt-hole to cram a valise with everything I thought I might need.

Goodman had not returned. I thought of leaving him another note, but couldn't decide what that should say. So I shut off the lights and stepped into the corridor—and then I stopped.

My hand went to the pocket in which I was collecting all the bits concerning the case, and thumbed through the scraps until I found the notes I'd made in Richard Sosa's flat.

A number jumped out at me, because I'd just rung it. Sosa had written down the number of The Travellers' Club on Thursday, on the diary page beside the telephone. And, I thought, he rang the number, either then or on the Friday, to send out of the country the only person apart from Holmes and me who could link Mycroft to the investigation of Thomas Brothers.

I hoped to God he'd only sent Lofte away. I did not want that valiant individual on my conscience as well.

Somewhere in the building, a clock chimed the quarter. I woke with a start, and hurried down to the street to hail a taxicab.

Chapter 49

Javitz was standing outside the gates of the house on the quiet and dignified road, a large, bruised man looking very out of place with a small girl on one side and a white-haired housekeeper on the other. He leant heavily on his crutch, the child kicked her heels from the top of the low wall, the woman was wringing her hands. He had acquired an elderly carpet-bag, now lying at his feet; his hand was on the taxicab's doorhandle before the hand-brake was set.

"Come on, 'Stella-my-heart," he said, sounding more like a father than a man on whom a stray had been pressed. She hopped down and scrambled into the taxi, Dolly in hand, to stand at my knees and demand, "Where is Mr Robert?"

"I don't really know," I told her. "Mr Jav—"

She cut me short. "But he was with you. When will he come back?"

"He didn't tell me," I said. "Mr Javitz, do you need a hand?"

By way of answer he threw his bag and crutch inside and hopped against the door frame to manoeuvre himself within.

"I want to see him," Estelle persisted.

"But sir," the housekeeper was saying.

"I'll do what I can," I said to Estelle. "Here, let's pull the seat down for you."

"Terribly good of you to put up with us," Javitz was saying to the woman. "We have to be away, see you around."

And then both his legs were inside and he was shutting the door in her face.

The driver slid down the window to ask where we wanted to go, and I merely told him to head back towards London while we decided. He slid up the window. I turned to Javitz.

"What on earth was all that about?"

He cast an eloquent look at Estelle, who blinked her limpid eyes at me and said, "That means he doesn't want to talk in front of me. Papa looks like that sometimes."

"I imagine he does," I said. "Does your Papa also tell you that you're too bright for your own good?"

"Sometimes. *I* don't think a person can be too bright, do you?"

"Certainly too bright for the convenience of others," I said, then told Javitz, "I'm not sure where to take you. They could be watching my friends' houses. For sure they'll be keeping an eye on the local hotels. I even tried to reach Mr Lofte, who struck me as a valuable ally in any circumstances, but he's gone back to Shanghai."

"Do you know yet who this mysterious 'they' is?" he asked.

It was my turn to cast a significant "not in front of the children" glance at the small person on the seat across from us. She rolled her eyes in disgust and looked out of the window.

"What about a park?" Javitz suggested in desperation.

A park it would have to be. It had the advantage of being one of the last places any enemy of Mary Russell's would expect to find her on a Sunday morning.

I paid the driver, unloaded my crew, and we set off slowly across the manicured paths on what was surely one of the last sunny week-ends of this lingering summer. Estelle tipped her head up at us and asked in a long-suffering voice, "You probably want me to go away, don't you?"

"Not too far," I agreed.

She turned away with a soft sigh, but I dropped the carpet-bag and said, "Estelle?"

She turned, and I knelt down and, cautiously, put my arms around her. She flung hers around me and held on for a long time, the only sign she'd given of being frightened or lonely. I murmured in her little ear, telling her that I hoped we'd see her Papa soon, and that she'd meet her Grandpapa. That she was a very brave and clever girl, and her parents would be as proud of her as I was. That she'd have to be patient, but I was working hard to straighten everything out. When she finally let go of me, there was a bounce in her step.

Javitz had settled gingerly onto a bench.

"How is the leg?" I asked him, sitting down beside him.

He stretched it out with a grimace, which he denied by saying, "Not too bad," then modified by adding, "Getting better, anyway."

"I am so sorry about all of this."

"Hey, not to worry. The War didn't stop altogether with Armistice."

"Yes, but you were hired for a piloting job, not as nurse-maid to a small child."

"Yeah, well, you did hire me to help you save the kid and her father," he pointed out cheerfully. "That's more or less what I'm doing." Why was he sounding so hearty, I wondered? Over the telephone he'd been in a state of agitation.

"This whole thing is taking rather longer than I'd anticipated."

"I have nothing else on at the moment. Couldn't fly for a while, now, anyway."

"Again, sorry."

"You didn't crash the crate, I did."

"After someone took a shot—" I stopped; this was getting us nowhere. "What did you need to tell me about Robert Goodman?"

"That's not his name."

"I never imagined it was."

"Then you know who he is?"

I shook my head, since the family whose house we had motored away from was one I did not know personally and Holmes had neither investigated, nor investigated for. "I'd have to look him up in *Debrett's*."

"The Honourable Winfred Stanley Moreton. His father's an earl."

"Should I know him?"

"His name was all over the newspapers this spring."

"I've been out of the country. What did he do?"

"He's nuts!"

"That, too, is fairly self-evident."

"I don't mean just cheerfully fruitcake, I mean loony-bin nuts. Straight-jacket and locked doors nuts. And, he's a fairy."

Since for days now I'd been thinking of Goodman as Puck, this assessment hardly surprised me. However, it appeared that was not what Javitz meant.

"And, he was involved in a murder, with one of his fairy friends."

That word got my attention.

"Murder? Goodman?"

"His name is—"

"Yes, yes. He was tried for murder?"

"This spring. Well, no, not him, but a friend of his—Johnny McAlpin—was tried for murder, and everyone seemed to think that Goodman—Moreton—knew more about it than he was saying."

"Mr Javitz, you really need to explain this to me."

He tried, but the legal details were rather fuzzy in his mind. The sensational details, however, were quite clear.

The death itself had occurred in the summer of 1917, in Edinburgh. The victim was a middle-aged man well known as an habitué of the sorts of clubs where the singers are boys dressed up as girls. The murder went unsolved all those years, until this past January, when the newly jilted boyfriend of Johnny McAlpin started telling his friends how McAlpin had once drunkenly bragged about killing the man and getting away with it.

The police heard, and arrested McAlpin. He, in an attempt to spread the blame as thinly as possible, named every friend he could think of— including Win Moreton, who was among those dragged in to testify.

Bearded and wild-haired and sounding more than a little unbalanced, Goodman made quite a splash on the stand. He refused to acknowledge the name "Moreton," would say only that McAlpin had once been his friend, and was narrowly saved from being gaoled for contempt of court when his sister brought to light a file concerning her brother's history: Moreton had indeed known McAlpin, the two men having both drunk at the same pub during April and May, 1917, but Moreton had left Edinburgh in June, three weeks before the murder, and there was no evidence that he had been back.

Moreton was a decorated hero, in Edinburgh for treatment of shell shock that spring, but had never been violent even at his most disturbed.

McAlpin alone was convicted. However, the trial of the Honorable Winfred Moreton in the court of public opinion, had been both loud and unequivocal: He had to be guilty of something, and murder would do as well as any other charge.

The story itself sounded more colourful than factual, so I finally interrupted Javitz to ask how he'd heard all this.

He bent down and pulled an oversized envelope from the carpet-bag, thrusting it into my hands. I unlooped the fastener and looked in at a mess of pages, newspaper clippings, letters, and pocket diaries. I eased a few out of the pile, and read enough to catch the drift of their meaning.

Meanwhile, Javitz was explaining how he had come across this, after the boy in the house had told him who "Goodman" was: He'd gone to the butler who took him to the housekeeper who showed him a clipping she kept in one of her ledgers and then, when he demanded to know more, led him to the butler's pantry and the collection in the envelope.

"You stole this?" I asked.

"Borrowed it—send it back to them if you want. But I needed you to see, and understand." The earlier heartiness had gone; he shifted, his leg troubling him.

I closed the envelope, trying to follow the currents. I felt that Javitz was honestly concerned at the idea of permitting a madman and accused murderer near Estelle. I also thought that he was more than a little worried at letting a man with dubious relationships near to his own person. I couldn't imagine what threat the five-and-a-half-foot-tall Goodman might be to a strapping six-footer, but sex and sensibility do not always go hand in hand.

Beyond his concern, however, I thought I detected traces of embarrassment, which I had seen in him before. He was a captain in the RAF, a hero and man of action, who had permitted me to shove him to the back with the children. That he had uncomplainingly set aside his personal dignity for the sake of a child—and moreover, continued to do so—was a sign of his true valiant nature. Reasoned argument would be no help, since his mind was already delivering that. I needed a means of permitting the man to retain his self-respect.

I let his story and his explanation fade away, watching Estelle solemnly constructing a Dolly-sized hut out of some twigs and dry grasses. Then I sat back.

"I can't tell you whether these newspaper charges are substantiated, although I'll find out. However, we still need to decide where to put you—and, if you honestly don't mind, Estelle. It shouldn't be for more than a day, at the most two."

He settled a bit, which allowed his embarrassment to come closer to the surface. When he realised I was not about to accuse him of cowardice or point out his irrational fear of a man who had never so much as looked at him sideways, he relaxed. Suddenly he sat up and dug out his watch. "You have to be at the funeral in, what, three hours?"

"A little more than that."

"Then you don't have time to spend on me and the kid," he said.

I exhaled in relief: If assuaging his guilt drove him to volunteer for nanny duty, who was I to argue? I hastened to assure him, "Three hours is plenty. Tell me, how do you feel about Kent?"

It took me half an hour to locate a taxi with a driver who was not only taciturn, but willing to take a fare all the way to Tunbridge Wells. I put on an American accent and explained that my injured brother was shy of conversation but willing to pay generously for silence, and that he and his daughter needed to go to the largest hotel in the town. Tunbridge Wells was a watering hole and tourist destination busy enough to render even this unusual pair—large American male and tiny Eurasian child— slightly less than instantaneously the centre of attention.

I told Javitz to explain to the concierge that the luggage had gone astray on the ship, and gave him enough cash to clothe and feed himself and the child for two days, as well as distribute the sorts of tips that guarantee happy, hence silent, hotel staff.

But I admit, it was with a great deal of trepidation that I watched the taxicab pull away.

Forty minutes later and dressed in my funeral clothes, I walked up the steps to the unlikely address for Peter James West. To my surprise, the warehouse showed signs of an inner transformation, with added windows and doors geared for humans rather than lorry-loads of goods. I grasped the polished brass of the lion's head knocker and let it fall sharply against its brass plate. The sound echoed through the building within, and I waited for footsteps.

Chapter 50

Walking to church in the company of his wife and daughter was the high point of Chief Inspector Lestrade's week. He tried hard to ensure that his work did not stand in the way of accompanying his family every Sunday. Once there, he participated with gusto in the hymns and prayers. He had many of the collects committed to memory. He got to his knees with humility and concentration—particularly following a week such as the past one, which left him much to pray about.

He even enjoyed the sermons. This new pastor, who had replaced the old one when senile dementia began to make services rather more creative than comfortable, was one of the new generation of enthusiasts, and Lestrade wasn't yet sure how he felt about this. One of the things he liked best about church was the abiding knowledge that all over the world—San Francisco and Sydney, Calcutta and Cairo—men and women were gathered for the same words, the same sentiments, and more or less the same sermon.

Progress was fine, but modernisation?

He might need to have a word with the lad in the pulpit, to suggest that certain topics were better suited for a discussion over the tea-pot than for a Sunday morning sermon. Such as—yes, there he went: The man probably thought he was being delicate, but his advocacy of universal suffrage was sometimes a little heavy-handed.

No doubt Miss Russell would appreciate these new-fangled sermons.

Imagine, picking the lock of a Scotland Yard officer in order to have a chat at three in the morning! Sooner or later, that young woman was going to find herself in a trouble that the joint efforts of Scotland Yard and Sherlock Holmes weren't going to get her out of. Still, one had to appreciate her enthusiasms, compared to the pleasure-seeking light-headedness of many of her generation.

Thank goodness for Maudie. His wife had been something of an enthusiast herself when they'd first met, but look how nicely she'd settled down into motherhood. He couldn't see Miss Russell going quite so far, but still, there had to be interests that were not quite so extreme and ... masculine.

(A gentle stir ran through the congregation, the ecclesiastic equivalent of "Hear, hear!" Lestrade cleared his throat to show agreement with the point, listened intently for a few minutes, then allowed his thoughts to wander again.)

Still, the poor girl had to be upset over the death of her brother-in-law. How shocking that idea was, even days later. Almost as bad as the death of a king. He looked forward to seeing who showed up for the funeral. Because the man's authority was, as it were, *sub rosa*, it wouldn't be a Westminster Abbey sort of affair, but he wouldn't be surprised if representatives of the Prime Minister and the Royal Family were dispatched.

His mind played over the possible diplomatic representatives of both those governmental bodies, men who were low-key, but important enough to indicate that Mycroft had been valued by those in the know. He, Lestrade, would of course represent Scotland Yard. Which suit should he wear? The new one might best assert the competence and authority of the Yard, in pursuit of the man's killer. On the other hand, its faint modernity (Maude's choice, about which he was still uncertain) might add a dubious thread of frivolity. Perhaps the older, blacker one, stolid and—

The congregation stirred again, and again Lestrade shifted and gave a nod. However, this time, the stir did not die down. Rather, the ripple of movement grew, and after a moment, the minister fell silent, a look of confusion and incipient outrage on his youthful face.

No, Lestrade thought: *Surely the Russell girl wouldn't interrupt—*

But it was not Mary Russell. It was one of his own Yard officers, so new one could see the ghost of a constable's helmet above the soft hat he wore. Lestrade turned to his wife to mouth, "Sorry," then rose to push his way past the other knees in the pew, mouthing the same apology to the scandalised priest in the pulpit.

The man in the aisle leant forward to give a loud whisper. "They think they found Brothers, up in Saint Al—"

But Lestrade reached out to seize the plain-clothes man's arm with such force that the words cut off in a squeak. As Lestrade frog-marched him up the aisle, he hissed, "For pity's sake, man, remove your hat in church."

This younger generation simply had no concept of proper behaviour.

Chapter 51

Peter James West sat at his desk, idly picking a design into the blotter with the wicked point of Reverend Brothers' knife. The curve of its blade was a satisfying touch of the exotic East; the sheen of the steel made him hope the metal had in truth begun as a meteor.

So, they'd found Brothers—not that they'd identified him yet, but they would before long. He'd hoped to be given a few more days. Still, he couldn't see that it mattered much. There was nothing to tie him to the mad religious leader from Shanghai. Nothing but the knife. West held it up to the light, admiring it again. He wondered if Brothers' last moments had included a brief appreciation of the symmetry of his death, being caused by an artefact that had been present at the moment of his birth.

He'd even been tempted to send the knife with Gunderson on Wednesday, for the sheer pleasure of owning an instrument that had killed not only Thomas Brothers but Mycroft Holmes, as well, but in the end decided that was too much like something Brothers would have thought. Instead, he'd merely told Gunderson to keep the killing silent, and sent him on his way.

West himself appreciated symmetry, in death or in life. The arrangement of items on his desk was balanced: IN tray here, OUT tray there, pens beside the one, a framed photograph next to the other (small, showing himself shaking hands with Prime Minister Baldwin at a garden party). The furniture in his sitting room was similarly balanced: a settee bracketed by two chairs, a mirror facing a framed watercolour, two carved figures on the left side of the mantel balancing two porcelain vases on the right. His tie always complemented his suit; his shoes matched his belt; his overcoat, his hat.

In life, too, symmetry was both the means and the end. One presence removed, another takes its place.

Human beings were happiest when the shapes around them were familiar. This was as true for the men on the ground—the troops, if you will—as it was for those in command. Revolutions failed not when the change ushered in was too minor, but when the new social order became too grossly unfamiliar for comfort.

The current radical shift in deployment—men who were generally scattered in low-visibility positions around the globe, brought home for the effort—would be permissible only if it quickly faded. He had needed men—unusually large numbers of men—and his position had allowed him to summon them without question. But questions there would be, if the situation went on.

However, it should not be necessary. After this evening, those elements of change that did not fit would be quietly packed away. Tomorrow, or by Tuesday at the latest, Gunderson would return from his second trip to the Orkneys—this one a tidying operation—and the men who'd been quietly summoned from Paris and Istanbul and New York would be just as circumspectly returned to their places. Before the men above West could draw up their list of questions, the situation would have stabilised again, the turmoil smoothed over, the reins of authority—so much authority!—resting in new, more competent hands.

Mycroft Holmes would be mourned. Ruffled feathers would subside. The work of Government would go on.

A sharp knock came from the door. West raised his head: Who would come here on a Sunday afternoon? Even if Gunderson finished quickly, he knew not to come here. He slipped the knife into the closely worked Moroccan leather scabbard that he, like its previous owner, wore over his heart (another touch of symmetry), then stood. As he adjusted his clothing over the knife, he studied the perfect spiral its tip had picked into the green blotter, closing inexorably in on the centre. As his men would do at the funeral.

Peter James West went to answer the door.

BOOK FOUR

Sunday, 7 September–
Tuesday, 9 September
1924

Chapter 52

The file concerning the Honourable Winfred Stanley Moreton, also known as Robert Goodman.

Letter from "Robert Goodman" to Sir Henry Moreton,
Moreton House, Richmond, Berkshire:

3 April 1917
Craiglockhart, Edinburgh

Dear H,

Sorry. Sorry, sorry, letting the side down and all that. A disappointment to all.

No, that's not fair to you, not after you spent half your leave travelling the length of Britain to see your dodgy brother. Really you should've stayed at home with the children. Children are all that matter. Give yours their uncle's love. Sal too, of course, although she won't want it.

I was thinking of spending time in Cumberland, once they give me permission for a few days away. The house is closed, but I'd sleep rough in any event. Not sure when.

Sorry, again, to disappoint. Sorry my handwriting's so bad. At least I can hold a pen now, more than I could when I got here. Sorry too you didn't like my friends down the local, they're not altogether a bad lot.

—me

Letter from "Robert Goodman" to Lady Phoenicia Moreton Browne, Moreton House:

15 May 1917
Craiglockhart

Dear Pin,

They told me today about Harry. I am sorry for Sal and the children, but I cannot say I am surprised. All the good men are dying over there. I hope you thank the Powers every day for James' foot, or he'd be dying over there too.

Sorry, not a great day here.

Anyway, I don't know what to write to Sal, but could you tell her I'm thinking of her? I think I'd better not come to the funeral, I'm not exactly at my most presentable.

And since you two will be wondering, leave me out of any discussion of the future. I'd like use of the Cumberland place, if Father doesn't mind, but the only time I intend to pass through Berks or London again is when they're dragging my corpse to the family vault. Everything else belongs to the children, so do with it as you like. Any papers that need signing will reach me here.

Although that may not be long. To everyone's surprise including my own, I'm making something they seem to regard as a recovery. My medical board is scheduled for mid-June. They'd have to be pretty desperate to want me back, but even if they do, I'll have some leave first, and will spend it in Cumberland. It's the only place I want to be. The thought of the woods keeps me alive.

Kiss the baby for me.

Yr brother

Report from W.H.R. Rivers, Craiglockhart Hospital for Officers, Edinburgh.
"Robert Goodman"/Winfred Stanley Moreton

9 June 1917

Generally the reports I write concerning a patient under review for release begin with that patient's name. However, in the case of this patient,

I shall use "Captain Moreton" when referring to his life previous to November 1916, and "Robert Goodman" to describe the period afterwards, for reasons that shall become evident.

Robert Goodman arrived at Craiglockhart in early March 1917 with a severe case of war neurosis. The previous November, "Captain Moreton's" position near Beaumont Hamel was shelled and overrun, his entire company was either killed outright or evacuated, and Moreton was declared missing. His family was informed of his death and his possessions returned to them.

Two months later, in mid-January, an ambulance disappeared from a field hospital twenty miles down the line. Five days later, it and the missing driver, Robert Goodman, turned up in the French lines near Champagne, some sixty miles away. Goodman was arrested for theft and desertion and returned to the BEF for court martial. However, there was some confusion as to his actual identity.

As I understand it, Goodman had simply appeared at the British casualty clearing station in late November, driving an ambulance full of wounded, himself in a muddy and mildly concussed state. His ambulance had been shelled and his identity papers and half his uniform were missing, but after a rest he appeared well and declared himself ready to work. Drivers were short at that point and the hospital desperate for help, so the irregularity of his papers was temporarily set aside.

In January, Goodman disappeared as abruptly as he had come, only this time he took with him his ambulance. Although details are unclear, it would seem that he had gone south into French lines. As before, he simply was there one day amongst the French ambulances, delivering wounded to the French tents. When questioned, he claimed to have been seconded there from the BEF. The unlikeliness of the claim took several days to be researched, during which time Goodman continued to drive, and also to make urgent and increasingly incomprehensible enquiries about a missing child.

It was at about this time that a rumour of an unattached ambulance driver had begun to circulate along the Front, when one of the many trench newspapers had a small piece about the so-called Angel of Albert, who rescued wounded men when all seemed lost. In fact, an officer new to

Craiglockhart two weeks ago happened to tell me of the Angel, so it would appear that the mythic tale is still active.

In any event, "Goodman" was eventually arrested, and he and his stolen ambulance returned up the line to the British forces. Upon closer enquiry, he was identified as the long-missing Captain Moreton. Men have been shot for less, even officers. However, during his time as a driver, for the British and particularly for the French, he had performed admirably, including an heroic rescue of several French officers and soldiers. During his court martial, three high-ranking French officials and one from the British forces spoke for leniency. (I understand that, since then, Goodman-Moreton has been given a medal by the French government.)

Under these circumstances, his court martial chose to attribute his desertion and subsequent crimes to shell shock, and he was sent to Craiglockhart.

When he arrived, although until the previous month he had been performing efficiently as a driver, he was unresponsive and physically incapable, prey to uncontrollable tremors, and with a severe stammer that rendered speech nearly incomprehensible. (It should be noted that many of the officers arrive here with stammers, which can be interpreted as the body's rebellion against giving orders, or the result of shattered nerves. In either case, treatment is the same: rest, and talk.)

By the end of March, he had improved to the extent that he could walk and feed himself without mishap, and speech was slow but comprehensible.

However, we had found that to address him by his proper name led to a state of quivering incapacity characterised by uncontrollable but silent weeping. In a staff meeting two weeks after his arrival, it was decided that he would not be so addressed until such time as it seemed therapeutically desirable. I informed him of the decision, and asked him by what name he wished to be called.

He replied with the name of the driver, Robert Goodman, and although the choice is a telling combination of strength (particularly here in Scotland) and virtue ("good man"), here is not the place to go into an analysis.

Under this nom de fou, his progress continued. His stammer became less pronounced except under periods of tiredness or particular stress (such as a visit by his older brother at the end of March). His manual dexterity improved to the point that he could control buttons, table implements, and a pen, and he undertook short visits into the town. In mid-April, however, an attempt to reintroduce his name stimulated an attack of nerves that set him back for days.

With improved speech, talk therapy became more effective. After some weeks, Goodman revealed to me that a wartime incident with a child had sent him south into the French lines; however, he was unwilling to give further details concerning the incident. Questions made him weep.

By early June, it was our judgement that he was ready for his medical board. It should be noted that it is not the task of this hospital to "cure" a man, but either to ready him for a return to duty, or to speak for his inability to perform his duties and thus require discharge. In the case of "Robert Goodman," his lasting opinion appears to be that "the Other" (i.e., Moreton) had dropped the world into a state of war in the first place, and he, Goodman, wished nothing to do with the man. I do not believe he meant this literally—that his individual family was in some way personally responsible for the War—but that the country's ingrained system of aristocracy and privilege had made for a situation in which war was the only option.

If this officer is permitted to retain his identity of "Robert Goodman," I believe he can eventually become a functioning member of society. He has no wish to resume his place in his birth family or in his regiment, and I would strongly recommend that he not be forced into doing so. He has an abhorrence of violence that would make the duties of a front-line officer impossible. He is more than willing to serve as an ambulance driver, although he understands how unlikely that would be.

If the board certifies that he is to return to duty, my strong recommendation is that he be permitted quietly to enter the ranks rather than resume his status of officer: The responsibility of giving orders is what he fears most, to the extent that the friendships he has made here, amongst patients or the community, are men who are dominant to the point of bullying. Were he to resume his rank and his command, it would not surprise me to hear that he arranged to do himself harm.

The changes evinced in this patient's life are profound and, to all appearances, permanent. His family (I find myself tempted to write, "his former family") describes Moreton as methodical, tidy, and of a scientific bent; however, as Goodman he embraces spontaneity, spends his time with drawing pencils and clay (or knives and wood, once he was permitted them), and appears ill at ease when confronted by symmetrical array: A ready chess set, for example, gives him a mental itch until he has shifted a piece into an unlikely position. He sings, as apparently he has not done since adolescence, in a light but pleasant voice. He prefers simple songs and nursery rhymes over more complex melodies or hymns.

If the Board is taken aback by the seemingly light-hearted attitude of "Robert Goodman" when he comes before it, I beg that they keep in mind his twenty-seven months of unflinching service on the Front followed by two months of heroic driving to the rescue of his fellows ("The Angel of Albert"). If I may be permitted an anthropological remark beyond the scope of this patient report, I might point out that a society often reacts to trauma by turning its collective back on responsibility and embracing the frivolous. It should be no surprise that an individual might choose the same means of self-preservation.

I recommend a medical discharge for the patient, and until such time as his family becomes available to him again, a full pension.

As a last note, I recommend that the Board be made aware of the distress that will ensue if they choose to address the patient by his birth name.

Respectfully,
W.H.R. Rivers

The file also included seventeen newspaper clippings concerning the trial of "Johnny" McAlpin in Edinburgh, during which accusations were made concerning the history and mental stability of Moreton, who had met McAlpin in a pub near Craiglockhart Hospital during April and May of 1917. No charges were filed against Moreton, and he was thanked by the judge and permitted to return to his home in Cumberland.

Chapter 53

Robert Goodman had only been to two funerals in his life. As The Other Man, no doubt he had attended any number, in calm green cemeteries or in the filth and shattering chaos of the battlefield, but that was The Other Man and he, Goodman, didn't have to think about that.

So he was mildly curious about this one. It would not be in a small village church as the other two had been, both of them for neighbours who had reached the ends of their long lives and been ushered into the grave with as much relief as sorrow. This one would be for a man who had, he gathered, still been strong and hale, and whose sudden death had been a terrible shock for everyone who knew him.

He liked this young woman Mary Russell. If there were more like her in circulation, he might not have chosen to live quite so far out of the world. And such was his respect for her as a person, he thought that anyone she loved as much as she evidently had Mycroft Holmes might have been someone he, Robert Goodman, would have enjoyed.

So he was sympathetic, and sad for opportunities missed, but mostly he was curious. All sorts of currents swirled around the man's death, each of them promising to wash in some interesting artefacts to the funeral.

His life had become far too simple. It had taken an aeroplane falling out of the sky to make him aware of his lapse into tedium. But now, everything had become exciting and vital and unpredictable, in ways that made him itch to contribute.

And now that he thought of it, he probably could come up with one or two ways to add his own touch to the afternoon's obsequies.

Yes indeed; why not make the event something to remember, for all concerned? After all, who commanded that a funeral had to be funereal?

It was the least he could do for Miss Russell.

Chapter 54

R ussell had been here, in this bolt-hole, Holmes could see that.

But she had brought another person with her. To the bolt-hole. A man.

The clothing she had given the guest indicated he was small; the traces of hair in the razor said he was blond; his choices of reading material suggested either eclectic interests or easy boredom: Russell's feminist Bible translation by Elizabeth Cady Stanton, a picture-book on the Venetian Mardi Gras, and a biography of Benjamin Franklin lay on the floor beside the chaise.

It was also clear that the man had spent some considerable time here on his own—or if not alone, he had felt free to paw through every corner of the place under Russell's gaze. The man had even discovered the hidden cabinet, although he had not taken anything, merely re-stacking the gold coins into one teetering pile, and rearranging the eight valuable diamonds into what was perhaps meant to be an *R*.

Holmes very much looked forward to making the acquaintance of this small, blond, inquisitive man whom his wife trusted enough to leave unattended. Or, he corrected himself, whom his wife had brought here before she fell unconscious. And if that was the case, he looked forward to meeting the man all the more.

He returned the books to the shelf, locked the cabinet and re-stored the concealing volumes in front of it, scrupulously rinsed and dried the razor, and then began to dress in clothing suitable for the funeral of one's only brother.

Chapter 55

A song thrush sat atop a tree growing at the corner of a cemetery. It was a large tree, and an old cemetery. Generation upon generation of Londoners had been laid here, their bones dug up and re-buried, their lichen-spangled stones lifted and placed to one side like substantial ghosts lined up to bear witness.

The thrush had fed well that morning; the weak sun was welcome; its young were long gone from the year's nest. He was happy to perch and cock a bright eye at the curious comings and goings below.

Earlier in the day, the grave-diggers had come with their spades, making their casual way across the lawns to the scheduled resting place of this newest graveyard resident. Their orders were for a larger hole than usual: Having an oversized coffin stuck halfway down was humiliating to professional pride, and affected the generosity of the families.

So their shovels scraped longer than usual in the heavy London soil, and the hole they dug was as outsized as the man it was to contain.

At last, they were finished. The man in the hole tossed out his spade and raised a hand for the others to pull him up. They arranged the cloth over the raw soil mound, gentling reality for the mourners, then propped their tools across their shoulders and went to seek out their luncheons.

Two hours passed, in silence but for the bells of nearby churches. The thrush came and went, came and went and returned. Clouds gathered, then cleared. Three families came to lay flowers on gravestones; a courting couple lingered under the trees; a pack of neighbouring children ran through, their raucous joy not, oddly, entirely out of place.

Then silence.

When the sun was halfway to the horizon, a man came, dressed in formal black, though wearing a soft hat. He stood for a time at the edge of the hole, then turned to survey the surrounding trees, stones, and marble tombs. He walked up and down, taking up a position behind a large granite cross, then beneath the song thrush's tree, and finally stepped into the shadows beneath a grand family vault. The toes of his polished shoes caught the light, then they, too, retreated into the gloom. The man might not have been there at all.

The hearse that eventually came was the old-fashioned sort: high, black, and pulled by black horses with black feathered top-knots. The priest walked before, his black cassock peeping out from under a lace-trimmed white surplice, head bent beneath a Canterbury cap, prayer book in hand.

The coffin, both large and heavy, was taken from the hearse by six men. They settled it cautiously upon their shoulders, then stepped into an even pace, transferring the body to its eternal home.

Step; pause. Step; pause. Step.

Clouds grew across the sun, and the afternoon went dull. The mourners glanced upwards and fingered their umbrellas. A person looking on, from the high branches, perhaps, or a family vault, might have noticed how the people deferred to two or three of their fellows: Clearly these were important men, at a solemn occasion. Too solemn, too important for the jostling, bumptious press to have been notified.

The bird, back now, noticed primarily that there was no sign of a picnic luncheon.

The coffin approached, paused in the air, was lowered, and came to rest beside the hole. The six men stepped back, surreptitiously easing their shoulders. The priest stepped forward.

"I am the resurrection and the life, saith the Lord." The ancient words of grief and comfort rose up from the circle. One woman, tall and buxom, raised a handkerchief underneath her black veil. One man, his hair sandy and thin, his black suit slightly out of date, swayed infinitesimally, then regained control. Another man, this one with the nose of a boxer and a tie too gaudy for the occasion, looked intently around the neighbouring area, seemed not to find what he was searching for, and then raised his arm to pass his hand slowly over his greased hair, a gesture so deliberate it might almost have been intended to convey meaning.

The thrush atop the overlooking tree noticed motion at a distance. Men, perhaps a dozen in all, had taken up positions in a wide circle around the oblivious mourners. Now they began to move forward. These were large, hard-looking men; two of them had bruised faces, as if they had recently walked into a tree, or a rock; one limped. Several sparrows flew out from another tree, but the song thrush remained.

Then came another wave of motion. This, too, came from all over, but it had many more than a dozen sources. Along the cemetery's paths, over the low hill, from under the scattering of ancient trees, small groups of men and women converged on the hole and its coffin. The men wore dark suits, some ill-fitting; the women wore dresses appropriate to mourning. The women's hair was of all colours and lengths; two of the men were bald beneath their hats. All the men were at least six feet tall, all were thin, all were at least forty years of age; the women were uniformly tall, all were slim, none was over forty.

And all of the women wore spectacles.

Quiet and to all appearances solemn, the men and women closed in to insinuate themselves among the twenty-three mourners already gathered at the grave-side. The original group looked at the oddly similar newcomers with expressions ranging from surprise to outrage, but the men and women were polite, quiet, and patient.

The congregation now numbered almost ninety. The priest stared open-mouthed at the proceedings, then stirred back to his responsibilities. He found his place, and resumed. The shadow beneath the ornate vault remained still.

The narrowing circle of hard-looking men had stopped abruptly when the odd cohort of late-comers appeared, to let the men and women flow around them towards the grave. They consulted silently with their fellows, glanced at the burly man with the boxer's nose, then gave mental shrugs and settled back where they were.

Again, the words of the psalm rose up. Again, the tall, buxom woman raised the scrap of white cloth to her veil. The sparrows returned to their tree.

And again, came an interruption. This time it was music, riding thinly on the fitful breeze: a brass band. The mourners shifted and glanced at one another, disapproving of this thoughtless levity. The priest glanced up briefly, then pushed on.

However, the band did not go away. In fact, the raucous music seemed to be growing, as if some horribly inappropriate Salvation Army band had chosen this place of dignity and sorrow to practice its thumping tunes. Closer it came, and closer, until the tune became clear: "Rock of Ages," quickened to marching time. The priest raised his voice and speeded up a fraction. Some of the mourners exchanged glances, others hunched into themselves, determinedly oblivious. The sandy-haired man in the old-fashioned suit spoke to the younger man at his side, who put on his hat and stalked in the direction of the disturbance.

But before he had disappeared from view, those mourners unable to keep their eyes from following saw him jerk to a halt. He put out both hands, in a manner strongly reminiscent of a constable directing traffic, but his authority was insufficient: The music came nearer, and louder.

And then it was upon them, a marching band of all the loudest, most discordant instruments in an orchestra: tubas, trombones, and French horns (all of them ever-so-slightly out of tune) tootled along with not one, but two large drums (beat nearly in rhythm), a phalanx of flutes, clarinets, and piccolos, and a short pot-bellied man dwarfed by an enormous pair of brass cymbals.

At the front, marching high-kneed with an enormous, sparkly, bulbous red baton, was a wiry blond man wearing Victorian mourning clothes, an oversized fedora with a feather, and an expression of devout religiosity more suited to a cathedral choir. But even the trappings could not hide the sparkle of mischief that shone out from the green eyes, brighter than the flashes of sunlight off his oversized baton.

Those around the graveside panicked. The men clapped their hats on their heads; the women drew together. The priest, thinking to hurry matters along, raised his voice to declare, "Man, that is born of woman," but quickly realised the futility of his effort. He snapped shut his book and stepped forward to protest.

Without effect. The band finished their tune and immediately launched into the next—rather, they launched into two different tunes. It took several bars before the players of one melody dropped out, scrambling to find their place in the dominant one. The blond man stood with his back at the brink of the hole and pumped his baton with great enthusiasm and no sense of tempo whatsoever. The young man who had been sent to stop them returned to the man with the sandy hair and spoke—shouted—into his ear. The man bent to listen, then threw up his hands and strode over to address the blond conductor, with no result.

The threescore similarly dressed latecomers looked around at each other, at the original mourners, and at the musical invaders. They seemed mightily confused.

The heavily veiled woman broke first. With the handkerchief to her face, she turned and ran, stumbling in her heels over the close-cropped grass until she reached a path, when her gait settled into a brisk march, head down. She had made it as far as the nearest tree when a hard-faced man stepped out and ripped off her veil. She struggled, got one arm free, and swung the hand at her assailant's already bruised face with a resounding slap. He retaliated by shoving her face-first against the tree-trunk, grabbing her wrist, and fumbling with a pair of handcuffs.

The sandy-haired man saw what was happening and broke into a run to interfere; his young companion followed on his heels; the band, responding to the increased gesturings of the blond man, enthusiastically notched up its tempo and its volume.

As if a switch had been thrown, half a dozen of the original mourners were infected with the urge for rapid retreat. Five others followed on their heels. The look-alike men and women glanced at each other, at the coffin, and at the band before they, too, shifted away from the proceedings, slowly at first, then more quickly, until eighty-some people were fleeing the epicentre of the disturbance, like ants from a stirred nest.

The priest, torn between his congregation and his corpse, chose the living, abandoning the coffin to the brass band, its blond director, and the burly man who had ostentatiously smoothed his hair.

In a wide circle around the gravesite, the twelve hard-faced men had their hands full. A few of them managed to handcuff some of the look-alikes and were drawing them towards the grave. The band played on, loud and joyous and discordant. The burly man scowled at the band-leader, then turned on his heel, noticing the approach of several of his fellows dragging or shoving their protesting mourners. In the distance, the other two men had caught up the first assailant and his prisoner, whose luxurious black hair was spilling down around her shoulders. The younger man bent over the woman's bound wrists while the older one directed a wrathful tirade at the man with the bruised nose and freshly reddened cheek.

It seemed that, in moments, these two would break into open vio-lence. But before that happened, the man with the bruises cast a glance down at the sole remaining mourner. This time, the burly man's hand was not smoothing his hair, but stretched over his head, open-palmed, waving sharply in a clear message to cease and desist.

The inward movement of the hard men and their prisoners slowed, then stopped. One at a time, the men bent to struggle with the handcuff mechanisms. The freed men and women, looking frightened, hurried to join their untouched fellows who had gathered at a safe distance. The larger group took them in, patting and touching their reassurance. Sev-eral of the women pulled off wigs that had been knocked awry; several of the men yanked at the ties in their stiff collars. When all their original members were reunited, they moved as one down the paths and out of the cemetery's main entrance, where the original twenty-three mourn-ers had long since fled.

When the band came to an end of the present song, it briskly launched into the first tune it had played on arrival. Now, green eyes blazing with the triumph of his rout, the blond Lord of Misrule bran-dished his baton in the air, stepped away from the gaping hole, and marched, high-kneed as before, across the grass in the direction they had come. The band jerked and trailed into his wake, motion making them play even more out of tune and off the beat. Some of the hard-looking men, now drawn together around the boxer, made as if to stop them, but the man made a cutting motion with his hand, then turned and walked away, stiff-spined with fury. The twelve looked at each other, then at the band, before turning to follow.

The band marched off. The woman with the handkerchief, weeping in earnest now, stumbled after all the others with her veil in her hand, a sad and solitary figure crossing a nearly deserted graveyard.

The two men who had loosed her from her captor came back down the rise, standing for a time beside the bare hole and its abandoned coffin, before even they turned to make their way towards the entrance.

The cemetery subsided into its state of calm Sunday afternoon peace.

The thrush on the high branch was moved to song, although the season for singing had been over for many weeks. His music spilled over the deserted cemetery for a long time before the approach of evening made itself felt, and he flew off in search of a resting place.

It was full dusk when the figure slipped away from the grand family vault.

Chapter 56

I found Holmes by the time-honoured method of strolling up the street and waiting for him to pounce on me. The familiar *hsst* came from the doorway of an antiquarian bookstore. It was not open for business, it being Sunday, but the proprietor was at work, his door propped open to counteract the drowsy effects of his accumulated centuries of wood pulp and printer's ink.

Holmes had removed his cassock and lacy surplice, and set aside his piety along with the Book of Common Prayer. He physically jerked me inside and frowned at my funeral disguise, which was that of a dowdy young woman indistinguishable from any of Billy's relatives. He commented on the effectiveness of the disguise, examined me for sign of injuries, berated me for driving away our foes before they could reveal their leader, and chided me for reducing the obsequies to a shambles—all of which were his way of expressing his pleasure in seeing me. The last of the accusations, however, I felt I should deny.

"That was not I, Holmes," I protested.

He stopped. "It was not?"

"Well, not all of it."

"Are you saying that Billy himself came up with the idea of having every one of his friends and relations who possessed vaguely the correct physique show up in identical dress?"

"Oh no, *that* was mine. The brass band was something else entirely."

"Ha! The small blond man whom you introduced into the bolt-hole near Baker Street."

"He spent more time there than I did, but yes. Was that disapproval I heard?"

He summoned a look of surprise. "Why should I disapprove? Clearly you had reason to permit a stranger access."

Before I could respond, he turned to the antique antiquarian perched behind the counter and thanked him for the temporary use of his shop, then took me by the arm again to drag me towards the back. I shook off his grip—shook off, too, the fleeting memory of running hand in hand with Goodman through a dark forest.

"His musical interlude was, I will admit, remarkably effective," he remarked over his shoulder. "I had not anticipated quite such a number of opponents, lying in wait for us."

"Nor I. Holmes, where have you been?"

"First Wick, then Amsterdam," he said succinctly.

"Yes, Billy told me you were there, although he did not know why. Rather a long detour to London, was it not?"

"Damian was more comfortable when we ran before the wind."

"Is he all right?"

"His shoulder is healing. I left him in the tender hands of a lady doctor."

"You found a lady doctor in Amsterdam?"

"We abducted one from Wick."

"*Abducted?* Oh, Holmes, do you think—"

"Needs must, Russell. Can you climb in that frock?"

I sighed. "Needs must, Holmes."

The external ladder led to a flat above the bookshop, which by all evidence belonged to the bookseller himself. Holmes moved to the gas ring and put on a kettle, tossing my way a few details of the trip he and Damian had made, along with this doctor lady.

When I had unearthed a chair from a dozen ancient volumes and settled with my cup of tea, I returned to my question.

"When I asked where you were, I meant more recently. I expected to see you at the bolt-hole."

"Life became rather more complex than I had anticipated."

"You went down to Southwark," I suggested.

"Either they are good or I am getting old, because I nearly handed myself to them twice."

"If they got the better of Billy in his own home ground, they know what they're doing."

"And you?" he said. "Any problems on the way down from Scotland?"

"Ah. Goodman didn't give you the letter?"

"Goodman is your blond friend? No, I received no letter."

Of course not: Even I had needed a moment to see behind the priest's disguise. I took another revivifying swallow of tea and began my report on the past eight days. Thirty seconds in, he interrupted.

"Brothers is alive?"

"The book, Holmes. Brothers had his death journal with him, probably in his breast pocket where the bullet hit. I thought it odd that the Orcadian police seemed only marginally interested in the site, but Lestrade confirmed it when I went to his house this morning—news had reached him of a fire and loud noise like a gunshot, but since there was no body, that was all he'd heard."

"That does rather change things."

"But I can't see—" I jolted to a halt: I had not seen Holmes since Mycroft's death, and his brief description of the week's activities had skipped over that central event. I put down my cup and laid my hand over his. "I'm so sorry, Holmes. I read of it in *The Times*, on Wednesday. It was . . . couldn't believe it."

"Nor could I," he said flatly. "And I've now wasted a week."

"Holmes, I can't see any relation between Brothers alive and Mycroft . . ."

"Dead? Brothers had help from within the government, either directly or purchased for him by others. I was operating under the theory that he came here under the auspices of a Shanghai crime cartel, who then lost control over him at the same time he lost control of his reason. If he is alive, it throws another light on our target, but in either case, we are facing a group with considerable resources: men in Holland and in Harwich, an insider in the passport office, twelve men this afternoon. Mycr—"

"A sharpshooter in Thurso," I added to his list.

He raised an eyebrow, and fell silent. I told him all: Javitz; aeroplane; sniper; crash; wild man of the woods; telegrams and newspaper notices; five armed invaders, two of whom had been at the cemetery this afternoon; our trip to London; Javitz and Estelle. I told him what I had found in the apartment of the absent Richard Sosa, and what I had uncovered in Mycroft's flat: a note from Lestrade; sixteen documents that could change the world; a key; and one letter with an anomalous capital *I*.

"Sophy Melas," he said, when I told him the last.

"You know her? I mean to say, you know her from before, but recently?"

"We've met. And I knew that Mycroft had continued dealings with her, after she returned to this country. That was she at the funeral, in the veil."

"The only one in tears," I said. Then, distracted from my train of thought, I asked, "I saw the Prime Minister there, but who was the grey-haired man with the entourage?"

He gave the name of a high-ranking but painfully introverted Royal, commenting that Mycroft had assisted the man some years before. Other mourners had included Sinclair, head of the SIS, and Vernon Kell, the man in charge of the domestic Secret Service. Not, apparently, Peter James West, nor Richard Sosa.

"And of course Lestrade was there," I added.

"You went to his house, you say?"

"I let myself in during the wee hours, and found him waiting."

"I imagine he was well pleased."

"Well, I didn't want to wake his family. And he ought to have a better latch."

"Did his note alone lead you to believe a visit to his house would not be a trap?"

"It didn't strike me as his kind of ruse. Besides which," I added, "it was three in the morning and I'm a lot quicker than he is. I thought it a reasonable risk."

"As, too, breaking into Richard Sosa's flat."

"The only indication that I was there was a small ivory carving I knocked to the floor when I moved the curtains. I put it back, but I can't be sure I had the precise place. If there was one—Sosa seemed an odd mixture of great caution with slips of carelessness."

"Which might make one wonder, were not most criminals apprehended because of a moment's carelessness."

"So, Holmes. What next?"

"This pilot of yours: Will he keep the child—will he keep Estelle safe for another day or two?" I was glad he'd finally come around to his granddaughter.

"Captain Javitz is a determined and honourable man, and he and Estelle get along like a house afire. And he's a bit embarrassed at one or two recent displays of weakness, which means he'll be scrupulous about guarding her. As for Goodman, I'm not sure what he'll do. The last I saw of him—other than at the head of that awful band—was at the bolt-hole this morning. He's like a jack-in-the-box, always popping in and out. Later I saw that he'd taken the letter I'd written to you, giving details about this past week—I thought I should set it all down in case Lestrade decided to arrest me. I put the Sussex address on the front, and stamps. I hope he remembers to put it into the post." And to seal it first.

"You have doubts?"

"It is beyond me to predict what the man will do. He's an extraordinary creature, like something from another world." Time enough later to tell him what I knew of the man's history. "Perhaps we'd best go back to Baker Street, just to be sure. I'll need a change of clothes, in any case; it might as well be from there."

"A man who cannot be trusted to post a letter is someone you trusted with the bolt-hole?" He did not sound angry, merely curious.

I could not explain my confidence in this odd man, not even to myself.

"I had to do something with him, Holmes. Billy was out of the equation, most of our friends are known, Mycroft's flat felt exposed, and I didn't want to risk an hotel. When you meet him, you can decide if I've compromised the place too badly." *And you have five other bolt-holes*, I thought but did not say.

"Very well, let us go now. There will be rough garments there, I believe." He picked up the tea-pot and cups, returning them to the sink.

"Rough?" I repeated to his back. I did not care for the sound of that word. "Why do we need rough garments, Holmes?"

He turned in surprise. "Oh, if you wish to retain the frock, by all means, do so, Russell. I merely assumed you would prefer more practical garb for the purpose of grave-digging."

Chapter 57

H olmes, no," I protested, trotting after him down a passageway that would have been dark even were it not coming on to evening. "You can't be serious. Grave-digging?"

"How else are we to know who lies there?"

"Why would you imagine it is anyone other than your brother?"

"I tried to get into the mortuary yesterday night and was told the coffin was already sealed. When I pressed the man, I learned that they had received the coffin in that state on the Thursday morning."

"Is that unusual, when embalming is not required?"

"I . . ." He could not answer: Either he did not know, or it was not unusual.

"I'm surprised you didn't break in then and there."

"I would have, but there was never a time when the building was empty. Who would have imagined mortuaries were so incessantly busy?"

"Holmes, I think you're being unreasonable."

"You said yourself, you couldn't believe Mycroft was dead."

"That was a figure of speech!"

"Well, mine was not. When I see his corpse with my own eyes, I will believe, but not before then."

I had found it difficult to use the words *death* and *murder* when talking to Lestrade that morning, but this went far beyond any mere aversion to hard truth. In another man, I would have assumed that brother-worship had taken an alarming turn and required physical intervention and a long period of quiet conversation. But this was Holmes, after all: Despite his age, I doubted I could tackle him successfully.

So I kept silent and did my best to keep up with him.

The streets behind Marylebone Road appeared deserted—these were, after all, office blocks, and it was a Sunday evening—but Holmes paused for several minutes at the top of the street so we could survey all of the doorways and windows. When he was satisfied, we made a swift detour through a service entry, came out next to the bolt-hole's entrance, and in moments, we were inside and invisible.

But not before I had spotted something odd on the ground just outside the entrance. "Wait, is that—" I reached for it and said, "Holmes."

"Quiet," he shot back, standing rigid inside. I drew breath, and discovered what had attracted his attention: the odours of cooking, highly unlikely here.

"It'll be Goodman," I said. "He left this outside, stuck to the paving stones. An owl feather. His favourite bird, and not often seen in London."

His eyes gleamed as he studied me in the faint light, then he turned and went on.

When we stepped into the tiny apartment, the first thing to greet our eyes were Robert Goodman's stockinged feet against the wall. He was standing on his head.

"Hello, Robert," I said, waiting for him to resume an upright position before I attempted introductions. But he stayed as he was, merely pointing a toe at the table and saying, "Sir, I believe there is an epistle I was instructed to deliver."

Holmes looked at the table, then back at Goodman, and said, "It is, I agree, a topsy-turvy world."

Instantly, Goodman let his legs fall to the floor and jumped upright, face pink and hair flattened. He shook his clothing back into place, rescued the neck-tie he had tucked between the buttons of his shirt, ran his hands over his hair, and stuck out his right hand.

"Mine host," he said.

"Mr Goodman, I presume," Holmes replied. "I understand it is you I have to thank for the musical interlude during the services for my brother."

"You needn't thank me," Goodman protested, although that was not what Holmes had meant.

"Nonetheless. My brother would have been most...entertained."

Goodman's face relaxed into happiness. "I'm sorry your granddaughter couldn't have been there."

Holmes' eyes came to me in silent reproach for the amount this stranger knew of us. "You think the child would have enjoyed it?"

"Heavens no. She'd have had to cover her ears."

Holmes said dryly, "You think the child a natural music critic?"

"Ah, that's right—you have not met the poppet. Perhaps you don't know? Estelle has perfect pitch. She'd have found the discord physically painful."

Now, Holmes simply looked at him. Goodman nodded as if he'd replied, and said, "She looks forward to meeting you." He went into the minuscule kitchen, which was more a matter of putting his head into the cubicle.

"Mr Goodman, I believe you have something on the stove for us?"

"I do," our guest replied. "Although I have to say it was a challenge, coming up with something edible out of that pantry. Perhaps the tins are intended as weapons, rather than comestibles?" he added politely, his head appearing around the door.

Holmes retreated with the letter to the inner room while I took out plates and silver. I was rinsing the dust from some glasses when I heard Holmes say my name, sharply. I looked in at where he sat on the bed.

"Why did you not tell me how Mycroft signed his name?" he demanded.

"How did he sign his name?"

"With the letter *M*."

"Is there significance in that?"

"Have you ever seen my brother sign a letter with only the initial?"

"He does all the time," I protested. I could see it in front of my eyes, that copperplate *M* curving around a dot.

"In a letter to *me?*" he persisted.

Now that he'd mentioned it, I had to agree, it was generally Mycroft's full name, even in telegrams. But I had seen that *M* as well, and recently. Then I had it: "The letters from Mycroft that Sosa had in his desk. Those were signed with just the initial."

"Precisely: his business communications. The initial began as his mark to indicate that he had seen a document, and evolved into a substitute formal signature. I believe Smith-Cumming adopted the technique with his letter C on documents, until that letter took on a life of its own and was taken to mean *Chief*—his successor, Hugh Sinclair, signs with the C."

"So, what? This letter to you is a business communication?"

"I should say he meant us to understand that he was writing in an official, rather than a fraternal, capacity."

I could not see that it made any particular difference. "If you say so, Holmes," I said, and went back to laying the table.

When he came out, he had changed his formal suit for a pair of frayed trousers and an equally working-man's shirt of a dark colour, which he was rolling up to the elbows. He set an ancient dark-lantern on the floor beside the door: He had not by some miracle let go the idea of digging up Mycroft's grave.

Goodman had created a kind of bean ragoût that he poured over a mound of rice—remarkable, considering the raw materials to hand. Holmes chewed the first bite with careful consideration, then gave a small moue, as if the taste had proved some inner theory. Goodman tucked in with gusto, and launched into the story of how he'd come to locate and hire a band with such absurdly woeful skills, weaving in a great deal of entertaining but questionable detail, aware of, but ignoring, the grey eyes that never left him.

When the plates were empty, I abandoned the men to the washing-up and dug through the stores for a costume appropriate for grave-robbing: trousers and a dark shirt similar to those Holmes had donned, ancient brogues, and the gloves Holmes used when he was driving a carriage. I chose another shirt and took it into the other room. The cook was scrubbing a pot. Holmes was drying the plates and putting them on the shelf. One of them had made coffee.

"Mr Goodman chooses to join us," Holmes told me.

"I didn't imagine he could resist." I held out the shirt. "That white shirt will be too visible at night, if we're caught. This one should fit you well enough."

Goodman laid the pot upside-down next to the sink and reached for his neck-tie, undressing with no more self-consciousness than a child. I turned my back. Holmes looked on, bemused.

I had rather hoped that, considering the circumstances, we might find the coffin sitting at the edge of the hole, the interrupted burial having been delayed until the morrow. However, the mound of earth had been filled in, the sod returned to its place. The height of the mound suggested the addition of a substantial volume.

We rolled away the turf and Holmes pulled on his driving gloves, then set to with a spade he had stolen from the workman's shed. I guided him with the dark-lantern, keeping it low and sheltering it behind my body.

After a quarter hour, Goodman dropped down from his perch on top of a grandiose vault and took the spade. A quarter hour after that, I returned from a wide survey of the surrounds and assumed the gloves and spade.

A faint rain began to drift across us, a mist rising from the ground to meet it. A faint half-moon occasionally looked through the clouds, catching on Goodman's pale hair, the gleam of his teeth, the glitter of Holmes' eyes.

The advantage of overturning a fresh grave is obvious, and this one was as fresh as they get. Halfway through our second circuit of diggers, with Goodman in the hole, the spade hit wood. To my surprise, he dropped the handle and scrabbled his way out of the hole as if he'd felt a hand on his leg.

Holmes let himself down and began uncovering the coffin.

It emerged quickly, its former polish somewhat scraped and dented. Holmes tossed out the spade and pulled a screw-driver from the back pocket of his trousers. When he had worked his way around and the fastenings were loose, he traded the screw-driver for a length of lightweight rope, knotting it around the handle. He picked it up; Goodman interrupted.

"Allow me," he said with exaggerated politeness, holding out a hand. Holmes laid the rope's end across his palm. Goodman wrapped it around his fist, waited until Holmes and I were standing across the grave from him with the lamp shining down at the wood. Then he pulled, working against the weight and the press of remaining soil against the hinges. The wood came up; the air went heavy with the stench of corruption; the light wavered and went still; and we looked down into the silk-lined coffin.

The face below us was nestled into a pale satin pillow.

The face was that of a large man, his dead features slack and beginning to swell.

Not Mycroft.

Chapter 58

Holmes could not quite stifle his grunt of relief; however, his only words were to tell Goodman to hold the lid. He let his long legs down until his shoes rested on the edges of the coffin, and I shone the light on the corpse's upper body as Holmes tilted it, but as I'd thought, the coffin was not deep enough to contain two.

He had been killed, not by a knife as the newspaper had reported, but by gunshot: three shots, in fact, one of which had stopped his heart and brought an end to his bleeding. He had not been embalmed; no autopsy had been performed; he had been dead for several days.

Holmes pulled himself back onto the grass, his legs dangling, while I continued to direct the light over the man's face. Death obscures the features and drains away the personality, but the fresh pink scar along his left eyebrow tugged at my memory: I had put it there myself two weeks earlier.

"You know him," Holmes said.

"Marcus Gunderson."

Silence held for a solid minute, before he murmured, "Curioser and curioser."

"Our opponent is clearing the field," I said. "Removing anyone who can tie him to this whole business. He'll find Sosa next."

"Perhaps Sosa is in hiding with Mycroft."

The blithe illogic of this was so startling, I could feel even Goodman's scepticism from the darkness. Just because Mycroft wasn't here didn't mean he wasn't dead elsewhere.

"If Mycroft is hiding, why did he not get into touch with us?"

"Have you finished?" asked a voice from across the grave. Holmes hastily retracted his legs. The coffin lid came down; the rope sagged loose; Holmes screwed down the lid again, then reached for the spade. The air grew sweeter.

"Is there any information you have not given me?" Holmes asked as he began to fling soil back into place.

"Nothing that comes to mind," I said.

"Why, then, is Gunderson here in place of my brother?"

"He sounds irritated." Goodman's voice from the darkness was amused.

"Not that it doesn't please me immensely," I said, "that he isn't here, but honestly, what does this mean?"

"Think, Russell. Who would be capable of this? Who could trace you to Scotland and have a sniper waiting for you overnight in Thurso? Who could learn from the telephone exchange where a trunk call had originated, and two days later have armed men in Amsterdam? Who would have the authority to remove a body from the purview of Scotland Yard, produce a false identity and falsified autopsy results, and package it for burial with no trace of official protest?"

Goodman's arm came out of the dark and appropriated the spade, which Holmes had been leaning on during this speech. Holmes moved to one side, and the hole continued to fill.

"Mycroft could have done all of that," I pointed out.

"Granted. Although my brother might hesitate to send a sniper after his sister-in-law."

I ignored the levity, although Goodman made a quiet *Ha!* "Anything Mycroft was in a position to effect, I imagine his secretary could have duplicated with forged orders. Certainly until Wednesday, when Mycroft was found. Or, not found," I added.

"Either side could have done this. But it was definitely intended to be taken as Mycroft."

"But Holmes, if Mycroft was alive, surely he'd have got us a message?"

"Perhaps he's in Kent with your Mr Javitz and—"

He caught my sharp gesture even in the near-dark, but too late. The sound of digging stopped.

"You moved them?" came the voice from the grave.

With a wrench, my brain shifted direction: Our preoccupation with governmental misdeeds and assassinations meant nothing to Robert Goodman compared with the welfare of a child. "I did. I'm sorry I didn't tell you, but I talked to Captain Javitz after you left this morning and he had . . . concerns, so it seemed best to send the two of them away. They'll be safe."

"What concerns?"

How to answer him? By saying that his family's servants had betrayed him to the American? That the pilot now suspected our eccentric rescuer was not only truly insane, but friends with a homosexual murderer as well? That I had to depend on Javitz to watch Estelle, and had no choice but to do as he asked?

"It's complicated."

"He knows," Goodman said flatly.

I felt Holmes' gaze bore into me, but I dropped onto my heels, stretching a hand out to the small man's shoulder. "Robert, I owe you so much. May I ask one more favour of you? That we not have this discussion just now?"

For the longest time, the glitter of his eyes in the faint light did not shift. Then he said, "Does *she* know?"

"No."

"Do not tell her."

"I won't."

And without another word, he returned to his shovelling.

I could feel the question yearning from the man at my side: *Know what?* Another would have asked. Holmes said merely, "That my brother is not in his coffin suggests that this entire episode could have been in service of his needs. That he wished to appear dead."

"For the third time, why not leave a message?"

"I could think of a hundred reasons," he snapped. "He is held captive. His post to *The Times* was intercepted. He decided that a message was either inadvisable or unnecessary."

"Unnecessary? How were we to guess the newspaper report was false?" I used the word *guess* deliberately, knowing it would raise his ire.

"*I* knew there was something wrong the moment I read his obituary."

"Well, yes!"

"Wrong with the report, that is. The general public does not know Mycroft Holmes from Adam, so why should *The Times* print a formal obituary? And in any event, even if a man has been old and ill, how often does his obituary appear *the very next day?*"

I started to protest, then stopped: Javitz had noted just that thing, and I had dismissed it. Still: "And you think Mycroft would have expected us to make a whopping great leap of ratiocination based on a too-quick obituary?"

"I think when we find him, he will be amused that we had to dig up his coffin to be certain."

" 'Amused,' " I repeated darkly, looking at my filthy clothing and blistered hands. "Will he also be amused when his misplaced confidence in our deductive abilities gets us arrested for grave-robbing?"

"We have not actually stolen anything," Holmes pointed out mildly.

"Tell that to the arresting constable. Are you ready for the turf, Goodman?"

We tamped down the soil as best we could and shifted the turf back over the grave. In a day or two it would look much as it had, particularly if the rain continued, but even if the grave-diggers noticed that it was not as they left it, what would they do? Dig it up and find precisely what they had left there?

We darkened the light, left the spade in the shed, and crept unnoticed from the silent graveyard, taking our filthy selves through the wet streets to the bolt-hole.

Chapter 59

Peter James West returned the telephone to its cradle and walked across the room to stretch his reflection across the dark, rain-swept city. And only an hour ago, he'd been ready to call an end to it and see what he could salvage from the rubble of his carefully constructed plans.

The knock on his office door that afternoon had summoned him half an hour early to the taxi, which had meant an extra half hour sheltering in the damp recesses of the vault, waiting for the mourners to arrive. And there he had stood, growing ever colder, as his plans melted away like the mud at the edges of Mycroft Holmes' grave. Now, hours later, he could acknowledge a grudging respect for the two-pronged attack on his careful plan. Buckner hadn't a chance—although he couldn't see that Gunderson would have done any better.

The blond man in charge of the band must have been Moreton, the mad woodsman of Cumberland. The question was, had the woman only met him last week, or had she deliberately sought him out? He'd thought the man a pet she'd picked up along the way, as she had picked up (or so it appeared) the pilot and the child. If so, it showed a degree of sentimentality he'd not have expected of the young wife of Sherlock Holmes. If not—if the band-leader's inclusion had been planned—it indicated a degree of forethought that could prove dangerous.

Could that even be where Sosa had got to, as well, sheltering beneath her wing? And if not with her, where was he? Had his employer's death brought him face to face with the consequences of treason, and driven him to flee the country? If so, he hadn't taken his ill-gotten gains with him. And if the man tried to gain access to his accounts, West would hear about it. In any event, Sosa would surely be picked up soon—he lacked the nerve or the skill to go to ground for long.

But all the gloom and despair faded with the telephone call. There was a move in chess (idiotic game, a pale imitation of reality) where a lowly pawn could be made into a queen, and turned against the opponent with devastating consequences.

The telephone conversation had been to say that his pawn had been queened. He now had the tool with which to prise out the last remaining remnants of the old age, and make it new.

Painstaking, untiring, scientific method backed by modern technology: This was the new age of Intelligence. The age of Peter James West.

Chapter 60

It was fortunate that the building was empty at night, because during the work-day, someone would surely have noticed the volume of water running through unseen pipes. I claimed the first bath, which meant that Holmes' water ran cold. I felt no regret for his discomfort.

My hair was dry by the time he came out, his skin resembling a fish's pale belly. Goodman placed a steaming bowl of soup before him along with the plate of fresh-cooked scones he had apparently summoned from the air, and I let Holmes finish his meal before raising my questions.

"So, if Mycroft could have orchestrated this entire affair, but did not, who else is there? Who is in a similar position?"

"As you said, Sosa comes to mind. He has always been more an assistant than a mere secretary. And, he might well expect to inherit some portion of Mycroft's authority."

"What about West—what's his name, Peter James? I went to see him, but he was not at the address Lestrade gave me. I thought he might come to the funeral."

"West is one of the young men Smith-Cumming brought in after the War, and I'd have thought him of too low a rank to possess that degree of ambition. In another twenty years, perhaps. His boss, Sinclair, would be more likely: Sinclair and Mycroft have never seen eye to eye on what constitutes the greatest threat to the empire, and he's more than once expressed his disapproval of Mycroft's parallel and, as Sinclair regards it, amateur Intelligence firm.

"I was rather surprised to see him at the funeral—and, looking less relieved than saddened. Sinclair has taken the widespread conviction that Germany was the ultimate evil and transferred it onto Russia. He maintains the Bolsheviks have to be crushed, instantly and forever, lest they penetrate to our very soul. Mycroft agrees to an extent, but refuses to permit the limitation of interests. Thus far, the powers-that-be have agreed that Mycroft possesses a balanced view, but this has only convinced Sinclair that Mycroft is deluded and obstructive."

He stretched out an arm for a sterling cigarette case and gaudy glass ash-tray from Blackpool. When the stale cigarette was lit, he slid the case towards Goodman, who did not take it. We sat for a time, meditating on the ramifications of in-fighting among the branches of Intelligence.

"I have to agree," I said at last, "this entire scheme is convoluted enough to be something Mycroft cooked up."

"That would be a pleasant dream: my brother and his assistant, smoking cigars and moving pieces around a chessboard whilst his machinery turns."

"We need to find him," I said, stating the obvious.

"We need to find all of the missing pieces," Holmes corrected me. "We need to have a word with Sosa's mother, to see if he had a favourite refuge. And Brothers, who might be with one of the church's Inner Circle."

"I'd suggest we look for Mycroft first."

"Agreed," Holmes said. He put out his cigarette and fixed an eye on our guest. "Mr Goodman, where might you look for my brother?"

"At home," the small man said promptly.

I winced, recalling the state in which I'd left Mycroft's flat, but objected, "He wasn't there yesterday."

"All the more reason for him to be there today," Holmes said.

Goodman came with us, of course. I could not see that he would either cause, or come to, harm, and although I thought for a moment that Holmes would request him to stay behind, he did not.

We went in through the St James's Square entrance and followed Holmes' bobbing candle in single-file through the narrow labyrinth. The faint cracks around the doorway indicated that the light was still on in the study, and Holmes slid the peep-hole aside that I might examine the room, comparing it with how we had left it.

I took my time, then stood back.

"I don't see his gold pen on the desk-top. I'm pretty certain it was there Saturday."

Goodman reached for the latch, but Holmes grabbed his wrist. I had to agree. "Robert, he's right. Last time it only seemed to be a matter of arrest, but now there may be something more dangerous in there."

"All the more reason," he said, and before either of us could stop him, his other hand had worked the latch and he was putting his shoulder to the hidden door.

This time, I put my hand on Holmes' arm.

We waited for this peculiar man to make a second leisurely survey of Mycroft's flat. No shouts came, no gunshots. In a minute he was back, again holding an apple with a bite missing.

"Someone's been here," he commented indistinctly, then dropped into a chair, picking up an abandoned book from the nearby table.

Holmes shoved the door open, and I followed him inside.

At first, I could see no evidence of intrusion past the disorder I had myself left. Then: The chair I had used to prop under the door-handle was not as I remembered leaving it. Lestrade's note, which I had left in case Holmes came here, lay at a different angle. And the bowl of fruit— surely there was more than one apple missing?

The sitting-room window made it imprudent to turn on those lights, but the kitchen had doors. I made my way there, let the doors swing shut, and switched on a small light.

Yes: Someone had been here since I searched the room the previous afternoon.

In a few minutes, Holmes' voice came from without. "Was the revolver still in his bedside table when you were here yesterday?"

"Yes—is it missing now? Here—hold on a moment," I said. I dimmed the light to let him in, then turned it on again. "The tea caddy is empty, an assortment of foodstuffs are missing, and the chair Mrs Cowper sits in has been moved a few inches. Also, the pills she puts on his tea-tray every morning? The bottles had more in them yesterday."

He stared at me, then through me, a look I knew well. "What did you tell me about the key?"

"That Robert found? I merely speculated that the hiding of both key and letter—with the capital *I* on *Interpreter*—were intended to combine into a message that the key is in the interpreter. Or as it turned out, the key *is* the interpreter. Rather, his wife."

The expression that dawned across Holmes' face gave lie to his assertions of optimism. His face was transformed, and his eyes rose to the ceiling, as if thanking God. With an almost child-like glee, he rubbed his hands together as his gaze darted around the room, coming to rest on the royal portrait behind the housekeeper's misplaced chair.

The dumbwaiter, the height of modern amenities when it was installed a generation ago, had proved more trouble than benefit for most of the building's residents. Mycroft's renovations this past year had included a panel screwed to the wall over its opening, but he had not blocked the hole entirely, merely hung over it Mrs Cowper's portrait of His Majesty King George V.

Holmes jerked open the cutlery drawer for a knife, then crossed the room in three broad strides to attack the panel's screws. Two turns of the wrist and a screw fell away. He bent to retrieve it, holding it out on his palm: The full-sized head was attached to a mere half-inch of shaft. The screw had been sawed off until it was no thicker than the panel.

All six screws had received the same treatment, and none of them had any function but appearance, but when he jabbed the silver blade under the edge of the panel, it did not give. And not, as I first thought, because it had been painted shut: The panel was held in place from the back.

At home, we could instantly lay our hands on a wide variety of tools suitable for burglary or architectural destruction, but Mycroft had never gone in for the practical side of his profession. Still, Mrs Cowper kept a well-equipped kitchen: I hoped I never had to explain to her what we had done to her meat mallet and butcher-knife.

Dish-towels and pot-holders helped muffle the sound of splintering wood, but we had to shut off the lights once to fetch a large pillow from the sitting room, and a second time when the inquisitive Goodman requested entrance.

Finally, the panel's inner latches came free. Picking away the more vicious splinters, Holmes drew the torch from his pocket and put his head into the dark hole, twisting about to examine all angles.

When he stepped away, he looked as proud as ever a brother could be. He held out the torch, and I took his place.

Where there once would have dangled sturdy ropes joining the box to its pulley device at the top, there was now nothing but a dusty square shaft that reminded me of the emergency exits of some of the bolt-holes. Its roominess surprised me until I called to mind the box that travelled up and down: It had thick, insulated walls, and even then was big enough for . . .

I twisted about, as Holmes had done, and saw them: narrow boards, some ten inches apart, bolted to the wall beside the entrance and disappearing upwards into the gloom. It looked almost like—

"A ladder!" I withdrew my head and met Holmes' dancing grey eyes. "Oh, surely not. Mycroft couldn't climb those."

"Last year's Mycroft, no. But this year's model?"

"Good heavens. You don't imagine . . ."

"That my brother decided to shed weight in order to use this? It would require considerable determination and foresight."

Mycroft's Russian-doll of a mind, renovating a kitchen to conceal the noise and dust of building one secret entrance, at the same time creating another, even more closely hidden one.

Goodman had nudged me aside to look at our find. His height made it difficult to see, so he dragged Mrs Cowper's chair over to climb on. He thrust his torso inside. In a moment, his hand came back, holding a wide metal strip with a small hook at one end.

Holmes examined it, then bent to fit the hook into the wire mounted on the portrait. "It's a means of replacing the king before the door is fully shut," he said.

"Where does the shaft come out?" I asked Holmes, keeping my voice low. "Is the basement kitchen still in use?"

"I believe he was interested less in the depths than what lies above."

"What is that?"

"The Melas flat," Holmes replied with satisfaction. Then his face changed as he lunged past me, too late for the second time in minutes.

"Goodman, *stop!*" he hissed, his hand locked on the Green Man's ankle. Goodman did not retreat, nor did he reply, he merely waited, giving Holmes no choice but to let go. He thumbed the torch on and climbed through on the small man's heels, with me bringing up the rear and praying that the boards had in fact held Mycroft's weight, and could thus be trusted to hold a series of lesser bodies. It was at least forty feet to the ground, and I had two men above me.

The torch in Holmes' hand bounced madly, illuminating nothing so much as the soles of Goodman's shoes. I had only gone up a few feet when everything came to a halt. Trying simultaneously to cling to the wall and peer around Holmes, I saw Goodman's left hand exploring the wall beside the ladder, a storey above Mycroft's kitchen. Holmes stretched his arm back so the light fell on the wall; I heard a faint click.

Sudden light flooded the shaft, and Goodman leant forward to place his hand on the lower edge of the entrance.

Then he froze, his weight braced on one hand, suspended above our heads.

Holmes shifted, and said in a low voice, "Mycroft? If that is you, kindly put away your gun and allow Mr Goodman to enter."

The light dimmed somewhat as a figure appeared through the hole in the shaft wall. "My dear Sherlock. And Mary, too, I see. Yes, reports of my demise were somewhat exaggerated. I trust you brought dinner?"

Chapter 61

Mycroft looked bizarrely thin, as if his features had been grafted onto another man's body. However, he moved with ease around his borrowed kitchen, playing the host and making coffee despite the sticking plasters on two fingertips of his right hand. The revolver lay on the work-table beside an equally gaunt packet of biscuits.

"Am I to understand that Mrs Melas told you about this flat?"

"She did not," I answered.

Goodman said to me, "That's what she was waiting for you to ask." Mycroft had been more dubious about Goodman even than Holmes, eyeing him as one might a small child in a roomful of delicate knick-knacks.

"Yes, I should have known that you would not overlook the usefulness of an adjoining flat." That I had missed the significance of the renovations might have been humiliating, had Holmes not also failed to see them.

"I was beginning to wonder if I should have to sneak out at night and raid my neighbours' cupboards."

"I did make it as far as your own flat on Saturday," I told him.

He turned with a look of surprise. "That was you, Mary? Thumping about for hours?"

"Hardly hours. And yes, it was I."

"You left an unholy mess."

"I know. Sorry."

"I thought it was the police again—I expect they are the source of the ringing telephone downstairs that has been plaguing me all week-end. Although thank heavens, the ringing seems at last to have ceased. In any event, I kept anticipating that they would find their way up the dumb-waiter shaft."

"It was well concealed."

"By that portrait?" he said in astonishment. "How could anyone who ever met Mrs Cowper take her for a devoted Royalist?"

Another failure for which I had no answer.

The coffee was ready, the meagre edibles arranged on a fine plate. Mycroft led us to the Melas sitting room, a dark place furnished when Victoria set the fashion, with maroon velvet curtains so thick we had no worry of escaping light, and laid out eggshell cups and saucers that might have been a wedding gift to Sophy Melas and her Greek-interpreter husband. The coffee was pitifully weak, the milk tinned, the few biscuits stale. Goodman ignored the refreshment in favour of a thorough circuit of the flat, listening over his shoulder as Holmes told Mycroft about Damian's injuries and the threats he had encountered in Holland and Harwich. I then gave a quick synopsis of my own adventures, during which Goodman lost interest and kicked off his shoes to curl onto a divan in the corner. By the time I finished, a light snore came from his corner of the room.

Then it was Mycroft's turn.

"I think," Mycroft began, "this all began in June, fifteen months ago, when Cumming died." He took in the uncomprehending looks on half his audience, and explained. "Sir George Mansfield Smith-Cumming was the head of the foreign division of the SIS. In 1909, Intelligence was divided into domestic and foreign divisions—although the Navy and Army still had their own Intelligence services, of course. Cumming did some good work during the War, but afterwards the combination of his ill health and questionable decisions shook the service badly. In November 1920, you will recall, the IRA executed fourteen of his men. A catastrophic blow—and one which may have contributed to the next year's decision to reduce drastically the SIS budget.

"After Cumming's death, Hugh Sinclair took over, and although I find him somewhat single-minded on the dangers of Bolshevism, he is a competent man, who does what he can with limited funds."

He cleared his throat, and dribbled another dose of coffee-flavoured water into his cup. "However, economics is not the point—or not the particular point I have in mind. Intelligence in this country—the gathering of information on potential enemies—has a tumultuous history. In general, spying is seen as an ungentlemanly pursuit that becomes an unfortunate necessity in times of war. Each time conflict starts up, the country scrambles to generate spies and procure traitors, ending up with information that is incomplete or even wrong, and some highly questionable employees. Without method and forethought, we are left dangerously exposed.

"After the War, the various Intelligence divisions combined, shrank, or in a few cases, split off entirely. Vestigial elements remained, rather as my own department does. Military and civilian forces were thrown together: Names changed, power was grabbed, and the only thing the government could agree upon was, as I said, that the Intelligence budget wanted cutting. And cuts were made, insofar as the public record was concerned.

"In point of fact, several of the military and civilian bureaux, instead of being absorbed into the overall SIS, have continued blithely along their own lines. When Sinclair took over last year, he had a devil of a time finding which of those wartime groups had actually disbanded. Cumming had been willing to put up with these 'Intelligence Irregulars,' one might say— little more than private clubs or Old-Boys networks, really—because their information was occasionally useful. Sinclair, however, wanted them disbanded."

I frowned and was about to ask how these various groups were funded if the central agencies were being cut back, when Holmes spoke up.

"You'll have to tell her, Mycroft."

My brother-in-law shifted as if his chair had become uncomfortable; I would have missed the giveaway gesture had I not been looking directly at him. Goodman's rhythmic breathing continued without interruption; Mycroft lowered his voice, and began.

"Some thirty years ago, I found myself in a position to change this . . .

impermanent nature of the empire's Intelligence service. It was towards the end of the war between Japan and China, in 1895. A considerable amount of money had been ... circumspectly allotted to influence the war in favour of China. There is no need to go into the series of events first delaying the funds and then obscuring their presence, but suffice it to say that when war had ended, much of the money was still there, in limbo, threatening to become something of an embarrassment were Japan to discover it.

"Those responsible for committing the funds assumed they had been spent, either during the war or as a portion of the indemnities. I was one of the few capable of tracing them precisely. To ask for their return would have opened up a can of worms that the Prime Minister did not wish to see opened. So I ... removed the potential source of international chagrin by making the money disappear."

"What? Wait—you *stole* government funds? *You?*"

"I stole nothing. I merely relocated them. With the Prime Minister's full knowledge, I may add, although nothing was put to paper. The amount was considerable, and I invested it sensibly. The annual return keeps my operations running."

I looked at Holmes, who was diligently studying the end of his cigarette, then back at his brother. I couldn't believe it. Embezzlement? *Mycroft?*

My brother-in-law went on, as if he had confessed to taking home the office dictionary. "As I said, in the months since Cumming's death, power has shifted in several directions. My own rôle in the Intelligence world has always been primarily that of observer, and although I do have direct employees, generally speaking I commandeer men from elsewhere when I require them.

"My illness came at a bad time. Decisions were being made with great rapidity last December, after the election but before Labour took over. One might even describe the mood as 'panicked.' The outgoing Prime Minister together with Admiral Sinclair set a number of Intelligence elements into stone, then brushed away the dust and presented the incoming Labour party with a *fait accompli*. And since Labour had been on the outside of policy, they could not know that this was not how things had always appeared.

"I lost two key months to illness. When I was fit enough to resume work in February, I thought at first the changes around me were due to the new régime. And as you no doubt heard even in foreign parts, there was consternation and loud doom-saying on all sides: The Socialists were expected to bring the end of the monarchy, the establishment of rubles as the coin of the realm, a destruction of marriage and family, and dangerously intimate political and economic ties with the Bolsheviks. Eight months later, the worst of the country's fears have yet to be realised, and MacDonald has surprised everyone by being less of a firebrand than the village greengrocer.

"I expect you followed these issues to some degree during your travels. But when I returned to my office, it was nearly impossible to sift rumour from fact and policy from gossip. I felt there was something awry, I sensed a leak and a degree of manipulation, but everything had been overturned all around me, and in any case, the interference was very subtly done.

"Then in April, someone blackmailed my secretary."

"Ah," I said. So he did know about Sosa.

"Now, over the years I have collected nearly as varied a list of enemies as you, Sherlock. The immediate threat was from within, but whether it came out of the central SIS or one of the vestigial organisations was remarkably difficult to determine.

"So I set up a trap. And because my opponent had at least one finger inside my camp, it was possible he had more. I moved with caution, and attempted to appear oblivious.

"Which is terribly difficult! How do you manage it, Sherlock? Playing the idiot, I mean?"

"It helps to wear dark lenses," Holmes remarked. "To conceal the intelligence."

"Metaphorical dark glasses, in my case," Mycroft said. "I have found the appearance of age and infirmity quite helpful in maintaining the façade of oblivion. And I might have managed to complete my trap and bait it, had it not been for the abrupt arrival of my nephew on the scene."

"Because of Brothers?"

"The Brothers case proved both a blessing and a curse. On the one hand, that wretch's acts drove a cart and horses through my tidy ambush. All of a sudden, the police were underfoot, with an all-out hunt for Damian, then for the two of you.

"However, once I began to look into the situation for you, I realised that it might be another in the series of incidents where I suspected my invisible opponent's hand at work. It had become clear that Brothers had a guardian within the government, someone who greased official rails. One might think that there are a limited number of men who can establish new identities and arrange bank accounts, but in practice, a person who holds authority in one department can generally manipulate the machinery of another. And it can work informally, as well, or even indirectly: informally, in that when one knows the right people, one need only drop a word in a fellow club-man's ear to have a protégé's application speeded, his request granted. And indirectly, because a tightly knit group of school- and 'varsity-chums will grant one another favours without asking where the request originated.

"I was in the process of narrowing down the candidates when five uniformed constables came to the office to demand that I accompany them to New Scotland Yard. I have to say, I did not know whether to laugh or to take out my revolver."

"Why did you not telephone the PM?" Holmes asked.

"Because I thought this might be the additional factor that brought my list of candidates down to one. I knew Lestrade had to be acting under orders—why else not simply come and talk to me?—but I wanted to know whose.

"Unfortunately, I do not think he knew himself. During our interview, he seemed almost sheepish, as if he'd been asked to take part in a play with rather too much melodrama for his taste. Still, it gave me a pathway to investigate, since there are a limited number of ways in which Scotland Yard can be reached.

"And I might have found it by now had it not been for the motorcar that pulled to the kerb thirty feet from the Yard's entrance. In the back sat a large man with a scar across his left eyebrow and a gun in his hand."

"Gunderson," I supplied.

I became aware of an odd, breathy noise; it took me a moment to identify it as Goodman's snores.

"And the driver?" Holmes asked.

"Another criminal type. Certainly no public-school boy."

"They masked you?"

"A sack over my head. He then made me get on the floor, and we drove back and forth for twenty minutes or so before ending up very close to where we had begun, at a warehouse in Lambeth—an old warehouse, no doubt slated for development and therefore quite deserted. I could hear Ben's chimes and smell the river, but I was well and truly trapped, and any noise would go unheard.

"I was minimally fed every eight hours, the water often lightly drugged. Until this past Wednesday, when the three o'clock meal was not only brought me by a new set of feet, it was so heavily drugged, I could see the powder residue in the cup. So I poured it on the floor, and waited.

"Two hours later, Richard Sosa arrived."

I jerked upright in disbelief. "They sent your secretary to kill you?"

Mycroft returned my look of disbelief. "Kill me? What are you on about? Mr Sosa came to rescue me."

Chapter 62

Mycroft's three o'clock meal—Wednesday? He was almost certain it was Wednesday—sat in the corner of the room, taunting him. He had seen the foreign matter in the cup, tasting it gingerly before pouring it onto the floor, and decided not to risk the solid food.

If death was finally coming for him, he wanted to meet it on his feet.

Ninety minutes later, he heard a noise, but it was not the noise he expected. It sounded like glass breaking.

After five minutes, it happened again, only closer. This time he moved to the far corner of the room, raising his eyes to the square of light overhead.

The next repetition came two minutes after the second; after another two-minute pause, his window proved to be the fourth. It began when the square developed a dark patch—ah, Mycroft thought: The breaker of windows had discovered that glass splashes back, and spent three minutes improvising a guard before his second attempt.

A sharp rap in the centre of the shadow split the glass. Palm-sized shards of glass rained down; the shadow was removed, and glass fell as the pipe jabbed at the widening hole. When the hole reached the window's edge, the pipe withdrew. Seconds later, a torch beam hit the floor, searching the corners until it froze on Mycroft.

"Mr Holmes!" said a welcome voice that wavered upwards to a squeak.

"Mr Sosa," Mycroft said in astonishment. "An unexpected pleasure."

"Oh, sir, I am so glad to see you. I hope you are well?"

Mycroft's lips quirked. "Much the better for seeing you, Blondel."

"Er, quite. I am glad," the secretary repeated, fervent with relief. "Shall I, that is, if you wish, I could go and fetch a locksmith?"

"Either that or a heavy sledge. The door is solid."

"I do have...that is, I wasn't certain if you...I have a ladder."

"A ladder?" Mycroft had judged his prison on the top of a sizeable building: Summoning a ladder the height of the room would be a considerable project.

"Not a ladder as such, it's rope. A rope-ladder. If you feel up to such a thing."

"Is there sufficient anchor up there? I'd not care to get nearly to the top and have it come loose."

"Oh no, no no, that wouldn't do at all. Yes, there is a metal pipe nearby, and I have a rope as well. To fasten around the pipe, that is, and tie to the ladder."

"Mr Sosa, I don't know that I've ever had opportunity to enquire, but—your knowledge of knots. How comprehensive is it?"

"Quite sufficient, I assure you, sir," he answered earnestly. "As a boy, I taught myself a full two dozen styles and their chief purposes. I propose a sheet bend rather than a reef knot. And to fasten it to the pipe, a double half-hitch should be quite sufficient. No, sir; my knots will hold."

"Very well, let us make haste."

"If you would just—"

"Stand back—I know. The quality of mercy is not strained, it droppeth down as the gentle glass from heaven. Bash away, Mr Sosa."

Sosa bashed, until the frame was cleared of glass. He then disappeared, for a disarmingly long period, while Mycroft stood below, his hands working hard against each other.

A young eternity later, an object little smaller than the window leapt through the hole and plunged downwards. Mycroft stumbled back, seeing it as Sosa being thrown inside by the returned gaoler—but then the large darkness caught and rapidly unfurled, dancing its way all the way down to the floor: the ladder.

Mycroft rested his hand against his pounding heart for a moment. The torch-light hit him and he heard his name. He dropped his hand and picked his way over the glass to the ladder, tugging it with little conviction. It seemed sturdy.

He gave a last glance to his prison, and the formula scratched into the wall, then committed his stockinged foot to the first rung.

Five rungs up, the ladder dipped alarmingly, and he clung to the insecure rope as if it would do an iota of good. He waited, feeling motion on the line. Then came two sharp tremors, as if its tautness was being slapped.

"Mr Sosa, may I take it that the two raps were to indicate the rope is secure?"

Two tremors came down again; reluctantly, Mycroft inched up another rung, then another.

At the top, he saw the problem: The knots had held admirably; the pipe had been less secure. He gave up on gentle motions and threw himself over the frame onto the roof.

Sosa, red-faced and trembling from the effort of keeping the metal pipe from bending catastrophically, sank to the roof and put his head in his hands.

After a minute, not far from open tears, the secretary staggered to his feet and came over to pat his employer on the shoulder, back, and arm. Mycroft began to feel like a prize dog, and feared that in another minute, the man would embrace him.

"Remind me to increase your salary," he said.

This distracted Sosa. "Sir, I did not do this for the salary," he protested.

Mycroft laughed. He laughed for quite a while, finding it oddly difficult to regain control of his face, but eventually he forced levity to arm's length and stood up.

"My afternoon meal was heavily drugged, with what appeared to be Veronal."

"Did you eat it?" Sosa asked in alarm.

"Of course not. But my captor will assume I did, and will return before long so as to catch me unconscious. I believe, Mr Sosa, you have come only just in time."

"Oh, dear. Perhaps not."

Mycroft looked up in alarm, hearing the dread in his secretary's voice, then moved over quickly to see what had attracted the man's attention.

Down on the empty street below, a large figure got out from behind the wheel of a van that looked remarkably like those used by a mortuary to transport bodies.

"Fast, man," Mycroft urged. "If we can get down the stairs and take him by surprise, I can use this stout pipe you most thoughtfully—sorry, what was that?"

"I said, wouldn't you rather use your gun?" The revolver looked incongruous balanced in the secretary's thin palm, but most welcome.

"Mr Sosa, you are a gem among men."

They were an unlikely pair of avengers, a thin balding man in a high collar with dust on his knees and a look of resolute terror on his sweating face, following a shoeless, unshaven, once-fat man in a filthy suit belted by an aged Eton tie, rapidly tip-toeing down a rickety metal stairway and through a derelict hallway.

The muffled gunshots that followed, heard by two waking prostitutes, a nurse snatching a quick cigarette outside St Thomas' hospital, six ex-Army madmen in Bedlam, and three members of the House of Lords in solemn conclave with a glass of sherry on the Terrace, were dismissed as a back-firing lorry.

Chapter 63

Heavens, Sosa has been at my right hand for twenty-six years," Mycroft told us indignantly. "I'm surprised that you imagine me such a poor judge of character."

"I, well," I said, biting my tongue to keep from saying, *Nor had I imagined you an embezzler.*

"The hypothesis was, Mr Sosa wished to inherit your position," Holmes said. Mycroft looked at me askance, and did not deign to acknowledge such a ridiculous suspicion.

"Sosa came to me immediately after the blackmailer approached him. He'd been ordered to turn over certain minor pieces of information, thus saving himself from scandal and earning a small sum as well. The photographs were of his sister and, shall we say, politically rather than socially embarrassing, while the information requested was indeed of little importance. The sort of thing that could be learnt elsewhere with a bit of digging."

"It was a toe in the door," Holmes remarked.

"Precisely. A thing that might tempt a man to succumb without preying on his conscience over-much. I naturally gave Sosa permission to pass on the information."

"Thus setting a trap."

"The first faint preparation for a trap. More like a thread to grasp. A delicate and convoluted thread, little better than the mere suspicion I'd had to that point, but I seized it, and I have spent the past five months trying to follow it to its source."

"A twenty-pound trout on five-pound test line," Goodman's sleepy voice murmured from the corner.

Mycroft looked around in surprise. "Yes, a telling analogy. Attempting to reel my opponent in.

"And then, as I said, you two arrived back in the country, and we were instantly overtaken by Damian's problems."

"Why keep you alive?" Holmes asked.

Another man might have been taken aback by the callous question, but Mycroft merely said, "I spent much of my captivity meditating on that question, and eventually decided that I was being kept, as it were, on ice, until my death could serve a function."

"How did your secretary find you?" I asked.

"I keep Sosa apprised of the general outlines of any of my projects, including this one. He became uneasy on the Thursday I disappeared, when I failed to return to work in the afternoon. Then in the evening he had a telephone call from his blackmailer instructing him to send Captain Lofte back to Shanghai. When Friday not only found me absent, but saw the deposit of a sizeable sum into his bank account, he grew alarmed, and began to work his way down the *dramatis personae* of our recent portfolios. Brothers was still missing, but now his general factotum, Gunderson, was as well.

"Mr Sosa may be a mere secretary, but he has not worked with me all these years for nothing. He placed the telephone call to Captain Lofte, but he also made arrangements with the neighbours at Gunderson's and Brothers' homes, to send word if either man returned. He applied himself wholeheartedly to the hunt, with little result. I fear the poor fellow was worn quite thin by the time he heard of activity in Gunderson's rooms on Tuesday night. The moment he received the news, Wednesday morning, he took up a position across the street from Gunderson's lodgings house, in an agony of trepidation lest his quarry had already left, or he would miss him when he did.

"Five hours later, at two-thirty in the afternoon, Gunderson came out carrying a small bag, and headed for the river.

"Gunderson never looked behind him. Although if he had, what would he have seen? One drab clerk among a thousand others, harried and indistinguishable.

"Yes, I am quite pleased with Mr Sosa.

"Gunderson went straight to the warehouse. And since the route to my prison led up a stair-well with many broken windows, Sosa could follow the man's progress to the top storey. He waited for Gunderson to leave again, which was almost immediately—he had been dispatched to bring me my final, heavily drugged afternoon meal. Sosa watched him go, then summoned his courage and crossed over to the warehouse.

"There, his skills failed him—he had absorbed quite a bit of theory over the years, but little of the practicum. An oversight I shall have to remedy, in the future: It would have simplified matters had he been able to pick locks.

"But he could not. However, upon circling the building, he saw a set of fire-stairs, precariously attached and missing some of their treads, but for the most part sound.

"It took him two hours to round up what he needed, and he came near to breaking his neck getting up the metal steps in his office shoes, but he persisted, and made it to the roof, where he went along the row of sky-lights with a length of pipe. On the fourth such window, he found me."

He described how Sosa, terrified by his own audacity, had rescued him. "I then told him to keep back when I went to confront Gunderson, but the poor fellow seemed to think he was Allen Quatermain and would not leave me. When Gunderson turned and saw us, an old man and a milksop, of course he pulled his gun. I had little choice but to shoot him. And to my irritation, he was inconsiderate enough to die before he could tell me who had sent him.

"But with him he had a parcel, the contents of which were most intriguing. My shoes and belt were there, and a clean shirt—not one of mine, but in my size. Also a clothes' brush, razor, and bottle of water, indicating that he intended to render me more or less presentable. But the contents of a large envelope were the most suggestive of all: my note-case, into which a photograph of a rather attractive and scantily clad female had been inserted; a card for a night-club called The Pink Pagoda;

a torn-off section of the London map showing the area about The Pink Pagoda, with an X drawn across a nearby alley; the forms necessary for a London mortuary to conduct a burial; and the autopsy for a man matching my size and general description, signed by an out-of-town pathologist, and dated the following day.

"Poor Mr Sosa, the events of that afternoon nearly did him in. Flying bullets and the presence of a dead man were bad enough, but then I made him wait there with me until dark—hoping that Gunderson's boss, or at least a colleague, might come looking for him, which they did not—because in my weakened condition I could not manhandle Gunderson's body down to the mortuary van by myself. And after that, he had to drive, then help me dump the body. I think by this time his mind had gone numb, because he did not even protest when I told him we needed to wait until the police had showed up, before carrying out the charade that Gunderson's employer had intended for me.

"I had found a flask of gin in the glove compartment of the van, and made my secretary take a swallow to steady his nerves. And when the time came, he flashed his identity at the police with what appeared to be bored panache, but was, in fact, sheer terror. Then we snatched the body from out of their hands and delivered it, with the papers, to the funeral home.

"After that, I had Sosa drop me at the Angel Court entrance, and I ordered him to go to an hotel I knew near Maidenhead, and check in under an assumed name. I also ordered him to drink the remainder of the gin and go immediately to bed—he is a teetotaller, but I expected it might be a choice between alcohol and a complete breakdown, and thought the effect of drink would be simpler to deal with."

With that, Mycroft picked up the final biscuit and sat back, as if his tale was at its end.

"So you've been here since Wednesday?" I prompted.

"I have a long-standing arrangement with Mrs Melas, that I might use her upstairs flat if ever I needed a retreat. She even came to see if I might be here, while I was in my prison—she left a note on the desk for me, asking that I get into touch. Fortunately, she hasn't been back since."

"She believed the reports of your death, as we did. *I* did," I corrected myself, although Holmes' claims to the contrary were not entirely convincing.

Mycroft winced. "Yes, I feared the report would trouble you. There was little I could do. Any public message-board such as the agony column was sure to be watched. As I said, my opponent has a remarkably subtle mind."

That gave me pause, to think that the messages Holmes and I had posted to each other might have been not only noticed, but understood. However, one would also have had to know where the bolt-holes were to trace us to them, and there this faceless opponent had met his limits.

"I knew you would return to London, once you had dealt with Brothers. With luck, you would even find me before I began to eat Mrs Melas' leather chair. But you say that Brothers is not dead. How do you intend to find him?"

Brothers be damned, I thought, and interrupted. "Did you send Mr Sosa away?"

"On Thursday, it must have been," Holmes noted. "Once he'd brought you the morning papers."

"And food. Yes, I sent him to the country with his mother, and had him get into touch with your Mrs Hudson and my own Mrs Cowper. We have a wide number of acquaintances at the moment who are taking in distant scenery."

Poor Mrs Hudson, banished yet again for her own good. At least Dr Watson was out of it this time.

"We cannot afford any more hostages to fortune," Holmes agreed.

"That was my thought. However, I had not suspected that Mr Sosa was made of such stern stuff. He returned to St James's Square at mid-day on Thursday, where I had agreed to be available to him, were he to want me, and brought me a pair of Gladstone bags stuffed with edibles and the news. However, he was badly shaken: That morning he had decided that he could scarcely spend the day in the same shirt he had worn the day previous, and went home to pack a valise. There he found signs of a most expert break-in and the insinuation of several pieces of incriminating evidence amongst his things. He gathered his mother and fled; the two of them were in the mortuary van with her cat and canary. I gave him strict orders to abandon the stolen motor and take her away for at least two weeks. After the invasion of his home, I believe he will obey me. I only hope I can talk him into returning to my employ, once this is over."

"Good," Holmes said to his brother. "Tell me, what do you propose to do about your faceless opponent?"

"Now that I have you, I'd thought—"

"Wait," I said. Damian was lodged in Holland somewhere and Javitz was protecting Estelle—but if our opponent was all-knowing, there remained one member of our party to consider: "Goodman."

The man attached to that name gave a snort and sat upright on the divan, blinking against the light. I said, "That is your family's estate, in Cumberland, where you live?"

"My . . . yes."

"You could be traced from there?"

He shrugged, to indicate its remote possibility. I turned to Holmes.

"If our opponent has figured out who Goodman is, and if he's desperate enough, he could use them—the family is away, fortunately, but the servants are there, and vulnerable."

Goodman snorted again, this time a sound of derision. "*That* family? Were he sane, a threat to a mere servant would not bend a son of the family. But mad? One cannot manipulate a madman. No sensible man would try."

With that, he turned over on the divan and went back to sleep.

We three looked at each other, and admitted the wisdom of the fool's pronouncement.

"You were saying, Mycroft?" Holmes asked.

"I was saying, with your assistance, I believe we might revive the trap I had been constructing before Mr Brothers stumbled into our lives. There may be fewer of us than I had anticipated. However, I believe we can adapt it to our reduced numbers."

The conversation that followed led us nearly to dawn, and the plan Mycroft laid and Holmes and I amended was a good one: simple, solid, and requiring little luck to succeed. Our opponent might not realise yet that Mycroft was alive, but he must be aware that Gunderson was missing. It was unfortunate that Mycroft had lacked the personal stamina, or the reliable manpower, to set watch over the warehouse. Nonetheless, the combination of blood on the floor, bullets in the walls, and a broken sky-light would surely put the most phlegmatic of villains in a state of panic.

Mycroft need only walk in the door of his Whitehall office to send any rats scurrying for their holes. With me at the building's telephone board and Holmes at its exit, one or the other would lead us to their source.

Before the sun rose behind the curtains that Monday morning, our plans were laid.

Mycroft stood, moving like an old man. Holmes and I were little better. I looked at the mantelpiece clock: nearly six.

"You will leave soon?" I asked Mycroft.

Holmes was frowning at his brother's stiffness and spoke first. "The afternoon will suffice."

"Really?" I dreaded to hear what other activity he had in mind. "So what now?"

"A few hours of sleep might be for the best."

"Sleep, Holmes?" I exclaimed. "Do we *do* that?"

"As best we might, given the age of Mrs Melas' beds."

When we began to stir, Goodman woke and stretched full-length on the striped divan, looking remarkably like Estelle. Then he jumped to his feet.

"Unless you need me to guard the door or repel boarders, I'll be gone for a bit. Shall I hang the picture back over the hole downstairs, on the chance someone wanders in?"

Holmes started to object, but I was more accustomed to Goodman's habit of popping in and out of view, and told my long-time partner, "He knows the back entrance, he knows to take care that no one sees him use the hidden doors, he'll be careful."

"And I'll bring a pint of milk," Goodman said.

"But not an entire arm-load of groceries," I ordered. "Nothing you can't slip unseen into your pockets. We don't want you to look like a delivery boy."

He put on his straw hat and marched with jaunty steps to the kitchen. I had a sudden pang of doubt—we could be trapped here—but stifled it, and went to find a bed. It wanted airing, but a slight mustiness would not keep me from sleep.

I felt I had scarcely closed my eyes when a presence woke me. I forced an eye open, and saw green; blinked, and the green became an eye; pulled back my head, and Goodman came into view, his face inches from mine.

I sat sharply upright, glanced over, and found Holmes, incredibly, still asleep—who would have thought Goodman could enter this place without waking either of the brothers? When I turned back to my human alarum clock, my vision was obscured by an object that, when I had pushed it away sufficient to focus, proved to be a folded newspaper.

His other hand came around the side of the page, one finger pointing at the print. "Is this for you?"

I took the paper, and read:

> **THE BEEKEEPER** wished in trade for the object of his affection central Bensbridge, alone, 2:30 am, reply acceptance in evening standard.

Chapter 64

R obert Goodman sat on the rooftop, watching London rush to and fro between his dangling toes. The view was omniscient—in the theatre of the streets, his seat was in the gods. Which was only appropriate, considering the Person on whom he was meditating.

Are you frightened of anything?

Suffer the little children, to come unto me, because they will speak the truths only fools know. Oh, the Son of Man knew what he was talking about, that was for certain.

And the Son of Man did his own sitting on the heights, thinking on the morrow, wondering if he might not simply slip away and leave his friends to sort it out.

A simple child that lightly draws its breath / And feels its life in every limb; what should it know of death? Interesting, that the Bard of Avon had so few children in his writing while Wordsworth had so many. If Wordsworth had been a playwright forced to deal with actors, would he, too, have replaced children with sprites and fairies?

A simple child should know nothing of death, or fear, or hunger. But children did, all the time. Estelle Adler certainly did, poor mite—mother murdered, father hunted. But what was that to him?

An ambulance driver had responsibilities, but they were not those of an officer. A driver's demands were immediate, clear-cut, and rode light upon the conscience: Men died, but if one had done one's job, those deaths could be laid at the foot of someone else. Some officer.

Even then, even *Before*, his very soul—that Other whom he once was—had cringed from an officer's relationship with the men in his command. Not through cowardice: He would risk life and limb to bring a man home, even one who was not going to reach the field hospital alive. But he would not lead them. He would not love them and comfort them and cajole them into the path of flying metal. He'd have put a lump of metal into his own brain first.

Are you frightened of anything, Mr Robert?

An omnibus paused between his toes, sucking up a row of tiny figures, evacuating others. The Son of Man could walk among those figures and go unnoticed, for to their minds, they were the gods. Modern gods, whose mighty commands rang down the telephone wires; who parted the waters with steamers and digging machines; who rained fire from the heavens over the poor cowering wretches in the trenches; who thundered rage in the engines of their trains and the blare of their motorcar klaxons.

Take away this cup, for I am afraid. If the Son of Man couldn't talk his way out of what was coming for him, how could any other son of man?

A tiny dot of brilliant blue caught his eye, and he bent forward to watch it: a woman's hat, a spot of defiant *joie de vivre* sailing the drab sea before it was swallowed by a shop.

With the bright spot gone, he became aware of the pull of the street, far below. *Mad world, mad kings, mad composition!* There was earth beneath the tarmac and tile, real earth, and its call was, ultimately, not to be denied. Who was to say it would not be today?

Without a doubt, the time had passed for men like him. The city below him was a machine, its people mere moving parts generating goods and money. Cold rationality had spread across this fair land: Its nobility were those who stole for good purpose. Which he could understand— gods made their own rules—but these took no joy in life. The gods of this England were film stars and dispensers of tawdry advice, and they embraced brittle frivolity rather than the deep and supple exuberance of woodland creatures. In this England, Ariel would wear a straight-jacket, Hamlet would be fodder for the gossip columns. Hadn't he seen Oberon

and Titania this very morning, aged and worn as the feather in his borrowed hat: a man and a woman, older than their years, sitting on a park
bench in their cast-off overcoats and sharing a scrap of ill-cooked food?
The king and queen of the fairy world, eking out their days amongst the
wind-blown biscuit wrappers.

Goodman pulled the feather from his hat band. This primary flight-
feather of *Strix aluco* had greeted him one morning outside his front
door, a gift from the tawny lady whose home was in the old oak, whose
voice often called to him at night. His fingers smoothed the barbs to
order, but there remained a gap. One barb was missing. When had that
happened? He worked at it with his fingertips, as if his flight from the
roof-top depended on the feather's perfection, but even with the bar-
bules linked, there remained a hole near the shaft.

Are you frightened of anything, Mr Robert?

The hole in the owl's feather was the shape of an elongated tear-drop.
Turned slightly, it reminded him of the shape of a child's eye. A half-
Chinese child's eye.

He shuddered, and let go the feather, leaning forward, forward until a
gust of wind caught it, whipping it around the corner and out of sight.

A child's eye.

Late November, in the depths of an eternal war, a war with no beginning, no end, only stink and muck and death. One rainy day all his men
had been taken from him, and in exchange he had been given an ambulance filled with groaning bodies and a dead driver. And so he became
Goodman and no longer had to be The Other who ordered his men into
the bullets, and he drove like a demon to claw the bleeding away from
Death.

Then in December, The Powers Above had decreed that a particular
piece of ground must be won, a tiny hillock of no more importance than
any other hillock won or lost over the past twenty-eight months. It was
to be a surprise push. It was certainly a surprise to the citizens of a much-
shelled village, trying to scrape a few potatoes from the liquid ground.

And a child. God only knew where her parents were—under a collapsed building, leaking into a field. But the child was there, a grubby
thing in a too-short dress and a too-large hat who had climbed—or been

placed—on a bit of surviving wall, where she kicked her heels and watched the parade of passing motors and horses; soldiers marching in one direction, soldiers staggering or being carried in the other.

No fear, no curiosity, just sitting and watching, hands in her lap, as if she'd been sitting and watching the whole of her young life.

One glance, and the passing soldiers and ambulance drivers could tell she was not right. A closer look, and Goodman had seen the almond curve to her eyes, the protruding tongue-tip that imparted a look of great concentration. She was what they call Mongoloid, what his mother—what The Other's mother—had called one of God's innocents. The child had sat there like a talisman for three trips to the Front, and then she was gone. The wall was gone. He drove two more trips before he stopped to see. The hat was there; she was not. She was not there all the way until dark, but that night she was back, her epicanthic eyes watching him, that night and a string of other nights. Once the battle had moved on a few miles, he returned to the village and found an old woman who knew of the child, who confirmed that the mother had died and the father was gone to war. The old woman did not know where the child was. He asked soldiers. He haunted the hospital tents. In the end he drove off in his ambulance, far down the line to where the French uniforms began, in pursuit of a rumour of troops who had adopted a mute orphan as their mascot. But it was not she.

Then he was arrested, and it was discovered that Goodman had been born on a battlefield when The Other had died. He expected to be lined up and shot, but word came of a medal, and as a favour to the French, they sent him to Craiglockhart instead. There he met Rivers, and told him, just a little, about the girl on the wall.

Only after, when he'd crawled off to Cumberland and found the old woodsman's hut and let the land remake him, had she gone away, for good.

Until an aeroplane came at him out of the sky and gave birth to a very different child with the same almond-shaped eyes.

And now below him lay the child's nest, her hive, the loud, confusing, cold-hearted world into which she had been born. She might appear a being *that could not feel the touch of earthly years*—Wordsworth's children, again—yet in no time at all the *shades of the prison-house* would close in on her and she would grow up. There was nothing he could do to stop it. She could not live in a Cumberland estate among the owls and the hedgehogs. Her people lay below him. In his pocket was the drawing her father had done, the child become a woman: That was her world.

Her world, not his: He had no place here. But because of a child with a certain shape to her eyes, he must try to see the life in the machine, to see the sweetness in what they produced. He must do what he could to make it a place worthy of her.

He wished he'd had time to talk to Mary Russell's man about bees. The books in his bolt-hole suggested an interest in the creatures, yet this was a man who'd spent his life with the darkest side of the human race. Would he look between his feet at a city landscape and see a hive, or a machine? Would he behold the labours of his fellow man and see the sweetness of intellectual honey, or yet more machines in which they would enmesh themselves? The man's eagerness to support his brother's preoccupation with Intelligence—what a misnomer!—suggested the latter. Nonetheless, he was Estelle's grandfather, and therefore worthy of assistance.

Are you afraid of anything, Mr Robert?

Oh, dear child, I most certainly am. I am afraid of fear, so afraid. I am terrified of the bonds that tie a man down, the weight of other lives on his shoulders, the responsibility for stopping unnatural acts.

He was grateful to have made the acquaintance of Mary Russell: *A perfect woman, nobly planned / To warn, to comfort, and command.*

Command me, dear lady, he thought. *Warn me and comfort me and give me orders, for I am in need of a clear-cut task. I have long cast off my officer's class. I need to know that someone else is in charge.*

Still, the music to the funeral had gone well, and that was all his own doing. Perhaps he needed to venture his own contribution to the current problem.

What could he bring to this next act in the play?

He got to his feet and stretched out one arm in a gesture unseen by those on the street below. "Sweep on, you fat and greasy citizens," he shouted at them, then laughed aloud.

Having thus granted London his god-like permission to continue its scurrying life, he put on his hat and turned for the stairway.

He had, he recalled, promised a pint of milk. And his pockets were capacious, his coat large enough to conceal a beltful of sustenance—cheese and biscuits from the shop on the ground floor of this very building, apples from the man on the corner, a packet of coffee, a small loaf of bread. That Mycroft fellow looked as if he'd appreciate a slab of bacon.

Oh, he thought, and a newspaper. Mary's husband seemed particularly taken by the things.

Chapter 65

Bensbridge' I assume to be Westminster Bridge, and he wants a reply in the *Evening Standard*, but what the devil does he mean by 'the object of your affection'?" I demanded. Goodman, newspaper delivered, had washed his hands of the matter and retired to the kitchen. He was humming to himself and exploring the cupboards.

"I do not know. Although addressing himself to Sherlock suggests that he believes me dead."

Holmes and I rose at the same instant.

"There's a public telephone down the street. Do you want to go, or shall I?" I asked.

"Take a taxicab to the offices of the *Evening Standard*," Mycroft said. "There will be a telephone near there."

"You're not thinking of agreeing to his demands?" I protested.

Holmes' face was a study in storm clouds. He made a circle of the room, then snatched up Mycroft's gold pen and a piece of paper. "If we do not place a reply—by noon—we remove the option of choice. One of us needs to stay here, and...you are the less immediately visible." He held out the page, on which he had written three words:

The beekeeper agrees.

I hesitated, but the revelations of the night before, which I had pushed from my mind under the urgent need for rationality, washed back with a vengeance. Suddenly, the thought of being locked up with my brother-in-law filled me with revulsion. Without further argument, I thrust the page into a pocket and made for the kitchen. As I climbed through the dumbwaiter hole, I heard Holmes say to Mycroft that he needed some things from downstairs.

I went fast down the shaft and through Mycroft's flat to the guest room, noticing in passing that Goodman had cleaned up the débris from the panel. Holmes found me ripping garments from the wardrobe.

"Russell."

"*Theft,*" I spat. "Embezzlement for the good of the nation! Oh, Holmes, how could you?"

"It was necessary."

"The ends justifying the means? The tawdry excuse of every tyrant through history."

"Mycroft is no tyrant, Russell."

"Isn't he? Stealing money from his government to set up his own little monarchy. What is he doing with all that money, that can't be done openly? Bribes? Assassinations? I know there's blackmail—*blackmail*, Holmes! Those letters of his that 'would taint our name forever.' You detest blackmailers, yet you permitted it!"

"The 'noble lie' has to convince the rulers themselves."

I rejected the sadness in his voice by making mine louder. "I think I prefer the sentiments of *Phaedo* to those of *The Republic*: 'False words are not only themselves evil, but they infect the soul with evil.'"

"Do you not imagine that my brother is well aware of that? Do you not see that thirty years ago, he consciously chose to shape a life of virtue on top of that one act?"

"What I'd imagined was that Mycroft was above such things. What I'd hoped was that he did his best to counteract the slimy deeds that Intelligence spawns, the bribes and blackmail and God knows what death and misery. What I'd hoped—" I broke off and slammed the drawer. What I'd hoped was that Mycroft was better than that.

"Good men may be driven to unethical decisions. I have been, myself."

I grabbed a comb and began to drag it through my hair, trying to ignore the figure in the edge of the looking-glass.

"Are you and I arguing," Holmes asked eventually, "or are you arguing with yourself?"

I threw the comb into its drawer, kicked my shed garments into the corner, and jammed one of the wider cloches over my head. I looked at my reflection, but after a time, I had to look away.

Mycroft had always been a bigger-than-life presence, even before I met him; to find...*this* at the man's core shook me. When it came to Mycroft, I had somehow decided that he managed to undertake the business of Intelligence without the unsavoury aspects of the craft, even though I myself was regularly driven to house-breaking, lying to the police, assault...Holmes was right, I was being simplistic. Childish.

Fortunately, he had the sense not to say so.

"All right," I said. "Yes, he pays. That doesn't make it right, but it's a brutal world and the work he does is necessary. I am disappointed. Profoundly disappointed. But I will help." I picked up my purse.

"I left Damian at the Hotel Delft in Bleumenschoten," Holmes said. "And Dr Henning, of course. Under the name Daniel de Fontaine."

I flagged down a cab on Piccadilly, went to the *Standard*'s offices to leave the advert, then walked down the street to a quiet public call-box.

It took ten minutes to achieve a connexion with the hotel in Tunbridge Wells. The man who answered was friendly and sounded intelligent, but he assured me that no one by the name of Javitz had checked in the previous day. My heart instantly tried to climb up my throat.

"Not—" I forced myself under control: Shouting at the man would not help me. I took a deep breath, and changed what I had been about to say, and the way in which I said it. "Oh dear, perhaps they were forced to use another hotel. Were you full up, yesterday?"

"No, madam, we were not."

"Well, perhaps—" Perhaps what? They didn't like the looks of the place? Estelle threw a tantrum and demanded to be returned to

Goodman's family home? They'd had a mechanical breakdown on the road to Tunbridge Wells, a flat tyre, a deadly crash?

They'd been picked up by Mycroft's foe?

Do not panic. Do not. "Perhaps if I describe them, you can tell me if you've seen them. He's tall, American, has an injured leg, and the child—"

"Ah yes, you mean Mr Russell."

I found I was leaning against the wall, and the box was full of a rushing sound.

"Madam? Hello, Exchange, have we been cut off?"

"No," I said. "Yes, I'm here, sorry. Yes, Mr Russell. He came in yesterday?"

"With the child, yes, charming little thing. What was the name you used?"

"Oh, nothing, it's just one—he occasionally uses another name so his step-father doesn't find him. The step-father doesn't, er . . . doesn't care for the child."

It was the best I could do at the moment, but the voice over the telephone line was as indignant as I could have asked. "I see. Well, I shall take care to forget the other name."

"Whatever it was," I added.

"Indeed."

"May I speak to Mr Russell, then?"

"I am sorry, madam, they are not in the hotel at present."

"When did they leave?" I asked sharply.

"Not ten minutes ago," he answered, to my relief. "I believe the little girl expressed a desire to paddle in the sea, so he arranged a car and driver until the afternoon."

"Very good," I said. "May I leave a message for him? To say that his cousin Mary will ring again at tea-time?"

"I shall let him know the moment he returns," the man assured me. I thanked him and rang off, resting my forehead against the telephone's black body. Had the hotel man been in front of me, I would have rested it against him.

The "object of our affection" to be traded on Westminster Bridge was not Estelle, at any rate. Was it Damian?

I waited for an hour before the exchange put my call through, only to be cut off not once, but twice, each time having to begin the process anew. Then when I reached the Hotel Delft, the woman who answered the telephone spoke only Dutch; she broke the connexion a third time. On the fourth attempt I used French instead of English, which delayed her long enough that I could try German, as well, and although she seemed to speak neither with any fluency, she did recognise words of both languages, and I could guess from her voice if not her words what answers she was giving.

Yes, she knew M de Fontaine and his *something* companion. (*Redheaded*, perhaps? Did Dr Henning have red hair?) They were there for two nights and then not. Friday and Saturday? I asked—*vendredi et samedi? Mais pas le dimanche?*

There followed a rattle of Dutch, which I took to be the affirmative but linked to a question of—I pressed the telephone into my ear as if it might aid comprehension. Then I heard a word in the torrent that sounded familiar in several languages.

"Valise?" I asked. "Did you say 'valise'?"

Thirty seconds of something that meant: yes.

"What about his valise?"

The voice paused, then came out with six laborious and heavily accented syllables. *"Sa valise sont ici."*

"Whose valises are still there?" I demanded. "His, or hers? Or both?"

But precision was beyond her abilities, or even agreement in case and gender. She rattled on, her voice climbing, and then the telephone went dead.

I did not have the heart to attempt a fifth connexion.

I made two more calls. The first was to Sophy Melas, who was at home and sounded puzzled but unworried when I asked her if she'd had any unexpected callers other than Goodman and me the other night. The answer was no; I rang off before she could question why I called. The other was to my own house in Sussex. Its buzz continued in my ear, although there was no knowing if that was because Mrs Hudson had gone, as she'd been told, or because she'd stayed and been abducted.

I put the earpiece into its rest, and tried to think what else I could do, what other hostages to fortune lay out there.

I could think of none.

I bought eggs, cheese, and a loaf of bread on my way back to Pall Mall, retraced my laborious path through Mycroft's flat and into the dumb-waiter shaft, hanging the portrait over the hole as I came. In the Melas kitchen, I left my contribution on the table.

I found Mycroft in a dressing room whose furniture testified to Mrs Melas' taste. He was standing at the window, hands clasped behind his back, staring intently at the narrow crack between the two halves of the curtain. I cleared my throat, and he turned, startled.

"Ah, Mary. Good. What news?"

"Is there something out there?" I asked.

He gave an uncomfortable laugh and brushed past me. "Merely the air. I find myself longing for a glimpse of the sky, having exchanged one prison for another."

"It won't be long," I said, an attempt at reassurance.

Holmes and Goodman were missing, although the smoke in the air told me Holmes had been there until recently.

Mycroft pointed at the morning's paper, sprawled across the table, with headlines about the attempt on Mussolini's life.

"Brothers is dead," he said. "In St Albans."

The news jerked me out of the stilted conversation in my mind (...*what might otherwise be described as blackmail operations*). "St Albans? How on earth did he get there?"

"I do not know," he said, his frustration under thin rein: Mycroft Holmes was not a man who waited to receive his information from the daily papers. "Sherlock decided it was worth the risk of venturing out, to see what he can learn."

"To St Albans?"

"I believe he will make do with a telephone call to Lestrade. And before you ask, yes, he collected a disguise from downstairs."

I picked up the newspaper that Goodman had brought us, and found it open to a brief note, little more than two column inches, concerning the identity of a man found dead of knife wounds in St Albans on Saturday.

Knife wounds. I read the sparse information with care, but it was only given space on the page because of the irresistible juxtaposition of an oddball religious leader and a brutal attack. The piquant touch of it being in St Albans rather than London or Manchester helped explain its appearance in a national newspaper.

Mycroft was in the kitchen, carving bread, cheese, and sausage into meticulous slices. "Did Holmes take Goodman with him?" I asked.

"I am not certain when Mr Goodman left, or where he was going."

That sounded like Robert Goodman. I began to tell Mycroft what I had learnt, or failed to learn, over the telephone, when I was interrupted by a small noise from below. In a minute, Holmes threaded himself through the dumbwaiter hole. He was wearing a stiff collar with a pair of pince-nez on a ribbon around his neck, and had no doubt left the bowler hat downstairs: He'd been dressed as a solicitor's clerk.

With an addition: He pulled from his pocket a bottle of Bass Ale and set it beside the sink.

Without comment, Mycroft added more bread to the platter and carried it through to the sitting room. I fetched three glasses, holding one under the froth that boiled up when Holmes opened the bottle.

"Estelle and Javitz are at the sea-shore," I told him. "Damian, I'm not so sure about, partly because of language difficulties. I'm to telephone back to Tunbridge Wells at tea-time, and I'll try the Dutch hotel again then as well." I gave him the details of both conversations as he finished pouring and we took the glasses in to where Mycroft sat. Then it was Holmes' turn.

"Brothers died of a single knife-wound in a nearly empty house in St Albans," he said. "The police identified him by the distinctive scar beside his eye, although they are puzzled by the presence of both gunshot and knife-wounds on one man, particularly as the bullet wound had been treated and was in the process of healing. The fire had been left on in the room, which accelerated decomposition, but the coroner believes the man died on Tuesday or Wednesday. A neighbour saw two men get out of a taxi at the house on Tuesday afternoon. One of them had his left arm in a sling, which is how Brothers was found. She did not notice when they left.

"That's Brothers out of the way—and, as far as our opponent is concerned, you as well, Mycroft. He'll be aiming at Sosa, and I suppose me and Russell, before he can feel quite secure. I wonder how far he will go before he judges that he is free from threat? Will he remove Brothers' assistant in Orkney? Perhaps a few key members of the church's Inner Circle?"

"Surely he must at least suspect that you're alive and Gunderson is dead?" I asked Mycroft. "Gunderson has been missing for five days, and you said yourself that evidence at the warehouse testifies to things having gone awry."

"Short of digging up the grave, he can't be certain that Gunderson didn't deliver my corpse to the mortuary, then lose his nerve and flee. And without knowing what 'precious object' he possesses—or claims to possess—Sherlock and I decided it was best not to push our opponent too far. The last thing we want him to do is cut his losses and go invisible."

"So you've changed your mind about going to the office this afternoon?"

"We have," Holmes answered for his brother. "Russell, about your friend Goodman."

"Yes, I'd have expected him to return before this."

"He is a concern."

"No," I said flatly. I could tell from his tone what he was suggesting, and I would have none of it. "Robert Goodman would not give us away."

"How can you know that?"

I turned my face to him. "Because you are Estelle Adler's grandfather. There is some tie between those two, I can't begin to explain it. But he would do nothing that would make her lot any worse. Nothing."

"Then where is he?"

"I don't know. Maybe he's gone to see her." It was a spur of the moment suggestion, but once it had come to mind, I had to say that it would be very like him, to turn his back on matters of monumental political import to go and play tea-party with Estelle. Had I mentioned Tunbridge Wells in his hearing? I might easily have done.

"Well, if he does return in time, how do you suggest we deploy the man? He is quite effective at the head of a marching band, but would he be of use in a tight place?"

"He would stand up for us, yes. But if you're asking, would he use a gun?" I thought about the contents of the envelope Javitz had given me. In the end, I had to say, "I shouldn't want to ask him. And I really wouldn't want my life to depend on it."

Chapter 66

We had little more than twelve hours to assemble a foolproof plan to save a life, and an empire. We resolutely turned our minds to the maps and drawings Holmes retrieved from Mycroft's study downstairs, doing our best to ignore hunger, mistrust, and anxiety.

At four o'clock, I left the building to seek out another telephone. The powerful sense of release brought by hearing Javitz's voice coming down the line was only somewhat countered by Estelle's querulous demands that I produce Mr Robert. I assured her—several times—that I was doing the best I could, then distracted her with a question about how Dolly had enjoyed her visit to the sea-shore, and eventually convinced her to return Javitz to the conversation.

"This should be over tomorrow," I told him. *One way or the other.*

"It would help if you could get Goodman to ring here," he said, although I was relieved to hear him sounding resigned rather than desperate.

"I've, well, I don't know where he is. In fact," I hurried to say, "he may turn up down there. If he does, make sure you don't let him talk you into coming back to Town before I've spoken with you."

When I had rung off from Tunbridge Wells, it was time to try Holland again. This time, I was at the phone for nearly two hours, achieving two actual if short-lived connexions. A man came onto the line, and we quickly located a common language in French. Our first conversation, which lasted approximately forty-five seconds, determined that "Daniel de Fontaine" and his nurse were still registered at the hotel, although he wasn't entirely certain where the two were at this time. However, they had placed a series of telephone calls to England for which he very much hoped M de Fontaine's friends would guarantee payment since—

And we were cut off. I fear I shouted at the exchange operator, which never helps one's cause, but eventually I was again speaking with the Dutch hotelier. I began by hastily assuring him that all his costs would be reimbursed, and more, by the young gentleman's generous friends, but that I had to know where he was.

And at that, we reached an impasse. The man wasted a couple of minutes with a delicate description of how unfortunately short of funds these two guests appeared to be running, and was only slowly reassured by my increasingly desperate assertions that money was no problem. Finally, he permitted himself to be steered back into the matter at hand, namely, that the young gentleman had gone out walking on the Sunday afternoon—the two of them often went out walking, M de Fontaine seemed a great lover of the open air, although on this occasion the lady appeared to have chosen—

"Please!" I shouted. "Where is he?"

Taken aback, the hotelier admitted he was not certain. The lady had come down in the afternoon and enquired as to her companion's whereabouts, and became increasingly agitated when the hotel was unable to produce him. Although a handsome young man like that, perhaps he was not taken with a woman with hair that colour—and the temper! *Ooh la la!* Such a temper, it would be entirely understandable if he were to have chosen to go elsewhere for a day or two. And truth to tell, the hotel staff was keeping a close eye on the possessions in those two rooms, since it was not unheard-of for guests to lay a false trail and quietly slip away, leaving their bills unpaid. . . .

"*I* will pay the cost. Do not throw them out. Permit them whatever it takes to make them comfortable."

Why a voice over the telephone should be considered a substantial guarantee I could not think, but the man seemed reassured. However, that was about all he had to tell me. The red-haired woman had stayed the previous night, but she had left the hotel early and not been seen in the hours since. Yes, he would make her welcome—and M de Fontaine, as well—whenever they returned. Yes, he would tell them that I would telephone again tomorrow, and that they were to stay at the hotel until they heard from me.

I put up the earpiece; dread lay heavy in my bones.

I made one last telephone call, to Billy's home number. As I had hoped, he answered, sounding belligerent. I spoke five clear words and rang off.

Back in the Melas flat, Goodman was still missing. Holmes listened to my news with no expression on his face, but when I attempted to reassure him that perhaps Damian had merely needed some time to himself, he waved away the possibility with a sharp gesture.

"Mycroft's telephone rang, from Saturday until Sunday and not since then. The local exchange would know where those calls were coming from."

Neither Mycroft nor I argued with him. In any case, we would know before long just who the "object of affection" was.

Mycroft set about producing a supper of remarkably heavy scones (lacking butter, they more closely resembled the flat breads eaten by the Bedouin), saving the eggs for a last meal before we left.

The prime question was, how far could we trust Lestrade? I felt he would come down on our side in a pinch; Holmes suspected he might come down on our heads. Mycroft cast the deciding vote, for compromise: We would telephone to Lestrade at home, letting him know that we badly needed a police sharpshooter, but we would wait to tell when and where to appear. We could not risk an all-out police presence, with roadblocks and desperate shooting, so we would keep him in the dark until the last moment.

One had to feel sorry for Lestrade's wife: He was not going to be sanguine about the arrangement.

Westminster Bridge crosses the Thames on its northward turn, with the Victoria Embankment meeting the Houses of Parliament on the west and the County Hall, St Thomas' Hospital, and Lambeth Palace gathering on the east bank. It was a sixty-two-year-old iron bridge some 1200 feet long and 85 wide, with generous footways and a pair of decorative street-lamps atop each of its seven piers. There was seldom a time when the entire length of it was deserted, but half past two in the morning would find it as empty as it got.

Across the street from the Houses of Parliament was the St Stephen's Club, and behind it the ornate building that housed the London Metropolitan Police department, known as New Scotland Yard. Five years earlier, deep in mid-winter and in a case as frightening as any we had known, Holmes and I had been shot at in the office of one Inspector John Lestrade. It was a small office, several long stairways from the ground, but despite the plane trees, it had a marvellous view of Westminster Bridge.

Mycroft would be at the west end of that bridge, sheltering on the precincts of Parliament itself, where he was known to the guards. A telephone call to Lestrade at two a.m. would give the chief inspector enough time to bring his marksman to the Yard, but insufficient preparation to rally numbers of troops that might get in our way.

I, in the meantime, would wait on the bridge's eastern side, taking shelter on the steps leading down to the Albert Embankment. Behind me would be the assistance I had conjured up with five words to Billy: "Eleven at your wife's sister." His wife's sister was a seamstress: The reference was a code he and Holmes had used before, and this time it brought him to Cleopatra's Needle on the Embankment at eleven o'clock. Between us, Billy and I summoned a pair of motorcycles (motorcycling was an exhilarating new skill I had picked up in Los Angeles, a few months earlier). Our opponent would almost certainly be in a motorcar: On two wheels, Billy and I could stick to him like tacks. Even if the plan went as we intended and our foe drove away alone and unharmed, we could not take a chance that he might escape us entirely.

At half past ten, when I was getting ready to leave and meet Billy, Goodman was still missing. Standing in Mycroft's kitchen, I reluctantly admitted to Holmes that I was worried.

"What, you think he walked into a trap? Does anyone know who he is?"

"It would be difficult to unearth his identity, but not impossible."

"And you say he would not readily give us away."

I grimaced at the thought of what an unscrupulous man might do to Robert Goodman. "Perhaps he's gone to Tunbridge Wells. Or home to Cumberland."

"Is that likely?"

"Without taking his leave of Estelle? I'm afraid not."

At one o'clock, with Billy set and the motorcycles in place, I made my way back to the flat to see that all was as had been planned, and to report that Billy and the motorcycles would be in place. Holmes had already left, but Mycroft would wait for an hour before setting off.

I wished him luck, and moved towards the kitchen.

"Mary?"

I don't know what I expected. An apology, perhaps, or thanks. Instead, Mycroft said, "Remember, it's essential that the man not be harmed. I have to know what he knows."

I nodded, and turned away, wondering if I would ever again feel comfortable with him, knowing about him what I did.

Of course, I reminded myself as I climbed down the ladder, that assumed we all survived the night.

Chapter 67

A family can be a burden, at half past two in the morning. Peter James West was counting on that.

He could have chosen a different time and place. It would have been simple enough to draw Sherlock Holmes into the countryside at noontime, to do the deed—he would have come. But laying this final element of his long-worked plan at the feet of Parliament set a seal on the transfer: No one but he might ever know, but that was enough.

He only wished Gunderson were there. He knew Gunderson as a carpenter knows his hammer, and would have no hesitation to order the man to shoot. Or, to shoot Gunderson himself, for that matter. Had he known for certain that his assistant would not be back from Orkney today, West would have re-scheduled this meeting—he'd considered moving it, but in the end, he'd gone ahead, putting Buckner behind the wheel instead. The man was a dunce, but he could handle a motorcar. And how complicated could it be, trading one man for another at gunpoint?

He'd be glad when this entire operation was over; working with criminals threatened to infect even Peter James West with stupidity.

He and Buckner went down the cellar steps. In front of the padlocked door, he pulled down the long silken cap with the holes in it, which was uncomfortable and made him feel ridiculous, but which could be a last line of defence if things went wrong.

Buckner looked at him. "D'you want me to wear one a' them?"

"It won't be necessary."

"Why not?"

Because I'm going to dispose of you, anyway, you idiot. "You won't be getting out of the motor, but I may have to. The streak in my hair is a little too recognisable." And if we are forced by some mishap actually to go through with the trade, rather than take both men, I should prefer that Adler not know who took him. That way, the only stray out there was the young wife. And Sosa, although he hardly counted.

"Gotcher."

"Open the door."

Buckner found the key, worked the lock, and stood back. Nothing moved from within. Adler had not been very comfortable the previous evening, when he was dragged from the back of the lorry that had brought him from Holland (telephone calls, again—when would people learn that a string of trunk calls to a number under surveillance could lead back to the source?) but he'd been well. Food, drink, and a night's rest should have restored him somewhat.

"Mr Adler, I have come to take you to your family," West called.

No motion. West sighed. "Buckner, kindly bring our guest out—alive and conscious, if you please. Wait: Give me your gun first."

Buckner dug out the weapon and handed it to West, then hunched his shoulders and barrelled into the dim space. Damian Adler was waiting for him, but with no weapons and a bad arm, he was no match. Buckner bounced him against the wall and shoved him out of the door to sprawl at West's feet.

West held out a set of police-issue handcuffs, which Buckner slapped on with a relish that could only come from a man who was more accustomed to being the recipient of the treatment.

By the time they got Adler cuffed and on his feet, the younger man was sweating—with pain, not fear. He glared furiously at his masked captor. "Who the hell are you, and what have you done with Dr Henning?"

"I have done nothing with your companion, Mr Adler. And you do not need to know who I am. Up the stairs, if you please."

The prisoner backed away and Buckner grabbed his arms, which brought a grunt of pain. "Mr Adler, please cooperate. I am giving you back to your family." Most of it. Albeit temporarily. "Now, up the stairs."

They got him up the stairs, into the yard, and seated in the front of the motor. West had Buckner loop a rope around Adler to keep him from making some kind of heroic attempt at the controls, then drop a sack over the man's head—the selfsame one Adler's late uncle had worn, twelve days before.

Symmetry.

West tugged at his mask, wishing it weren't quite so suffocating, and climbed into the back behind the driver. He stretched his hand forward with Buckner's gun. "I'd suggest you put this in the door pocket instead of about your person. You don't want it to go off by accident."

"Righto," Buckner said, and pushed the starter.

It was ten minutes past two in the morning. He had given Buckner the first stages of directions earlier: Wind through the streets of Southwark and cross the river on the Vauxhall Bridge before circling back east. At twenty minutes after the hour, he began to give the next set of directions that would take them onto Westminster Bridge.

The fourteen-foot minute hand of the great clock stood just before the half hour when the motorcar went under the tower.

"Stop here for a moment," West said. He opened the door and stepped onto the roadway to study the bridge.

At this hour of the night, little stirred on London's pavements. Mist hung over the Thames, and the smell of decay neared its turn. The Houses of Parliament stood beside him, toes in the water; at his back lay all the machinery of empire. Somewhere, a horse-cart clopped, sounding tired.

The roadway was deserted, the pools of light along its noble length pushing back the darkness. West started to get back into the motor, then stopped. What was that at the far end, half-hidden by the almost imperceptible curve in the roadway? Rubbish? Or—a child, at this time of night? No, it had to be a man, but even from a distance he could see the figure was too small to be the Holmes brother, or even the American wife.

"Is that someone sitting on the footway?" Buckner asked.

"It is."

"What's he doing?"

The figure was hunched over, looking at something on the ground. No, not just looking: He was doing something, his hunched shoulders moving. He was in his shirt-sleeves and wore a summer hat that should have been retired a week ago.

"Should I turn around?" Buckner asked.

West stepped up onto the running-board. With the added height, he could see that the figure's back was turned.

"Hey," Buckner said, "maybe he's doing a drawing? There was this kid down the Embankment a couple months past, did a chalk drawing of the *Mona Lisa* before the police moved him away. The wife and I watched him for a while—he was pretty good."

Buckner was married? West studied the figure, and gave another close survey of the surrounding buildings. No motion at all.

The minute hand three hundred feet overhead moved to the half hour; so quiet was the night, West heard the shift of machinery before the strike of bells.

Eight notes rang over the bridge, and faded.

West folded back inside the motor. "Go halfway out and stop in the centre of the bridge. Leave the motor running. Be prepared to leave rapidly."

"Gotcher."

Repressing a strong impulse to slap his driver on the skull with his gun, West closed the door. The motor purred forward and stopped, precisely in the centre of the bridge.

West pulled out the knife that he had taken from Thomas Brothers. With it in his hand and the gun in his overcoat pocket, he slid across the leather seat and opened the passenger-side door. He stepped out, letting the door swing back but not latch, then pulled open the front door and used the knife to slice through the rope holding his prisoner in place. The knife that had killed the prisoner's wife, three and a half weeks before.

"Get out," he said.

The blind and handcuffed artist blundered his way around and upright. West pulled him away from the motor, then moved up behind him and pressed the knife against the loose portion of the flour sack. Adler went still.

* * *

"Too close," Lestrade said. Three hundred fifty yards away, the marksman was glued to his sights, his finger ready. He did not move, but Lestrade could feel disapproval radiating off the man's shoulders at the interruption. "Sorry," he said, and took a step away from the open window.

The man kneeling in the window had his sights not on the standing figures, but on the roof of the motor, on a line drawn with the driver. Holmes had been adamant: The man in charge must be taken alive. It was a matter of the empire's security, that this villain give up his secrets.

And as if Holmes had heard Lestrade voice his doubts, had known that Lestrade intended to tell the marksman to fire wherever needed, a quarter of an hour later the telephone had rung again. This time, it was the Palace.

The standing figure was free to murder everyone in sight, and unless Lestrade's shooter could absolutely, positively guarantee a shot that merely wounded the man, the villain would be free to run.

All Lestrade could do was curse and pray, with equal vehemence. But in silence.

I could not see either Holmes, standing near Boadicea, or Mycroft, inside the Parliamentary garden across the roadway from him. Nor could I see Billy, tucked into the street behind me, ready to pounce. But I saw the motorcar, creeping slowly onto the bridge. And a minute later I saw the two figures, pressed in close embrace on the passenger side.

And I could see Robert Goodman all too well, thirty yards away and playing, of all things, jackstones beneath one of the lamp standards on Westminster Bridge. What the hell was he up to?

Holmes tore his eyes away from the tableau in the centre of the span—Damian, it had to be—and looked across Bridge Street to where Mycroft stood, hidden by shadows. There was no signal—no need for one, in truth—but when the clock hand touched the next minute mark, the darkness shifted like the workings of the mighty clock, and Mycroft walked out into the light.

He stood facing the motorcar.

The two figures moved—for an instant Holmes could not breathe, thinking they were struggling—but they were merely moving, away from the pools of light and into the dimmest reaches between them. When they were but a doubled outline, a voice came down the roadway. "Mr Holmes?"

"One of them," Mycroft answered, and removed his hat.

That would do for a signal, Holmes decided, and walked out from his own darkness, to stand, also hatless, in the pool of light opposite Mycroft.

The shocked silence was broken by Mycroft's voice.

"I'm afraid your Mr Gunderson won't be returning to your service. He is lying in a mis-marked grave, not far from here."

Longer silence, then: "It matters not. Our agreement stands."

The two brothers exchanged a look from their opposite lamp-posts, and Holmes walked onto the bridge.

I had my field glasses trained on the other end of the bridge, shifting back and forth across the roadway. I could hear faint voices, but not what they were saying. However, I could see Holmes start forward. I reached into my pocket to finger the keys of the motorcycle, parked and waiting in the lee of the hospital.

Holmes had closed half the distance between him and the motorcar when he heard a voice from ahead, and saw motion where the doubled figures stood—saw, too, what had caused it.

The blond figure that had come onto the bridge a minute before the motorcar appeared was gathering something from the pavement and getting to its feet. Goodman—it had to be he—turned towards the centre and began to walk in his quick, easy stride. His hands were free and seemed to be empty, and at each step his right hand reached out to slap the handrail in a cheery gesture. He was singing in a low voice, an old and half-familiar tune, wrapped up in his own world, to all appearances utterly unaware that there were others on the bridge.

Holmes could only keep moving, and hope the man holding Damian had steady nerves.

"Stop, there," the man called, aimed at the small oncoming figure, who kept singing, kept patting, kept walking.

Holmes was a stone's throw from the two figures when the man ordered him, too, to stop. He did so, hands outstretched.

He was close enough now to see that both men were masked, Damian entirely, the other man with a head-covering cut away to reveal eyes and mouth. The mask glanced over his shoulder at the oncoming figure, still oblivious and still close to the railing, then came around again to demand of Holmes, "Is this something of yours?"

"Nothing of mine," Holmes replied, which was the absolute truth.

"Watch him," he called over his shoulder to the driver, then to Holmes, "If he makes a move for his pockets, I'll cut your son's throat."

Holmes fought to keep his voice reasonable. "Look at the fellow—he's either drunk or a lunatic, and apt to do anything," he protested, then added more mildly, "You really ought to climb back in your motor and get away while you can. You've seen that my brother is alive and well. If you're as clever as I think you are, you could be across the Channel before the police can lay their blocks."

"Oh, I don't think this is entirely over."

Holmes did not recognise the voice, which in any case was not only muffled by the mask, but had an artificial sound to it, both in timbre and in accent. If he had long enough to study the sound, he might trace its true origins. He doubted he'd be given the chance.

"Get into the motor, Mr Holmes," the disguised voice said.

"I need to see the prisoner first."

"You don't recognise him without his face? Very well."

The man dropped the knife just long enough to tug the sack off his prisoner's head.

* * *

Blinking against the dust, Damian saw his father, standing to his left with the bridge stretching out behind him and the mass of Parliament's houses rearing up behind: Despite everything, his fingers twitched as if to reach for a sketching pencil. However, with the bite of the blade again at his throat, he did not move further.

Now, out of the side of his other eye, he saw motion: a small man in worn trousers, a pale hat, and shirt-sleeves, marching happily across the bridge as if all alone on a woodland path. The man with the knife at Damian's throat was watching him, too—Damian would have bet that any nearby eyes would be drawn to him. The figure's self-absorption was so marked, it even penetrated the apprehension of the prisoner.

Then the man stopped, causing a shudder to run out in all directions. He was standing directly beneath the bridge's central light, looking now at the two figures held together by a razor-sharp piece of worked meteor. Deliberately, he removed his hat and set it atop the handrail. His hair was a tumble of straw, his eyes green even in lamp-light, and in his left hand was a small rubber ball.

He bounced it once, caught it without looking, and spoke. "Are you the father?"

I could not believe what I was seeing: Goodman was walking openly down the length of the bridge, simply asking to be shot. I took a step out of the shadows, feeling the careful clockwork of Mycroft's plan stutter and grind.

No, oh Goodman, no, please don't.

What were they saying?

"You want me to shoot him?" said the voice from the motorcar.

"No," said the man with the knife. "Let us avoid gunfire if we can."

His question unanswered, the green eyes shifted to look farther down the roadway. The small man raised his voice to ask, "Is he the father?"

When Holmes, too, gave no reply, the figure stepped away from the railing. Three others reacted instantaneously.

"Stop!" West snapped, over Buckner's voice asking, "You *sure* you don't want me to shoot?"

"He's a poor bloody simpleton, for heaven's sake," Holmes shouted.

The blond man stepped down from the wide footway, and stopped. He bounced and caught the ball a couple of times, looking intently at the prisoner. "You're the father. Estelle's father."

Damian jerked, oblivious to the knife cutting into his skin. Estelle—who *was* this man?

"Yes," he said. It came out half-strangled, but it came out.

The green eyes beamed at him as if the word were a gold trophy. The eyes were young and fearless and full of mischief; the eyes were older than the hills.

"I really think you should let me shoot—"

"Enough!" West barked. He recognised the small man now: the band-leader, the wife's pet woodsman, caretaker of the estate in Cumberland. "Buckner, get out and keep these two in place while I get rid of this."

The motorcar door opened and the driver stepped out, turning his gun on the two tall men, prisoner and soon-to-be prisoner. His boss rapidly crossed the roadway until he was standing face to face with the bothersome drunkard. "You," he said. "Be gone."

"Ha!" Goodman's response was a laugh. "Yes, I am gone, and I return. But you?"

West moved before the last word had left Goodman's mouth.

Goodman made a sound, and looked down at the blood spilling across the front of his shirt.

The moment the masked figure moved towards Goodman, I began to run, knowing I would be too late, knowing I had to try. I sprinted down the impossibly long bridge, and saw the Green Man stagger back, his shirt-front going instantly dark. He tripped on the footway, going to one knee then recovering to move, doubled over, towards the railing. He laid his chest across the metal (for an instant, the image of Estelle flashed through my mind, draped across the tree-round foot-stool before Mr Robert's fireplace). One leg rose, painfully slow, and a heel crawled its way across the railing, to hook onto the far side. His arms embraced the wide iron, and then he rolled, and vanished into the darkness beyond.

He was gone.

Four men watched the blond man stagger back. They heard the small cry when his belly touched the iron railing, but he kept moving, onto the wide rail, moving like a wounded animal crawling to its hole.

The blond man rolled over, and disappeared.

There was no splash. West, knife in his hand, waited. He swivelled, making certain that the two men stood where they were and that his man was on guard, then walked over to the side, sticking his head over the railing to look.

And a hand came up, as if born of the bridge, or the night. A hand that had led lost souls through the woods and drunk tea with a child and loaded men onto the bed of an ambulance. A hand that raised up and wrapped around the back of Peter James West's head.

Holmes took one step forward, thinking only of Mycroft's need for the man, but froze when the driver shouted a warning.

Then behind came a figure he knew well, sprinting down the horribly exposed bridge. In a moment, the driver would hear, and would turn—and now he was turning, his gun moving towards her and Holmes was in motion, shoving Damian in the direction of the struggling figures and shouting, "Keep that man from going over—Mycroft needs him!" then "Russell!" he was shouting, and running for all he was worth.

The Yard marksman, with a clear line on his target, eased down the trigger a split instant before the man turned around.

* * *

Damian's hands were tied—literally—but his father had spoken, and he would do all he could to obey. Six long leaps took him to where his abductor was fighting against the pulling hands, heels free of the pavement now, and he slammed into the man, throwing his weight across the sprawled body, pinning him against the bridge. Damian's shoulder screamed at the blow, but he lay hard against the rigid back, locking the man to the railing, staring past his shoulder into a pair of brilliant green eyes.

The expression in them, oddly, was one of disappointment.

I closed on the struggle, which had been joined by Damian, coming out of nowhere to throw himself onto the man in the mask. A *zzip* flew alarmingly close past my head, followed instantly by a pair of gunshots, one close and one farther away. I ducked, tearing my attention from the railing in time to see Holmes crash into the driver and wrench the revolver from his hand.

I leapt up and ran again, reaching the knot of legs and torsos before any of them went over. The black mask had slipped, and now drifted into the dark, although all I could see of our opponent was a flash of white against his otherwise dark hair. He jerked another half inch towards the edge; Damian grunted with pain but redoubled his efforts.

"Stop!" I shouted. "Robert, stop, let me help you, I can't—"

"Let me have him," said the voice from below.

"No, Robert, please, take my hand, I'll get you to—"

"Please," his voice asked. Such a reasonable request. "Please."

Time stretched out while I gazed down into those eyes. I could see Death there—I had worked in hospitals; I knew what Death looked like—but Robert Goodman was there as well, the Green Man, Estelle's champion, speaking to me without words. His hands were shaking with effort, his toes were jammed precariously into the base of the railing. I could see what it was costing him to hang on.

Voices reached me, from a distance:

Damian, into my left ear: "I'm to stop him from going over. Father said. Mycroft needs him."

Holmes, from somewhere behind me: "I'm coming, Russell!"

From farther away, Mycroft shouting: "Hang on to that man!"

And Goodman, saying without words, *Please. Please.*

My eyes filled with tears before I put my hands on Damian's shoulders and peeled him away.

Two men vanished off the side of the bridge, with a single splash.

Holmes brushed me aside, gun in hand, to crane over into the river. Mycroft followed, cold with fury, incapable of speaking to me. Soon the bridge was swarming with uniformed constables who ran down the banks with torches, waiting for the bodies to surface on the outgoing tide.

I picked up the hat from the rail, noticing that it was missing its feather, and dropped it over the side. The pale straw was visible for an instant, then it passed out of the lamp-light and was gone.

At the far end of the bridge, where I headed to tell Billy that we would not need his skills, another object caught my eye: a small rubber ball that had rolled down the lip of the footway until it came to rest against some dry leaves. That, I put in my pocket.

The mortal remains of Peter James West were discovered a week later, among the debris at the side of the river near Tilbury. Of Robert Goodman, there was no trace.

Epilogue

The Green Man's tale is one of mythic sacrifice. The figure personifies growth, the vegetation that springs up so joyously in the spring only to be brutally mowed down in the autumn. He is vitality personified, short-lived yet eternal, a cycle of life and apparent death.

When Peter James West disappeared over the bridge into the Thames, his passing left a vacuum in the Empire's array of power, and any vacuum brings disorder to things around it.

Mycroft was there, inevitably, to breach the holes and restore order, although without West—for it had been he who went into the water—the extent of his machinations proved almost impossible to uncover. The Labour government was voted out a few weeks later following a piece of highly dubious political chicanery that bore all the hallmarks of West's office. Holmes claimed that his brother did not blame me for the overthrow of a government, but I did not entirely believe him. In any case, it was a long time before I was to have an easy conversation with my brother-in-law.

When I told Estelle that her friend Mr Robert was gone, she threw herself upon me and wept, and I found that under the impetus of her tears, my own were loosed as well. She wept again when Damian told of her mother's death, three days later on the train to Edinburgh.

In Edinburgh, we met the Holland steamer. The first passenger to disembark was a small, intense woman who stormed from the boat like a red-headed fury, both relieved at the safety of her former patient, and irate at her own failure to protect the man who, clearly, was more than a patient to her. From Edinburgh, we travelled to Wick, there to stay in a house hired outside of the town. I found it remarkably restful, to sit before the fire, helping Estelle with her lessons and reading an accumulation of old newspapers, drinking strong Scottish tea in the morning and strong Scots whisky in the evenings.

There we stayed until Lestrade left a message for us in the agony column, assuring us that Damian had been cleared of all suspicions. But by that time, Damian was in no hurry to be back in London. And the doctor was considering the benefits of packing up her *locum* practice for good and moving south.

Between one thing and another, Holmes and I did not return to Sussex until the third week of October, having been diverted by events along the way (none of which surprised me: Holmes has always been a remarkable magnet for problems). At long last, we settled back into our home, and had nearly a week's peace before I drove to Eastbourne to pick up Damian and Estelle. They were spending a few days with us before leaving for Paris. Where, as Damian pointed out, a young woman of mixed heritage might be granted the freedom to be herself: Paris was not blind to skin colour and eye shape, but it found other attributes to be of greater concern.

Holmes and I both expected that before long, Dr Henning would join them there.

It was the last day of the month, All Hallow's Eve, and as I helped load their luggage, the rain that had held out all day spat down around us. Estelle shrieked, Damian laughed, and we quickly bundled into the car to motor up onto the Downs.

"Is this a new motorcar, Mary?" Estelle asked.

"It is indeed. Do you like it?"

"It's lovely. May I honk the horn?"

"When we reach the house, you may."

"I can play jackstones now," she told me.

"You can? That's very clever of you."

"She worked at it for hours," Damian said. "She has the determination of a bulldog."

At the house, the horn duly sounded, I bundled them all inside and finished the unloading myself. When all was inside and the motor secure, I went up and changed, coming down with damp hair and the exhilaration of storm in my blood.

Estelle was sitting in front of the fire, working her way through a demonstration of jackstones. Her small hand was remarkably efficient, her concentration, as her father had said, extraordinary. She was singing under her breath, her voice tiny but true, her own words set to the tune of "John Barleycorn" that Goodman had taught her.

She came to an end of the stones and jumped to her feet, her grey eyes shining.

"Uncle Mycroft sent me a present," she declared. "Papa said I had to wait until we were here before I opened it."

"Well, you're here."

She seized my hand and dragged me towards the kitchen.

Among the bags and valises we brought from the motorcar at the station were a pair of boxes which, on closer examination, were not actually from Mycroft, but which had been posted the previous week to his London address. One was a wooden cigar box addressed to me; the other was a wooden tea crate with Estelle's name on it.

Damian had picked up one of Mrs Hudson's knives, only to have it snatched from his hand with loud protests. While she was finding him a screw-driver, I picked open the twine on my own parcel and curiously looked at the contents: a lump of some hard black substance the size of a child's fist, and another fire-stained object the size of my thumb. I picked up the heavy black stuff to examine it more closely, to be distracted by Estelle's exclamations at her box.

Wood-shaving spilt onto the kitchen table when the top came free, revealing a small curve of some rich brown colour. Damian brushed it off before handing it to his daughter: a delicate wooden disc, some two inches wide, made of oak. Another lay in the shavings beneath it, and another, then: a tea-cup into which a man's fingertip would barely fit.

I watched, slack-mouthed, as the child and her father unpacked an entire tea-set of hand-carved, exquisitely finished wooden plates and cups, sugar bowl and milk jug. The tea-pot itself was a perfectly round oak gall with a curved-twig handle and a hollowed-reed spout.

Mrs Hudson had started to brush together the spilt shaving when she noticed a foreign object among them. She placed it to one side and continued her brushing, but I looked at it, and my hand went out to pick it up.

A feather. Specifically, the primary flight-feather of a tawny owl.

I looked at Holmes. Our eyes were simultaneously drawn to the heavy, cold lump I still held in my other hand, and I convulsively let the object fall back into its box. I could not suppress a shudder of revulsion as I slapped down the lid and reached for the twine.

The black lump was a mass of meteor metal; the burnt object was the remains of an ivory haft.

I could not imagine the heat necessary to return that knife to its primary state.

I looked up to find Damian's eyes on me. "What is that?" he asked.

"Oh, just a rock sample I asked for," I said smoothly, reaching for the twine to bind the cover down tight.

I left the box on a high shelf, and we adults solemnly adjourned to the next room to join the dollies' tea-party.

But late that night, Holmes and I left our sleeping family to walk down to Birling Gap and take the hotel's skiff, rowing far out into the moonless water. There I undid the twine for a second time, and let what was left of Thomas Brothers' knife vanish into the cleansing depths of the English Channel.

Acknowledgements

With thanks to Tammy Albee and Chris Sagar for the Russellisms in chapters 12 and 63; to Dick Griffith for helping me hot-wire an old car; to Linda Fitzpatrick of Fife's Scottish Fisheries Museum and Louisa Pittman (former "Mate," future PhD, current humble student) for giving me a boat (on paper, anyway); to Adrian Muller for sharing his family and his Dutch; and to the gents at the Hiller Air Museum for nursing along my Bristol Tourer.

For Patricia Toner and all the other readers who helped raise funds for Heifer International's beehive project, and her husband, Richard Luther Sosa (who is both better-looking and of stronger stuff than his namesake), and daughter, Meghann Toner (who should have been the doctor).

And a hive-full of thanks to Zoë Elkaim, Vicki Van Valkenburgh, Bob Difley, Alice Wright, Erin Bright, Wanda Kalgren, Nikki Rowe, and Caitlin Rowe, for their generosity and cleverness in keeping together all the manifold nooks and crannies associated with www.LaurieRKing.com. Bless you, ladies and gent, I couldn't have done it without you.

About the Author

LAURIE R. KING is the *New York Times* bestselling author of ten Mary Russell mysteries, five contemporary novels featuring Kate Martinelli, and the acclaimed novels *A Darker Place, Folly, Keeping Watch,* and *Touchstone*. She is one of only two novelists to win the Best First Crime Novel awards on both sides of the Atlantic. She lives in northern California, where she is at work on her next Russell and Holmes mystery.

If you enjoyed

The God *of the* Hive,

please read on for a preview
of the exciting new mystery featuring
Mary Russell & Sherlock Holmes,

Pirate King

Chapter 1

RUTH: I did not catch the word aright, through being hard of hearing...
I took and bound this promising boy apprentice to a *pirate*.

H onestly, Holmes? *Pirates?*"
"That is what I said."

"You want me to go and work for pirates."

O'er the glad waters of the dark blue sea, our thoughts as boundless, and our souls as free...

"My dear Russell, someone your age should not be having trouble with her hearing." Sherlock Holmes solicitous was Sherlock Holmes sarcastic.

"My dear Holmes, someone your age should not be overlooking incipient dementia. Why do you wish me to go and work for pirates?"

"Think of it as an adventure, Russell."

"May I point out that this past year has been nothing but adventure? Ten back-to-back cases between us in the past fifteen months, stretched over, what, eight countries? Ten, if one acknowledges the independence of Scotland and Wales. What I need is a few weeks with nothing more demanding than my books."

"You should, of course, feel welcome to remain here."

The words seemed to contain a weight beyond their surface meaning. A dark and inauspicious weight. A Mariner's albatross sort of a weight. I replied with caution. "This being my home, I generally do feel welcome."

"Ah. Did I not mention that Mycroft is coming to stay?"

"Mycroft? Why on earth would Mycroft come here? In all the years I've lived in Sussex, he's visited only once."

"Twice, although the other occasion was while you were away. However, he's about to have the builders in, and he needs a quiet retreat."

"He can afford an hotel room."

"This is my brother, Russell," he chided.

Yes, exactly: my husband's brother, Mycroft Holmes. Whom I had thwarted—blatantly, with malice aforethought, and with what promised to be heavy consequences—scant weeks earlier. Whose history, I now knew, held events that soured my attitude towards him. Who wielded enormous if invisible power within the British government. And who was capable of making life uncomfortable for me until he had tamped me back down into my position of sister-in-law.

"How long?" I asked.

"He thought two weeks."

Fourteen days: 336 hours: 20,160 minutes, of first-hand opportunity to revenge himself on me verbally, psychologically, or (surely not?) physically. Mycroft was a master of the subtlest of poisons—I speak metaphorically, of course—and fourteen days would be plenty to work his vengeance and drive me to the edge of madness.

And only the previous afternoon, I had learnt that my alternate lodgings in Oxford had been flooded by a broken pipe. Information that now crept forward in my mind, bringing a note of dour suspicion.

No, Holmes was right: best to be away if I could.

Which circled the discussion around to its beginnings.

"Why should I wish to go work with pirates?" I repeated.

"You would, of course, be undercover."

"Naturally. With a cutlass between my teeth."

"I should think you would be more likely to wear a night-dress."

"A night-dress." Oh, this was getting better and better.

"As I remember, there are few parts for females among the pirates. Although they may decide to place you among the support staff."

"Pirates have support staff?" I set my tea-cup back into its saucer, that I might lean forward and examine my husband's face. I could see no overt indications of lunacy. No more than usual.

He ignored me, turning over a page of the letter he had been reading, keeping it on his knee beneath the level of the table. I could not see the writing—which was, I thought, no accident.

"I should imagine they have a considerable number of personnel behind the scenes," he replied.

"Are we talking about pirates-on-the-high-seas, or piracy-as-violation-of-copyright-law?"

"Definitely the cutlass rather than the pen. Although Gilbert might have argued for the literary element."

"Gilbert?" Two seconds later, the awful light of revelation flashed through my brain; at the same instant, Holmes tossed the letter onto the table so I could see its heading.

Headings, plural, for the missive contained two separate letters folded together. The first was from Scotland Yard. The second was emblazoned with the words *D'Oyly Carte Opera*.

I reared back, far more alarmed by the stationery than by the thought of climbing storm-tossed rigging in the company of cut-throats.

"Gilbert and *Sullivan?*" I exclaimed. "Pirates as in *Penzance?* Light opera and heavy humour? No. Absolutely not. Whatever Inspector Lestrade has in mind, I refuse."

"One gathers," Holmes reflected, reaching for another slice of toast, "that the title originally did hold a *double entendre*, Gilbert's dig at the habit of American companies to flout the niceties of British copyright law."

He was not about to divert me by historical titbits or an insult against my American heritage: This was one threat against which my homeland would have to mount its own defence.

"You've dragged your sleeve in the butter." I got to my feet, picking up my half-emptied plate to underscore my refusal.

"It would not be a singing part," he said.

I walked out of the room.

He raised his voice. "I would do it myself, but I need to be here for Mycroft, to help him tidy up after the Goodman case."

Answer gave I none.

"It shouldn't take you more than two weeks, three at the most. You'd probably find the solution before arriving in Lisbon."

"Why—" I cut the question short; it did not matter in the least why the D'Oyly Carte company wished me to go to Lisbon. I poked my head back into the room. "Holmes: no. I have an entire academic year to catch up on. I have no interest whatsoever in the entertainment of *hoi polloi*. The entire thing sounds like a headache. I am not going to Lisbon, or even London. I'm not going anywhere. No."

Chapter 2

PIRATE KING: I don't think much of our profession, but, contrasted
with respectability, it is comparatively honest.

My steamer lurched into Lisbon on a horrible sleet-blown November morning. My face was scoured by the ocean air, I having spent
most of the voyage on deck in an attempt (largely vain) to keep my
stomach from turning inside out. My hair and clothing were stiff with
salt, my nose raw from the handkerchief, I had lost nearly half a stone
and more than half my mind, and my mood was as bloody as my eye-
balls.

If a pirate had hove into view—or my husband, for that matter—
I would merrily have keelhauled either with a rope of linen from the
captain's table.

My only source of satisfaction, grim as it was, lay in the knowledge
that several of the actors on board were every bit as miserable as I.

The eternal, quease-inducing sway lessened as we left the open sea
to churn our way up the Rio Tejo towards the vast harbour—one of
Europe's largest, according to someone's guide-book—that in the days
of sail had made Portugal a great empire. The occasional isolated castle
or fishing village along the shore slowly proliferated. Our view panned
across a lighthouse, then picked up an odd piece of architecture planted
just offshore to our left, a diminutive fort in an unnecessarily exuberant

Gothic style. (Was that the style of the guide-book—Annie's?—had called "Manueline"?) Someone in the crowd of shivering fellow passengers loudly identified it as the Tower of Belém; my mind's eye automatically supplied the phrase on an internal subtitle:

"That's the Tower of Belem!"

I shook my head in irritation. I had watched more moving pictures over the past few days than in the past few years: My way of seeing the world had changed dramatically.

Beyond the Manueline excrescence rose *Lisboa* itself—*Alis Ubo* to the Phoenicians, *Ulissipont* to the Romans. Our first indication of the city was the spill of masts and belching smoke-stacks that pressed towards the docks. As we drew nearer, a jumble of pale walls and red tile roofs rose up from the harbour (it looked like a lake) on a series of hills (the guide-book had claimed seven, on a par with Rome) punctuated by church spires (a startling number of those) watched over by a decaying castle.

Pirates, I sniffed as I eyed the castle gun-ports. Any sensible member of the piratical fraternity would have steered well clear of this place.

I pulled my thick coat around me, made a fruitless attempt to clean my spectacles, and went below to assemble my charges.

My job—my official job—was to shepherd, protect, nurse, and browbeat into order some three dozen inmates of a mobile lunatic asylum. I was the one responsible for their well-being. It was I who ensured the inmates were housed and fed, entertained and soothed, kept off one another's throats and out of one another's beds. I was the one the inmates ran to, sent on errands, and shouted at, whether the complaint was inadequately hot coffee or insufficiently robust lightbulb. On the first night out from England, I had been roused from a fitful sleep by a demand that I—I, personally—remove a moth from a cabin.

A fraternity of actual pirates could not have been more trouble. Even a travelling D'Oyly Carte company would have been less of a madhouse.

But I was working neither with buccaneers nor with travelling players: The letter with the heading of the firm responsible for the Gilbert and Sullivan performances had merely been by way of introduction. Instead, I found myself the general coordinator and jack-of-all-trades for a film crew.

In the early years after the War, Fflytte Films had appeared to be the rising star of the British cinema industry: From *Quarterdeck* in 1919 through 1922's *Krakatoa*, Fflytte Films ("Fflyttes of Fancy!") seemed positioned to challenge the American domination of the young industry, producing a series of stupendously successful multi-reel extravaganzas with exotic settings and dashing stories. Then came *Hannibal*, which ran so far over budget in the preliminary stages, the project was cancelled before the second reel of film was fed into the cameras. *Hannibal* was followed by the wildly popular *Rum Runner*, but after that came *The Writer*, which took eight months to make and ran in precisely four cinema houses for less than a week. *The Writer*'s failure might have been predicted—a three-reel drama about a British novelist in Paris?—except that Randolph St John Warminster-Fflytte ("Fflyttes of Fantasy!") was a director famous for pulling hugely successful rabbits out of apparently shabby hats (*Small Arms* concerned the accidental death of a child; *Rum Runner* was about smuggling alcohol into the United States; both had returned their costs a hundredfold) and a movie about a thinly disguised James Joyce might have been as successful as his other ugly ducklings, particularly when one threw in the titillating appeal of the *Ulysses* obscenity ban.

However, since the film had skirted around the actual depiction of the obscene acts in question, it went rather flat. So now, with three costly duds on his hands and the threatened loss of his aristocratic backers, Fflytte was returning to the scene of his three previous solid successes ("Fflyttes of Fanfare!"): the sea-borne action adventure.

This one was to be loosely based on the Gilbert and Sullivan operetta. *Loosely* as in wobbling wildly and on the verge of a complete uncoupling. Not an inch of film had gone through the cameras; the Major-General was drunk around the clock; the cameraman's assistant had a palsy of the hands that was explained to me, *sotto voce*, as the result of a recent nervous breakdown; the actress playing Mabel had taken the bit into her teeth with this, her first starring rôle, and was out to prove herself a flapper edition of Sarah Bernhardt (if not in talent, then in imperious attitudes and a knack of fabricating alternate versions of her personal history); and the twelve other young ladies playing the Major-General's daughters—yes, thirteen daughters altogether—formed a non-stop cyclone of lace, giggles, and yellow curls that spun up and down the decks and occasionally below them—far below, to judge by the grease-stains on one pink dress thrust under my nose by an accusing maternal person. Even the eldest of the "sisters," a busybody of the first order, had blinked her big blue eyes at me in practiced innocence from more than one out-of-bounds state-room.

We had not left the Channel before I felt the first impulse to murder.

"Producer's assistant," then, was my official job. My unofficial one—the one Holmes had manoeuvred me into—was given me by Chief Inspector Lestrade in his office overlooking Westminster Bridge. He had stood as I was ushered in, but remained behind his desk—as if that might protect him. A single thin folder lay on its pristine surface.

"Miss Russell. Do sit down. May I take your bag?"

"No, thank you." I dropped the bag I had thrown together in Sussex—basic necessities such as tooth-brush, clean socks, reading material, and loaded revolver—onto the floor, and sat.

"Mr Holmes is not with you?"

"As you see." Was that a sigh I heard? He sat down.

"You two haven't any news of Robert Goodman or Peter James West, have you?"

"Is that why you asked me here, Chief Inspector? To follow up on the last case?"

"No, no. I just thought I'd ask, since both men have vanished into thin air, and whenever something like that takes place, it's extraordinary how often Sherlock Holmes happens to have been in the vicinity."

"No, we have not heard news of either man." The literal, if not actual, truth.

"Why do I get the feeling that you know more than you're telling?"

"I know a great number of things, Chief Inspector, few of which are your concern. Now, you wrote asking for assistance."

"From your husband."

"Why?" Lestrade had always complained, loud and clear, that there was no place for amateurs in the investigation of crimes.

"Because the only police officers I had with the necessary skills have become unavailable."

"Those skills being . . . ?"

"The ability to make educated small-talk, and mastery of a type-writing machine. It is remarkable how few gentlemen are capable of producing type-written documents with their own ten fingers. Your husband, as I recall, is one who can."

"And yet the city's employment rosters are positively crawling with educated *women* type-writers."

"I had one of those. A fine and talented young PC. Who is now home with a baby."

"Oh. Well, now you have me."

"Yes." Definitely a sigh, this time. "Oh, it might as well be you."

My eyes narrowed. "Chief Inspector, one might almost think you had no interest in this matter. Is it important enough to concern Holmes and me, or is it not?"

"Yes. I mean to say, I don't know. That is—" He ran a hand over his face. "I dislike having outside pressures turned on the Yard."

"Ah. Politics."

"In a manner of speaking. It has to do with the British moving picture industry."

"Do we have a moving picture industry?" I asked in surprise.

"Exactly. While the Americans turn out vast sagas that sell tickets by the bushel, this country makes small pictures about bunnies and Scottish hillsides that are shown as the audience is taking its seats for the feature. I'm told it's because of the War—all our boys went to the Front, but the American cameras just kept rolling. And now, when we're beginning to catch up, we no sooner produce a possible rival to the likes of Griffith and De Mille when a rumour—a faint rumour, mind—comes to the ears of Certain Individuals that the man they're backing may be bent."

I put the clues together. "Some members of the House of Lords are worried about the money they put up to fund a picture; they mentioned it to the Chancellor of the Exchequer over sherry, and Winston sent someone to talk to you?"

"Worse than that—the Palace itself have invested in the company, if you can believe that. And the trouble is, I can't say for certain that there's nothing to it. The studio has been linked to...problems."

"I should imagine that picture studios generate all sorts of problems."

"Not generally of the criminal variety. There are some odd coincidences that follow this one around. Three years ago, they made a movie about guns, and—"

"An entire moving picture about guns?"

"More or less. This was shortly after the Firearms Act, and the picture was about a returned soldier who used his military revolver in a Bolshevik act, accidentally killing a child."

"The Bolshevist terror being why the Firearms Act was introduced in the first place." The 1920 Firearms Act meant that every three years, Holmes and I were forced to go before our local sheriff for weapons permits, demonstrating that we were neither drunks, lunatics, or children.

"That and the sheer number of revolvers knocking around after the War waiting to go off. Which more or less concealed the fact that someone sold quite a few of said firearms in this country, unpermitted, shortly after the picture came out."

"What does that—"

"Wait. The following year, Fflytte did a story about a young woman whose life was taken over by drugs—*Coke Express*, it was called. The month following its release in the cinema houses, we had an unusual number of drugs parties along the south coast."

"Yes, but—"

"And last year, one of their pirate movies was about rum-running into America. It came out in November."

"I was busy in November. What happened?"

"McCoy's arrest. 'The Real McCoy'? The man's made a small fortune smuggling hard liquor into the United States."

"Hmm. Is this perhaps the same studio that was making a film about Hannibal?"

"Fflytte Films, that's them."

"Odd, I don't recall hearing about a sudden influx of elephants racing down the streets of—"

"I knew this was a mistake. Never mind, Miss Russell, I'll—"

"No no, Chief Inspector, sit down, I apologise. Surely there must have been something more concrete to interest you in the case, even in a peripheral manner?"

He paused, then subsided into his chair. "Yes. Although even that I can't be at all certain about. We were beginning to ask some questions— in a hush-hush fashion, so as not to set the gossip magazines on fire— when the studio's secretary went missing. Lonnie Johns is her name."

"When was that?"

"Well, there's the thing—it was only four or five days ago. And there's nothing to say that the Johns girl didn't just quit her job and go on holiday. The girl she shares a room with said it wouldn't surprise her, that Lonnie's job would shred the nerves of a saint."

"But Miss Johns didn't say anything to her, about going away?"

"The room-mate didn't see her go—she'd just got back herself from a week in Bognor Regis."

"Any signs of foul play at the flat?"

"Neither disturbance nor a note, although some of her things did seem to be missing, tooth-brush and the like."

"If the girl had run off to the Riviera with a movie star, she'd probably have told everyone she knew," I reflected.

"Normally, we'd barely even be opening an enquiry into a disappearance of a girl missing a few days, but time is against us. The entire crew is about to set sail out of England, and if we don't get someone planted in their midst, we'll lose the chance. And when my likely officers were unavailable, I thought, just maybe Mr Holmes would have a few days free to act as a sort of place-holder, until I could get one of my own in line for it. But never mind, it was only a—"

"And in addition, if it does blow up in the face of a gaggle of bluebloods and splatter them all with scandal, it would be nice if Scotland Yard were nowhere in sight."

"Miss Russell, I deeply resent the im—"

"Chief Inspector, I have nothing in particular on at the moment. I'll be happy to devote myself to the Mysterious Affair of the Coincidental Film Crew."

He looked shocked. "You mean you'll *do* it?"

"I just said I would."

"I thought you'd laugh in my face." He gave me a suspicious scowl. "You aren't a 'fan' of the cinema world, are you?"

"By no means."

"And yet you seem almost eager to take this on."

Motion pictures, or Mycroft? I reached out to snatch the folder from his hand. "My dear Chief Inspector, you have no idea."